TRACK OF
THE GRIZZLY

Other novels by Alfred Dennis

Chiricahua
Lone Eagle
Elkhorn Divide
Brant's Fort
Catamount
The Mustangers
Rover
Sandigras Canyon
Yellowstone Brigade
Shawnee Trail
Fort Reno
Yuma
Ride the Rough String
Trail to Medicine Mound
Arapaho Lance: Crow Killer Series - Book 1
Lance Bearer: Crow Killer Series - Book 2

To see more books by Alfred Dennis visit
www.alfreddennis.com

TRACK OF THE GRIZZLY

Crow Killer Series - Book 3

by

Alfred Dennis

WCP

Walnut Creek Publishing
Tuskahoma, Oklahoma

Track of the Grizzly: Crow Killer Series - Book 3

ISBN: 978-1-942869-28-3
First Edition, Paperback
Published 2018 by Walnut Creek Publishing
Front cover painting: derivative work of Charles Marion Russell/To The Victor Belongs The Spoils / Wikimedia Commons/Public Domain
Library of Congress Control Number: 2018954180

Books may be purchased in quantity and/or special sales by contacting the publisher;
Walnut Creek Publishing
PO Box 820
Talihina, OK 74571
www.wc-books.com

This book is dedicated to my friends and
book agent Karen and David Galbraith.
Great job, thank you.

CHAPTER 1

The changing of the seasons was near, and soon the weather would turn cold in the high country. Jed could feel the change as the air had a nip in the daylight hours and the leaves on the trees were turning colors. Autumn was what the farmers in the lowlands down below called the muddy season. The dark eyes of the man took in the valley with its browning grass and yellowing leaves. He could feel the cool wind, that blew across the broad meadows, brushing softly against his face. Jedidiah Bracket, the warrior the Arapaho had named Crow Killer, stood at the edge of the small creek. He studied the valley, knowing well, the time for trapping the clear streams, ponds, and forests would soon arrive.

The piebald paint horse, two mules, and two Blackfoot ponies grazed further out on the valley floor. The tall, dark-skinned, young man let his eyes follow the distant mountains and tree lines. He knew summer in the high elevation was shorter than down below, but still the green times had passed so quickly this season. Alone in the high valley, with only himself for company, the young man had time to reflect on the many battles and adventures he had been involved in since becoming a Lance Bearer of the Arapaho.

Earlier in the spring, after waving farewell to Red Hawk, Walking Horse, and Little Antelope on the bank of the Yellowstone River, Jed had been alone and had seen nary a living soul all summer. His time had not been wasted, as the hay barn was full to overflowing, wood was stacked in cords against the cabin, and his traps were well oiled. Everything was ready so he could begin bringing in valuable hides as soon as the winter cold thickened the fur bearer's coats. During the summer, Jed had alternated his time between preparing for the coming cold times, and patrolling his valley and passes against any encroaching enemies. He doubted the Nez Perce would come again to his valley to raid, as they were too afraid of the demon they thought the Arapaho would become when attacked. He hadn't heard anything, but he figured his friend Blue Darter was now head Chief of the Piegan Blackfoot, so there should be no problems from them. However, Walking Horse's words of warning always reminded him to be watchful of everything and never leave anything to chance.

The young Arapaho did not forget the deadly grizzly bears, or Red Hawk's words of warning. The Crow had warned him several times before riding south with Walking Horse that the big grizzly and her cubs had his scent and could return to his valley any time. He had predicted the she bear would pick her time and come down from the mountain in all her fury and rage, when he least expected her. All summer, as Jed hunted, he searched out the valley and the game trails for any sign of her presence, but not a trace of her or her cubs were found. Smaller bear tracks had shown themselves from time to time, but the bigger track of the huge killer bear was not seen. He hoped Red Hawk's words of warning would prove to be wrong. Hopefully, she would move back south with her cubs and leave him and his valley in peace.

Still, Jed never let down his guard. He knew a bear was unpredictable, a roamer by nature with a wide range of mountains and valleys to hunt on. He knew the grizzly could come down out of the higher mountains at any time. If he lived to be a hundred, he could never forget the rage or angry roar of the huge bear as she chased after him and Bow Legs, as she ran them from her kill. Red Hawk said she had his scent because Jed had touched Billy Wilson, leaving his smell forever burned into her small brain. The Crow said she would never leave, never forget his smell, or quit his track. Jed remembered the grizzly's attack on the Blackfoot warriors of Deep Water and Lone Bull. He couldn't explain her actions that day or why she had suddenly appeared to attack the Blackfoot warriors. Maybe the bear was an omen of some kind as Blue Darter had said.

Red Hawk, perhaps in his superstitious way, had answered the question. The warrior had said the grizzly wanted no one to kill Crow

Killer but her. Jed shook his head, Lige Hatcher had been wrong when he spoke of the grizzly, because this bear was intelligent and worse, she was a man stalker and killer. Never would he forget the huge grizzly's bloody teeth, dripping saliva, burning red eyes, or ferociousness. Jed knew she was much more dangerous than any man, causing him to be extra cautious, searching warily for her tracks every time he rode out to hunt for meat. Grizzlies were animals and Hatcher had said she was a dumb brute, but Jed knew different, as this bear acted almost as a man would. In her own way, the killer bear was a thinking killing machine. Even now, Jed could feel her watching him from somewhere on the mountain. The mere thought of her small, beady eyes made his blood run cold and the hairs on his neck stand on end.

Absently, Jed turned his thoughts to Chalk Briggs' wagon train. The season was getting late, but the passes leading west to Oregon should still be clear. Higher up in the tall mountains, the train would have to cross passes where early winter snowstorms could endanger the train if they were caught in the heavy drifts. He remembered well how wagon trains were subject to many hardships on the trail. Rain, mud, snow, rock slides, storms, sickness, flooding rivers, and the always present danger of hostile Indians rode with the immigrants every step of every mile, as the train rolled west. He recalled with admiration, from his short time on the wagon train, how strong people made the dangerous journey, but for many their last. Jed respected Lige Hatcher and Chalk Briggs, and he hoped the train had made safe passage across the grueling miles.

Walking to where the animals grazed, Jed removed the hobbles and led them back to the creek for water. Out of habit, and since the fight with Deep Water, the Blackfoot, plus fear of the grizzly, Jed was keeping the horses and mules corralled at night. Red Hawk had warned that the bear would one day come for him, so until that time came; he intended to keep the horses close so he could protect them. He also remembered the many times the Crow had warned him, saying the Hawken Rifle could not kill the grizzly. The white man in him said this was just Indian superstition, but the Arapaho in him nearly made him believe Red Hawk. Shaking his head in disbelief, he all but laughed at the thought. Possibly, he too started believing the big grizzly was a demon as the tribes said. He knew better, as she wasn't indestructible, at least he hoped she wasn't.

He almost hoped the heavy snows would come early, at least the cold would send the killer bears into hibernation. Jed wasn't exactly scared of the bear, but he knew she was a killer and he respected her. When he was out hunting, she was always foremost on his mind. The bear was smart, so he searched every path and animal run for any sign of her. So far, after a summer's search, her tracks had eluded him. Maybe Red Hawk had been wrong, causing him to worry for no reason.

During the summer months, he worked on the corral and barn, re-enforcing the heavy log rails, making them almost impregnable. He knew the fence would not hold a nine hundred pound bear out for very long, but it should slow her down long enough for him to get off a shot before she broke through and killed a horse. On the valley floor, if the grizzly charged out of the dark, the horses would have no chance of getting away from her. At least one of them could be killed, maybe more if her cubs still hunted with her. At a short distance a bear was faster a foot than any horse, and their long claws and razor sharp teeth were deadly.

Fastening the heavy gate, Jed returned to the cabin and his coffee. Since the departure of Hatcher and Elizabeth, then Red Hawk, Walking Horse, and Little Antelope, the cabin had become lonely. Jed missed the young Assiniboine, Silent One, who, although unable to speak or hear, was good company and a loyal friend. Shaking himself out of his mood, Jed started deer steaks frying over the open hearth. To stave off his loneliness, he kept busy, as there was still plenty to be done before the fur trapping season started.

Stepping out, in the early morning hours, Jed touched the coffee cup to his lips and looked about the cabin. The horses stood in the corral waiting and nickering at him, eager to be led out to pasture. Dumping the dregs from his cup, Jed picked up his rifle and started for the corral. Somewhere, further off in the long valley, a bull elk bugled, calling across the grasslands. The call always made Jed smile, as his valley was home to many herds of elk, deer, and smaller animals.

At times, he wished the shaggies would return to the high meadows and save him the long ride to the lower valleys. This year, he would go east earlier to get his buffalo hides and meat, and not wait until the storms could trap him in the passes as they almost had last year. Traveling so far with fresh meat, the temperature would have to be below freezing to keep it from spoiling. His timing was important, but there was plenty of time because the bad storms would not come for at least another month.

Laughing as he turned the horses and mules loose, Jed watched as they bucked and played, running across the valley floor. The black mule always outlasted the horses, as she seemed to run for hours without tiring in her easy striding lope. Only the piebald was hobbled this morning, kept close in case he was needed. Turning back for the cabin, Jed filled a bucket with creek water on his way. Somewhere far out an elk trumpeted his challenge, another sign winter was nearing. With the coming of the cold times, the bull elk and buck deer became more aggressive, trying to put on the last bit of fat for strength as they fought over the females during the rut. The females put on fat to stave off the hungry times ahead.

Sitting outside the cabin at a new split-log table, Jed laid out a tanned elk hide and lighter deer skins. In his lax time, he would cut the hides to make moccasins, which were needed for the wet winter months of trapping. Continually wading in the shallow water of the ponds and lower downstream in the damned water of the creek, many pairs would be needed to last him over the long months ahead. This was one lesson he had learned the hard way from his first trapping season last winter. His feet had remained cold and chapped almost his entire first season in the high country. Jed remembered hearing the old mountain men, visiting the wagon train, talk how their feet had become swollen with rheumatism for days on end during the trapping season.

Engrossed in his work, Jed didn't see the piebald's ears prick up, out on the valley floor. Further out, the loud snort of the red mule and the long bray of the black mule took his attention. Dropping the skins, Jed grabbed his rifle and bridle, hurrying in a dead run to where the piebald was hobbled. The mules were nervous with their ears affixed toward whatever they had located to the south.

Most times, whatever the animals alerted on was harmless, but Jed never neglected their warnings, always riding out to investigate every

alarm. Crossing the valley in a slow walk, Jed watched the piebald's ears
for any sign of intruders. He trusted the horse's senses, which were much
stronger than his own. Hearing, smell, and sight, the horse could detect
an enemy, even an elk or deer, many minutes before a human could.

Following the tree line on the west side of the valley, Jed rode the
piebald back and forth through the timber while watching the trail and
the horse's ears. Reining in, he studied the small animal path, then
surveyed the trees and brush. The piebald suddenly alerted, raising his
neck and pricking his ears. Cocking the rifle, Jed turned the horse in a
circle. After finding nothing, he looked further down the trail.

"So you have come, little bear." The hairs seemed to rise on his neck
as he detected the huge tracks in front of him on the trail. "You're a big
one all right."

Jed knew the bear wasn't close because the horse wasn't reacting
nervously to its smell. Below him, the large toe claws showed plainly in
the soft trail and a large heap of scat, further along, showed the bear to
be a big one. Jed remembered the attack on Billy Wilson so he wasn't
about to push further into the underbrush and give the grizzly an
opportunity to attack him from the cover of the brush. The piebald was
good at detecting an enemy, but if the bear got downwind of them, he
may not be able to smell her. He remembered Billy Wilson, and later the
Blackfoot warriors and their horses, but they had never detected or
smelled the bears before they were attacked and killed. Jed had listened
to Hatcher tell of a bear charging from a standstill was faster than a
greyhound dog in four strides. He knew in the heavy underbrush, he
could be caught before the horse could turn and escape from the danger.
As Walking Horse had taught him, there was always another day for a
kill, so don't be foolish and get caught unaware.

Backing the piebald down the trail, Jed whirled the animal and raced
out onto the valley floor where he could see what was around him. The
piebald fidgeted, and now he sensed the bear behind them. Jed stared
into the dark passageway of the trail, as something moved back in the
tall timber. Sitting the piebald in the valley, Jed contemplated
dismounting and moving back into the trees. Shaking his head, he
decided not to stalk the bear in his domain, as it would be both
foolhardy and probably disastrous. Further back in the heavy, dense

woods, she has the advantage in her element. He would be foolish to walk into her jaws, so today he would retreat and wait.

Riding the horse further back into the valley, Jed watched the tree line for any sign of movement. The piebald kept his attention focused on the heavy brush that grew lower along the tree line. Jed shook his head, thinking it had to be the grizzly. Even now, she was stalking him, getting closer before making her charge as if he was an elk or deer. He couldn't believe it, as the bear had no fear of man at all and she was fixing to charge him in daylight. Hatcher and Red Hawk had talked a lot about bears, but never had they known one to stalk and charge a man unless there were cubs present. Jed had faced many a warrior intent on killing him, but never an animal as large and dangerous as a grizzly. He still remembered her speed from the time she had chased after him and Bow Legs. Even with their head start, she was almost upon them as they raced their frightened horses away from her. Jed figured the timberline was at least one hundred paces away. Backing the horse, he wanted a more comfortable distance between them if she charged.

Checking his priming, Jed cocked the rifle and waited, watching the tree line and the horse's ears. The piebald stood still with his neck arched, as his ears and eyes fixed on a clump of bushes pushing closer onto the grassy floor. Suddenly, the sensitive nostrils flared, then the big horse snorted an alarm. Jed watched the brush, his heart racing in anticipation, as there was no doubt she was there, and the horse had her position located exactly. Jed's eyes squinted as he thought he could see the ear of the grizzly poking out from the bushes. The bush was far, and it could be merely a leaf formed like a bear's ear. At this distance, he couldn't be sure.

Raising the Hawken slowly, he sighted in to the left of what he thought was the ear. Nothing moved so it was a gamble and he might waste a shot, but it was his only chance today. He could move closer and provoke her into charging, but he wasn't sure the horse could get away from her first quick burst of speed. If it wasn't her ear, he was seeing, he could retreat further onto the valley floor while he reloaded. Setting his set trigger, Jed squeezed easily on the second trigger. The roar and buck of the heavy caliber rifle, the shying of the piebald, plus the scream and thrashing in the underbrush all happened at the same time. The horse was used to a rifle firing, but with the bear roaring and the bushes thrashing wildly just yards ahead, the horse was startled, causing him to whirl sideways. Jed only had a quick sighting of the thrashing bear as the bullet impacted, but there was no doubt it was the bear. With all the roaring, there was little doubt, he scored a hit somewhere on the animal.

Quickly reloading, Jed listened and watched as the horse quieted and again focused on the far tree line. Nothing moved or sounded, everything across the open space was quiet. Jed had been taught by the best, to always give the shot animal time to bleed out before moving in. Any large animal was hard to kill, but he had been warned by Hatcher, the grizzly bear was the hardest of them all. Many times, hunters had been killed by their own impatience or badly mauled by a dead bear that suddenly came back to life.

Several minutes passed, and it was time to move. He contemplated on going into the timber after the bear, which may only be wounded, or ride away, not knowing if he killed her. Touching the lance in his arrow quiver, Jed knew he would go in after the bear. To do less would show cowardice, something he could not do. He knew if the grizzly wasn't dead, she would be waiting and the advantage would be all hers. He knew he had hit her somewhere, but didn't know how badly she was wounded. Dismounting, he pulled the hobbles from his belt, then shook his head as he changed his mind.

"No, old son, if I hobble you and she gets by me, you wouldn't stand a chance. Just don't leave me on foot out here." Jed replaced the rawhide hobbles.

Pushing his lance into the soft soil of the valley, Jed tied the rein loosely to the shaft then patted the horse's sleek neck. He knew if the bear came out of the brush, the horse could pull loose easily and get away. Rechecking the rifle, Jed started slowly toward the tree line. Sweat beaded on his forehead, as nothing he had ever faced or done was as scary, but at the same time was invigorating and exciting as this. He knew he should turn back, but something drove him forward. His nerves were taut, but he was determined to move forward into the unknown. Today, one of them, maybe both, would die if the grizzly wasn't already dead.

Not a sound came from the dense underbrush as Jed retraced his tracks back across the flat area to where he thought the bear might be lying. Sweat penetrated his hunting shirt as he moved noiselessly forward. Ears strained, eyes focused, and scanning the brush and trail ahead, Jed moved forward with every nerve at its highest. He had fought many a battle with his enemies, but nothing brought his senses to life and focus like stalking the bear was doing. Suddenly, he didn't know how, but he could sense somewhere ahead, the bear was alive and watching, waiting for him to move closer. From only yards down the brushy trail, the sudden roar and shaking brush sounded as the huge grizzly stood up and started toward him on the narrow trail.

With no time to aim, Jed pointed the long rifle and fired as the grizzly slammed into him, knocking him back off his feet. Temporarily stunned from his head hitting the hard ground, Jed tried to move, but the bear's heavy weight had him pinned. He could feel the heart beating and the stench of the animal's awful breath. Finally working his right arm free, Jed pulled his knife and plunged it deep into the bear several times, then pushed with all his strength, rolling the grizzly from atop him. Quickly rising to his feet, Jed used his war axe to finish the dying animal.

Covered in blood and still shaking from the exertion, Jed stood back and looked down at the huge form. Turning the bear's head, he found his first shot had taken off the animal's lower jaw and his second shot had entered the bear's chest. The missing lower jaw saved him. If the bear had been able to bite, there was no doubt he would be dead. With two bullets in the grizzly, the animal should have been dead, unable to charge him. Hatcher and Red Hawk had said a grizzly was one hard animal to kill, and now, he believed it.

Examining himself, Jed couldn't find anything but minor scratches and cuts from where the bear had swiped him with her claws, during her final death throws. His new hunting shirt hadn't fared so well, covered in blood and ripped to tatters, it was ruined. He had been lucky, as fate and the ones above had been smiling on him this day. Pulling his skinning knife, Jed started his first cut on the carcass, then stopped. The bear wasn't her; it was a boar, probably one of her cubs. Quickly reloading the rifle, Jed surveyed the surrounding woods, then went to work skinning the massive animal.

The piebald wasn't happy about carrying the bearskin back to the cabin, but he was well trained and stood while Jed hefted the bloody hide onto him. As he led the horse back to the north, Jed shook his head, it wasn't the old bear but at least he killed one of them. He couldn't believe it, as the grizzly waited and charged him instead of running away like a normal animal would after being wounded. There was no doubt in his mind these grizzlies were killers, afraid of nothing and very dangerous.

Today the spirits smiled on him, but still there were two killer bears left roaming the mountains. Somewhere out there, the grizzlies would be waiting and watching, focused on their prey, Crow Killer, the human who had dared touch their kill. Jed wasn't sure he believed Red Hawk and his thinking that the bear would never forget his scent or leave his trail, but he knew they were out there somewhere, roaming these mountains. Now, the bears were the enemy. Jed was determined to keep vigilant and pay close attention to his surroundings when out hunting.

Pegging the huge hide to the barn wall, Jed stood back and shook his head in amazement. He didn't figure it as large as the sow grizzly, but it was a monster of an animal, at least eight feet tall and weighing probably eight hundred pounds. The cub was running with his mother, but at this age, he should already be out on his own, looking for a mate. Looking at the hide, Jed's spine tingled, he had been a mighty lucky pilgrim today.

Pouring himself some hot coffee after bringing in his stock, Jed sat down wearily and stared off across the valley. Somewhere out there, the old bear was waiting. When she found the dead carcass, Jed wondered if she would follow the blood smell he had left across the valley back to the cabin. Tonight would be a long and vigilant night. There was no way he would be able to sleep, even with the mules keeping watch from the corral. His nerves were too tight and he wouldn't be able to close his eyes for a minute because he had to stay awake and be ready. He had very little experience with grizzly bears, but after today there was no doubt in his mind, one of them, either the sow grizzly and her cub or he had to die.

Morning found the valley quiet and peaceful as birds called out, crows cawing about the cabin, and a lone eagle soaring high above the valley. Leaning his rifle against the table, Jed stretched his aching shoulder and sipped a cup of coffee. Looking down at the bloody bear claws, he had laid out on the table to dry, he was tempted to place them on an ant hill. If he let the ants do the work of removing the dead skin and meat that would take a few days, and something, like a squirrel or pack rat might steal them.

"Old Lige and Red Hawk sure ain't gonna believe this tale." Jed shook his head, as he picked up the claw. "Shucks, I hardly believe it myself."

A week passed as Jed prepared for the cold times by getting his trap lines ready, then patrolling the valley and animal trails for any sign of the other two grizzlies. Nothing, nary a track or hair of the bears could be seen anywhere. Jed was relieved, but still couldn't figure out the bears. He knew sooner or later the old sow would come looking for her cub and vengeance. That is, if Red Hawk was right and if a bear knew about vengeance.

The heavy claw necklace was finished. Jed held it up to the fading sunlight as he admired his handicraft. Too heavy and burdensome to wear every day, the necklace would be a novelty and talking piece when he wore it into Baxter Springs come warm weather. Hanging it on the wall inside the cabin, he wished for two more to hang alongside it. These bears were evil, scary, and the incarnate of the devil. After his encounter with the cub, Jed learned to respect and fear them even more.

Out on the valley floor, just as he was about to bring in his horses and mules for the night, Jed noticed every animal had their ears pricked toward the north pass. Gathering up his rifle, he quickly hurried the herd into the corral and fastened the gate. Something or somebody was coming his way, friend or foe, man or beast, he had no idea. In the high lonesome, he never knew who his next unexpected guest would be.

Wading across the creek, Jed knelt out of sight behind a large sycamore and waited. Almost an hour passed before the black mule brayed a greeting and a lone rider leading two pack animals appeared out on the valley floor. Focusing on the nearing rider, Jed stood up and raised his hand in greeting.

"Lem Roden, what you be doing way up here by yourself?"

Smiling as he reined in, the old scout nodded and grinned. "Howdy, Jed."

"Howdy yourself, Lem. Light and we'll go to the cabin." Jed took the lead ropes of the packhorses. "S'pect you could use a little coffee right about now?"

"Sure wouldn't say no to a good deer steak either." Roden nodded at the horses. "Your pa sent back your horses."

"Well, what you waiting for, light down and let's eat." Jed turned.

Roden couldn't help but see the huge grizzly hide as they unloaded the packhorses and unsaddled his horse. Entering the cabin with the heavy packs, Jed put the steaks on, then returned to help Roden with the rest of his possibles. Sitting at the table, Roden noticed the bloody hunting shirt lying by the door.

"If I don't miss my guess, looks like you had trouble the last few days."

Turning the steaks, Jed nodded. "Little bit, Red Hawk said she'd be back."

"The killer grizz that y'all said killed Billy Wilson?"

"That ain't her out there in the barn."

"It ain't?"

"Nope, one of her cubs, I figure." Jed poured coffee.

"Well, he was a big one for sure."

Filling the plates with meat and biscuits, Jed pushed a plate over to Roden. "That he was."

"You reckon the old she bear is still around here?"

"I figure she is." Jed sat down. "Ain't found no sign of her yet."

"Hopefully, she'll leave out, head back to her own hunting grounds." Roden looked down at his coffee. "But, I doubt it."

"Hopefully. Now tell me, Mister Roden." Jed bit into his steak. "What are you doing this far up?"

The scout looked up and shrugged. "Drying out."

"Drying out?"

"The saloon and civilization was just too tempting." Roden nodded. "Just like this steak looks tempting. I was getting mighty hungry, Jed. I had to get far away from that saloon and its temptations."

"Have you seen my stepdad?"

The grey head bobbed up and down. "He's not the same man. He seems sad, real sad."

"I imagine." Jed thought of Seth and Billy. "He has a reason."

"I reckon he has, but them boys of his were just plain no account."

Jed thought of the brothers and the meanness that was in them. "They were at that."

"Said he'd see you in the spring." Roden sipped on his coffee. "I believe he's looking forward to you coming in."

"You heard anything of Lige or Chalk Briggs' train?"

"Not since they pulled out." Roden pushed back his plate. "Lige told me about the fight. Reckon I missed a good show with the Blackfoot."

"It was a show alright, can't say it was good though."

"Was the part about the bears true or was old Lige just prying on my leg a little?"

"It's true enough, they saved our bacon that day." Jed nodded. "I don't know how they came to be there, but they sure put the run on most of them Blackfoot warriors."

"And you think they may still be out there stalking you?" Roden nodded. "Besides the one you killed, I mean."

"She's out there alright, I can feel her." Jed sipped on his coffee. "Be careful, Lem, whenever you're outside, be alert and very careful."

"That bad, huh?"

Jed laughed. "She'd have your scrawny little self for a snack."

"That's why you got your animals locked up so tight?"

"That's it, just trying to slow her down a little if she comes in the night."

"Sounds to me like the old gal has really got you spooked, Jed." Roden nodded. "Put the scare into you pretty good, I'd say."

"She's the most dangerous thing, man or beast, I've ever run up against." Jed shrugged. "Yeah, she has me plenty worried. She's one intelligent animal."

Roden cleared his throat. "You wouldn't be needing a skinner to help you this winter, would you?"

"You're a hunter, Mister Roden, not a skinner."

"Just call me Lem, and I was a hunter." Roden shrugged. "A man in my position can't afford to be choosy."

"Alright, Lem. Yes, I could use a skinner." Jed admitted. "I had one last year and we done pretty good."

"The young Assiniboine they killed?"

"His name was Silent One."

"I'm in debt to your stepdad for my horse and outfit." Roden looked over at the packs. "I'll have to pay him back come spring."

"You get settled up with the owner of your last horse?" Jed laughed.

"Thanks to Ed Wilson." Roden chuckled. "I thought old Sam McBride was gonna ring my neck before your pappy stepped in."

"Yeah, I remember that Swede. He had a temper on the train out here, and big as a house he was."

"Still does and still is, and I settled up with the store man for the supplies Seth Wilson took from his store."

"Why? You didn't take them."

"No, but I was wearing them when he spotted me in the settlement."

Jed smiled. "Well, I reckon it all worked out okay."

Roden looked at Jed. "By the way, old Bate Baker told me to tell you, he wasn't buying beaver plews this year."

"Don't matter, we'll probably be taking our furs to Bridger come spring and the thaw."

Roden blinked as he looked over at Jed. "What about the girl?'

"Ellie?"

"Yep, she's looking forward to seeing you." Roden grinned. "I think she's got her sights set on you, Jed."

"She belongs in Baxter Springs taking care of sick folks."

Roden shut up, as he said his piece. "I think old Bate is just bluffing you on the furs."

"Tell me, Lem, what is the going price of beaver back east?"

"They ain't bringing what they did in the shining times, but they'll still bring enough to feed a hungry man and buy his powder."

"Come morning, we'll ride out and plan out our trap lines." Jed nodded. "I'll think on Mister Baker and the beaver."

"I brought in forty more traps." Roden finished his steak. "Your pap sent them up."

"Good, we'll put them to good use."

Buzzards covered the sky, hovering over the dead body of the grizzly Jed had killed. Sitting back in the valley, as the black vultures floated lazily on the wind, Jed and Roden watched the birds circling over the place where the bear lay. Jed studied the far tree line, then abruptly turned the piebald away. He doubted the grizzlies were anywhere near the dead body, but he wasn't ready to confront the bears again today. Today, he had trapping on his mind.

Roden was a trapper, who had trapped with the likes of Bridger, Smith, Beckworth, and Wallace. He knew his business, pointing out several places as they rode where animal runs showed and traps should be set. Jed liked the old scout. He knew the mountains and was a congenial kind of man, quiet spoken with few words, and was always in a good mood.

"Them carrion eaters give me the heebie-jeebies." Roden studied the circling buzzards. "I can't stand the ugly things."

"They're ugly alright."

"Had me a woman once. Longer I lived with her, the more she began to look like one of them birds." Roden seemed to quiver. "Old Nellie had herself a long skinny neck, beaky nose, and beady eyes. She reminded me of them buzzards alright."

"What did you do, Lem?"

"Lit out, that's what I did." Roden nodded. "On the fastest horse I could find and believe me, he wasn't near fast enough."

Jed laughed. "Well, it seems you survived. Now, what about the trapping around here?"

"Well, the timber and trails look ripe for trapping."

"I never trapped this far from the cabin last season."

Roden nodded. "There is plenty of sign here and plenty of food for the varmints. We should take many pelts on this end."

"Sounds good." Jed looked over at the old trapper. "We'll split the skinning between us."

"That's fine, Jed."

"One thing, you be careful out here all alone until these bears go into hibernation." Jed looked about the timber. "If you want, I'll take the south end this season."

"No, you stay north, I'll take this end." Roden shook his head. "But, if they persist, we'll need to track 'em down and kill 'em."

"I'm for it, but I can't find them." Jed scanned the huge valley and mountains. "It will be very dangerous going in the timber hunting for them, and as you well know, these mountain ranges are vast with many a hiding place."

"Sooner or later they'll get careless and let us see them. Roden nodded. "Especially, when they get hungry enough and have to come out."

"Red Hawk predicted before he rode out, that she'd come after me in her own good time."

Both men sat in front of the cabin, sipping on coffee and enjoying the early morning freshness. Roden studied the horses as they moved slowly across the valley grazing, then turned his attention to the tall mountains.

"I figure we got about another month before the cold really hits, and the furs become prime and ready for the traps."

"Last year, me and Lige were working on this cabin about now." Jed remembered the early snows of his first winter in the high lonesome. "The very day we completed it, snow started to fall."

"I think it will be a while yet before the snows hit."

"I hope you're right."

"If a man wanted to, he'd have time to ride into the settlements and pay his respects to someone." Roden shrugged. "If a man wanted to, that is."

"Mighty long ride to pay respects."

"These mountains, they have a way of getting to a man." The scout smiled slowly. "We all need a break from them now and again."

"I know, but maybe I'm different. I love these mountains, Lem." Jed inhaled the clean fresh air. "I really love it up here."

"They can turn a man into a loner, cold, and a hermit in ways." Roden shook his head. "Jed, I've seen men stay alone so long they became mad and didn't even realize it."

"I can't leave my stock or cabin."

Shrugging, Roden laughed. "That's what I'm here for."

"I don't think I should leave you up here alone just yet." Jed was thinking of the bears.

"I'll be just fine. Last I took stock, I was full grown."

Jed shook his head. "Those bears are out there, Lem. They're just waiting and watching for us to make a mistake."

"Hoss, this old brigand has dealt with many a bear in my time."

"Not like these, I'll bet." Jed looked at the scout. "I'll study on it."

"Boy, I've been traipsing these old hills for almost thirty years, I'll be just fine." Roden argued. "You go, don't worry about me none."

Jed looked out across the valley. "It would be good to see about my brother, Walking Horse."

"Walking Horse?"

"If I ride out, it'll be south to the Arapaho."

"She'd sure like to see you before the cold times and your step-pappy may need you." Roden shrugged. "He's mainly why I'm suggesting you go."

"I'll study on it." Jed repeated himself, then took up his rifle and started for the creek. "I'll take a quick walk and see if I can get us some fresh meat."

Jed knew Roden was right. Ed Wilson was his step-pa and a man who had lost both his sons. Maybe he should ride into Baxter Springs to check on him, and maybe help cheer him up some. Still, he thought of the Arapaho and wanted to see about Walking Horse and Little Antelope. It was late in the season so he couldn't ride to both places before the cold times arrived, and soon it would be time to start setting his trap lines.

Slipping slowly through the underbrush and along the small animal trail, Jed scouted out the upper ridge behind the cabin for deer. From this high up, he could see the smoke from the cabin fire filtering through the trees and the herd of horses grazing peacefully out on the valley. They didn't really need fresh meat, but he wanted to be alone, to think. Sitting down with his back against a small mountain pine, Jed relaxed and let his eyes rove over the beautiful mountains that stood looking down on the huge valley like tall sentinels.

Somewhere further along the mountain, a loafer wolf howled out his lonely call, probably the same big wolf that Jed had seen so many times on his hunts down the valley. The wolf was a large grey male, a loner, always staying to himself, never in the company of other wolves. The mournful cry came again, echoing across the valley causing the horses in the valley to shift their attention to him. In some ways, the wolf reminded Jed of himself, alone in the tall mountains. Roden had been wrong, the mountains weren't getting to him, just the opposite, he enjoyed being alone in the quiet peacefulness of the valley. Still, Roden's words echoed in his ears, and he worried about the scout's veiled warning about his stepdad, Ed Wilson. Roden was old school, and he would never tell a man what he thought he should do, but he would make his comments, then become silent. Then there was Walking Horse, and he wondered how he was and how the Arapaho people and Little Antelope were doing. He had to choose before the cold times came, whether he should ride into Baxter Springs or south to the Arapaho Village.

Jed tried to convince himself to ride south to the Arapaho, but his mind thought of Ellie. What was she doing and did she really want to see him as Roden said? Again, his mind swung to Walking Horse, hoping he was healing and growing stronger. Was Little Antelope okay? Shaking his head, he raised up slowly as a small buck walked down to the creek for a drink. Slipping stealthily down the ridge, Jed stopped and raised his rifle as the deer threw up his head. The echo of the rifle across the mountains had barely quieted when Jed knelt over the young deer, quickly gutting the buck, and slinging him over his shoulder.

He had to think on what he was going to do. What was the right thing to do? Dropping the deer at Roden's feet, Jed shook his head. On the walk back to the cabin, he finally made up his mind. Tomorrow, he would ride for Baxter Springs. If he was needed as Roden reported, he should return and check on Ed Wilson. His stepdad, the only father figure he had ever known, maybe needed him more right now than Walking Horse. He owed the man for all he had become, for treating him as a son, and for coming to the mountains to warn him of Seth's intentions. Ed Wilson was a good man, one of the best, and how his sons turned out so bad, Jed had no idea.

CHAPTER 2

Reaching the Snake River, Jed swam the piebald and one extra packhorse across the all-too familiar crossing. Behind him, over the mountain, he had bid farewell to Lem Roden, warning him to always stay alert should the grizzlies come calling while he was gone. Jed didn't want to leave his valley or Roden alone, but now that he was almost to the immigrant trail, running east and west, he grew excited. A few miles down the road was Baxter Springs, Ed Wilson and Ellie, and he was eager to see both of them again. Maybe Roden had been right, maybe the loneliness of the mountains was getting to him.

Reining in his horses as he neared Jake Carter's small homestead, he studied the outbuildings several minutes before the tall farmer came from the barn, walking toward him. The man had changed little, tall and skinny with a huge Adam's apple.

"Jedidiah Bracket ain't it?"

"It's me alright, Mister Carter. How you been?"

"Existing, Jed. This is rough country for a Pennsylvania farmer." The tall man shrugged. "A very harsh land makes a man look back."

"I can imagine it would be for you. Pennsylvania is a long way from here." Jed nodded. "But, looking back can be dangerous, Mister Carter."

"I miss the east, and my woman misses the east."

"I stopped here to thank you for helping me."

"I helped your pa and Roden is all." Carter shrugged. "No thanks are needed, but I thank you for your consideration."

"Thank you just the same."

"You're riding into Baxter Springs, I see."

"I figure on it."

Carter glanced up at Jed. "Let me help you again, boy. Don't ride into the settlement, bypass it."

"What's the trouble with me riding in?"

"Last time you left there, threats were made."

Jed shrugged. "I remember what I said. They weren't threats then, they were promises."

"Luke Grisham took it personal and says he'll kill you if he lays eyes on you."

"What's his kick?"

"I reckon it's about Sally Ann getting killed." Carter shook his head. "Truth is they're all scared. They figured sooner or later you'd come back for revenge."

"That's all finished now." Jed shook his head. "The killers of my wife are dead."

"Seth Wilson was your own brother." The farmer shook his head. "That don't bother you none?"

"Yes, Mister Carter, he was my brother and he's paid for what he done." Jed looked hard at the tall man. "And no, it don't bother me at all that he's dead."

"Rumor has it, his own pa killed him."

Jed ignored the last words of the farmer as he turned the piebald down the road. Wilson had killed his own son to save another son, but the people of Baxter Springs could only guess, and Jed meant to leave it that way. Ed Wilson was too proud to speak of it, and neither would he.

Passing through Baxter Springs, the piebald stood out like a sore thumb. Everybody knew the horse and the man riding him. Jed stared straight ahead, his shoulders squared and straight. His proud bearing and calm demeanor showed not only pride but also defiance. Jed never glanced sideways at the doorways or windows, just rode straight through town, heading toward the Pennybrook and the Wilson farm.

Riding into the farmyard, he was surprised, almost shocked, as Wilson walked out into the yard. The man had aged, turned grayer, older, but it was the same strong man that Jed remembered.

Sliding from the piebald, Jed looked at the man. "Pa."

"Jedidiah, son, you're here." Wilson smiled. "Thank you for coming."

"I'm here, Pa. I'm here."

Tears formed in the older man's eyes as he pulled Jed to him and hugged him. "Boy, I'm so glad you came."

"You alright, Pa?" Jed remembered Roden's words.

"I am now, boy. I am now that you're here."

Jed watched the older man as he moved about the house, cooking over the hot stove. He could tell Wilson had changed since leaving the valley, as he had grown quiet and sad. Jed could understand losing someone he loved, because he had lost his mother on the trail west. Seth Wilson was responsible for killing his wife, Sally Ann, be it accidental or not. He was just like his brother, Billy, and they were both no good, but they were still Wilson's sons. Jed had no idea at the time he left Roden and his step-dad on the trail from the valley, that Wilson would take the death of Seth this hard. Looking about the house, Jed could tell the farm had been neglected. Very little work had been done inside the house and none at all around the outside. Trash and weeds were scattered about the cluttered yard.

"How's your crops this year, Pa?"

Wilson looked over at the table and shrugged. "I'm afraid they've grown up in weeds."

"About time to harvest, ain't it?"

"Actually, it's past time."

Jed pulled his plate across the table. "Starting tomorrow, we're gonna remedy that real quick."

"I haven't been quite the same lately." Wilson looked embarrassed as he turned toward the table. "You sure you want to help me with the fields?"

"That's what a son is for, ain't it?"

"Okay, son. I'll take you up on the help." Wilson smiled. "But, first we'll ride into Baxter Springs and see somebody you know."

"Ellie?"

"She'll give me the devil if I don't bring you in."

"Okay, Pa, we'll ride in." Jed nodded. "I need to see Bate Baker, the fur man, while I'm here anyway."

"Right after I milk old Jers." Wilson seemed happy. "Come morning, we'll go."

Baxter Springs was barely awake as Jed and Wilson plodded slowly down the main street and reined in at the trading post. It was early, and some of the town's businesses were just opening, but most were still locked up tight.

"You go in and see Bate." Wilson dismounted. "I'll go find Ellie."

Jed dropped the reins on the piebald. "I doubt I'll be more than a minute."

"You figuring on having trouble with Bate?"

"Not really, but I don't figure on doing business with him this spring. We'll see soon enough." Jed shrugged. "He doesn't like beaver plews."

Watching his stepdad walk down the dusty street, Jed pushed open the door to find the fur buyer already up and sitting behind his desk with his spectacles perched on his nose. A pile of papers laid before the heavyset trader, who was preoccupied, busily going over them.

"Morning, Mister Baker."

Pulling his wire glasses from his face, the buyer looked up at the tall man. "Jed Bracket, well now, what can I do for you?"

"Business."

"You got furs to sell this time of year?"

"Nope, I'm here to see what your prices are gonna be on the same quality pelts this coming spring?"

"Well, it's a mite early yet to know for sure."

"Your best guess will be pretty good." Jed looked over at the buyer.

Baker laid his glasses down and stood up. "Alright, but I'm just spitting in the wind, can't guarantee anything."

"Well, start spitting."

"I figure they'll be the same as last year." Baker cleared his throat. "But, I ain't buying any beaver plews, none."

"Well, thank you, Mister Baker." Jed turned for the door. "Be seeing you."

"You are coming with your pelts in the spring?"

"Nope." Jed stepped out on the porch and walked to the piebald.

Gathering the horse's reins, he started down the street toward the doctor's office. Turning as he heard Baker's steps on the porch, Jed stopped.

"You bring'em on in, come spring, Jed, we'll talk." The buyer smiled. "Let's not be hasty now, and bring in some more of those buffalo coats, like them you brung me last year."

"And beaver plews, Mister Baker?"

"And beaver plews." The fat man frowned as Jed walked away.

Reaching the building where Doctor Zeke had his office, Jed smiled as Wilson followed Ellie from the doorway. "Ellie."

Hugging him, the tall, dark-haired woman smiled, looking up into his dark eyes. "Jed what a surprise, it's so good to see you here."

"It's good to see you again, Ellie." Jed smiled. "Really good."

"When did you get here?"

"Passed through Baxter Springs last night."

"I didn't know. I've been cooped up helping Grandpa with a sick patient." Ellie cut her eyes up at him. "You could have stopped and said hi."

"No, I've been told my welcome around town could be mighty chilly."

"Depends on who's doing the welcoming." She smiled coyly. "You're always welcome here, you know that."

"Let's all go across to the café for some coffee." Wilson motioned to the buildings where the town's people were watching. "It sure beats us standing out here for the town folk to gawk at."

The small café was almost empty as they found a table and ordered coffee. Jed blushed slightly as he looked over at the beautiful woman. With all the troubles back in the valley, he never realized how pretty she was and how much he missed her. He couldn't keep his eyes from the beautiful face.

"Tell me, Jed, what are you doing here?"

"Well, for one thing, I came to see you and my pa." Jed smiled. "Tomorrow, we're fixing to start harvesting his crops."

"When will you go back?"

"I'll stay however long it takes to get in his corn and hay crops."

Ellie smiled. "So you'll be here for at least two weeks or more?"

Wilson nodded. "It should take that long at least, providing Jed has the time."

"I've got until the cold times come."

"But your valley is unprotected, your cabin and horses."

"No, Lem Roden rode in last week and he's watching over things until I get back." Jed looked across the table. "I thought you knew that."

"So that's why he needed a horse and an outfit?" Wilson nodded thoughtfully. "He didn't say he was going back to your valley."

"Yep, rode in big as life and asked for a job skinning pelts." Jed nodded thoughtfully. "Hate to admit it, but he was a pretty welcome sight."

"I imagine it does get lonely up there all alone." Ellie smiled over at him. "Is everything else alright in the valley?"

Jed didn't mention the bears. "Everything is fine, just fine."

"No more Indian trouble?" Ellie asked.

"No more trouble for the time being."

"What have you been doing since I saw you last, Miss Ellie?" Wilson emptied his coffee cup.

Looking over at Wilson, she smiled. "Just helping my grandfather and keeping house. But, I'm all caught up and sure could use a job for a few days."

"What kind of a job?" Wilson was curious.

"Well, I'm a pretty good hand with a team and you are going to need a driver for the corn gathering."

"What?" Jed sputtered at her words. "You want to help with the harvest?"

"Don't look shocked, Mister Bracket. I won't eat much and I work cheap."

"You are hired, young lady." Wilson chimed in before Jed could say more. "And we're glad to have your help, ain't we, Jed?"

"Yes, sir, we'd appreciate the help." Jed couldn't believe it. "Hope you can cook."

"Good, it's agreed then." Ellie smiled over at Jed. "And yes, I can cook."

"What is your grandfather to think, you going off alone with two strange men?"

"Why, Jed Brackett, there's nothing strange about either of you." Ellie laughed. "You're odd maybe, but not strange."

"I'll have Jed come in tomorrow morning with a rig and pick you up." Wilson grinned slyly.

"I'll be ready." Ellie stood up. "Now, I have to fix Grandfather some breakfast."

"Dress to ride, Ellie." Jed chimed in. "I'll bring you a horse."

"You're the boss."

Walking back out onto the front porch, Jed watched Ellie walk away, then turned to Wilson. "Pa, if I didn't know better, I'd think you two already had this idea all hatched up."

"We're innocent, Jed, purely innocent." Ellie replied back over her shoulder.

"I didn't hear Pa say a word."

"And you won't either." Wilson laughed for the first time since Jed returned to Baxter Springs.

Jed shook his head as they walked back to where the horses stood. Mounting quickly, the two men headed back out of town in a short lope. Jed couldn't believe Ellie would come to the farm to help them with the harvest. There was little doubt his stepdad had planned the whole thing, but that couldn't be since he had no idea Jed would be coming to Baxter Springs.

The corn field hadn't been cultivated in weeks, and in places there were weeds almost as tall as the corn. Ellie sat in the small farm wagon and drove the horses while Jed and Wilson pitched ears of corn into the oak wagon. Several times, Wilson laughed as Jed completely missed the wagon as his eyes were focused on the figure of Ellie, sitting on the wagon seat, instead of watching where he was throwing.

"The wagon's full, Jed. I'll rest here a bit while you and Ellie take the corn to the crib and unload."

"Okay, Pa, we'll be right back." Jed stepped into the wagon and nodded. "Take us to the barn, driver."

"Yes, sir." Ellie laughed. "This is fun."

"As much fun as swimming across the river after dark?"

"Almost, but I could use a refresher course."

"What?"

"Mister Crow Killer, this corn gathering is a dusty, dirty job." Ellie clucked to the horses as they started across the Pennybrook. "When we get through today, I'll need a bath."

"Yes, ma'am, soon as Pa says quit, we'll go for a swim."

Another wagon was half full, then the last row in the field was picked and Wilson called it quits for the night. Tomorrow, they would start on the larger field by the bend of the Pennybrook, just east of the house. Wilson had planted at least twenty acres of field corn, enough to feed his horses and cow through the long winter and enough to be ground into feed and cornmeal. Two log corncribs stood beside the barn, and one was already half full. A farm's good fortune depended on a good corn yield. Jed knew twenty acres of corn was a lot for one lone man, a team of horses, and a twelve inch breaking plow to work. He knew Wilson had worked hard getting the corn in the ground before he gave up.

Finished unloading, Jed unharnessed the team and turned them into the corral. Gathering his milk bucket, Wilson walked to the barn where the Jersey cow and calf stood waiting at the milk lot.

"You kids go wash up while I milk."

"We're going to the swimming hole to bathe, Pa." Jed kinda blushed as the older man smiled. "We won't be gone long."

"You do that, son, and take your time while I fix supper."

"I'll do that when I get back, Mister Wilson."

"No, ma'am. Tonight, I'll do the honors." Wilson nodded. "Y'all go have fun and get acquainted."

A clear, deep pool in the deeper part of the Pennybrook was only a short way from the house. Jed laughed as Ellie eased off into the clear water, clothes and all. Slipping from his hunting shirt and moccasins, Jed bailed off into the creek from a rock. Just before he plunged into the water, Ellie's eyes blinked in shock as she took in the massive chest and arm muscles. Never has she seen a better proportioned or physical specimen of manhood. Now, she understood how easily he had lifted her up on her horse. Covered with his deerskin hunting shirt, his muscles didn't show, but the warrior known as Crow Killer was huge, almost unbelievable in size.

"Did you bring any soap, Jed?"

Looking over at her wet hair, he laughed. "Never use it."

"What?" Ellie laughed. "How do you get clean?"

"Sand."

"Sand, why that's dirt."

"Maybe it's dirt but it's clean dirt, and it's in the water all day, ain't it, Doctor?"

Shaking her head, she grinned. "Well, I reckon that's true enough."

Slipping behind him, Ellie pounced on his shoulders, trying her best to dunk him beneath the waterline. Laughing as he lifted her bodily over his head and tossed her head first into the water, she came up sputtering. Several times, she tried her best to get him under the water, but to no avail.

"I give up."

"Me too. We better be getting back to the house."

"You scared of the dark?"

"I'm more scared of you." Jed splashed water at her. "Pa will have supper ready, and we sure wouldn't want his old blue hound to get it."

Ellie was up early, frying side meat, eggs, and biscuits while Wilson milked the cow, and Jed fed and harnessed the team.

"Say, boy." Wilson smiled as he bit into a fluffy biscuit. "She's a heck of a cook. You better latch onto her."

Looking over to where Ellie stood in front of the hot stove, Jed nodded. "Sounds like good advice, Pa."

It was only midmorning, but already they were on their second load of corn and heading for the crib. Jed laughed several times as Ellie pulled and jerked on the big workhorses as they stole corn from the stalks, taking one bite before dropping and ruining the whole cob.

"What's your remedy to stop them from stealing corn?"

"A good talking to, out behind the barn would do nicely." Jed shook his head.

Wilson laughed. "They're just bullies, Ellie. They know you're smaller than they are."

"You drive awhile and I'll pitch corn, Mister Wilson."

"You sure, Miss Ellie?" Wilson winked over at Jed. "It's mighty hard work, and some folks have trouble getting the corn in the wagon."

"I can do it." Ellie laughed, as Jed blushed. "I'm pretty strong for a girl."

For three hours, corn flew into the wagon and was transported to the crib, then Wilson finally called a halt for dinner. Jed knew Ellie was exhausted, but she wasn't letting on or complaining. They were working steadily, as one corn crib was already full and the other was half full. After a good dinner, Jed lifted her into the wagon and then headed for the field.

"We'll finish by dark."

"That's good news." Ellie looked at her sore hands. "Great news."

"Not really." Jed laughed. "Unless you're quitting."

"What do you mean?"

Wilson laughed. "He means that tomorrow, we've got hay to cut for the winter."

"Is that bad, Mister Wilson?"

"Well, it requires a little more backbreaking work with a scythe."

For almost two weeks, day after day Wilson, Jed, and Ellie cut, picked, and dug their way through a season of crops. Finally, they brought in their last wagon load of hay along with other farm vegetables that could be canned or put up in the root cellar beneath the house. Not used to hard work, Ellie was exhausted from long hours in the field, but she refused to stay behind at the house.

Doctor Zeke came to the farm in his buggy while making a call, mostly to check on her. After frowning at the three of them covered in dirt from their labors, he shook his head and drove away.

"I don't think Grandfather approves of a woman being dirty." Ellie laughed as she waved at the disappearing buggy.

"Well, we're finally catching up, kids." Wilson announced with the last load of hay. He perked up as he looked about at his corn cribs and cleared fields.

"Good, I guess tomorrow I better get back to town and see about my grandfather." Ellie seemed sad. "I've neglected him these last two weeks."

"Jed will see you home tomorrow, Ellie."

"I guess you'll head back to your mountains, Jed?"

"If Pa doesn't need me, I'll be leaving in a couple days."

Shaking her head, Ellie stood up from the table. "Oh, no you won't, Jed Bracket."

"What?" Jed was shocked at her sudden outbreak.

"You owe me for a week and a half's work."

"Okay, how much?"

"I'll be paying you, Ellie." Wilson grinned.

"No, you won't, Mister Wilson." Ellie pointed her finger at Jed. "Mister Crow Killer here owes me the money."

Jed shook his head in dismay at her insistence on being paid. "How much do I owe you, Ellie?"

"A dance."

"What?"

Wilson smiled, as he knew exactly what she was getting at. "Next Saturday night is the fall harvest dance in town, and you're taking me."

"That's what I owe you?"

"That's it." Ellie placed her hands on her hips and smiled. "You can stay at least that long."

Wilson laughed out loud. "Best idea I heard all week."

"It's ridiculous, I can't even dance."

"Well, sir, you've got about two days to learn." Ellie smiled. "The fall crops in the settlement are gathered. Now, everyone celebrates with a grand dance and plenty of food."

Midmorning found Jed and Ellie riding the farm wagon down the middle of the main street, pulling up at the doctor's house. Several sets of eyes watched them curiously as they passed through the settlement.

"Thank you, Ellie, for all the help." Jed lifted her from the wagon.

Taking his hand, she smiled into his eyes. "It was fun, the most fun I've ever had."

"It was hard work." Jed looked down at her callused hands. "I'm thanking you."

"Will you take me to the dance and party Saturday?"

"I promised I would. Yes, ma'am, I'll take you."

"I better get inside, my granddaddy isn't real happy with me spending two weeks alone at your pa's farm."

"Should I talk with him before I leave?"

"I don't think that would be a good idea just yet." Ellie laughed. "You'd probably be safer to say good-bye here."

"Okay, you know what's best, I reckon." Jed shrugged.

Touching him on the arm, she smiled. "I'll see you Saturday night, Jed."

Stopping at the general store, Jed went inside and walked to where Elmer Woods stood behind the counter. Seeing the tall figure before him, Woods retreated as far back from the counter as he could get.

"I'm not wanting any trouble, young man."

"No trouble, I just came in for a few supplies." Jed could smell the fear in the clerk.

Relieved, the man quit shaking. "Yes, sir, Mister Bracket."

Jed laid a list on the counter, then walked to the front window and peered down the street. It seemed like only yesterday, Sally Ann had stood in this very spot just before she had been shot. It almost didn't seem real, as the bullet holes in the wall and the stains on the floor had been completely erased. He remembered her beautiful smile, her exuberant spirit. Ellie in ways reminded him of Sally Ann, then in other ways, they were totally different.

"Here you are, Mister Bracket." The store man interrupted Jed's thoughts as he laid the supplies out on the counter.

"How much?"

Figuring on his chalk pad, the store clerk looked over his glasses. "Reckon eight dollars ought to do it."

Jed laid the money out on the counter, then shouldered his supplies. "I'll be seeing you."

"You're coming in the spring with your furs?"

"I might, but I was referring to the Saturday night dance."

Elmer looked at the tall man. "You can't be serious."

"Why not it's a free dance, open to everyone, ain't it?"

"There could be trouble."

"Luke Grisham?"

Elmer nodded shakily. "He's heard you were at your pa's. He's been making threats."

"Threats never killed anybody, Mister Woods."

"Threats killed Sally Ann."

Jed's knuckles whitened as he grasped his rifle, whirling on the storekeeper. "Leave her name out of this."

"Yes, sir." The timid Woods stepped back. "Don't go to the dance, Mister Bracket, for your own good."

"Thanks for the free advice."

Jed sat across the breakfast table drinking his coffee as Ed Wilson hovered over the wood stove, frying side meat. Jed arrived two weeks ago, and already Wilson seemed to come alive, becoming livelier and more vibrant. Jed hoped his pa had snapped out of his grief and mourning.

"You coming to the dance tonight, Pa?"

"Hadn't thought much on it, one way or the other." Wilson shrugged. "Ellie said there'd be some good vittles and sweets there."

"Sounds mighty tasty to me."

"You pulling out in the morning?"

"I am." Jed looked at the man's back. "Why don't you come back to the mountains with me?"

"My farm, I couldn't leave it."

"We'll hire someone to look after it this winter."

"I'd love to Jed, but no, not this year."

"Okay, Pa, but you are coming to the dance, ain't you?"

"I'm coming." Wilson nodded. "Sure wouldn't miss it for the world."

The building holding the dance and the street were lit up as Jed and Wilson rode their horses up to the hitching rail. People already started gathering as saddle horses and wagons were tied along the street and around the corrals. Jack-O-lanterns, oil lanterns, candles, and bonfires lit the street up like daylight. Jed dropped Wilson off at the hall, then walked down the street to Doctor Zeke's residence. He started to knock on the door when it opened.

Jed's jaw dropped as he beheld Ellie standing before him. The word beautiful could in no way pay her looks justice. The blue dress and long dark hair outlined her figure as she stood in the doorway.

"Ellie?"

"It's me silly."

"You're so beautiful."

"Not the same girl from the cornfields?"

Jed nodded. "Yes, the very same, but I hadn't really seen her yet."

"My granddaughter is beautiful, isn't she, but I'm prejudiced. The old doctor stood behind her, smiling. "You two go, the dance has started."

"Come with us, Grandfather."

"No, I have patients to look after." The old man declined. "You two go have fun."

Walking arm in arm, Jed and Ellie stepped through the busy doors of the town meeting hall to the stares of the gathered townspeople and farmers. Eyes fastened on the two new arrivals as they walked across the floor. Some were stares of curiosity and some were glares of pure hatred. A lady dressed in a beautiful blue cotton dress was with a man dressed in buckskins, looking every part a bloody Arapaho Indian. His long hair, black as a raven's wing, hung far below his broad shoulders. Some who had been on the wagon train with Jed knew different, and others figured him for a full-blood Arapaho, but none dared to say it.

The band started up as people gathered around the dance floor. Jed had seen dances back east when he was young then on the wagon train headed west, but never had he seen anything like the decorated dance hall with all its refinery and fine food.

"I hope you learned to dance." Ellie laughed softly. "They'll all be watching."

"I can do a scalp dance, a victory dance, and a hunter's dance." Jed looked over the dancers. "Which would you desire, beautiful lady?"

"Why, sir, that's a compliment, the first you've ever given me."

Blushing, Jed smiled and took her by the arm. "Shall we dance?"

Jed was surprised, in his arms, she was as light as a feather on her feet. Quickly, he found Indian dancing and white man dancing almost the same, just with different steps. After several passes around the floor, Ellie was elated and smiled happily, as he was a good dancer with natural rhythm. Not only could he dance, Jedidiah Bracket was the handsomest man in Baxter Springs.

Two hours and several dances later, Ellie, Wilson, and Jed sat eating pie and cake, a delicious treat that Jed didn't get back in the mountains.

Jed could feel the hatred in the room as they were watched, but no one dared speak up. Jed didn't know why they hated him, sitting and eating with civilized people. Maybe they were afraid of him, jealous because Ellie was the granddaughter of the only doctor in town or because she was a lady in the company of a heathen Indian.

The hour was getting late and it was a long ride back to the farm. Jed was about to tell Ellie it was time to leave when Luke Grisham came forward and asked Ellie to dance. Jed could tell the man was drinking, as the stench of hard spirits emanated from him.

"We were just fixing to leave, Mister Grisham, but I thank you anyway." Ellie turned her face from the man.

"It's early, Ellie. Surely you've got time for one dance with an old friend." Luke reached out his hand and grabbed her arm forcibly. "Why don't you dance with a civilized white man for once tonight?"

Only the sound of a hard slap sounded as Jed slammed his hand down on Grisham's wrist. "The lady told you no, Grisham."

Stepping back, Grisham shook his wrist and nodded at the door. "I'll see you outside, Injun."

"Oh, Jed, no." Ellie grabbed his arm. "No trouble, please."

"Keep her inside, Pa." Jed remembered all too vividly how Sally Ann had gotten into the line of fire accidentally.

"No, Jed, no please."

Walking into the well-lit yard, Jed found Grisham, standing beside Beck, in front of several of his friends. The younger crowd surrounding them was hostile, still believing Seth Wilson and Adam Beale had been murdered. Jed knew the scene inside with Ellie had only been a ploy to start a fight with him, and make Grisham look like the good guy.

"Well, Mister Bracket, you offered us a fight last time we met." Grisham grinned, as he had been drinking heavily, giving him the nerve to put up a brave front for his young friends. "You still offering?"

Jed could see the long knives clasped in their hands. Several of the watching townspeople stepped forward, wanting to stop the trouble they knew was coming. Several rifles appeared in the younger men's hands, stopping the older, unarmed men from advancing.

"From here, it sure don't look like you boys are giving me any choice." Jed looked over at the porch where Wilson was holding Ellie.

"We ain't, Injun." Willie snickered. "None at all. We aim to scalp you right here and now."

"Why don't you boys put down them pigstickers and we'll just have us a free for all. That way nobody gets hurt real bad."

"You scared, boy? We're gonna gut you like a fish, then maybe peel your stinking red hide off you." Beck bragged. "You ain't fit to be here with a white woman, Injun."

"That's pretty rough talk, Willie." Reaching down, Jed slipped his skinning knife from his leg sheath. "If I can't talk you out of it, let's get to it."

A big fur trapper by his appearance stepped forward. "You need any help, Luke?"

"Nah, Mister Cross, it's just one lousy Injun, not enough to go around." Grisham laughed drunkenly. "Thanks anyway."

Both men closed in on Jed with their knives waving threateningly before them. Jed circled to his left toward Willie, slowly moving into striking range. Suddenly, with the speed of a striking rattler, Jed's flying feet caught the smaller man full in the throat and nose, knocking him senseless.

"Now, Luke, it's just you and me." Jed looked down at the unconscious man, then advanced slowly on the scared Grisham. "What do you say to that, big mouth?"

"Shoot him, shoot him." Luke looked wildly about him.

"I wouldn't, boys." Wilson and two others held rifles on the younger followers of Grisham.

Grisham looked about frantically. He had no place to retreat to as Jed moved forward in a crouch. Faster than the eye could see, Jed's powerful leg swiped Grisham's legs from under him, laying the loud-mouth flat on his back.

"No!" Ellie screamed as Jed's knife flashed down toward the cringing man. "You heathen!"

Looking up at the porch, Jed released the whimpering drunk and turned away from the gathered people, walking to where the piebald was tied. Grabbing his rifle and reins, he swung up on the horse and galloped down the street, ignoring the yells from Ellie. Covering the miles to the farm in a hard run, Jed gathered his possibles and supplies, quickly loading them on his spare horse. Hearing the sound of another horse coming in a lope, Jed swung up on the piebald and waited.

"Looks like you're pulling out, Jed?" Wilson pulled the workhorse to a stop beside the piebald.

"You gonna be alright, Pa?"

"Yes, I'll be alright now, thanks to you." Wilson nodded sadly. "What about you, son?"

"If you need me, I'll come back."

"I'm sorry about what happened back there." Wilson shook his head. "Most folks around here are decent. You don't have to leave."

"I don't belong here with civilized folks, I've learned that now." Jed shook his head. "You heard her. I'm a heathen like she said."

"She was scared for you, son. She didn't mean to call you a heathen."

"She meant it." Jed kicked the piebald. "Good-bye, Pa. You know where I am if you ever need me."

Wilson sat his old horse and watched the piebald disappear into the dark. "You've never really been given a chance, Jed, and for that, I'm truly sorry."

Jed passed through Baxter Springs quietly, keeping to the dark shadows and out of sight. He knew Grisham was probably still in town drinking and he didn't want any more trouble. In three or four days, he'd be back to the valley where he intended to stay. Never again did he intend to return to Baxter Springs, except to pick up supplies and sell furs.

CHAPTER 3

*E*llie rode her horse to Wilson's farm at midmorning and dismounted. Upon hearing the blue hounds bark, Wilson walked to the door, hoping Jed had returned. After jerking open the screen door, he stopped short when he found Ellie standing by her horse.

"Ellie, what are you doing here?"

"I've come to see Jed, Mister Wilson." Her dark eyes looked over at the corral, hoping to find the piebald.

Wilson shook his head. "He's gone, girl. He pulled out last night."

"He didn't even stop to say good-bye."

"He wouldn't, it's not his way."

"I didn't mean what I said, Mister Wilson." Tears bubbled up in her eyes. "I was just trying to stop him from killing Grisham."

"You don't understand, killing is his way of life." Wilson touched her shoulder. "You can't take a man, living like he has, in the wild element and change him overnight."

"I don't understand him." She shook her head. "He can be so soft at times."

"Yes, he's a good man, but now he's lived as an Arapaho Lance Bearer." Wilson nodded. "Where he lives, it's kill or be killed."

"Will we see him again this year?"

"I don't think we will." Wilson shrugged. "Not in Baxter Springs, unless he is needed."

Mounting her horse, Ellie looked down at Wilson. "You're wrong, Mister Wilson, we'll see him again soon. I know we will."

"Miss Ellie." Wilson placed his big hand on her bridle rein. "A man like Jed… well, you've got to take him as he is. He can't be changed, not even by you."

"Maybe you're wrong, Mister Wilson."

Shaking his head, Wilson watched the woman cross the Pennybrook. "Maybe I am gal, but I don't think so."

Jed reined in at the rock ledge overlooking the beginning of the large valley and the far grove of trees hiding his cabin. Fear grabbed at his stomach, as no smoke appeared over the tree line and buzzards floated high in the sky far out in the valley. Anxiously, Jed kicked the piebald forward, pushing the tired horses down the last part of the steep trail. Hitting a hard lope at the bottom, he pushed the horses fast toward the cabin. Crossing the creek, Jed noticed the corral was torn down in shambles and his neatly stacked firewood turned over, strewn about the cabin wall.

Cocking his Hawken, Jed dismounted and stalked quietly to the cabin. Long deep scratches scarred the logs and door, showing where a bear had tried to tear down the door. Pushing hard, he found the door latch broken and the door barred from the inside.

Banging his rifle against the cabin, Jed hollered for Roden. "Lem, you in there?"

"I'm here, boy. I'm coming."

Jed could hear the scrapping of the heavy log that barred the door, keeping it securely shut against anything. Seeing the bloody shirt of the scout as he opened the door, Jed looked back over his shoulder.

"What happened, Lem?"

"They came Jed, before I knew what happened." Roden leaned against the door weakly.

"How many were there?"

"Two of them things, big ones." Roden looked about nervously. "I was lucky, I dodged in here and got the door barred."

"You hurt bad?"

"No, but I lost my rifle outside when they charged me." Roden looked past Jed. "I was afraid to go out after it, figured they could be out there waiting for me."

Jed looked about and found the rifle lying beneath the overturned table. Picking the Hawken up, he checked the priming. "It's been fired, Lem."

"I know." Roden nodded. "I think I might have gotten a ball in one of them devils as I rolled backwards."

"You were lucky." Jed shook his head. "I shouldn't have left you."

"Weren't your fault, boy." Lem smiled. "They're devils, Jed. Believe me, they're huge and mighty fast."

Jed looked out across the valley where buzzards were gathering on the grass. "What's dead out there? Where's the horses and mules?"

"Couldn't say for sure where the horses are, but it's certain something's dead out there." Roden stuck his chin out.

"I'll take a look. You get back inside while I go see." Jed tied up his packhorse. "I'll take care of that arm as soon as I get back."

"You be careful out there." Roden looked worried. "They're killers, if you could have seen the way they charged in here."

"I'll be mighty careful." Jed nodded. "You can count on that."

Mounting the piebald, Jed kicked the tired horse and crossed the creek. Snorting and sidestepping as they neared whatever was dead, Jed had to kick the animal hard to get him to move closer to see whatever lay dead in the tall brown grass.

It was the old red mule. The buzzards and scavengers had done their job well, almost completely devouring half of the carcass. Shaking his head, Jed turned the piebald back to the cabin.

"What's out there?"

"The old mule."

Roden shook his head. "Dang, they must have killed her before they came here."

"Don't matter now, she's dead." Jed looked at the corral. "Let's fix that shoulder and get you something to eat, and then I'll repair the corral."

"You know they'll be back."

"I know, but this time we'll be ready." Jed nodded.

"We're lucky, I hadn't penned up the horses yet for the night when they roared in." Roden looked over at the corral. "Them devils would have killed more of your stock if they were lotted."

"And you too, if they caught you afoot out in the valley."

"I'll drink to that." Roden agreed.

Roden was sore, but he wasn't hurt bad. The bear had struck him as he rolled through the door, only nicking him across his left shoulder and arm with its claws. He had been lucky to get the door barred before they tried pushing inside.

Fixing deer steaks and biscuits, Jed quickly fed Roden and wrapped his shoulder. Finished with what he could do for the old scout, Jed moved outside and went to work repairing the corral. Finished with the corral, Jed built a large bonfire, then went to work putting the yard back in shape and restacking the woodpile.

"You seen our horses?" Jed looked over to where Roden sat at the outside table.

"I tried to see them through the north shutter, but nothing."

Leading the piebald and his packhorse into the corral, Jed closed the gate and sat down beside Roden. "I'll ride out in the morning and try to find them."

"You be careful, Jed. I think I got some lead in one of them." Roden looked about in the dark. "I may be wrong, but they could be watching us right now."

"I doubt they'd come with this fire burning." Jed fingered his rifle.

"I'm afraid you're wrong this time. Them things ain't scared of anything, not even fire."

"Well, we know one thing for certain, they'll be back if we don't kill them first." Jed sat down. "I've got to find the horses tomorrow, then I'll start hunting for bear."

"Just wait a few days until I can go with you." Roden touched his sore shoulder. "I want in on the kill."

"Lem, I don't think we've got a few days." Jed shook his head. "We've got to kill them soon. You know they'll be back and this time around we may not be so lucky."

"I reckon we were lucky this time."

"Thanks anyway, but come morning, I'll ride out to look for our horses." Jed nodded. "Without them, we can't transport our plews."

"Just be careful and keep your powder dry."

After a night's rest, the piebald was rested and refreshed. Jed left the other horse locked in the corral where he would be safe. Admonishing Roden to stay inside the cabin while he was gone, Jed crossed the creek and headed for the northern most reaches of the valley. Traversing every square inch of the valley carefully before moving forward, Jed rode the piebald slowly, studying the ground for horse signs. He had confidence in the horse's ability to sense the bears, if they were near, but today he was taking no chances. The brown grass had died and wilted, leaving the coverage in the valley too short to hide the huge bears. Jed knew all he had to do was stay far enough out on open ground so the piebald could get out of the way of any charging bear.

All morning, he had ridden the north end of the valley. So far, no sign had been found of the horses or the black mule, so Jed turned the piebald back to the south. The Blackfoot ponies and the mule were badly needed for carrying his pelts to the settlements in spring. Riding slowly, Jed pondered finding the animals, and perhaps they had run off with a wild band of mustangs. He knew he would have to trade for horses if these were not recovered, but where would he find horses close by? Soon, the passes would be closed for many months and when they filled with snow, he wouldn't be able to ride to the tribes to trade.

Stopping, as the piebald threw up his head and looked across the valley, Jed tensed until a herd of elk raced away, disappearing from his sight. Looking up at the sun, Jed figured he had only a couple hours left of daylight before he would have to return to the cabin. To stay out in the open would be far too dangerous, and even if he had Roden backing him, it would still be a foolish thing to do.

Reining the horse through a narrow pass, leading into a small box canyon, Jed kicked the piebald into a slow trot. He only rode a short way into the canyon when the piebald raised his head, pinpointing the lost horses. Riding in slowly, Jed noticed the black mule and one of the horses had long fresh claw marks across their flanks. They both were lucky to have escaped the grizzlies. The bear hadn't done much damage to either animal. They only had scratches, not serious enough to keep the horses from being able to outdistance the bears, and escape.

Easing in among the grazing horses, Jed laid a rawhide loop around Roden's saddle horse and then around the black mule. The others were harder to catch, nervously moving away as he tried to get his rope on them. After haltering the two caught animals, Jed turned the piebald toward home, nodding thankfully as the loose horses started to follow him. Today, once again, the spirit people were watching over him, and he had gotten his horses back.

Almost back to the cabin, the loose horses smelled the dead red mule, refusing to follow the piebald any further. Instead, they stopped in the valley and went back to grazing. Leading the mule and horse across the creek, Jed rode up to the corral and quickly put the horse and mule in the enclosure.

Opening the cabin door, Roden stepped out into the fading evening light. "Found them, did you?"

"We were fortunate today, Lem. Now, if I can catch the other two, we'll be real lucky."

"I'll help you."

"Stay here, Lem. Keep watch and keep your rifle primed." Jed had an uneasy feeling he was being followed all the way home. "Something is out there, I can feel it."

Sitting down in a chair, Roden rested his rifle across the table as Jed crossed the creek and eased back to the last two horses. The horses were skittish and kept moving away as he closed in to lay his loop over their heads. Jed kept moving in slowly on the horses, pushing the piebald closer as the horses angled away from him. He knew it was going to take patience and a soft voice to gain their trust to allow him to get near enough to use his rope. The grizzlies had put a real fright into the half-wild Blackfoot ponies. For most of an hour, he circled the horses until he finally lucked out and flipped his rawhide rope across the smaller bay. Now, only one horse was left to catch. Jed watched the valley floor closely as the piebald was nervously throwing his head up and looking off to the south. He didn't have much time, as he had to get the horses locked up before full dark fell.

Finally, almost at sundown as Jed was about to give up and leave the last horse out in the valley, he managed to slip from the piebald, grabbing the last horse around the neck. Slipping the rope on the animal, he led both horses across the creek, lotting them and the piebald with the others.

"Boy, that took some doing." Roden smiled. "I didn't figure you'd get it done for a while there."

Jed looked across the valley. "There's something out there, Lem. I believe it followed me from where I picked up the horses."

"What are we gonna do?"

"All we can do tonight is build a fire and take turns keeping watch over the horses."

"You didn't see any sign that I might have hit one of those devils?"

"I'll tell you the truth, Lem." Jed shook his head. "I was afraid to get close enough to the timber to take a look see."

"No sign of vultures or crows?"

Jed shook his head. "Nothing."

"I'll get you some supper while you build a fire and feed the animals." Roden stopped at the door. "You know, if it's just wounded and still moving, the buzzards wouldn't come in."

"I wish I had brought some dogs back with me."

"Bear dogs?" Roden rubbed his chin. "That's a good idea. Old Morgan Lehigh used to have some downright vicious bear and cat dogs."

"No matter now, I ain't going back after them." Jed looked out across the valley. "This valley was peaceful when I first found it. Tomorrow, I'm going back out to make it peaceful again."

Roden shook his head as he watched Jed piling up dead wood for the bonfire. Hunting a man killer, any man killer, whether it's man or animal, was a dangerous undertaking. An animal was even more dangerous, this far back in the deep mountains, where the hunter was in their backyard. Men had guns, but the old scout knew animals had other senses that gave them the advantage in the deep woods, in the dark, and in brute strength and stealth.

Looking up as Jed came into the cabin, Roden placed food and a cup of coffee on the table. "How we gonna work it tonight?"

Jed shook his head. "You know, Lem, if you told me about this mess we're in with them bears, I'd call you a liar."

"Immigrants might not believe you, but any old-time mountain man would." Roden nodded. "Most all of us have had their run-ins with the bruins."

Biting into a hot biscuit, Jed nodded. "I fixed us a ladder up to the roof. That's where we'll keep watch tonight."

"That's good, they can't get at us up there." Roden sat down at the table. "I heard a French Canadian trapper tell one time about a wolverine that caused him trouble."

"Bad?"

"He said that thing was worse than any bear. That wolverine tore up his cabin, his trap lines, and ruined his whole season."

"Did he kill it?"

Roden laughed. "Nope, he packed up and lit out."

"Well, I ain't never met up with a wolverine, but I'm not lighting out. Come morning, I aim to kill me a bear. "

"You know he said that wolverine had a nastier bite than a bear." Roden shook his head. "If they have, I don't want no part of one of them things."

"No, we've got enough trouble with two little old bears.

"Two little old bears you say." Roden grinned. "What about tonight?"

"We'll take shifts guarding the animals. When we change out, we'll guard each other while we build up the fire." Jed sipped his coffee. "We'll take the thirty caliber up there. It ain't real heavy, but it'll give whoever's up there, two quick shots."

"Good idea." Roden swallowed. "Funny thing, I ain't the least bit tired. I doubt I'll get much shut eye tonight."

"If anything breaks loose, don't leave the cabin until I give you the okay."

"Good thinking, I sure wouldn't want to run out into the yard, right into one of them things." Roden agreed.

As the night passed, the two hunters changed places and replenished the fire. Jed shook his head disgusted, as he figured the bears were too smart to come into the firelight and they probably sensed he was on the roof. Nary a horse alerted during the night, as Jed could hear their powerful molars busily chewing on the grass he had pitched them. If he had to keep the horses lotted much longer, he would have to cut more hay to refill the barn. He wished he had brought back some bear dogs.

"You get much sleep last night, Jed?" Roden questioned as Jed pushed open the cabin door.

"Not much, a few cat winks when I was down here."

"Are you turning the horses out today?"

"No, we sure can't hobble them, they'd be dead horses if them bears attacked." Jed nodded. "I'll leave them penned, and you keep an eye on them from here."

"I rolled you up some dried meat to carry with you today." Roden laid a wrapped bundle on the table. "You be careful out there."

"Thank you." Jed took the meat. "Hopefully, I'll be in before dark."

Roden shook his head. "No hopeful to it, you be here before the sun sets or I'll come looking for you."

Jed left the piebald penned in the corral with the other horses. Today, he would stalk the bears on foot. He knew the grizzlies were nearby, and he was sure they followed him when he brought the horses in. He knew they might find him before he found them. Slipping quietly through the trees, bordering the valley, Jed searched every clump of trees and every bush as he moved stealthily forward. Today, the wind was still, not a blade of grass moved as he scouted along a small game trail. He hoped the bears hadn't winded him and wouldn't sense he was stalking them.

Several times, Jed checked the priming of his rifle, as he couldn't afford a miss fire if one of the grizzlies suddenly charged out of the timber. Circling in behind the cabin, where the brush and timber was the heaviest, Jed's fears materialized. Before him, less than a few hundred feet up the game trail, were fresh tracks and claw marks of a huge bear showing plainly in the soft trail. The tracks were heading back to the south, letting Jed breathe a small sigh of relief. For now, the tracks were moving away from his cabin and horses, and hopefully they were leaving the valley.

For two hours, Jed stalked the bear to the south, following the deep claw marks the grizzly left in the trail. Moving quickly, Jed wanted to hurry even faster, but the threat of a sudden attack from the brush was too great to get careless. Jed found where the bear had stopped to eat dried berries along the trail and where it dug into a dead log for bugs or termite larva. By its calm actions, the grizzly didn't know it was being followed, as Jed was still downwind of the animal. By the solitary track showing, he knew he was following only one bear, but he didn't know if it was the big sow or her cub.

Climbing a tall outcropping of a steep rock formation, Jed slipped behind a boulder where he could survey the lower valley and dense brush that bordered it. Below him and off to the south, Jed could see crows lighting in a tall pine. Jed knew crows were mischievous, curious, and very noisy. However, something held the crow's attention. Somewhere down there, something was hurt or down, unable to move. There were just too many of the black birds gathered to be fighting over a few acorns.

Now, his stalk became more stealthy and slower as he slipped toward the brush, straight to where the birds were making a fuss. Twenty minutes passed as Jed, step by step, stalked closer. Finally, one of the sentinel crows cawed frantically, sending the whole flock into the air, flying away as they spotted him. Jed halted, studying the surrounding trees, looking for an easy tree to climb, just in case he needed a refuge.

Nothing moved, nary a leaf or blade of grass, as Jed crept slowly toward a dense pile of brush. The surrounding timber was quiet as death as Jed stopped, listening for any movement ahead, but nothing stirred. He looked up at the overhead sun and it was almost midday. The cabin was at least two hours due north from where he stood. He couldn't wait for whatever was ahead to move. He had no time to spare, as time was short and he had to push forward.

Moving slowly, Jed kept behind the larger trees, trying to conceal himself as he stalked whatever was ahead in the bushes. The crows weren't circling for no reason, as they spotted something from their lofty perches in the tall trees. Less than fifty feet from the tall bushes, Jed knelt and listened. He could hear the ragged breathing of something in pain. Sweat ran down his face as he waited. Finally, the suspense became too great. Standing up, he moved to where he could see what lay ahead in the bushes. Shock hit him as he found himself looking straight into the eyes of one of the grizzlies. The bear was hurt and Roden was right, as he said he thought he had shot one of them back at the cabin.

Seeing him, the big animal tried to rise on its front paws only to fall back, too weak to get up. Looking about the heavy timber and looking for a tree to climb, Jed cocked the hammer of the rifle and took careful aim. The heavy recoil and blast of the Hawken echoed up the mountain slope as the rifle discharged. Watching the hurt grizzly stiffen and stretch out in a death kick, Jed knew his bullet finished the bear. Quickly examining the carcass, Jed found it was the other boar cub.

Suddenly, from high on the ridge, Jed could hear the thrashing of brush, and there was no mistake, it was the noise of a heavy animal coming straight down the mountain. Turning, he broke into a dead run as he hastily reloaded the rifle. The cabin was at least four or five miles down the valley, much too far to outrun the grizzly, if she pursued him. Wanting to stay close to the timber, in case he needed to climb a tree, Jed raced as fast as he could. Behind him, he could hear the bear coming through the heavy timber, breaking limbs, and huffing as the animal tried to find him. Jed knew his one advantage was the grizzly's poor eyesight, but he also knew their keen sense of smell and hearing neutralized that one advantage. He couldn't believe the bear would charge toward the sound of a rifle, instead of running away, but nothing these bears had already done was believable.

Silently slipping through the timber, Jed looked occasionally behind him to try to locate the bear. Eerily, not a sound came out of the timber causing Jed even more concern. He didn't know where the huge bear was, if she had his scent or if she was closing in on him. Running as hard as he could, Jed thought about climbing a tree, but that could be disastrous if the grizzly remained hidden in the brush, keeping him treed like a coon. He knew, sooner or later, Roden would keep his promise and come looking for him. He could possibly ride right into her deadly claws. No, he had no choice but to keep running as long as he could.

Stopping in flight to catch his breath, Jed knelt beside a large oak and checked the priming on his rifle. If she came, the showdown would be here, now. He hoped Red Hawk's prediction that the rifle wouldn't kill her was wrong. There were no more tomorrows. Today, he would settle it one way or another. Living in fear and dreading the grizzlies next attack on his cabin was finished and over with. If she found him here it would all end, and fleeing like a coward was over. No hunter would see shame in running from an animal with the killing power of a grizzly, but Jed was through running. Today, in this place, if she attacked him, one or both of them would die.

Jed knelt and waited, with every sense keyed in on any sound the bear might make, if she came toward him. Nothing, not a sound came from the dense timber on the trail behind. Slowly, Jed stood and retreated down the trail. He didn't know why she hadn't shown herself, but he wasn't going back after her today, it would be foolish. The bear knew he was here and was probably watching and waiting in ambush for him. If she came here, he would fight, but he wouldn't be foolish enough to walk back into her deadly teeth.

Now, Jed knew about where she was, and tomorrow he would return to pick up her track again. Today, she had led him straight to the wounded cub. She hadn't winded or sensed him behind her, and with any luck tomorrow, he would be lucky again. Now, he would return to the cabin and help Roden get ready for the long night ahead.

Returning to the north in a trot, Jed watched over his shoulder expecting the bear to rise up somewhere along his back trail and charge. Even as the smoke from the cabin became visible, Jed didn't let up his vigilance, knowing this bear was dangerous and a killer. With her speed and endurance, she could be anywhere behind him in the heavy timber.

"You been running hard, Jed." Roden met the winded hunter outside the cabin.

Sitting down at the table, Jed nodded. "She may be right behind me, Lem. Watch for her while I catch my breath."

"What happened?"

Between deep breaths, Jed quickly relayed the day's hunt, the shooting of the wounded bear and the long race home. "I'll tell you, Lem, I've been more scared in my life, but I just can't recollect when."

"I'll bet." The scout shook his head in disbelief. "I've never heard of a bear acting this way, never in all my put togethers."

"Red Hawk said she had my scent." Jed shook his head. "She had no fear of my rifle. Apparently, he was right."

"The way you're telling it, this old bear thinks like a man would?"

"So far, my friend, she's out thought any man I've faced, and I've faced many a man." Jed frowned.

"Never heard tell of an animal of any kind charging a rifle blast, never." Roden scratched his chin thoughtfully. "Cepting maybe if they were wounded."

"Well, at least you killed another one of them things." Jed nodded thankfully.

"I wounded it alright, but you tracked him down and finished him off."

"That only leaves us one more to kill."

"She's probably the most dangerous of the lot." Roden shook his head. "I'll tell you, Jed, the old gal has me stumped. I've never heard of a bear acting like this critter does."

"She didn't come after me today, why?"

"Beats me, but I figure sooner or later she'll be coming." Roden sat down. "This one's mean and she's a thinker."

"We can't let down our guard, Lem." Jed nodded. "We'll have to be on our toes until we get her."

Roden shook his head. "You know, I had me a woman once that hated just like this old bear does."

"Another woman, why did she hate you?"

"Never figured that one out myself." Roden rubbed his chin thoughtfully. "Unless it were that other woman I took up with occasionally."

"You think that's why?"

"Maybe, or it could have been cause I left her and went trapping with Fitzgerald." Roden seemed to be thinking. "Anyway, next time she seen me, she tried to take my head off with a skillet. Yep, that one was a hater for sure. I've never seen the like of her hating till now."

"Uh huh." Jed figured Roden was just pulling his leg.

"You didn't jilt this old bear for a younger one did you, Jed?" Roden roared with laughter slapping his leg.

"Keep a sharp look out while I water the horses." Jed shook his head at Roden. The old scout could find humor in almost anything, but to Jed the old sow wasn't humorous in any way.

With supper finished, Jed had the big fire going and the horses penned up tight for the night. Sitting outside waiting for full dark, the men discussed the grizzly, trying to figure her out. Roden had hunted and trapped these mountains for, what seemed to him, a lifetime. He had heard of many a mountain man getting mauled, sometimes even killed by a grizzly. Never, in all his days trapping, had he heard of a killer bear continuing to stalk a man as this one was doing.

"I think she's got the taste of man's blood and she likes it." Roden sipped on his coffee. "That's what I think. Has nothing to do with you."

"You may be right, but I don't think so." Jed shrugged. "Red Hawk says she's got my smell, and now she wants me."

"You going out again come morning?"

Jed nodded. "I have to, if we're gonna have any peace around here at all this season."

"It's dangerous business going after her on her own ground." Roden looked at the fire. "But no more dangerous than trying to run our traps with her stalking us every minute, not knowing when she will strike next."

"Cold times and snow will come soon." Jed picked up his coffee cup. "Maybe she'll hibernate and leave us alone."

"She'll hibernate for sure, but who knows when." Roden emptied his cup. "Question is, will she stay hibernated?"

"Well, one thing's for certain, we can't hole up and trap at the same time."

"No, I don't reckon we can at that."

Again, the night passed uneventfully. Climbing down from the roof at sunup, Roden went inside and woke Jed up. Rummaging around, the scout fixed breakfast while Jed put the horses back out on pasture.

Noticing the piebald still in the corral, Roden looked over at Jed. "You taking the paint horse with you today?"

"Ain't no sense letting that bear hide go to waste, if I can save it."

"Wrong time of year for hides, it ain't worth the risk." Roden argued. "She could be waiting on you."

"I'm hoping she will be." Jed picked up his rifle. "Keep your eyes open, stay close, and watch the horses while I'm gone."

Luke Grisham and Willie Beck sat in the Baxter Springs Saloon half drunk, nursing a bottle of rotgut whiskey. Since the fight at the dance, both men were nurturing both a bottle of whiskey and a deep hatred for Jedidiah Bracket. Jed had made both of them the laughingstock of the settlement. Even some of their longtime friends had turned on them, disgusted with their actions at the dance. Seeing how easily Jed had beaten both of them so handily, most townspeople no longer feared the two bullies as they once did. No longer were they followed and listened to in awe by the younger men of the settlement.

Since the dance, both men kept to themselves, inside the saloon drunk, not working, just talking, and nurturing their hate for Jed. Decent people in the settlement were still afraid of the two drunken troublemakers, avoiding the pair as much as possible. Both men, when drinking, could be dangerous. Not actually the shooters in the girl's death, most people still contributed the death of Sally Ann Duncan on these two. Not knowing Amos Duncan had paid for Grisham and Beck to run Jed out of town, the townspeople now blamed the two men for starting the confrontation that led up to Sally Ann's death.

"We've got to kill him, Luke." Beck mumbled under his breath. "We've got no choice if we want to live here with our pride."

"You ain't too smart, Willie." Grisham slurred his words. "It's been tried before."

Beck snickered. "You mean Seth Wilson and Adam Beale?"

"Yeah, I mean the late Seth Wilson and Adam Beale, both dead because they tried the same thing."

"We ain't them, Luke." Beck shook his head, trying to convince Grisham. "We're a whole lot tougher."

"Really, you're kinda forgetting how easy he whipped us at the dance." Grisham shook his head. "That Injun is powerful, and he'd of killed me if Ellie Zeke hadn't yelled out."

"No, I ain't forgetting nothing." Beck frowned. "We'll just have to be smarter next time."

"What's your plan, Willie?"

"We've still got friends, and we got what they want." Beck snickered.

"What would that be?'

"This." Beck whirled the bottle of whiskey.

"You talking about the Nez Perce?"

"No, not them, they are more afraid of this Crow Killer than we are." Beck grinned. "We'll ride north and have a talk with the Shoshone."

"The Shoshone? Have you gone loco, Willie?" Luke was shocked. "They're liable to take our hair."

"No, they won't. We'll supply them with rifles and whiskey if they'll agree to kill our Injun friend." Beck poured them both another drink. "They'll want this stuff more than they'll want our hair."

"That's crazy talk, Willie. Why would we do that?" Luke downed another gulp of whiskey. "Waste our money and whiskey to get him killed."

"You're forgetting, Luke, we used to be well liked and respected here. Now, look at us." Beck looked about the saloon. "Here we sit with all our friends, the two of us."

"I'm telling you, leave it be. You're asking for trouble." Grisham shook his head. "Folks around here find out we gave them cutthroat Shoshoni whiskey and guns, and they'll hang us for sure."

"I want my respect back, and that's only gonna happen when he's dead." Beck slammed his hand down hard on the table. "I aim to see him dead, Luke, and the Shoshoni are gonna get it done for me."

"And you think if he's dead, that's gonna get us our respect back?"

"It'll take some time, but soon enough people will forget how he whipped us and start coming around again."

"You mean they'll start buying our whiskey again. That's what this is all about isn't it, Willie?" Luke shook his head. "Selling our corn liquor, not your respect."

"I'm putting the Shoshone on him." Beck cussed. "You in or out, old buddy?"

"The Shoshone are a long way from here."

"Exactly, it's perfect, he'll never see them coming." Beck laughed crazily. "Those young bucks are bloodthirsty and a little of our spirits will make them even more so."

"How are they gonna find him?"

"Ed Wilson that's how. Old Ed will know where his boy is."

"Wilson? You're crazy, Willie." Luke looked across the table. "He'll never tell anything."

"He will if the Shoshone get hold of him."

"You'd turn them savages on him?" Luke shook his head in disbelief. "We're not heathens."

"I want him dead, Luke. I don't care how." Beck stared across the table. "Now, if that makes me a heathen, so be it."

"First, we helped kill Sally Ann and now this. No, I want nothing to do with this scheme of yours."

"I'm gonna kill him, Luke. I have to."

"Have you lost your mind, man?"

"No, Luke." Beck grinned drunkenly. "My respect, my girlfriend, and my customers are what I've lost."

Grisham looked across the table at the man incredulously. "I'm out of this, out."

"You scared, or what?"

"No, not scared. You just gave me my first good look at myself and I don't like what I see." Luke stood up.

"With you or without you, I'm gonna see him dead."

"It'll be without me, Willie."

Beck watched as Grisham pushed through the saloon doors and disappeared. He knew he wasn't bluffing, and he meant to kill Jedidiah Bracket using whatever means he had to. His livelihood depended on it, or he would have to get a real job. In his sick mind, he blamed Jed for losing all his friends, even his girlfriend, Sara Fletcher, the night Jed made a fool of him at the dance. Most importantly, his customers had quit buying his makings. Before the dance fiasco, when he walked through town, people noticed him and catered to him, but not now. Grisham thought it was the liquor talking, but Beck was fixing to show him differently.

Disgusted with Beck and his drunken schemes, Grisham staggered through the saloon door into the sunshine. Looking up and down the street, he quickly ducked into an alleyway beside the saloon as he noticed Ellie Zeke walking up the boardwalk toward him. As the girl walked past where he waited, Luke called out, stopping her. Noticing her look of disgust, as she turned and took in his unkempt drunken form, Grisham waved her closer.

"Give me just a minute, Miss Ellie." Grisham pleaded as she started to walk away. "Just one minute, it's important."

"What do you want, Mister Grisham?"

"It's Willie Beck, ma'am, he's threatening your friend Jedidiah."

"Jed isn't here, how can he threaten him?"

"Warn Ed Wilson, he could be in danger too." Grisham looked up and down the street nervously. "This is serious, Miss Ellie. Jed and Wilson are both in danger."

"I thought you and Willie Beck were friends?"

"We are, but I'll have no part in this." Grisham shook his head. "Willie's gone crazy. I've done what I could, you've been warned."

"Willie is no threat to Jed or Mister Wilson." Ellie looked at the drunken man. "How could that little weasel do either of them harm?"

"No, but the Shoshone to the north could." Grisham turned back down the alley, then threw his final warning over his shoulder. "Warn them or it'll be on your head, Miss Ellie."

"Shoshone?" Ellie had heard the tribe mentioned by many of her grandfather's patients. They were a bloodthirsty northern tribe who had no love for the white settlers moving into their lands. "Why are you telling me this, Luke Grisham?"

"I told you already, I want no part of it anymore."

"If you're speaking the truth, I thank you."

"Don't thank me, woman, warn your lover boy and Ed Wilson." Grisham turned and looked at her. "Or you may not have a boyfriend to warn."

Ed Wilson was surprised to find Ellie waiting outside his front door as he exited the house. Hurrying into the yard, he helped her dismount, then hugged the tall woman. Taking the reins of her horse, Wilson tied him to the hitching post in the yard.

"Ellie Zeke, this is a pleasure." Wilson smiled broadly as he turned back and looked at her closely. "You, my dear, have grown even lovelier since I saw you last."

Smiling, the woman hugged him again. "It's good to see you, Mister Wilson."

"Come inside for coffee, girl." Wilson knew this was no social call, as he could see she had something worrying her. "Looks like you need some."

Ellie took a place at the oak table and thanked Wilson for the coffee. "We've got trouble coming, Mister Wilson."

Sitting down at the table, Wilson looked across at the woman. "Tell me, Ellie, what trouble? Why are you here?"

"Luke Grisham said Willie Beck was scheming to kill Jed." Ellie sipped her coffee. "Grisham said Willie's been drinking and acting crazy since the dance."

"A back shooting skunk like Willie Beck would hold a grudge against a man he thought disgraced him alright." Wilson nodded. "Which is exactly what Jed did at the dance."

"Enough of a grudge to kill a man?"

"Men like Beck are the heathens out here, Ellie, not good men like Jedidiah."

Dropping her eyes, Ellie nodded. "I know I was wrong that night, I'm sorry."

"It's okay, girl." Wilson smiled. "Beck is no match for Jed in any way. Did Grisham say how he intended to do this deed?"

"Something about the Shoshone to the north."

"Shoshone?" Wilson's face grew hard. "They're bad actors alright. I wonder how he intends to lure them this far south to kill one lone white man?"

"I don't know, but Luke Grisham says Beck intends to pay them to kill Jed." Ellie looked across the table. "He's going to send them after you first to find out where Jed is."

"I am of no importance any longer." Wilson shook his head in disbelief. "I have already lost two sons, and I will not lose my third, no sir."

"What can we do?"

"Where was Grisham when you last seen him?"

"He was near the saloon." Ellie sipped on her coffee, her hands trembling slightly. "He rarely leaves the place. I can't figure out where they get their money to drink and loaf around Baxter Springs like they do."

"That's easy to answer, the saloon owner buys most of his rotgut whiskey from them."

"You mean they make whiskey?"

"That they do." Wilson nodded. "From what I hear, ain't many folks buying from them nowadays, since they've lost their bad man reputations. Folks are disgusted with them."

"So that's why Willie Beck is so mad at Jed. He showed them for what they are and they lost their way of making a living without working." Ellie nodded.

"Don't forget, Willie lost face with his used to be girlfriend, Sara Fletcher." Wilson looked at Ellie. "You go back to Baxter Springs, circle the settlement, and try not to let anyone see you returning from here."

"Why?"

"We wouldn't want anyone to know I've been warned, now would we?" Wilson smiled. "Let them think we know nothing."

"Be careful, Mister Wilson." Ellie walked outside. "I've seen Willie around town. Most of the time he's drunk and he does act crazy."

"Don't worry, Ellie, many have tried to kill Jed, and he's still alive." Wilson helped her on her horse.

Looking down at the farmer, Ellie smiled. "You are part of that warning, Mister Wilson, and I don't want you hurt either."

"Thank you, girl, but I figure it's just that rotgut whiskey they're drinking that's making them talk this way." Wilson shook his head. "Them two are both mainly loudmouths."

"My grandpa says a crazy person is far more dangerous than a sane one." Ellie picked up her reins. "He says they sometimes possess the strength of two men."

Wilson thought back on Seth. "Perhaps he is right. Now, you ride on home."

"Mister Wilson."

"Yes, Ellie."

"Do you think Jed is still mad? I would like to see him, speak with him." Ellie looked down glumly. "I really messed this up, didn't I?"

Wilson smiled. "Winter is coming, and the passes will be closed. Hopefully, we'll see him in the spring after break up."

"That's such a long time away."

"Yes, it is." Wilson watched her ride away and headed for the barn. Looking up at the sun, he picked up his milk bucket. First, he would milk, then he would ride into Baxter Springs. He wanted to have a long talk with Mister Luke Grisham.

The sun was already down, and dark covered the settlement as Wilson hitched his horse in the alley beside the saloon. Slipping unseen, up the darkened alley, Wilson located the back door to the saloon by the raucous laughter coming from inside. Returning to the darkened street, Wilson stepped on the sideboard and waited. Checking to see no one was out on the front street to see him, Wilson moved closer and peered in the window. Luke Grisham, Willie Beck, and another man, Wilson didn't know, sat at the back of the room with their heads close together, deep in conversation. Watching as Beck exited through the back door, Wilson moved back into the alley and hid in the shadows behind the saloon.

The slender form of Beck was well lit up by the coal oil lamps of the saloon as he reentered the building. Finding an empty crate, Wilson sat down and waited. He figured drinking the way he was, Grisham would come out to relieve himself before long. Twice Wilson stood up as the door opened, only to sit back down as the wrong man came through the lit doorway.

Finally, the door opened, revealing Grisham's face in the light of the doorway. Slipping beside the door, Wilson waited for the man to return. Several minutes passed, as Wilson thought maybe Grisham had passed out, but then the noise of stumbling footsteps coming through the trash of the alley sounded. Starting to step out and grab the drunken Grisham, Wilson ducked back as the door opened again to reveal Willie Beck's drunken face. The surly man reminded Wilson of a weasel, and that wasn't speaking well for the animal. Beck was a thin, mean looking individual, carrying a natural snarl on his face.

"Thought you'd gotten yourself lost out here, Luke boy." Beck spit. "Listen here, when you come in don't say a word in front of York about us killing that half-breed Bracket."

"I ain't saying nothing." Grisham stopped. "And I ain't doing nothing, like I done told you."

"You will if you want to make a living around here and hold your head up again in front of folks." Beck seemed to giggle.

"Cooking moonshine, that's a living?" Grisham cussed. "You do what you want, Willie Beck, just leave me out of your Shoshone scheme."

"Whatever you say, Luke. I'm still gonna have them Shoshones cut him in so many pieces, his own mother wouldn't know him." Beck cackled, and turned back inside slamming the door, leaving Grisham standing alone in the dark with his parting words. "He's gonna be dead, dead, dead."

As Grisham reached for the door handle, Wilson's huge hand grabbed him, dragging him further back into the alley. Struggling and kicking, the drunken brain of Grisham was terrified as he tried to yell out, only to have only small squeaks come from his windpipe.

"Shut up, Grisham, or I'll quiet you permanent like."

"Who are you?"

"How is Beck figuring on killing Jed?"

"Ed Wilson, is that you?" Grisham squeaked. "I know your voice."

The huge arm of the farmer stiffened as Wilson lifted Grisham bodily by his neck from the ground, slamming him, kicking up against another building. Squeezing the man's neck harder, Wilson leaned closer. "I'm giving you your last chance, Luke." Wilson could feel the man strangling and loosened his grip so Grisham could speak. "Talk, or I'll choke the life out of you right here, so help me."

Grisham's hand took hold of Wilson's arm feebly. "Let me down and I'll tell you."

"Talk." Wilson relaxed his hand slightly. "Spit it out and be quick about it."

"I'll tell you, Mister Wilson." Grisham rolled his eyes toward the door.

Wilson looked up into what little he could see of Grisham's terrified eyes. "Anybody steps through that door, Luke, before you tell me what I want to hear, and I'll snap that scrawny neck of yours like I would a chicken."

"He's gonna use the Shoshone to kill him."

"When?" Wilson hissed, his nose almost touching the terrified man's.

"He wants me to ride north with him, day after tomorrow." Grisham could feel the rage in Wilson, and he knew he was a dead man. "Don't kill me, Mister Wilson, please."

"Who is this York?"

"Stranger in town, Beck hired him to cook whiskey for us while we're up north."

"Tell me, how's Beck gonna lure the Shoshone down here?"

"Rotgut whiskey and guns, that's how." Grisham tried to swallow.

"You promise them young buck's guns and whiskey, they'll do anything. You can bet they'll come here for sure."

Wilson swore. "He must be crazy, putting guns in the hands of drunken Indians. Get them liquored up, and they'll kill everything and everyone in their path."

"I tell you, he's crazy, Mister Wilson, crazy like a rabid dog." Grisham squeaked. "I told him, I wanted no part of his scheme."

"You want to live, Luke?"

Almost frozen with fright, Grisham nodded. "Yes, sir, please."

"Then you head down this alley, leave Baxter Springs and don't ever come back."

"Yes, sir." The white face bobbed in relief. "I'll leave."

"Hear me, Luke, you let me see your ugly face around here again, and I promise you, you're a dead man." Wilson released his hold on the man. "Tell me, why does Beck want my son dead, so bad?"

"He's crazy, thinks he's lost face with his girlfriend since the whipping we took at the dance and we can't buffalo folks into buying our makings anymore." Grisham stumbled backward.

"That's ridiculous, kill a man over losing a woman or whiskey?"

"I told you, Mister Wilson, he's gone loco, plumb crazy."

"Git yourself gone, Luke." Wilson kicked Grisham in the seat of his pants. "I'm kinda loco right now myself."

Chapter 4

Wilson watched the man drunkenly lurch down the dark alley toward the street, disappearing into the darkness. He knew he should have killed Grisham so he couldn't warn Beck, but as he held him in his grasp, he felt the man trembling. Grisham was terrified, and a coward like him would run, leave town, and never dare come back. Wilson knew he was a farmer, not a cold-blooded killer, and it just wasn't in him to kill.

Easing back to the front window, Wilson watched as Beck and the one called York talked quietly together, occasionally looking at the back door. Finally, Beck stood up and called out the door into the dark. Shrugging, he returned to the table and sat down. Gathering his gelding, Wilson rode slowly back to his farm. Grisham had said Beck would ride north in two days. There was only one small trail out of Baxter Springs heading north to Shoshone country. Wilson nodded, he knew the trail to the north well and it was completely isolated with no settlers. People didn't live that far away from Baxter Springs because of the Shoshone threat. Now, Beck was fixing to lure them here with whiskey and guns. The man had to be mad. They might kill Jed, but then liquored up on rotgut whiskey and with the taste of blood; there was no telling what they might do next. Unsaddling the tired horse and turning him into the corral, Wilson looked over at Seth's grave. Wilson had never broken the law in his life, but no matter what it took, he wouldn't lose Jed. He planned on being on the north trail, well ahead of Beck.

Late the next day, after turning the cow out of the corral with her calf, Wilson mounted and crossed the Pennybrook. Cutting northeast, he headed for the trail Grisham had told him Beck would take. Dusk was falling as Wilson finally cut the trail north of Baxter Springs and dismounted. No fresh tracks showed in the sandy trail. Mounting, Wilson rode due north, wanting to get far enough out of the settlements to make sure he wouldn't be interrupted by anyone passing on the little used trail. He wasn't worried about missing Beck, as this was the only broken trail other than small animal trails leading north. Wilson knew Beck wasn't a mountain man or scout, and he would have to follow this lone trail to Shoshone country.

Bedding down beside the small path for the night, Wilson chewed on a cold biscuit and sipped water from his canteen. Wilson was troubled and didn't like being there, as this wasn't the type of man he was. However, he knew Willie Beck, along with Grisham, was partly responsible for Sally Ann's death. He thought of Seth and Billy, they were both gone, dying a well-deserved death that they had brought on themselves. Jed was different, and he didn't deserve to die by the hands of a sneaky troublemaker like Beck. Wilson swore under his breath, no sir, he wasn't about to lose his last son to the likes of Willie Beck. Shaking his head, the farmer knew he wasn't a killer, but sometimes a man needed killing and this was one of those times. He would kill Beck, because he wasn't about to let Jed be murdered if he could help it. Jed was only a stepson to him, but perhaps because of his mother, whom he had loved so dearly, he considered the boy as one of his own sons. Jedidiah Bracket was a man anybody would be proud to call son.

Daylight showed itself as the new sun peeked out of the east, waking Wilson from a troubled sleep. Walking the big gelding down to a small trickle of water that crossed the trail, the farmer knelt and cupped his hands full of water. He hadn't slept much, as his conscience still bothered him to think of what he planned to do today. Retracing his steps back to the campsite, Wilson relaxed against a tree and studied the trail back toward Baxter Springs. He couldn't believe he was here, a simple farmer, planning on deliberately killing a man.

He didn't have long to wait, as he heard a horse coming along the trail almost at the same time the big farm horse pricked up his ears.

Checking his rifle, Wilson stood up and walked into plain view in the trail. The fast drumming of the horse's hooves told Wilson, that someone was riding pretty hard. A hundred feet from where he waited, the horse and rider suddenly came into view. The thin man reined in hard when he spotted Wilson standing on the trail, blocking it. Grisham hadn't lied, it was Willie Beck sitting the blowing horse.

"Ed Wilson, what are you doing here?" Beck looked at the rifle Wilson held. "You out hunting or something?"

"Or something I reckon."

"What does that mean?"

"I came to kill you, Willie."

"What?" Beck's face drained of blood. "Kill me, what for? I ain't done anything to you."

Wilson nodded coldly. "You heard me, Willie. You plan to kill my boy Jed. Now, I aim to stop you right here."

"You're just a farmer, Ed." Willie composed himself and smiled. "You ain't a killer."

"No, I ain't, but unless you turn that horse around, you're about to make me one."

"You'd shoot a man in cold blood?"

Wilson shook his head. "I don't consider you a man, Beck. You're something that crawled out from under a rock."

"You're wrong about me, Mister Wilson." Beck stammered. "I was just out riding, that's all."

"You ain't killing Jed Bracket."

"Who told you I was gonna kill anybody?"

"A little bird."

Only the blur of Beck's rifle moving and the loud discharge broke the silence as Wilson felt the bullet sting his arm. Pulling the trigger of his own rifle, Wilson blinked as Beck was knocked backward from his horse. Looking down at the moaning gut-shot Beck, Wilson knelt beside the dying man.

"You did it, Ed. You done kilt me." The head slowly turned. "I wouldn't have believed you could do it."

"You were gonna do the same to Jed." Wilson shook his head. "I'm sorry, boy."

"He shamed me in front of my woman at the dance." Blood seeped from Beck's mouth as he labored to speak. "He shamed me."

"You shamed yourself, Willie Beck. Now, rest in peace." Wilson was shaken, as his shot had only been a reflex action when Beck's bullet hit him. It didn't matter now, the bullet had found its mark.

Catching the dead man's horse, Wilson hefted Beck and tied his dead body to the saddle. Shaking his head as he looked at the body, he couldn't believe he actually killed him. He came here to talk Beck out of this nonsense, and try to turn him back, but not to actually kill the man. Mounting his gelding, the big farmer started back to Baxter Springs, leading Beck's horse.

Ellie stopped in mid-stride as Ed Wilson rode down the street, leading another horse with a body tied across it. Hurrying to where he reined in at the town Constable's office, she rushed to his side. The stiff body of Willie Beck took her attention, then Wilson's arm.

"You're hurt, Mister Wilson." Ellie looked at the bloody sleeve.

"Not near as bad as Beck is, I reckon."

"You killed him?" Ellie shook her head. "I didn't want this."

"That was the only way to stop a man like Beck, Miss Ellie." Wilson nodded. "He was crazy, and he would have turned them Shoshone loose on all of us."

A tall, stern looking man stepped from the office as several bystanders gathered about the dead body. Looking at the body and then over at Wilson, the Constable picked up the dead man's head and stared at him.

"Willie Beck." The tall man looked at Wilson's bloody arm. "You men take the body down to Doctor Zeke's office, and you, Mister Wilson, step into my office."

"He needs medical attention." Ellie spoke up. "His arm."

"I see his arm, it can wait." The constable motioned Wilson toward the door. "Soon as he answers a couple questions, I'll send him straight to you, Miss Ellie."

"If you need my testimony, Mister Wilson, I'll be here for you."

Entering the jail, the man looked over at Wilson curiously. "What did she mean by that, Ed?"

"Nothing, Constable Rourke, she's just excited is all." Wilson lied, not wanting Ellie involved in the killing. In a small town like Baxter Springs a woman's reputation meant a lot, and he sure didn't want to taint Ellie's. "She's just trying to help."

"I see." Pulling a tablet and pencil out, the constable sat down behind his desk. "Alright, tell me what happened."

"Not much to tell." Wilson looked at the paper. "We had a few words, then shots were exchanged. I killed him out on the north trail."

"He try to shoot you first?" The constable motioned to an empty chair.

Nodding, Wilson sat down. "He shot first, but no matter, I meant to kill him."

"Why?"

"He aimed to get my boy, Jed, killed by liquoring up the Shoshone." Wilson exhaled.

"You speaking of Jedidiah Bracket, your stepson, also called by some, Crow Killer the demon?"

Wilson nodded tiredly. "He's my stepson, but he's more like a son."

"He is the one called Crow Killer?" The constable repeated his question. "Isn't he?"

"He is."

"So you took it onto yourself to stop him?"

Wilson nodded. "That's about it, Jim."

"Why didn't you report this to me?"

Wilson shrugged. "Wouldn't have done any good. I had no proof."

"So, you just took the law into your own hands?"

"Appears that way, don't it?"

"For the record, you say you have no proof of his intentions?"

"Just my word, and that's always been good enough for folks around these parts." Wilson looked hard at the man.

Filling out the report, the constable finally nodded and looked up. "Sign this for me."

"That it?"

"For now, go get your arm looked after." Rourke pushed the paper across the table. "Looks like a pure case of self-defense to me though, but we'll see what the magistrate has to say."

Leading his horse to Doctor Zeke's office, Wilson was met at the front door by Ellie, who had been watching for him from the window. Stepping into the small room, Wilson took a seat while Ellie went to work on his arm.

"It's just a scratch, Ellie."

"Scratches get infected, Ed." Doctor Zeke entered the office.

"What did the constable say?"

"Just took my statement and had me sign it." Wilson shrugged. "Said he'd turn it over to the magistrate."

"Magistrate, ha." Doc Zeke scoffed. "Dan Krueger is a joke, and a fine one to decide anybody's fate."

"That he is." Wilson agreed.

"Will everything be alright?" Ellie dabbed at the torn arm. "There won't be any trouble, will there?"

"They'll have to sober up old Dan first, if there is gonna be a hearing." Doc Zeke frowned as he watched Ellie work over Wilson.

"I don't know, but my son is alive." Wilson sighed. "At least, there won't be any drunken Shoshone on our doorsteps."

"Thank you for helping Jed, but I'm sorry I got you involved in this, Mister Wilson." Ellie cleaned the small tear.

"He's my son." Looking to where the doctor had his back turned, Wilson nodded. "I ain't one bit sorry."

"Ellie told me all about Beck and the Shoshone." Doctor Zeke spoke up. "You done what you had to do, Ed. When the people of this town find out the truth, they'll thank you."

"You have deep feelings for Jed?" Wilson looked into the girl's face. "I'm not being nosy, girl, just a father's natural curiosity."

Ellie looked then into Wilson's eyes. "I love him." The woman blushed slightly. "I'm ashamed I called him a heathen, so ashamed."

"When do you reckon Lige will return?" Wilson spoke to the doctor.

"It's hard to say, Ed. We had word, from a passing hunter, the train made it through the passes." Doctor Zeke finished dressing the wound. "He could ride in within a month, maybe less."

Jed pushed the piebald slowly through the trees as he approached the place where he had finished off the younger grizzly. On the ride from the cabin, the horse showed no sign of smelling or sensing the bear. Now, as they moved in closer to the dead grizzly, the piebald threw up his head and snorted.

Slipping to the ground, Jed approached the carcass warily as his nerves were wired tight with every sense alert. Nothing moved in the surrounding brush as Jed stared down at the dead grizzly. Circling a wide span of the area, Jed searched the nearby timber for any presence of the older grizzly. Returning to the stiff body, Jed pulled his skinning knife and started to work on the hide. Roden was probably right about the hide being worthless, but Jed wanted it. Not for bragging rights or to sell in Baxter Springs, he wanted to hang the hide on his barn wall to know for certain the killer bears were dead. These grizzlies had given him many sleepless nights, but they had also saved them from the Blackfoot the day of the battle. To be able to see the hides hanging on the barn would give both him and Roden a sense of relief.

Dragging the hide through the dense brush, Jed caught the piebald and loaded the heavy skin. The horse was a little skittish as Jed pushed the smelly hide across his withers, then suddenly, he turned and threw up his head. Whirling, Jed studied the near bushes as he backed away, leading the horse to the safety of the broad valley. The piebald sensed something in the brush, but so far Jed hadn't detected anything of the other bear's presence.

Nothing showed, but still the piebald was spooked, shying sideways and looking back as they moved out onto the grassland. Holding the Hawken, Jed's hands were sweaty, as he could almost feel the close presence of the older bear. She hadn't charged and he didn't know why, but he wasn't taking any chances, as his eyes stayed glued to the timber. His eyes narrowed and he wondered if she was there, as the heavy underbrush moved behind him. Jed's nerves were tight, strained to the utmost and his attention so intense, that he didn't even notice the small snowflakes falling. Winter was here, but it wasn't the snow that held his attention. Right now, Jed didn't care about snow or winter, as his thoughts stayed focused only on the bear.

Suddenly, near the edge of the woods, the bear materialized, standing to her full height. Rearing up on her hind legs and holding out her forearms, she sniffed the air. Quickly throwing up his rifle, Jed fired as the bear dropped to all fours and retreated into the brush. Cussing himself for hurrying his shot, Jed contemplated his next move. Reloading the Hawken, he waited, watching the tree line where the bear had disappeared when he fired. Was she hit or did he miss the shot? Dropping the piebald's rein, Jed started forward with his eyes focused on the near timber. Moving forward in a crouch, Jed gripped the rifle tighter, his finger curled around the trigger.

The bear hunt would end today. He was not going to live his life looking over his shoulder and staying awake nights, guarding his cabin and horses. Jed wanted the old sow to charge, come out into the open where he could get another shot at her before he was forced to go into the timber after her. He knew he was being foolish, as this bear was a grizzly. Under the best of conditions, confrontation with any grizzly was dangerous, but this grizzly was even worse, she was a man hunter. Around the campfires of the wagon train, he had heard many stories of grizzly attacks, and none had a happy ending. At least with this enemy, he was aware of how dangerous she was and he knew her intentions. Jed was completely calm, ready for her if she charged out of the timber.

Reaching the spot where the bear had shown herself, Jed examined the ground for any sign of blood. Finding nothing, he backtracked the grizzly at least a mile through the deep underbrush and timber. He couldn't understand her, as she retreated, moving away from him, but it couldn't be from the blast of the rifle. Only yesterday, when he had finished off the wounded cub, she came charging toward the sound of the blast, straight down the mountain. However, today she was definitely retreating and her heavy claw marks, leading to the south, were plainly visible in the soft trail.

Scouting out the entire area and after following her trail toward the mountain, Jed quickly retreated and picked up the piebald. Shaking his head as he looked one last time at the timber before heading for the cabin, Jed couldn't figure out the grizzly's actions.

"I see you got it." Roden eyed the skin as Jed led the piebald across the creek and into the cabin yard.

"I got it, and I got a shot at the old sow, but I didn't get her." Jed pushed the hide from the horse's back.

"What happened?"

Jed quickly told Roden everything that had happened out in the valley. Putting the piebald inside the corral, he carried the heavy hide to the barn, pegging it up beside the first one.

"You know, Lem." Jed looked at the bear skin. "The old gal is a killer, and she's after our scalps for sure, but when she stood up, I had to admire her. She's a magnificent looking animal."

"Magnificent." Roden scoffed. "Just don't forget she's a grizzly, and a mean one."

"I ain't forgetting."

"Snowed a little today and it's getting colder." Roden looked up at the moving trees. "Winter's just around the corner, won't be long."

"Yeah, I was a little busy and didn't notice the snow for a spell back there."

"I'll bet that was one nerve-racking hunt."

Jed nodded, thinking back on the day. "That, my friend, is putting it mildly."

"Are we guarding the animals tonight?"

"No, she won't be coming back here tonight."

Roden looked at Jed curiously. "How you got that figured?"

"Just guessing, I reckon." Jed turned for the creek. "I'll get the stock while you fix some hot coffee."

Jed and Roden sat at the table enjoying their coffee and listening to the wind howling through the trees outside. Walking to the door, Roden motioned for Jed to look outside. Snowflakes were blowing heavily about the cabin, already beginning to cover the ground.

"It's too early for snow." Roden shook his head in disgust. "This weather is starting to be as unpredictable as that old bear."

"I'm not a bear hunter or expert, but I agree, she is unpredictable. I sure don't understand her in the least." Jed sipped on his coffee thinking back on the afternoon. "Not one bit."

Retreating inside, Jed relaxed in his chair as Roden put biscuits to cooking in the Dutch oven. "I'd had you some food ready, but I didn't know when you'd be riding in."

"Or if I'd be coming back?" Jed grinned. "How's that shoulder?"

"Sore, but I'm ready to get back to work." Roden looked up from the fire. "For your information, Mister Bracket, I knew all along you'd be back."

"I was just joking, Lem. Now, don't burn your biscuits." Jed poured himself more coffee. "Tomorrow, let's finish laying out our trap lines."

Lighting up his pipe, Roden nodded. "This snow won't last. We'll still have some warm weather yet."

Jed remembered last year's early snowstorms. "You're probably right. The trouble is, up this high, you never know."

Jed was up early, refreshed and ready to ride. For the first time in several weeks, he had a good night's rest. Looking outside as he sipped on his steaming coffee, he found a thin sprinkling of snow covering the ground and woodpiles. Not enough snow to last after the sun came up, but still the first snow of the season and a premonition of the colder times soon to come. Walking about the cabin, studying the new snow, Jed found fresh tracks of night animals around the cabin and corrals, but no bear sign. Wolf, fox, coon, and every stalker of the night, followed the bank of the small creek looking for food. Looking out across the valley, he smiled at the smell of wood smoke and the fresh cut wood laying about the chopping block. The pure smell of the cedars and pines lining the cabin filled his lungs, and he was happy. Even with the bear problems, no finer place existed on earth.

Relieved with finding nothing, Jed returned to the cabin where Roden was cooking breakfast. He didn't know why he felt the bear had moved away from the cabin, maybe even out of the valley, but he felt she was gone for the time being. The heavy caliber Hawken hadn't wounded her or there would have been blood somewhere on the ground. A bullet that large and powerful from the rifle would have caused bleeding if he had hit her. Hopefully, she would go into hibernation and let them run their trap lines in peace.

All day, the two hunters crisscrossed the south end of the valley, returning to the cabin almost at sundown. The snow completely melted as Jed and Roden shut their horses inside the corral. Hitting a trot with his Hawken across his arm, Jed crossed the creek and gathered the other loose horses.

The light snow already melted, but the temperature fell fast with the coming of dark, almost cold enough to freeze. Looking around the cabin for the whetstone, Jed settled down at the table. After skinning the two bears, his sharp skinning knife had lost its edge.

Placing a cup of coffee on the table, Roden looked down at the knife. "Bear hides are tough and they'll sure dull a good blade."

"I've never found anything harder to skin, except the neck hide on a shaggie."

"What's on your mind for tomorrow?"

Jed dabbed a little bear grease oil on the stone. "Been thinking, Lem, maybe we ought to head down lower and get us some buffalo tongue."

"If we're going, I reckon we ought to get started before winter arrives."

Picking up his cup, Jed nodded. "It's settled then. Gather up your possibles, and we'll head out, come daybreak."

"How about a good deer steak?"

"Don't reckon I ever seen a bad one." Jed tested the knife blade. "I might eat two."

Daylight found Jed and Roden high on the north ridge leading the rest of their horses. With any luck, they'd need all of them for pack animals on their return trip. Jed reined in and looked down at the valley and the small spiral of smoke drifting up from the cabin. Even though, he wouldn't be gone long, it still gave him a feeling of forlornness to leave his beloved valley.

"Where we headed?"

"Lower down in the valleys. I found buffalo east and north of here last year." Jed kicked the piebald.

"Sounds like Turner's Hole to me. Lots of shaggies down that way." Roden nodded. "Leastways, there were last time I rode through there."

"They were still there last year."

The air up this high in the passes was thin and cold, piercing Jed's elk hide parka like a sharp knife. Two days passed as they crossed smaller valleys and streams dotted with trees and small ponds. Down lower, the valleys weren't as picturesque as his higher meadows were, but still the country was beautiful, wild, and untouched.

"If we run out of critters up higher, we can move our traps down here." Roden puffed on his pipe, staring into the small flames of their night fire. "Signs I've seen say the varmints are plentiful."

"If they're still there. Tomorrow, in the next valley, is where we'll find the shaggies."

"That'd be Turner's Hole alright."

"Who named it that?"

"Butternut Turner, hunter and trapper, but he wasn't much of a runner." Roden pictured the tall genial hunter with the big Adam's apple bobbing up and down his throat. "Injuns caught him one day, stripped him naked, and told him to run for his life."

Jed looked across the fire. "What happened to him?"

Smoke curled out of Roden's pipe. "Poor old Butternut, he didn't run fast enough."

"Fear of getting caught should have made his feet fly." Jed pondered the thought of being chased by howling Indians. "Sure would have mine."

"Should have maybe, but they didn't." Roden tapped out his pipe. "Good-night."

Bottoming out of the last pass, Jed already spotted a small herd of buffalo grazing peacefully across the valley floor. "We'll make camp here tonight. Tomorrow, we'll get our shaggies and head back."

"We've still got plenty of daylight left."

"Not today, it'll take time to skin, quarter, and load animals. Let's wait till morning."

"You're the boss." Roden looked at the sky. "Leastways it's cold enough the meat won't spoil, and the higher we climb, the colder it'll get."

"Let's unsaddle and round up something to eat."

Smoke from the small fire drifted along the skyline as Jed rested against his sleeping robe. The coming day would be hectic as skinning the big shaggies would be a hard, heavy day's work. He remembered the squaws of the Arapaho skinning buffalo and they made it look easy, but he knew better.

"Jed." Roden called out. "We've got ourselves some company."

Looking up, Jed watched as six warriors crossed the end of the valley and approached the camp. Standing up, he checked the priming on his Hawken and walked to where Roden stood by the horses. "What tribe are they?"

"Rees."

"Rees?"

"Arikara, plenty bad Injuns, Jed." Roden shook his head. "Bad luck on our part to have run into this bunch."

"Or theirs."

"They're young bucks, but from the time they leave their momma's breast, they're mean and vicious like rattlers." Roden frowned. "Be mighty careful, Jed, they're born fighters."

"So am I, Lem, if forced."

Six young braves sat their horses in a line, facing Jed and Roden. None spoke, they just sat, looking across the empty space between them. Jed had seen the same look from the eyes of young warriors many times in his short life. Full of fire and vinegar, the young bucks were out to earn a name and count coup on an enemy. The older looking of the Arikara rode forward several steps and pointed at Jed.

"Reckon he wants to talk." Roden nodded at Jed. "You best be careful out there."

"Reckon so." Jed mounted the piebald and rode forward. "I'll be ready."

"You do that, these Rees don't play fair."

Jed stopped looking across the short space, dividing him and the young warrior.

Several seconds passed, finally the Ree spoke up. "You here, our land. You hunt shaggies, you pay me."

Many times, he had heard these same words. "What do you want?"

"Why you come here, Arapaho?"

"Like you said, we come for buffalo."

"No, these our buffalo. You go." The warrior raised his war club. "You leave this place!"

"Nope, we came for buffalo and we're not leaving without them." Jed's face became hard. "Ride on in peace, or start fighting."

"Peace, hah." The young warrior spit out.

"We do not want to fight. You go."

"We let you have buffalo. You give us two horse." The warrior pointed at the horses. "We take those two."

Jed was curious how the warrior knew the English language. "You ain't taking a hair from any horse, no horses. We need them."

"Then, we fight."

"It's your funeral, Indian, not mine."

"What this word mean?"

"Death."

"It is a good day to die." Whirling his horse, he didn't hear Jed's last words.

"No, young feller, no day is a good day to die."

Jed watched as the warriors rode out into the valley and turned their horses. He had seen the same tactic before a fight so many times in his battles as a Lance Bearer. As Jed slipped from the piebald and rejoined Roden, the old scout nodded.

"What does he want?"

"Two horses."

"Figures, what else?"

"Ain't that enough?" Jed looked across at the warriors. "How did he learn white man's talk, way out here?"

"Jesuit Priests taught them. They're supposed to be Christian Indians."

"Christians, and they want to fight?"

"Just cause they speak English and are Christians, sure don't mean they're peaceful." Roden laughed. "They will fight, you can bet on it."

"Yeah, well here they come."

"I reckon they done up and lost their Christianity." Roden aimed his Hawken. "Too bad."

"Let's let them have this one pass, they're only armed with bows and arrows."

Arrows bedded into the ground as the warriors passed by yelling their war cries. "If they charge again, we ain't got time to discuss the situation."

"I don't think they were trying to hit anything."

Roden nodded. "They weren't. They were raised on them bows, cut their teeth on them. They sure wouldn't have missed an easy target like us standing here."

"Then what are they doing?"

"Just testing your mettle, Jed, bluffing." Roden spit. "They know how well we shoot these rifles. They're just trying to bluff us out of a horse or two."

Jed raised his hand at the waiting warriors, then his rifle. "If they come again, we'll fire."

"If they come again, you better."

Jed watched as the Arikara lined up for another pass, then abruptly turned their horses and rode away. Roden let down his rifle, then returned to the fire, chuckling.

"What's so funny?"

"Them young bucks, they love to try to bluff a pilgrim." The scout laughed. "This time it didn't work."

"How's that?"

"They ain't stupid. They had us three to one, but we had the rifles." Roden laughed again. "Just young bucks showing off how brave they are."

"That bravery could have gotten them killed."

"Yep, could have or maybe one of us." Roden picked up the coffeepot.

Early the next morning, four young buffalo laid about the small valley as Jed and Roden stepped out from their stand and approached the downed shaggies. Roden studied the end of the valley nervously, then looked over at Jed.

"Let's get them skinned, and pull out come sunup, tomorrow."

Jed followed Roden's eyes. "What's the problem?"

"Just a nagging feeling we're being watched." Roden's eyes studied the valley. "My neck hair is standing on end and when it does that, look out."

"Let's get back to camp and pick up our other horses."

"Too late, Jed." Roden nodded toward the lower pass. "We got more visitors."

"The Rees?"

"No, I don't believe so." Roden stepped back. "Worse this time. Let's get back to the horses and get ready for a fight."

"No, you get back behind me and keep your rifle ready." Jed looked to where Roden was staring. "I'll stay right here and act like I don't see them."

Thirty minutes later, two white hunters and an Indian rode up to where Jed was skinning the first buffalo. Looking up at the rough looking men, Jed wiped his knife and straightened.

"Sure nice of you to skin out our shaggies, Arapaho." The older hunter looked down at Jed. "Yep, mighty nice."

"Your shaggies?" Roden spoke up from behind Jed. "Since when is Turner's Hole yours, Bedoeux?"

"So you know who I am?" The hunter grinned a toothless grin. "That's real nice. Now, I don't have to be introduced."

"I know you and your running mate there alright, and that stinking Delaware." Roden nodded.

"Our trackers said two men, an Arapaho and a white, was in our valley hunting our game."

"The six Rees here yesterday, they your trackers?" Jed spoke up.

"You speak pretty good English for an Arapaho." The big hunter studied Jed curiously.

"I had a good teacher."

"You're pretty smart mouthed for an Injun." The other hunter spoke up, looking around. "Where's the rest of your bunch?"

"They're around here somewhere, I reckon."

"Your friend's right, this Injun here with us is a Delaware." The older man kicked his horse closer. "He could fix that smart mouth for you, real easy."

"I doubt it." Jed looked at the Indian. "I've got work to do. You men ride on."

"He is a smart one ain't he, Jean?" The smaller hunter barely started to swing his rifle as the bullet from Roden took him full in the chest.

Faster than the other man could react, Jed's war axe crashed against his forehead, killing him instantly. The Delaware sat still, not moving his rifle an inch.

Walking over to the Indian, Jed motioned to the two dead hunters. "You wanna join your friends here?"

"No."

"Load'em, then take their stinking bodies outta here."

"You kill white hunters, Arapaho." Broken English and hand signs came from the Delaware in a jumble. "Maybe, white law hang you."

"I'll hang you, if you don't do as I say mighty quick, or kill you right here." Jed raised his war axe.

Roden walked forward and stood beside Jed as the Delaware led the two horses carrying the bodies of the hunters back up the valley. Watching, as the Delaware disappeared, Jed shook his head.

"You knew them, Lem?"

"I know them alright, and that's why I fired when he made his move." Roden nodded. "They're French Canadians down from Canada with their Ree scouts, and that Delaware is Curasenay, one mean Delaware Indian. They've done for a lot of trappers to steal their furs."

"Bad men, huh?"

"Worst thieves and killers in the north country." Roden nodded again. "They were fixing to kill you. They've been hunted for years, up and down both sides of the border, but they were smart and too wily to catch up with."

Jed looked up the canyon. "The Rees help them?"

"Both of these Frenchies were blood brothers to the Arickara, and that's how they evaded the law for so long."

When Roden explained why he had fired so quickly without warning, Jed understood his reasoning. He felt better, because killing the two Frenchmen like they did was almost cold blooded. "I reckon they were fixing to kill us and steal everything we have."

"You reckoned right. They sent their Rees ahead to see how many we were. Then they came in here all innocent like, figuring they could handle it without help. Well, that was their mistake, coming in alone."

"What about the Delaware?"

"Don't know what he'll do now. We should have killed him when we had the chance."

"Why?"

"He was fixing to cut your throat, that's why." Roden swore. "That Delaware has put many a good man under in his time."

Shaking his head, Jed turned. "Let's get these buffalo skinned and get outta this valley."

"Keep a sharp eye out for them Rees to come back. I'll fetch the horses." Roden studied the valley. "Don't think they'll be back, but it sure wouldn't surprise me none in the least."

The horses and the black mule were heavily loaded as Jed led the way back along the trail leading out of the valley. Nothing had been seen of the Arickara or the Delaware as they skinned the buffalo and broke camp. With the four hides, Jed could make at least two more heavy coats to go with the coat Silent One had finished before he was killed. They would make a considerable profit, as he knew how valuable the heavy coats were to Bate Baker, the fur buyer. Jed knew from last season, the coats would entice Baker to buy the beaver plews.

Jed noticed ice forming on the water as they splashed across the many small streams that crossed the trail they were following. As they climbed higher into the high mountains, the temperature dropped as they rode back west, toward home. Winter was coming, and it was just around the corner, as the air was already frigid. Jed had no way of knowing what month of the year it was, but he figured it was still early fall, too early for the cold to be so intense.

Reining in at the summit, overlooking the valley, Jed stiffened. Below, he could see smoke coming from the cabin. Someone was there and had a fire going in the fireplace. Kicking the piebald on down the trail, Jed was in a hurry to see who was at his cabin. He had heard about cabin jumpers, but not this high in the mountains. Splashing across the creek, Jed spotted two horses in the corral. He recognized the tall bay horse immediately, it belonged to Lige Hatcher. It was the same bay Ellie had ridden here from the wagon train. Reining in, Jed hallowed the cabin, waiting with his rifle ready as the door opened.

"Ride on in, Jed, we're peaceable." Lige Hatcher and Ellie stood in the doorway smiling.

Reining in at the corrals, Jed slid from the piebald and shook hands with Hatcher. Turning to where Ellie stood, he walked over to her as Roden and Hatcher greeted each other. Jed was slightly embarrassed, remembering the last words that had been spoken at the dance. "Ellie, how are you?"

"I'm fine, Jed. How are you?"

"I'm fine, just surprised you're here, but pleased." Jed smiled. "What in the world are you two doing here this time of year?"

"I wanted to see you, and then we're off on our way to the Arapaho People."

"You're headed to the Arapaho?" Jed was shocked. "To the south, this late in the season?"

"Papa wants to go check on Walking Horse, and I wanted to see you." She blushed.

"It is good to see you again." Jed hugged her, taking her hand. "Let me unload, then we can talk."

"I'll help you."

Jed held up a hand. "These packs are heavy."

"I'm not a baby, Jed." Ellie laughed. "I'm a full-grown woman."

"Yes, ma'am." Jed agreed. "I can mighty well see that for myself, but you go rustle us up something to eat and get in out of the cold."

It was good to be home. Now, with Ellie and Lige here, it was even better. He still felt guilty about killing the two Frenchmen. He had killed many times, but it had always been in fair combat. The two Canadians never knew what hit them.

"If you're thinking on the Frenchmen, don't." Roden guessed his thoughts as they unloaded the horses. "In most places we would be considered heroes. Maybe, even get a reward for killing them two."

"I hear what you're saying, Lem."

"Do you? The young one was named Betile, and he was pulling down on you when I shot him." Roden looked over at Hatcher. "Tell him, Lige, out here it's kill or be killed."

"He's telling you right, Jed." Hatcher nodded. "Lem told me who you boys killed, and they were plumb no account."

"I seen him making his move."

"You've killed far better men than them two." Roden spit. "Let it go. You've got something much more interesting inside the cabin to fill your mind."

CHAPTER 5

The warm cabin was beckoning the three men as they finished unloading and tending to the stock before moving inside. With Hatcher's help, the animals were quickly unloaded and their packsaddles removed. The green hides were brought into the cabin, out of any passing varmint's dangerous jaws. The meat they carried back was already frozen solid and would keep until they could cure it for the winter.

"We had a good hunt, Lige." Roden was drinking coffee and watching Ellie as she fried buffalo tongue over the fire. "A real good hunt."

"Four hides, tallow, and enough meat to last all winter if we get it cured quick enough." Jed agreed.

"It'll keep, Jed. This cold will hold for at least a week, maybe more." Roden spoke up.

"Ellie says you're headed for Arapaho lands." Jed looked over to where the woman stood beside the fire. "Kinda late in the year, ain't it?"

"Nah, we'll make it." Lige looked over at Ellie. "She needs to check on her brother and meet her people, especially the woman who raised her."

"You got back from the train early this year." Roden swallowed his coffee. "You figure on trailing for Briggs next year?"

"Ain't heard no different, so reckon I am." Hatcher nodded. "That's why I want to check on Walking Horse now, may not be any time later."

"You've still got to get back before the passes close." Roden shook his head doubtfully. "You're sure cutting it close, hoss."

"I've been through them many a time in my days." Hatcher looked across at Roden. "You well know that."

Jed thought of the grizzly, and she could be between the cabin and Arapaho lands. "One bear is still out there, Lige, and she's gotten meaner."

"A whole lot meaner." Roden piped up.

"I seen you killed two of them." Hatcher nodded, as he had noticed the bear hides on the barn wall. "Anyway, she's probably holed up somewhere real cozy and warm."

"Don't bank on it, Lige." Jed looked again at the woman. "Don't ride that way until the cold times really get here. She's a bad one."

"Can't wait that long." Lige shook his head. "The passes could get snowed in and closed."

Placing steaming hot buffalo meat and hot biscuits on the table before the men, Ellie stopped their arguing. Jed and Roden hadn't eaten since late evening the day before and they were ravenous as they swallowed the delicious meat.

"Lige, she's a good cook." Roden smacked his lips grinning. "A real mudslinger for sure."

"And she's beautiful." Hatcher laughed. "Don't forget that."

Jed said nothing but agreed with both men. The food was delicious and she was beautiful. Smiling over at the woman, Jed nodded as she smiled back. Finishing their meal, Jed helped Ellie carry the dishes down to the creek to wash them.

"We could have washed them inside where it's warm." Ellie smiled at Jed.

"I wanted you alone for a minute." Jed laid his rifle aside and looked over at her. "I have missed you, Ellie."

"And I have missed you, Jedidiah Bracket." Ellie moved closer to him. "I could have died when you left without a word."

"I was mad."

"I'm sorry I inferred you were a heathen." She touched his face. "I was so frightened for you."

"I am a heathen." Jed thought of the two Frenchmen.

"Jed, I have something to tell you." Ellie rinsed the plates in the creek. "It's your father."

"Ed Wilson?" Jed looked closely at her. "What?"

"He killed one of the men you fought with at the dance."

"Which one, Willie or Luke?"

"Willie."

"Why?"

Quickly, Ellie explained everything that had happened. Why Wilson had killed Willie Beck, and the reason they were here in the valley. She had talked Hatcher into bringing her here so she could warn Jed.

"What will happen to Pa? They gonna charge him with murder or something?" Jed looked at the woman.

"They were, but after me and Constable Rourke had a little discussion, they decided to drop all charges." Ellie laughed. "Willie Beck selling the Shoshone whiskey and guns didn't sit too well with the town fathers. I'll be surprised if they don't give Mister Wilson a medal."

"What about the other one, Grisham?"

"Luke Grisham hasn't been seen anywhere around Baxter Springs lately."

"Now, you're heading for Arapaho lands?" Jed shook his head. "Why?"

"Since we've come this far, Pa wants to check on Walking Horse. He felt guilty about leaving him last summer."

"That's a long ride and it's cold."

"I'm half Indian, remember?" Ellie smiled. "We Indians are tough."

"You're half Arapaho." Jed took her into his arms. "I don't know about tough, but you are very beautiful."

Hatcher and Roden were still talking about the bear as Jed and Ellie entered the warm cabin. Both men were hunters and trappers, and both had seen the old sow in action. They knew she was indeed a man killer, but still neither could figure her out.

"I've seen and heard a lot of bear stories in my day, Lem, but this one beats them all." Hatcher tapped his coffee cup. "I watched as the bears attacked the Blackfoot, but is this the same animal?"

"Dang right, she is, ain't no doubt of that." Roden nodded as Jed sat down. "She's a caution, ain't she, Jed?"

"I wish you'd reconsider heading south, Lige. You'll be crossing her territory." Jed thanked Ellie for his coffee. "This one's different from a normal grizzly. She's a man killer, smart, and dangerous. She'll track a man like a bloodhound."

Hatcher nodded. "I've been traipsing these mountains for thirty years, Jed. I'm headed south, one surly old bear ain't gonna turn me."

"Jed's right, Lige. This ain't the time to be going out there." Roden looked over at Ellie. "You don't want Ellie harmed."

"She ain't gonna be harmed."

"No, she ain't, Lige." Jed looked across the table.

"Meaning?"

"If you're set on going, I'll ride with you to the Yellowstone."

"You've got traps to set, Jed."

"With luck, I'll be back in a week." Jed finished his coffee. "It won't be cold enough for fur taking for a spell yet."

Hatcher looked at Ellie. "Alright, Jed. I'm riding south and if that's the way you want it, you're welcome to trail along with us?"

"That's the way I want it." Jed nodded. "Lem, if you'll hold down the fort, we'll pull out at daybreak."

Shaking his head dubiously, Roden took out his pipe and walked to the door, then stepped out into the cold air. Walking to where the horses contentedly chewed on the dry grass, the old scout placed his foot on a lower rail and puffed on his pipe. After a long day, the one thing that was relaxing to him was the pipe and listening as horses chewed with their powerful molars. Turning, as the wind gusted, Roden looked up at the swaying trees. Heavy flakes of snow started to fall, covering everything under it.

Shaking his head, he pushed open the cabin door. "Anybody figuring on traveling better come take a gander at these clouds pushing in." Roden held the door open as Hatcher and Jed walked over to look out the open door. "They're sure banking up out there."

Gazing off into the distance, all three men shook their heads at the dark clouds boiling in. "This one's gonna be a rough storm for sure."

Jed shook his head doubtfully. "You still planning on pulling out, come morning, Lige?"

"Just have to wait and see what tomorrow brings." Hatcher pulled on his own pipe. "I'm going, Jed. If this storm hits, and it sure does look like it might, I'll wait till it blows over, but I'm going."

"Hoss, you're crazier than a loon." Roden laughed and retreated inside, out of the cold. "Crazier than old John Colter was."

Hatcher looked over at Jed. "I'm not being hardheaded, Jed."

"What is it, Lige?"

"I'm worried about Walking Horse. I've gotta know how he is."

"You could leave Ellie here."

"I could, but she may be needed." Hatcher shook his head. "No, she'll be going with me."

"She was raised in civilization. You think she'll hold up to the cold?" Roden questioned.

"I hope so."

Jed thought back to their hard ride from the wagon train. "She's a Hatcher and an Arapaho. I'd bet on it."

"Who was John Colter?" Ellie heard Roden call the man crazy.

"Well, Lassie, he was the first man across these mountains, back in the shining times." Roden grinned.

"That made him crazy?"

"I thought it did. The dang fool walked two hundred miles, durn near naked, and without a rifle, in shoulder deep snow."

"Why'd he do that?"

"Blackfoot caught him, stripped him naked, and sent him running." Hatcher looked into the fire. "He outran them all and survived the elements, varmints, and hostiles. A real mountain man he was for sure. Yes, sir, they don't make'em like Colter anymore."

"Amen to that brother." Roden laughed. "Colter was a shiner for sure."

"Trying to save his life was crazy?" Ellie questioned Roden.

"I thought it was. The rest of us were holed up, all snug and warm, while he was freezing his backsides off." Roden shook his head. "Plumb crazy! What you say, Lige?"

Hatcher smiled. "I say it was the dangdest bit of soldiering I ever saw, and I was there when he walked through the gates of the post, buck naked."

"He was still naked?" Ellie blurted out.

Only the clearing throats and red faces answered her as the two old scouts turned back to their pipes and coffee.

The storm hit with a fury in the early hours of the morning. Strong winds blew the heavy snow sideways, covering everything in its path. Opening the door for a quick peek, Jed could feel the temperature had dropped many degrees, and he could see the snowflakes blowing in gales, blinding everything in its path. Jed remembered the storm last year, and this one was far worse. Closing the door, he bumped into Ellie, who was standing close behind him.

"It's bad, isn't it?"

"Pretty bad, Ellie, but we're safe and snug in here." Jed smiled. "We've got plenty of good food and plenty of wood for heat."

"And if we ride south?"

"That I can't say. Hopefully, the storm will pass and the snow will melt quickly."

Taking his hand, then looking up into his eyes, she softened. "I have faith in you and Pa to see us through safely."

"If it was just me and Lige, I would feel more comfortable."

"You're afraid for me?"

"I've already lost one woman I cared for, Ellie." Jed smiled.

"I know about Sally Ann Duncan." Ellie nodded sadly. "It was the saddest thing I ever heard of. I'm sorry."

"Sally Ann's gone now, and all I have is her memory, but I will not lose you."

"Is that a proposal, Jed?" Ellie looked at him softly. "Is it?"

Jed thought of the bear, the storm, and the days ahead. "If and when we get clear of all this, then I will make my proposal."

"When you decide, Mister Bracket, I'll be waiting."

"Reckon how many horses will your pa want for you?"

"What?"

Jed laughed as he pushed her toward the fire.

As threatening as it had looked, the storm lasted only one day. While the snow came down it was heavy, lying in drifts across the valley, covering every tree and the cabin in its beautiful whiteness. Stomping to the corral to feed the horses, Jed studied the new snow covering the ground. Nothing was amiss, the storm kept all the night animals burrowed deep in their burrows. Tossing the animals several armfuls of hay, he closed the gate behind him and retreated to the cabin.

Hatcher and Roden stood outside the cabin, puffing on their pipes. Both nodded as he approached. "It over, Jed?"

"I believe it's blown itself out."

"That's the way I've got it figured." Hatcher nodded and looked off across the valley. "What do you think?"

"If we're going, let's get to it, right now."

"The girl." Roden protested. "It's below freezing out here."

"She's Arapaho, she'll make it just fine." Hatcher shrugged.

"No, Lige, she's white, raised white in a civilized town back east." Roden shook his head. "She's not an Arapaho squaw and she's not used to this frigid weather."

"She's my daughter, Lem, and she'll be fine."

Jed interrupted the arguing. "I'll be back in ten days, Lem, then we'll start trapping in earnest."

"By then, the beaver pelts and other varmints should be prime and ready to skin." Roden agreed. "I'll have the traps laid out and ready."

"You watch out for that grizzly." Jed looked across the snow covered valley. "She's still out there somewhere. Don't let her take you by surprise."

"I'll keep my eyes peeled." Roden nodded. "She pert near got me once so I'll keep both eyes wide open."

"If you don't, Lem, she's liable to peel them for you." Hatcher laughed.

"Do me a favor, Lem, catch up the horses, while me and Lige drag out our packs."

"Will do."

Ellie had a good hot breakfast frying in the cast iron skillets and biscuits in the Dutch oven. "Cook another passel of them dough biscuits, girl, while we saddle up."

"We're going?" Ellie was surprised. "In this weather?"

"It'll be okay." Jed smiled at the worried woman. "The snow is over, and what's on the ground will melt in a few days.

"It'll be a little frosty, daughter, but we'll be fine." Hatcher hugged the doubtful woman. "We're gonna make a mountain woman out of you."

Pulling out the buffalo hide coat, Silent One had made, Jed called Ellie over to him and slipped it on her. "That'll keep you snug as a curled up porcupine."

Smiling, she put her cheek against the soft fur. "It's so soft and beautiful, thank you."

Lem stepped into the cabin and motioned for Jed to come outside. "You've got problems, Jed."

"What now?" Jed shook his head and looked around for signs of the bear.

"The piebald is crippled, could be a horse kicked him last night."

Turning, Jed hurried to the corral. "How bad?"

"He's not ridable today. His ankle is swollen pretty big."

Kneeling beside the piebald, Jed examined the horse which had become his most dependable ally, over the last year. He depended on the horse more than himself when smelling out the enemy, any enemy. Cussing under his breath, he massaged the ankle. The swelling was bad, hopefully it was no more than a deep bruise.

"No, he's not going. I don't want to take a chance and permanently cripple him."

"He'll come out of it, but it'll take a couple weeks to heal up."

"I'll ride one of the Blackfoot horses."

"The bay?"

"Yeah, he'll work." Jed patted the piebald's neck. "If you will, Lem, soak that ankle in the creek a couple times a day. I think he'll be fine."

"I'll take care of him like a baby."

"You're a good friend, Lem, and a good partner."

"Thanks, Jed. That's a real compliment coming from you." Roden smiled. "Trust me, I'll take care of your horse."

"While you're at it, you keep a sharp eye out for that grizzly." Jed warned again. "Lige thinks she's gone into hibernation for the winter, but I wouldn't bet on it."

"I'm siding with you in that thinking." Roden nodded. "That old sow is smart. She sure gives me the willies."

"If that old gal catches you outside and not watching, she'll give you worse than that." Hatcher laughed. "Keep your powder dry, old friend."

"Not funny, Lige. She ain't catching this old hoss unawares again." Roden swore. "No, sir, never again."

Roden watched as the three riders rode south toward the far passes, disappearing into the brilliance of the sun's gleaming rays, reflecting against the snowy landscape. It was cold, and he sure didn't envy them the long hard ride, especially the woman. Arapaho women and children were raised in the hard winters and snow of the north, and they seemed immune to the cold. They understood and were accustomed to the hardships of cold and hunger. Roden wondered if the woman would be able to hold up to the rigorous trip that lay ahead of her. The heavy buffalo coat, falling beneath her moccasins, would keep her warm, but it was a long hard ride with many cold rivers to cross.

The smaller bay horse felt odd under Jed, compared to the heavier framed piebald. His gait was rougher and he didn't have the fast running walk of the paint horse that was so comfortable to ride. Jed took the lead, riding ahead of Hatcher and Ellie by a hundred paces. If the grizzly surprised them, he didn't want Ellie in harm's way. The old sow should be in a cave somewhere, hibernating for the winter, but this bear was unpredictable and dangerous. One storm had passed through the valley, but he didn't know if that storm was going to be enough to send her to bed for the winter.

Taking a final glance back down the mountain, as they topped out over the south ridge, Jed took in everything as if he was trying to remember his valley. Hopefully, with good luck and clear trails, the ride to the Arapaho lands shouldn't take more than three or four hard day's ride. Kicking the bay, he didn't wait for Hatcher and Ellie to catch up to him, pointing the horse on down the trail.

Two days later, the snow began to melt, showing the ground beneath only in places across the mountains, mostly under the round cedar trees. The storm had barely reached this far south before playing out. Riding into sight of the big river, Jed remembered when the two trappers Abe and Vern had tried to ambush him at this crossing. Looking about the two trapper's dead campsite, Hatcher and Ellie reined in beside him as he slid from the bay horse. Studying the fire blackened stones of the cold campfire, Jed shook his head.

"We'll camp here tonight." Hatcher looked across the big river. "Come morning, it's gonna be one cold crossing."

"I've got a raft hidden back on the Snake for crossing my pelts. I sure wish it were here for her."

"Yeah." Hatcher looked over at Ellie. "It would be nice to have one here."

"I'm gonna drag up some timber and see if we can fix her something to cross on." Jed nodded. "We've got a long ride ahead of us. It's too cold to get her and our possibles wet."

"Sounds good. I'll get a fire going while you see if you can get something tossed together. We'll go across at first light."

The night air was cold and crisp as the stars showed brightly overhead. The river was alive with different calls, as every animal that lived along its banks made some kind of sound. Further up the mountains, a pack of wolves set up a chorus of howling, with their lonely voices sounding forlorn.

"You warm enough?" Jed looked at Ellie as she ate her supper.

"Fine." The woman smiled. "This coat won't let the cold through it."

"Having fun?"

"Uh huh, it's so wild, but yet beautiful and peaceful here in the mountains."

Jed thought of the dead trappers and their violent deaths a year or so ago. "I reckon it's beautiful enough."

Hatcher sat with his back against his saddle. "It is that, Daughter, but remember the word wild. Stay close to the fire and don't wander away from it in the night."

"You told me that last night, Pa."

"I know I did, but you listen anyway." Hatcher pointed his finger. "You hear me, girl, you stay close to the fire."

Jed smiled, Hatcher could tell her, but that didn't mean she was fixing to listen. Ellie had a mind of her own. Nevertheless, out here danger lurked everywhere, and any traveler riding these trails should be very cautious. Indians, wild animals, poisonous snakes, or anything could be lying in ambush, waiting for their next victim. This time, Jed knew Ellie would listen to Hatcher's words, as she was completely out of her element.

Come early morning, Jed had the makeshift raft loaded with everything they didn't want wet. Near the water, Jed stood beside the three horses, stripped to his leather breeches. Ellie couldn't take her eyes off his muscular chest and arms. She felt sorry for him, as the morning air was crisp and cold, and the water would be even colder. She wasn't embarrassed in the least that her father was watching as she looked at Jed.

"I'll hold you with the rope, then I'll try to pull you across." Jed mounted the big bay horse Ellie rode. "I ain't promising anything, so be ready to swim."

Hatcher nodded over at Ellie. "You take that heavy coat off just in case we capsize this thing, girl."

As Hatcher poled the light raft out into the current, Jed mounted the bay and rode him into the cold water. Slipping from the swimming horse, Jed paddled alongside the animal as they worked their way across the fast current. With the rawhide rope around the bay's neck and chest, Jed was surprised the powerful horse could pull the raft across the river so easily. Reaching the far bank with the raft right behind them, Jed quickly pulled the light craft up onto the bank.

"You did a whale of a job on that craft, Jed." Hatcher laughed as he tossed Jed his clothes. "Bet that water was cold."

Ellie eyed Jed as he quickly dressed and pulled on his elk hide parka. "That looked like fun."

"In another day, you'll find out how much fun when we reach the Yellowstone." Jed grinned, looking at her clothes. "Uh huh, might get real interesting indeed."

"Keep your thoughts to yourself, Jedidiah Bracket." Ellie blushed slightly, then smiled.

Hiding the raft, Jed quickly covered it with dead branches and dry leaves, then rejoined Hatcher and Ellie where they waited with the horses. Turning the bay horse, he headed for the Yellowstone, miles ahead. Soon, they would be entering Crow hunting grounds, then after crossing the great river, they would be in Arapaho lands and hopefully the Arapaho Village would be nearby.

Midafternoon, Jed spotted the Crow warriors as they rode their horses across the flatland and circled them. He was surprised the Crow were this far from their villages, as the big hunts were over. Raising his hand, Jed recognized the same aggressive warrior, who had escorted him and Bow Legs to the Crow Village on their last crossing of the Yellowstone.

"You have come again to our lands, Crow Killer."

"I remember you, Two Tails, from my last visit to your lands."

"Where do you journey to?"

"We go to the Arapaho Village across the big river."

"You will not pass again across our lands." Two Tails shook his war axe. "Red Hawk is far away. He is not here to protect you this day."

"You think I need protection?" The words were more of a statement than a question. Jed could see the led horses marked with Cheyenne markings and a bound young warrior being pulled along behind Two Tails' horse. "You have been on a raid."

"Yes, we have taken many horses and this Cheyenne dog." Two Tails threw out his chest, giving the rawhide rope a cruel jerk.

Jed had to admire the youngster's courage, as no whimper or show of fear came from him. "Who is this young warrior?"

"Warrior, bah!" The Crow glared at Jed. "He was supposed to be guarding these horses when we captured him sleeping like a baby."

Jed rode closer to the captive. "What is your name?"

Only sullenness came from the young one as Jed looked down at him. Two Tails pushed between Jed and the boy. Kicking the youngster hard in the chest, the warrior laughed cruelly as the captive fell to the ground.

"He is a Cheyenne dog. That is all you need to know." Two Tails raised his war axe. "Now, turn your horses, Crow Killer, and leave our lands."

"You are Crow Killer?" The youngster hearing the name spoke up. "Is it really you?"

"Yes, I am Crow Killer." Jed looked at the shocked boy.

The youngster stood up, squaring his shoulders proudly. "I am He Dog, brother to Yellow Dog of the Cheyenne People."

"Yellow Dog?" Jed looked at the boy closely. "Your sister is Little Antelope?"

"Yes."

Jed turned to where Two Tails sat his horse arrogantly. "I will buy this prisoner from you."

"He is for our women's pleasure. He is not for sale." The warrior flattened his hand signaling no. "He will first be skinned alive, then roasted over their fires."

"How many horses?"

"You did not hear my words, Arapaho."

"I heard them." Jed asked again. "How much?"

"Look!" A Crow warrior raised his arm. "Red Hawk comes."

Jed looked to where the many colorful mounted Crow warriors suddenly appeared strung out across a high knoll, then with a yell they charged their ponies down the hill. The warrior, Two Tails, paled as he watched Red Hawk and his warriors racing toward them.

Hatcher looked over to where Ellie sat her horse. "Do not be afraid, daughter, it is Red Hawk."

"I am not afraid."

Reining in his spotted stallion hard, Red Hawk smiled over at Jed. "It is good to see you again, my brother."

"It is good to see Red Hawk."

"What do you do here? You should be hunting the fur bearers." Red Hawk looked around. "Where is the great painted horse?"

"He is crippled right now." Jed looked over to where Hatcher and Ellie sat their horses. "I was bringing my friends back to their people, the Arapaho, and to check on Walking Horse."

"And the one with the sharp tongue, maybe." Red Hawk laughed, then walked his horse over to where Hatcher sat. "It is good to see you and your daughter again, Rolling Thunder."

"It is good to see my friend, Red Hawk."

"You will come to see my father Plenty Coups before you leave." The handsome warrior smiled over at Ellie. "We will have a feast and dancing in your honor."

"I will do that. Thank you for the invite."

"Bring your daughter. Maybe I will trade for her." Red Hawk laughed again, then backed his horse to where Two Tails sat blustering. "It is too bad about your horse. I was hoping to have a race to see who has the best animal."

"Maybe it is a good thing he is not here. You might get embarrassed." Jed smiled.

Red Hawk nodded. "This is true, my friend."

"They are both great horses, especially the spotted horse you're riding."

"You two were speaking heated words when I rode up." The warrior winked at Jed. "Continue."

"Seems Two Tails here, doesn't want us to ride across Crow lands."

Looking over at the warrior, Red Hawk frowned. "You have been told before, this one is my brother. He has free passage over Crow lands."

"He is an Arapaho Lance Bearer." Two Tails shook his fist at Jed. "A dog!"

"You dishonor my father and the safe passage this one carries around his neck." Red Hawk pointed at the amulet Jed carried. "You will heed Plenty Coups word."

Jed spoke up before Red Hawk could finish. "I want to buy this young captive. He is the brother-in-law of Walking Horse."

"The sharp-tongued one's brother?" Red Hawk stared down at the defiant youngster curiously. "Yes, they resemble each other, mostly with their frowns."

"He is my prisoner, Red Hawk. I will not give him up." Two Tails raised his war axe. "Not even if the great Plenty Coups says to do this thing."

"It is Crow law." Red Hawk agreed. "I cannot take a prisoner away from the one who has captured him."

"I'm taking him. If Two Tails will not sell his prisoner, then I Crow Killer challenge Two Tails to fight for him."

"It is for Two Tails to accept your challenge." Red Hawk shrugged. "I cannot interfere with a challenge."

"Name your price, Two Tails, or fight for your prisoner." Jed pulled his war axe.

The warrior hesitated, as he knew he was caught. If he did not accept Jed's challenge, he would lose face in front of the other warriors and Red Hawk. A Crow warrior disgraced by refusing a challenge from an enemy warrior could never walk with pride among his people again.

"I accept your challenge, Arapaho." Two Tails slid from his horse. He had heard Red Hawk tell of Jed's strength and prowess with a war axe. "We will fight with only knives."

"Anyway you want it." Jed slid from his horse. "Bare hands is fine with me, if you want it that way."

Ellie heard the heated words, but didn't understand what was happening. Looking over at Hatcher, she questioned him without speaking as Jed dropped the reins of the bay horse.

"They're fixing to have at it over the boy."

"You mean fight?" Ellie looked to where Jed was removing his heavy, elk hide parka. "Why?"

"The boy is the brother of Little Antelope. They captured him and will let their women torture him. Jed can't let that happen to the boy."

"Jed could be killed or hurt seriously." Ellie watched as Jed handed Red Hawk his rifle then stripped to his bare torso. "Stop it."

"That would be impossible. Even our friend, Red Hawk, cannot stop a fight once a challenge has been given." Hatcher shook his head. "Didn't you hear me? That boy is your kin."

"I don't want him fighting for any reason." Ellie looked at Jed. "It's barbaric."

"Maybe so, Daughter, but that's the way it works out here, barbaric or not."

Taking both of the contestant's knives, Red Hawk laid them close together on the ground as the two combatants crouched, muscles wired, prepared to lunge forward. Dropping his hand, Red Hawk stepped back as the two warriors sprang like mountain cats at each other. Powerful hands grabbed at their opponent's arms as they fought to keep the other away from the knives. Back and forth across the flat ground, the two surged, each oblivious to the many eyes watching them. Their only thought was to get a knife and keep their opponent from getting his.

Falling backward, Jed tossed Two Tails over his head and managed to get his hands on one knife, while the Crow grabbed the other.

Crouched, ready to strike, the blades flicked forward like a snake's tongue. Muscles bulged as the fighters crashed together, grabbing at each other's knife arm, straining with all their might. Blood began to show as each man reached out with the sharp blades, slicing at their foe, causing blood to flow down their arms and torsos. Neither man hesitated nor drew back from the pain, so absorbed in their quest to kill their opponent.

Ellie wanted to turn her face as blood ran down Jed's arm and chest, but she couldn't. She had to watch, and urge him on with her eyes. Again and again, the two separated, then crashed back together, trying their best to end the struggle. Suddenly, as their bodies collided again, Two Tails moaned and stiffened, then slipped slowly to the ground. He charged right into Jed's blade, driving it deep into his own body.

Standing back, gasping for air, Jed looked down at the dying warrior, then around at the circle of warriors. "Does anybody else wish to claim this prisoner?"

None spoke as Red Hawk picked up Jed's hunting shirt and parka, then walked over to where he stood. Removing the rope from the prisoner's neck, a warrior pushed He Dog toward Jed.

"I am sorry, my brother, I had to kill this warrior." Jed pulled on his hunting shirt. "I think of the Crow as my own people."

Looking down at the dead warrior, Red Hawk shook his head. "Don't be, I never liked him even when we were young boys. This one always disobeyed his chief's wishes and caused trouble. He will not be missed."

"Thank you again, my friend." Jed accepted the parka and rifle.

"Go now, let the beautiful daughter of Rolling Thunder tend to your wounds." Red Hawk looked over where Ellie sat. "I watched her eyes while you fought with this one. She was scared for you, but brave the way a woman should be for her man."

"Then you're not gonna try to buy her from Rolling Thunder?" Jed quipped.

"What about the sharp-tongued one?" Red Hawk asked. "What does she think of this one?"

"She is the wife of Walking Horse, you know that."

"Yes, but does she?" Mounting his horse, Red Hawk reached down and shook hands with Jed, then rode to where Hatcher and Ellie sat their horses. Nodding, he looked across at them, then back at Jed. "Bring them and come to the Crow lodges, my brother."

"I will do that."

"He is the greatest of all warriors." Red Hawk looked over at Ellie. "Always honor him, as I do."

Kicking his horse, Red Hawk led his warriors away in a dead run, quickly disappearing over the near ridge. Rushing to Jed's side, Ellie examined the wounds thoroughly while Hatcher spoke with He Dog.

"I'm beginning to think you really are a heathen, Jed Bracket." Ellie dabbed at his wounds. "You're lucky this time, these are just flesh wounds."

"Will you still marry a heathen?"

"I'll think about it." Ellie smiled. "Is that a proposal?"

"It's pretty close I think."

Jed watched as the Crow warriors who had ridden with Two Tails quickly loaded him on a horse and followed after Red Hawk to the south. He had challenged the warrior, knowing he would kill him, but it had either been Two Tails' life or the life of the youngster, He Dog. In ways, Jed knew he was a heathen, but out here things were different, as this was a violent land and to survive, he had to be violent. Two Tails had intended the youngster to be tortured by the squaws of the Crow, so there was no other way to save him from a savage death.

The crossing of the Yellowstone was wet and cold, and the water chilled the swimmers to the bone. Jed didn't have a raft to float Ellie across so she had to swim with the horses. The heavy buffalo coat was carried high on the withers of her bay horse and remained dry. Quickly building a fire as they exited the river, Jed placed her wet clothing near the fire to dry. Now, the coat kept her warm and covered as she cooked over the open flames.

"Where you reckon Slow Wolf's village is right now, Jed?" Hatcher sat back, puffing on his pipe.

"Unless they've already moved back in the canyons, preparing for the cold times, they should still be at the little river camp."

"We'll ride there first."

"Red Hawk said the buffalo hunts were over." Jed stiffly pulled on his parka. "If that is so, I figure our people are finished with their meat taking also."

"They should be. The snow will be flying anytime now." Hatcher studied the young Cheyenne who had said little as they rode to the river. "Jed you plan on staying long with the Arapaho, or are you heading back right away?"

Looking over at Ellie, he nodded. "I'll be headed right back. Can't let Lem do all the work now, can I?"

"No, reckon not." Hatcher looked to where Ellie was staring at Jed. "When will you be heading to Bridger?"

"Hard to say. I may winter with the Arapaho and meet up with Chalk in the spring."

"What about Ellie?"

Hatcher shrugged. "She'll stay with me, I reckon."

"If Slow Wolf sends He Dog back to the Cheyenne, you could ride with them." Jed looked across the fire. "You'd be closer to Bridger's Post that way."

Hatcher nodded. "True enough, but I was hoping to do some hunting with Walking Horse."

"He will not have to send me back." He Dog spoke up. "Yellow Dog will come for me."

"You think Yellow Dog follows the Crow raiders?"

"He follows." He Dog nodded. "He comes here with blood in his eyes."

"We'll stay here tonight and let Ellie's clothes dry. Come first light, we'll head out." Jed watched Hatcher toss more wood on the fire. "Maybe Yellow Dog will show up."

"Yellow Dog come soon." He Dog repeated.

"Take me for a walk, Jed." Ellie placed her hand on his. "I need to walk."

"It's mighty cold away from the fire."

"I'm warm with this coat on."

"Okay." Jed helped her up and looked off down the river. "We'll return soon, Lige."

"Take your time." The old scout smiled. "He Dog and me will have us a talk."

CHAPTER 6

The Yellowstone rippled and lapped up against the bank as they walked slowly along its shores in the twilight of the evening. The slight breeze blowing was chilly, cold enough to make Ellie shiver slightly, even under the warm buffalo coat. Only the sound of their moccasins, crunching on the river gravel, could be heard as they strolled along the bank.

"I will miss you when you go back to your valley." Ellie pulled him close. "I will be lonely all winter."

"You shouldn't be lonely. You'll have your family all around you."

"I know, but most of them are complete strangers."

"The Arapaho people have big hearts and they will warm up to you very fast. Jed hugged her. "You'll see."

"But they are not you."

"It'll only be for a short time." Jed smiled down at her. "I will come for you in the spring."

"What if Pa rides on to Fort Bridger and winters with the Cheyenne?"

"No matter where he takes you, I'll come for you."

"I'll be waiting." Ellie smiled. "No matter how long it takes."

Out of the dark, several horsemen rode up as Jed and Ellie returned to the blazing fire. Grabbing his rifle, Jed relaxed when he recognized the big frame of Yellow Dog entering the light of the fire. Dismounting, he walked to where He Dog had leapt to his feet, grabbing him in a powerful bear hug.

"My brother, you are alive." The warrior looked his younger brother up and down. "I feared you were dead."

"I live, thanks to Crow Killer. The mighty one killed the Crow dog that captured me and stole our horses." He Dog nodded at Jed. "You should have seen the fight. Crow Killer is, as they say, a great warrior."

"Maybe like a demon?" Crazy Cat laughed.

He Dog shook his head. "He is far worse than a demon. He has the strength and heart of ten warriors."

Turning, Yellow Dog took Jed's arm in a powerful grasp. "I will forever be grateful to my friend, Crow Killer."

"It is good to see you again, Yellow Dog." Jed smiled down at He Dog. "The young one exaggerates like any good Cheyenne, but he did say you would come for him."

"We followed fast, but maybe we would have been too late if Crow Killer hadn't saved my brother."

"And me, Brother." Jed whirled to find Walking Horse standing behind him. "Are you glad to see me?"

For a few seconds, Jed could only stare at the warrior before him. Walking Horse had grown strong again, almost regaining all of his muscle and weight. It had been three months since he last saw the warrior. Time and plenty of good food had done wonders.

"Walking Horse." Jed was shaken with emotion as he grabbed the warrior. "My brother, you have recovered."

Walking Horse smiled as he heard the emotion in Jed's voice. An emotion an Arapaho Lance Bearer normally wouldn't show. "Yes, I have grown strong again, thanks to you and my sister. What do you do here, my brother?"

Jed turned to where Ellie and Hatcher stood beside the fire. "I came with your father and sister to check on you and our people."

Walking Horse shook hands with Hatcher, then hugged Ellie as he introduced her to Yellow Dog.

"It is good to see, Rolling Thunder." Stepping closer, Yellow Dog smiled, as he eyed Ellie. "You did not tell me your sister was so beautiful, Walking Horse."

Jed and Hatcher, both translated the warrior's words as they joked with her.

"Another suitor." Jed laughed. "Just what I need."

"Who else speaks for her?" Yellow Dog frowned. "Tell me, I will have his heart."

Jed laughed, as he knew the Cheyenne was just paying Ellie a great compliment. "First, there's me, Red Hawk, and about half the men in the white settlements."

"Ah, that is too many to fight." Yellow Dog wrapped his arm around He Dog and laughed again. "Too bad, little brother, seems she is already taken."

Hugging Walking Horse, Ellie shook her head as Jed told her their words. "Don't I get a say in who gets me?"

"Not out here, daughter." Hatcher nodded his head. "Out here, I set the bride price. I say who gets you for his woman."

"Oh really?" She looked over at Jed. "And what is normally the bride price?"

"Horses mainly." Hatcher smiled. "In this case, many horses."

"Horses, and just exactly how many horses am I worth?"

"Well, now, I don't know for sure." Hatcher rubbed his chin thoughtfully. "Most warriors like a little more meat on their squaws, and they want their women strong to do heavy work."

"Oh really?" Ellie pretended she was upset.

"Rolling Thunder is right. You are a little skinny to bring a big bride price." Yellow Dog laughed, watching her expression after she heard Hatcher's words translated.

"Too skinny?" Ellie frowned. "Well then, maybe I'll have to gain some weight."

"We need a woman with meat on her bones to keep us warm in the wintertime and build fires to do our cooking." Crazy Cat chimed in.

"Perhaps, I'm too skinny to cook you great warriors some deer steaks right now." Ellie shrugged.

"No, sister, you are not that skinny, and I am frail. Remember, I need my nourishment." Walking Horse pretended weakness.

"Okay, you poor thing, I'll cook up some deer meat while you all decide my future." Jed's translation of her words made the warriors all chuckle.

Big Owl, Crazy Cat, and the rest of the warriors took seats around the fire after greeting Jed and Hatcher. Finally, Yellow Dog became serious and looked over where He Dog sat.

"Tell me, Brother." The dark eyes stared hard at the youngster. "How were our horses stolen and you taken prisoner, without any alarm?"

Dropping his eyes, He Dog straightened his shoulders. "It shames me to say, my brother. I was sitting on my horse asleep when the Crow warriors sprang on me."

"Our father will not like these words."

"It is the truth." He Dog blushed. "They captured me as they would a child, while I slept."

"You will be punished." Yellow Dog looked over at the youngster. "For now, we are all happy Crow Killer and Rolling Thunder saved you."

"Tell us of this great deed and how Crow Killer killed the warrior, Two Tails?" Crazy Cat asked.

Proud to tell of the fight, He Dog went into a long tale, embellishing it to make it seem longer. "It was a great battle. The Crow was a giant with incredible strength. What a battle. Crow Killer killed the enemy but he should have scalped him. I would have."

"What about the other Crows that watched the fight?"

"You could see the fear in their eyes. After he killed the giant enemy, Crow Killer challenged any, who would not free me, to do battle." He Dog laughed. "They turned me loose quick."

"What about the great Red Hawk?" Crazy Cat asked.

"When Crow Killer challenged Two Tails to fight." He Dog shrugged. "Red Hawk would let no other Crows interfere."

"And our horses?"

"Be thankful you got me back, Brother. We can steal more horses." He Dog laughed. "One day, I will be a great warrior, much more valuable than a few scrawny horses."

"Scrawny? They stole two of my best buffalo runners." A warrior called Sharp Eye spoke up. "Scrawny?"

"I am sorry, my uncle. In my judgement, they were scrawny."

"He doesn't think much of himself, does he, my friends?" Yellow Dog frowned, then laughed, pushing He Dog over backward. "When our father gets through with you, maybe then, you won't be so proud."

"He may not be a great horse watcher, Yellow Dog, but he tells a great story." Big Owl hooted.

"The horses that were stolen, belonged mostly to the Crow anyway. We stole them first." He Dog shrugged, looking about the warriors. "I think they aren't worth getting all upset about."

Sharp Eye looked over at the river. "This young man has a swollen head. Maybe a good soaking in cold water will shrink it back to size."

Four warriors sprang on the hapless youth, picking him bodily from the ground and racing to the river.

"I do not think my father will like this very much."

"Your father is not here, we are." Sharp Eye laughed as He Dog hit the water with a big splash, coming up laughing as he paddled around in the cold water.

"Who wants to come in here and wrestle me?" One thing was certain, the youngster might be arrogant as all Cheyenne men were, but he was not lacking in courage.

The warriors could only shake their heads. "We are not so stupid, little one, to take a bath when it is so cold."

Laughing, the warriors pulled He Dog bodily from the water and pushed him toward the fire.

Ellie watched the proceedings from where she was cooking. "They can punish him later. They'll give him pneumonia in that river." She looked over at Jed, frowning.

"They ain't punishing him, Ellie. They're showing how glad they are to have him back safe."

"Sure is a funny way of showing it, trying to kill him." She piled hot steaks on the few plates Jed carried. "Would he have really scalped the dead warrior like he said?"

"He's young but he would have, like that." Jed snapped his fingers. "We're heathens, remember?"

"Very funny, Mister Crow Killer." Ellie frowned again. "Would you?"

"Would I what?"

"Scalp a human being."

Jed thought back on the fight with Standing Bull the Blackfoot, the only warrior he had ever scalped. "I have scalped."

Ellie almost dropped the deer steaks as she turned to look at Jed in shock. "You've scalped a man?"

"Only once, but he needed scalping if a man ever did." Jed looked into her eyes before she turned away.

"No man deserves scalping." Ellie refused to look at Jed. "That's barbaric."

Jed remembered the glass-eyed warrior. "If you think that's barbaric, Ellie, you should have met the Blackfoot warrior named Standing Bull. He was barbaric."

"Not bad enough to take his scalp."

"Yes, he was, and yes, I did." Jed frowned at her slightly. "If that makes me barbaric and a heathen, so be it."

Finding the village, a half day's ride from the river, Jed nodded over at Hatcher, then with a loud scream, he alerted the people to their presence. The whole village seemed to explode as the villagers ran from their lodges to see who had yelled. Singing and laughing as they recognized Crow Killer, the Arapaho, they swooped down on him and the rest of the riders, pushing in close, trying to touch their great Lance Bearer. Jed reined in the bay as he noticed the small figure of Little Antelope walking toward him. Slipping from his horse, Jed waited as the smiling woman approached.

"You have come home, my warrior."

"How are you, little one?"

The snow-white teeth, he remembered so well, sparkled as she smiled. "Now, I am completely happy again."

Walking Horse, with Ellie and Hatcher in tow, walked to where they were standing. "Look woman, your sister has returned and Crow Killer has brought your brother, He Dog, safely back to us as well."

"I see, my brother. Thank you, Crow Killer, for his life. Now, I will go speak with him, my husband." Little Antelope took Ellie by the hand and walked to where the warriors were surrounded by the villagers.

"She has missed you, my brother." Walking Horse looked quietly at Jed.

Jed knew that custom in the Arapaho Village was that a woman always greeted her husband first when he returned from a battle or hunting. He knew Little Antelope shouldn't have spoken to him before Walking Horse. Still, Walking Horse considered Crow Killer his brother and trusted him completely where Little Antelope was concerned. There was no jealousy in his heart.

Nodding, Jed smiled. "I have missed both of you."

Hatcher cleared his throat and studied the village. "I will go speak with Slow Wolf and White Swan."

"White Swan no longer walks the earth, my father." Walking Horse looked at Hatcher. "He has gone to meet his ancestors."

"I am sorry. He will be missed." Hatcher remembered when he and White Swan were both young together. "He was a great medicine man and my friend."

Hearing the words, Jed felt emptiness, as he had come to think of the old medicine man as his own grandfather. It had been White Swan's visions that had foretold of the big valley, the appearing bright light, and even the many battles he had endured in his quest. No more would his wisdom of the smoke and stones be of help to the people, and no longer would his medicines cure the people. Yes, he would be greatly missed.

"He was a great leader."

"Yes, but he was old. It was his time." Walking Horse nodded solemnly. "A man, even the great White Swan, cannot outlive his years forever."

"Still, it is hard to lose one like him."

"My sister says you will marry her." Walking Horse changed the subject. "She thinks much of you."

"Yes, after the cold times leave the land." Jed laughed. "If I can marry her before Red Hawk does."

Walking Horse smiled. "Red Hawk likes the pretty squaws."

"He is a good friend of Walking Horse and Crow Killer." Jed looked over at the warrior. "We must try to keep our friendship alive, my brother."

"It will be hard. The Arapaho and Crow have always been enemies."

"Turn your warriors against the Pawnee."

"That will be easy if the Arapaho and Pawnee should meet." Walking Horse pointed toward the women. "Come, Little Antelope will want to prepare food for you and Rolling Thunder."

"I have missed her cooking."

"I know your feelings for Little Antelope, and her for you." Walking Horse nodded.

"Yes, you do. The feelings of a brother for a good friend and a sister." Jed nodded. "You are the luckiest of men, my brother, she adores you."

"Yes." Walking Horse clasped Jed's arm. "Let us seek out Slow Wolf and Yellow Dog, then we will go to the lodge for our supper."

The drums beat long into the night as the villagers celebrated the return of Crow Killer and the rescue of He Dog. Buffalo tongue, steaks, and deer meat sizzled over the glowing fires as a circle of dancers pranced and cavorted around the huge bonfire. Several times, Jed pulled Ellie out into the circle and laughed as she protested.

"Remember, you made me dance the white man's dances when I didn't know the steps."

"I remember, but you are white, Jed." Ellie frowned.

"You are doing well, but you are Arapaho." Jed smiled down at her.

"So, I am a squaw to you?"

"Yes, you are a squaw. Be proud you carry Arapaho blood in your veins."

Several times during the feasting, warriors asked that he tell about the fights with the grizzlies back in the valley. All night around the great fire, He Dog told of Crow Killer's heroic fight with the Crow, which pleased Jed as he was not asked to tell about the fight himself.

Slow Wolf welcomed Jed into his lodge during the dancing, and for an hour he listened as Jed told of his adventures in his valley. The chief was curious as Jed told of killing the two grizzly cubs, but the old sow evaded him and then finally left the valley. Slow Wolf told Jed of the Pawnee and how they kept their word, staying away from the Arapaho Village and their horse herd.

"I am sorry for the loss of the great Medicine Man White Swan." Jed looked over at the chief. "He was like a grandfather to me."

Slow Wolf nodded sadly. "He was as a father to me."

"I will miss him."

"Go, my son. I have seen the daughter of Rolling Thunder." Slow

Wolf kidded with Jed. "Do not let Yellow Dog or one of the others steal her away from you."

"Yellow Dog doesn't want the woman, he just wants to pretend he does."

"I wouldn't bet my best pony on that, my son." Slow Wolf stood up stiffly. "Go, dance with your woman."

"How do you know she is my woman?"

Jed listened as Slow Wolf chuckled and shook his head. "I am old, my son, but my eyes are still bright. I can see the way she looks at you."

Late in the night, Jed and Hatcher retired to their robes, sending Ellie with Walking Horse and Little Antelope into their lodge. After the long ride, the fight with Two Tails, the small wounds he had received, and the dance left him sore, tired, and ready for sleep.

In the early morning, Jed was awakened as Little Antelope smiled down at him, shaking him by the shoulder. "Will my warrior sleep all day?"

Squinting up at the little woman, Jed shook his head. "It is barely daylight, Little Antelope."

"I have your food prepared. Wake up Rolling Thunder." The little woman looked to where Hatcher was snoring. "Bring him before the food cools."

"Thank you."

"I am glad you are here."

"Thank you, little one." Jed raised sorely on one shoulder. "I have missed you."

With her back turned to him, she asked over her shoulder. "Will you take the daughter of Rolling Thunder for your squaw?"

"Do you wish me to?"

"She will make you a good woman." Little Antelope turned and handed Jed a pot full of bear grease. "Have her put this on your wounds. It will take the soreness out."

"Thank you, little one." Jed watched as the small woman walked away.

The inside of the lodge of Walking Horse was warm, and smelled of hot steaks and onions cooking over the small fire. Jed and Hatcher stepped into the roomy lodge and took their seats across from Walking Horse. Looking over at Jed, Ellie brought gourds of food to the two men.

"I have examined Walking Horse's wounds." Ellie smiled. "He is healed and healthy. All he has to do now is eat and regain the rest of his weight."

"Thank you, Daughter." Hatcher smiled as he took his food. "It makes my heart happy that my son is well again."

"When do you go back to your valley?" Walking Horse bit into his food. "Will we be able to hunt while you are here?"

"No, I must ride back with the new sun tomorrow."

"So soon, Jed?" Ellie looked up.

Sadly, Jed nodded. "Lem Roden is alone, and the grizzly is still out there somewhere, plus our traps must be set soon."

"A man hunter is a dangerous animal, even more so than an enraged buffalo bull." Walking Horse remembered Red Hawk telling of the bear attacking the Blackfoot.

"She is a man hunter for sure. She has the taste of human blood." Hatcher added.

"You will hunt for her?"

"Only if she comes back to my valley." Jed remembered stalking the bears, and it made a chill run up his back.

Little Antelope moved to Walking Horse's side and sat down. "Perhaps your sister will help some of the people who are sick while she is here?"

Jed translated her words to Ellie. "Ask her what is wrong?"

"Our medicine man, White Swan, has been gone for several suns." Little Antelope looked over at Ellie. "Some of our people need a medicine man."

Ellie nodded. "Tell my sister, I will see the sick ones today."

"You can use Crow Killer's lodge." Little Antelope looked over at Jed. "He likes the outside better."

"Stay one more sleep, Crow Killer." Walking Horse asked. "We will hunt the elk and deer tomorrow, as we once did."

"One more sun only, no more."

"Good."

Riding behind Walking Horse, Jed remembered his early days as a Lance Bearer as he followed the warrior he learned from. Ahead of him on the trail, Walking Horse acted fully recovered, but he knew the warrior was still far from being fully back to his former self. The morning air was cold as the two warriors rode across the grassy swells they had hunted often and knew so well. Out there, the rolling grasslands were beautiful with the landscape so clean and untouched. Herds of elk and deer with a few antelope raced across the valley as they were startled from their morning grazing. Walking Horse pointed out a huge bull elk as they crossed a high swell. The bull was in his full prime and stood watching, fully alert to their presence as they passed further down the valley.

"He is the one we will take." Walking Horse reined in and slid from his horse.

"He is a good kill."

"Come."

Leading their horses slowly back down the valley, the two hunters kept out of sight of the watchful bull. Raising his finger, Walking Horse determined the direction of the wind, then nodded.

"If my arrow kills the bull, you will stay one more day and hunt with me." Walking Horse nodded.

"And if my arrow kills the elk?"

"Then, my friend, you can go back to your valley with the new sun." Walking Horse pretended sadness. "You have been greatly missed."

"And I have missed the people."

"Come, let us kill this elk for the people." Walking Horse slipped from his horse. "I will give you the first shot."

Leaving their horses ground tied, Jed and Walking Horse started stalking the bull elk. They had to get in range of the elk with their strong bows, which meant slipping silently forward, keeping out of sight of the bull for many steps. Peering up over the swell of grass, Walking Horse spotted the animal less than fifty paces downwind from them. Still, too far for their bows to reach accurately, Walking Horse fell to his stomach and with Jed following, crawled silently forward, staying hidden in the tall grass. Jed wished he had brought his rifle along on the hunt, as the big bull would have already been dead. Still, hunting with the age-old weapon of the Arapaho provided much more of a challenge to a hunter.

Raising his thumb, the two warriors peered over the grass, finding the huge elk less than thirty steps in front of them. Readying their bows, Walking Horse nodded. Both warriors rose to their knees, above the grass, and released their arrows. Walking Horse's arrow flew true, hitting the elk through the heart cavity while Jed's hit underneath the animal. Watching the elk run a short way, both men sat back and waited for the animal to bleed out.

Twenty minutes passed as they waited, studying the downed bull. The big elk was dead. He had not moved since he had fallen. Standing up, they started forward with their bows ready as four warriors stood up unexpectedly from another hidden knoll. Startled, both parties stopped less than forty steps apart, studying one another for several minutes before moving forward.

"Pawnee." Walking Horse looked over at Jed. "We have acted foolishly, my brother."

"Or they have."

Jed recognized one of the Pawnee as a warrior who had been at the Blue River, the day Bow Legs had lost his life. Reaching down where his arrow buried itself in the grass, Jed retrieved the feathered shaft, and quickly straightened.

Less than ten paces from the Pawnee, Walking Horse stopped and looked down at the dead elk. "My arrow killed the elk." Walking Horse pointed at his painted shaft sticking from the animal.

"And mine." The Pawnee turned the elk over, showing another broken shaft sticking from the bull. "Do you not see, Arapaho?"

"What is your name, Pawnee?"

"I am Wet Otter, subchief of the Pawnee Deer Clan." The Pawnee looked at Crow Killer and nodded. "The great Crow Killer is a poor shot with the bow."

"You remember me then, Wet Otter?"

"I remember you, Arapaho, from the day at the Blue water." The warrior glared at Jed. "You made big talk that day, but we had given our word not to fight."

"What do you do here in Arapaho hunting grounds?"

"We were passing through and needed meat." The warrior nodded. "We have a truce. Do you deny us meat?"

"The truce does not invite you here to our hunting grounds." Walking Horse spoke up. "This elk is Arapaho meat."

"It was my arrow that killed it."

Seeing trouble fixing to start, Walking Horse raised his arm. "I am Walking Horse of the Arapaho Lance Bearers and it seems you already know Crow Killer, my brother."

"We know who you two Arapaho dogs are." Wet Otter nodded at Jed. "I would not claim a dog like this one for a brother."

Walking Horse stepped forward, holding up his hand. "Will Wet Otter start our tribes to fighting again over an elk kill?"

Wet Otter swelled out his chest. "I did not ask for this truce, the Arapaho did."

"Take the elk. We will not break the truce over one elk." Jed nodded at the dead bull.

The Pawnee grinned. "Tell me, Crow Killer, brother of the bear, do you fear the Pawnee?"

Stepping closer to Wet Otter, Jed shrugged. "Do not be foolish, Pawnee. One elk, no matter how big or who shot it, is not worth dying over."

"There are four of us, Arapaho, and only two of you."

Jed laughed. "I will fight all of you alone, but I do not want this. Take the elk and go in peace."

"I, Wet Otter, Chief of the Pawnee says Crow Killer is a coward."

Jed held out his hand as Walking Horse started forward. "Wet Otter knows he cannot call an Arapaho Lance Bearer a coward."

Dropping his bow, the Pawnee pulled out his war axe and pointed at Jed. "I call you coward, Crow Killer. I will take your hair and your bear medicine this day."

Looking over at the other Pawnee warriors as they stepped back undecided, Jed nodded. "I did not want this, Wet Otter."

"I do. I will not walk away from a coward." Wet Otter raised his war axe.

Suddenly, in less than a blink of the eye, Jed whirled his right leg, crashing against the unprotected Pawnee's head, crumpling him to the grass. Walking over to the unconscious warrior, Jed sliced the golden necklace from his neck and stepped back, motioning to the other Pawnee.

"I could just as easily have taken his life." Jed held up the necklace. "Go, tell your people of the foolishness this one speaks."

One of the Pawnee shook his head in disbelief that Wet Otter had been so easily defeated. "He is only a minor Chief of the Pawnee. Perhaps when our high Chief Kills Eagle, finds out what he has done this day, Wet Otter will no longer be a chief."

Walking Horse only grinned as the Pawnee looked at their fallen leader in shock. "Take the elk, and take your minor chief out of our hunting grounds before Crow Killer kills all of you."

Moving cautiously back to the horses, Walking Horse smiled. "My arrow killed the elk so now you will stay with us another day."

Jed grinned to himself, as he had purposely missed the elk so he would have an excuse to stay. "Let's go find another elk."

Walking Horse laughed. "I know you, my brother. You are better with the bow than that. I think you missed the elk on purpose so you can stay with my sister one more day."

"You think you are so smart."

"I am smart, and handsome too."

"Now, you sound like Red Hawk."

Walking Horse nodded. "For a Crow, he is a good man."

Moving closer to the village, two deer were killed and tied across the horses, ready to take back to the Arapaho lodges. Jed could tell Walking Horse was tired. Even though tired, the warrior was happy. Hunting again with Crow Killer brought back memories of their first days together.

Leading their horses into the village, Jed took the meat into the lodges, leaving Walking Horse in front of his lodge. Taking enough back strap from one of the bucks to feed Walking Horse and his lodge, Jed returned to where Little Antelope stood beside Ellie.

"How did your doctoring go today, Doctor Zeke?"

"It was a long day. I'm really tired, but I am happy." Ellie smiled.

Handing the fresh meat to Little Antelope, he nodded. "The people already speak highly of you in the village."

"It felt good to help the Arapaho." Ellie smiled. "Now, you go speak with Papa while we prepare this meat."

Laughing, Little Antelope spoke in Arapaho to Jed's turned back. "She is not even your woman yet, and you already do as she says."

Swiping his finger across his throat, Jed entered the lodge. "Cook the meat, woman."

"What did he say?"

"He is a good man, my sister." Little Antelope replied in her broken English and Arapaho.

Ellie nodded. "You have deep feelings for him, Little Antelope?"

"Yes, but I have a husband. If I didn't, I would already be his woman." Little Antelope nodded.

"Can a woman care for two men?"

Little Antelope looked at Jed, then tried her best to answer her question. "Yes, I think this can be done, but a woman can only have one husband, she lives with, and she must be true to him."

Nodding, Ellie smiled. "Let's cook our men a good dinner."

"Will you marry Crow Killer?"

"Yes, if he asks."

Little Antelope nodded. "He will ask. He cares much for you."

"Are you alright with that?"

The little Arapaho smiled softly. "Yes, I wish him to have a good woman, and you, my sister, will make him the best of women."

"Thank you."

Two days later, in the early hours, Yellow Dog with his warriors and He Dog following, rode from the village. Ellie asked Hatcher to winter with the Arapaho and let her doctor the village. She knew many of the sick ones would need help to survive through the cold times.

As he waved good-bye to the Cheyenne, Jed swung upon the bay. Handing Jed a bundle of dried deer meat, Little Antelope looked up into his eyes and smiled. "Ride in safety, my warrior."

"And you, little one, be safe." Jed looked at the ones he had already said good-bye to. "I will miss you, all of you."

Slow Wolf, Walking Horse, Hatcher, and most of the village were there to see him off. Ellie sat a horse next to Jed, as she would accompany him a little way out of the village. Waving as they disappeared from sight of the village, Jed walked the horses only a little way before dismounting.

Holding her up close, he looked into the smoky dark eyes. "It will be a long winter."

"I will remain here in the spring. When you come for me, I will be here." Ellie hugged him.

"Do you have all you need to doctor the people through the winter?"

"I think so. If not, I'll make do somehow." Ellie nodded. "I met another medicine man that worked under White Swan. He knows wild herbs, and he will help me."

"Shadow Blocker?"

"Yes, he knows the ancient cures."

Jed liked the younger medicine man, but he also knew the deep jealousy among the healers of the tribes. "I think he is a good man, but remember he wishes to replace White Swan as the tribe's principal medicine man."

"I do not want to be the principal medicine man."

Kissing her, Jed helped her back on her horse, then mounted his own. "Good-bye, Ellie. I'll see you in the spring."

Leaning over, she kissed him again. "You didn't ask me."

Smiling, Jed looked into her eyes. "Will you come into my lodge when I return, Medicine Thunder?"

Laughing, Ellie nodded, as she knew the Arapaho people started calling her Medicine Thunder after her father, Rolling Thunder. She also knew Jed answered in the way of the Arapaho. "Yes, Crow Killer, I will come to your lodge when you return."

Kissing her one last time, Jed turned the bay horse for the Yellow-stone and kicked him into a hard lope, waving just before riding from her sight. He hated to leave her behind, but he needed to get back to his valley and start trapping if he was going to earn enough money to support a new bride. The weather was cold, but the snow held off, leastways here to the south. Jed had no way of knowing what the weather was in the high valley to the north, where his cabin was located.

Stripping quickly, Jed crossed the Yellowstone and turned upstream toward the north, heading for the big river. Above on the ridges, Jed spotted two Crow lookouts watching him. Crow Chief Plenty Coups and his son Red Hawk were true to their word and good friends. They kept their promise to keep a close look out over the Yellowstone crossing, making sure the Arapaho Village of Slow Wolf was not attacked by the Pawnee. With the Crow watching the river and Walking Horse regaining his strength, Jed felt comfortable the Arapaho were safe. Now, it was time for him to return to his valley. Jed wondered as he rode north, how long would the two enemies, the Crow and Arapaho, remain on friendly terms.

Kicking the fresh horse into a ground-eating lope, Jed started for the big river. With luck, he would be back at the cabin in three days. Crossing mile after mile of beautiful valleys and mountains, he found they abounded with game. Along the trail, he passed deer, elk, buffalo, and even wild bands of horses raced the wind before him.

Jed gripped the bay hard with his legs as the horse tried to lunge ahead and run with his brothers of the wild plains. Reining him in, Jed looked with admiration at the beautiful flowing manes and streaming tails of the wild ones. There were horses of every color and size. Next summer, he intended to return with Lem Roden to catch some of these horses to resell in the settlements. Most were too small to pull the heavy plow of the whites, but there were a few that would bring good money when broken to the saddle.

Late evening of the second day on the trail, Jed rode down to the bank of the big river and watered the tired bay. Already too late in the day to cross, Jed hobbled the horse and kicked together a small fire in a cove of the river. He dreaded the thought of another cold swim come morning, but the river lay before him and it would have to be crossed.

Pulling out Little Antelope's deer meat, Jed chewed on the tough meat slowly as he enjoyed the warm fire. Pulling his blanket across his body, Jed checked his Hawken and leaned back, studying the clear star-sprinkled sky overhead. Chewing on his supper, he thought on using the raft he had made for Ellie to ferry his possibles across, but that would mean he would have to cross the river twice. No, he would not use the raft. He would place his gear high on the horse's back to try to keep them dry.

The river was high from the heavy rains upstream and the water was cold. Early the next morning, Jed grew goose bumps as he waded into the water and started the long swim. Unavoidably, his clothes and sleeping robe had become wet as he crossed, but the rifle, powder horn, and possibles bag were kept dry. Holding onto the bay's long mane with one hand and holding the rifle across the horse's withers, out of the water, was tiring with such a strong current. Wading tiredly from the river, Jed pulled his damp clothes on. He led the horse afoot in a trot, trying to heat up his body.

Jed looked at the campsite of the dead trappers, Vern and Abe, in passing and continued in a trot up the narrow trail, leading north away from the river. He thought of Ellie, and only days before they had camped there, but now, the site seemed lonely. He remembered the trail well, as it turned and weaved, and how steep and narrow it could become. Late in the afternoon, as he neared the crest of the steep pass, the wind shifted out of the east, bringing with it a soft warm wind. Jed's clothes dried as he stopped to water the horse and chew on the dried meat. Only his parka and sleeping robe were still wet.

Up high in this peaceful place, Jed let his thoughts once again return to his parting with Ellie. He smiled, as it would be a long winter, but spring would return and he would go for her. Daydreaming of the beautiful woman and with his mind focused on her, Jed didn't see the horse's ears rise. Suddenly, a rush of a brown mass took the horse down with a mighty sweep of its powerful claws. Whirling, Jed discharged the rifle as the grizzly knocked it from his hands. Temporarily stopped by the roar of the rifle and smoke, the bear stood up to its full height, then lunged at the dying horse. With the bear attacking the kicking horse, Jed had time to retreat to a lone oak tree, climbing a low hanging limb, big enough to give him sanctuary.

Barely reaching the third limb, Jed climbed as fast as he could when the old, she bear grabbed for his moccasined foot. Kicking at the large snout, he barely pulled his foot away as her giant molars snapped together. Looking down, Jed couldn't believe his eyes, as the eight hundred pound or more behemoth was trying her best to climb the tree. Climbing higher, Jed looked down to where his rifle lay empty and useless below on the ground. Knowing what Walking Horse would say, Jed cussed himself for his carelessness, causing him to be in this predicament. Dropping his guard for only a moment with his thoughts consumed in daydreaming, and now he sat treed like a coon. However, below him wasn't merely a pack of hunting dogs, but a man killing bear. He had completely ignored Walking Horse's first lesson of warfare, always be aware of your surroundings when in a strange country.

Looking down, as the bear tore at the dead horse, Jed cussed himself again for his stupidity in letting his guard down. Sitting up in the tree like a possum and looking down at the bear, Jed found himself in the exact position he had worried about as he tracked the bear and killed her cub. Below, she could wait him out, weakening him, while she ate on horse meat, drank water, and stayed fat and sassy.

Studying the mountainside, above where he was perched, Jed looked at the rock outcropping, only yards from the limb he sat on. If he could somehow reach the one rock, he could see a passageway going up the mountain, much too small for the bear to get through. Luckily, he kept Little Antelope's dried meat tucked inside his shirt so he would have something to eat. He hoped the bear would become discouraged, as she had already attempted several times to climb the oak, only to fall back to the ground. Hopefully, she would become bored with him and wander off, but Jed feared this would not be. She had her kill and she knew he was up in the tree, so several days could pass before she gave up and left.

Out across the mountains, he knew the cabin was at least three days away as a crow flew. Below him, his prized rifle lay close to the dead horse, an unthinkable distance for him to reach before the bear could catch him in her mighty jaws. The strong bow of Walking Horse and his quiver of arrows lay at the base of the oak, where he had dropped them in his haste to climb the tree. Only a few feet away, the bow might as well be in the Arapaho Village, as it was out of his reach.

Jed could feel the bear was toying with him, waiting for him to dare come down from the tree. Shaking his head, Jed looked at his weapons, a skinning knife in his leggings and his war axe in his rawhide belt. The bear taunted him, keeping her back to him as she fed on the dead horse. His hands itched to get the rifle, as one well-placed shot would free him from this predicament.

He couldn't make his move in the dark, as he knew the bear was lying below, just waiting for him to make such a foolish mistake. Lashing himself to the tree trunk, in case he fell asleep, Jed leaned back against the small trunk. Below him, he could hear the bear moving about, protecting her kill from the night scavengers. Cold and shivering, somehow he had fallen asleep, awakening as the early morning sun peeped across the eastern skies.

Below him, the bear was nowhere to be seen as he surveyed the trail and the nearby trees. Jed knew how fast she could move and she could be hiding anywhere below, watching him up in the tree. However, he needed water, and eventually he would have to make his move. As he started to descend, he spotted her movement as she walked from the brush with her small beady eyes focused on him as she stood up at the base of the tree.

Jed watched the bear as she turned and lumbered back to the small hole of water where he had watered his horse, just before her attack. Tensing as he eased down the tree, Jed was just about to jump when the grizzly whirled and raced back to the tree, swiping at his legs. Retreating up the tree, Jed waited, and this time he would let her begin to drink before he tried to leave the tree. Jed was frustrated, as the bear didn't go back to the spring. She stretched out at the bottom of the tree and seemed to be sleeping peacefully.

Two hours later, after resting, the old sow stood up and walked to the horse's dead carcass. Ripping into the horse meat, she gorged herself, then took a look up the tree, focusing on her quarry. Seemingly satisfied, she turned and walked to the water hole. Jed tensed, this time he would not turn back. He knew how fast she was, but he had no choice. Without water, he would weaken and his chances of getting away from the grizzly would become less with each passing hour. He cussed himself again, as he had warned Roden many times about the bear. He let himself become distracted, and now, here he sat.

Watching intensely as the bear lay down on her belly to drink, Jed flexed his legs, then catapulted from the tree. Grabbing the bow and quiver, Jed raced for the safety of the rocks, then dove into the small passage. Behind him, he could hear the bear huffing and her heavy paws racing after him. Just before throwing himself bodily into the small opening, Jed felt her sharp claw slash his leg as he crawled into the rocks. Blood ran down his leg as he hurried along the small crevice that prevented the sow bear from reaching him. Jed had no idea where the rock passage would lead, but anything was better than the tree.

Packing his leg with sand and dirt, Jed stopped the flow of blood, then worked his way up the rock ledge. Below him, he could hear the bear tearing at the rocks, trying to navigate the passage. Exiting from the long rock crevice, Jed was surprised to find himself halfway up the mountain. Higher up, the mountain was mainly covered in smaller spruce and pine trees. None of the trees were big enough to protect him from the bear if he needed to climb again. Catching his breath, Jed studied the mountain trails and which course he would take when he finally made his break.

The bear was nowhere in sight and he had no way of knowing the man killer's location. He knew he had two choices, wait here and try to kill her with the bow, or make a break for the taller passes and try to stay ahead of her across the mountain. He knew the bear was a hunter, so she would have no difficulty tracking him with her sharp nose. If he waited, he knew she would eventually come, and then with nowhere to run, he would have to kill her or be killed. He could retreat and try to get his rifle, but the Hawken lay at least fifty feet from the rock crevice. It was too far to outrun the bear if she outsmarted him by doubling back, waiting for him to make a mistake. Bears guarded their kills, Jed remembered her coming out of the brush after him and Bow Legs near the body of Billy Wilson. She could still be near the dead horse, guarding her kill.

Taking a final look about the mountain, Jed raced from the rock passage and started across the mountain. Staying close to the ridge, Jed looked back, expecting to find the bear right behind him. Jed knew the cabin was due north and west of his present position. Taking a sighting on a far landmark, Jed slowed his pace and tried to conserve his strength.

The bear never showed herself, but Jed knew how dangerous she was and kept searching the scattered trees behind him. Fear of being caught out in the open with only these small trees for cover, pumped energy into his tiring legs. Running, mile after mile, he finally came upon a small water hole and quickly quenched his thirst. Crossing a tall ridge on the mountain, Jed stopped to look back, and there she was. He could see her huge frame as she lumbered slowly following his scent. Moving slowly, the old sow seemed to be taking her time following his trail, but there was no doubt about her actions, she was definitely on his trail.

Jed searched frantically for a way to throw her off his scent. Far below, he could see a body of water, but it was too small to keep her from crossing. Jed knew water wouldn't stop her, because bears spent much of their time in water, fishing. Larger trees loomed ahead, but Jed was reluctant to be helplessly treed again, with no way out. He knew the bear was at least an hour or more behind him, but she was faster and had more stamina for a long run. The old sow was crafty, and he knew she would catch up to him eventually.

Jed couldn't stop, otherwise she would catch him so he had to keep running. Touching the bow, he wondered if he took to a tree again could he shoot down at her and maybe kill the grizzly. There was no doubt, if she got close, he would have no choice but to climb another tree or be killed. All afternoon, as he ran, Jed never caught sight of the bear again. He had no idea where or how close she was. Dark was coming soon, and he was exhausted, feeling as if he had run for miles over tortuous terrain.

Jed looked across the mountains, and below was a valley and across the valley was another mountain range. Jed figured his cabin should be over the next mountain. He knew he didn't have the strength to keep ahead of the bear over another steep climb.

Almost at dark, another brown shape stood ahead of him, so Jed slipped behind a tree. Somehow, the deer hadn't sensed his approach. Quickly notching an arrow, Jed sighted in on the grazing deer and released his arrow. Looking down at the dead deer, Jed quickly gutted the animal, hoping the bear would stop long enough to fill her stomach before continuing after him. Dipping both feet in the deer's blood, Jed took off running down the mountain. Hopefully, the smell of the deer's blood would conceal his own smell and throw the bear from his scent for a while.

As darkness enveloped the high mountain, Jed reached the valley floor and started across. He had to hurry and cross the small valley so he could find refuge, if it was needed. He was tired, and his legs felt like wooden stumps. The slash on his leg stopped bleeding, but it was getting stiff. The bear no longer had his blood trail to follow, but he doubted the old grizzly needed it. He knew her nose was sharp, making her a dangerous predator.

His ragged breath labored with every stride as Jed forced himself to climb the steep mountain. He could go no further and finally found a tall tree. Jed hesitated at its base as he didn't want to climb, but he had no choice, he had to rest. Gulping down some cool water from a small spring, Jed returned to the tree and started to climb. Again, Jed managed to tie himself in the tree as sleep and fatigue fully engulfed him.

Arousing himself, as birds in the surrounding trees and the eastern sun awakened him, Jed untied himself from the tree trunk. Stiff and sore, he worked his numb legs as he studied the area around him. He had to locate the bear before working himself down the tree. The valley and the far mountain slopes were in plain view of where he sat but nothing showed, as deer grazed peacefully on the valley floor.

Not knowing where the bear was, Jed knew he had no choice and couldn't leave the tree. The grizzly could be waiting for him to descend the safety of the tree. Chewing on a piece of jerked meat, Jed planned his exit from the tree when he was finished. He was surprised, despite his tired legs and in the dark, he had managed to work his way halfway up the mountain grade. He wasn't sure, but over this mountain range, his valley should come into sight. He figured three days on foot, running hard, and traveling as a crow would straight across the mountains, perhaps he was closer.

Checking the rip in his leg, Jed tied a small piece of rawhide around the wound, binding it to his leggings, then took another bite of his jerky. In his hurry to escape the bear's claws, he never realized the extent of damage done to his leg. Luckily, the dirt had stopped the bleeding before it weakened him. Nothing showed below the tree or surrounding area so Jed started working his way to the ground. Quietly dropping to the ground, Jed listened for several seconds before starting stiffly up the mountain. Never has he fought an enemy like this one. She was out there, but he didn't know where. The unknown was scary.

As the climb continued, Jed's muscles started to loosen, letting him move faster up the steep grade. The night's rest in the tree, plus the virility of youth, returned his strength enough for him to run a few more miles. Stopping and looking back down the steep mountain, he had just climbed, Jed's eyes finally focused on what he looked for. The grizzly was crossing a bare grassy spot on the mountain, void of trees. Jed watched her for several minutes, as the bear appeared to be in no hurry, but Jed knew she was still following his track. He couldn't understand why she wasn't closing the distance between them. She didn't seem to want to catch up with him or she was having trouble following his track.

Turning, Jed started up the mountain in a slow trot. Trees heavily dotted the mountainside, but were beginning to thin out as he reached the peak. Jed hoped this was the last mountain and over this last ridge, he would see his own valley. Even if his valley lay on the other side of this mountain, Jed knew he had a long way to go to reach his cabin, while trying to keep ahead of the bear. Breathing hard, Jed topped out the mountain and studied the far valley. He had never explored this side of his valley as the steep mountain was covered with rock slides, loose boulders, and slippery shale. Studying the huge valley below, he knew it was his. Far to the north end, he knew his cabin and safety waited.

The rocky passage down the steep mountain would be slow and dangerous, giving the advantage to the bear. If she kept up her present pace, he would be able to at least stay ahead of her, but he also knew at any minute, she could switch speed and quickly catch up to him.

His mouth was parched dry, and this high there was no water unless he accidentally found a rock spring coming from the mountain. Jed was exhausted from the climb and wanted to rest. Shaking his head, his great heart responded; he wouldn't sit down or give up, and he would never let the bear win. His life depended on him keeping ahead of the killer bear, and he would run until he dropped from exhaustion. If she killed him, death wouldn't come without a fight. Taking a deep breath, Jed started down the rocky mountain. Refuge lay ahead, if he could only stay ahead of her for one more day.

Taking one final look back, Jed could not see the bear as he passed over the ridge. He slid and tried to stay on his feet as he descended the most treacherous part of the mountain. If he could reach the larger trees below, he could at least save himself in the refuge of its branches. Clearing the rocky shelf of loose rocks and gravel, Jed looked back up the mountain. His eyes blinked in disbelief. Watching him from the mountain crest, he had crossed less than an hour before, stood the grizzly.

Jed shook his head, as she seemed to be toying with him, letting him think he was going to get away. He had seen cats play with a live mouse the same way before killing it. As the bear focused on him and started down the mountain, Jed turned and raced through the small mountain spruce, hurrying to find a climbable tree where the bear couldn't reach him. He couldn't believe the sow was closing in on him so quickly.

Moving at a quicker pace, the bear was now less than thirty minutes behind him. He didn't want to, but a tree was his only hope for now. Racing down a game trail, Jed could almost feel the bear's hot breath on his back. He knew it was just his imagination, but it still made the hair on the nape of his neck stand up. The next time anyone asked him if he had ever known fear, Jed knew what his answer would be.

Crossing a small trickle of water on the trail, Jed stopped long enough to slake his thirst, then looked up the mountain a few feet. A small opening showed where the water was coming from. Quickly climbing to the opening, Jed found a small cave with an opening just barely big enough for him to slip through. The washed out cave was small, only deep enough for him to get back far enough to avoid the bear's reaching claws if she found him.

Looking up the game trail, Jed shook his head, as the old sow was coming at a lope right down the trail. He had no choice, taking one last look at the huge bear, he quickly worked his way into the opening. Flattening himself as far back as he could against the back wall, Jed waited. Below, he could hear the bear shuffling along the trail as she worked her way up to the small cave. Jed was curious, as he watched her for only a minute as she lumbered down the trail, but he thought she was moving as if she was hurt. He didn't think he had hit her, but his wild shot, when she killed the horse, was possible. How could a wounded animal track him as this bear has for an entire day and night across countless miles? Remembering Red Hawk's words, he had his answer; she knew his scent and she hated him. There was no doubt, this one was a man hunter and nothing would stop her.

CHAPTER 7

Jed pulled his legs back as the huge grizzly suddenly pushed her huge head into the small cave entrance and looked at him. Reaching with her front leg, she tried to claw at him in the cave. Notching an arrow, Jed found it impossible to draw the weapon inside the cave without getting into range of her groping front arms. Pulling his skinning knife, Jed waited until she flattened out her front paw as she felt for him, then he struck, stabbing the knife through her foot.

Quickly pulling back the knife, as she bellowed and roared in her rage, Jed pushed himself as far back as he could against the cave wall. She yelled in pain and flung herself at the entranceway. He could smell the hot, putrid breath and the stench of the bear as she clawed at the entrance. This close to her, he could feel the power, strength, and intense size of the grizzly. She was so close, far too close for comfort, and if he survived this battle, he would never underestimate a grizzly's power again. As she reached with her paw again, Jed struck with the knife, bringing another roar and spurt of blood. He couldn't believe it, her paw was severely damaged by the knife, and still in her hate, she reached for him.

Finally, with blood flowing from the stabbed paw, the bear shuffled back down the trail and looked up at the opening. Jed knew she was in pain, as the razor sharp knife had mutilated her huge front paw. Shaking her head in rage, the old sow slowly limped back up the trail, the way she had come. Crawling cautiously from the cave, Jed stood in the trail less than thirty feet from the limping bear and notched a razor sharp arrow. Drawing back the strong bow, Jed took a final look at the retreating bear and released the shaft. The arrow flew true, hitting the retreating bear in the back, just below her rib cage. Roaring in pain the big grizzly turned to charge, making Jed hastily retreat to the cave. Moving toward the cave a few feet, she stopped, shook her head, and then turned back, limping up the trail again.

Watching the wounded bear for several minutes as she limped away, Jed moved back down to the trail and waited. Turning back toward the lower valley, away from the bear, he stopped and shook his head. No more running, both man and beast were wounded, but today, Jed aimed to finish this once and for all. He knew the old grizzly would probably die from her wounds, but he had to make sure. Even though she was a man killer and had tried to kill him and Roden, she needed to be put out of her misery. He also knew she was still dangerous, probably more so now than ever. Snowflakes started to fall as Jed followed the bear, keeping to the side of the trail. She knew he was following her, and she stopped several times to turn to test the wind that carried the hated smell of man.

Quickly flanking the limping, slow moving bear, Jed notched another arrow and drove it powerfully at close range into her side. Whirling, she finally located him with her poor eyesight as another arrow penetrated her chest, almost to the feathered shaft. As the bear charged, Jed only had time to pull his sharp skinning knife before the enraged grizzly reached him. As she tried to stand and draw him into her sharp teeth and powerful jaws, both man and bear fell sideways, rolling down the mountain locked together in mortal combat. Jed desperately clung to the knife, his only means of killing the bear as they stopped in the middle of the trail. Jed could feel the claws raking his back as he stabbed the sow several times in the heart and neck. Blood gushed all over him as the grizzly relaxed, then quivered, as his last knife stab cut her jugular vein.

Jed was exhausted, unable to move as the bear lay dead under him. The stench of dead carrion emitted from the grizzly as she exhaled her last breath of life. Trying several times to rise before he finally succeeded, Jed sat down by the still warm body of the bear. Nodding his head in satisfaction, he smiled as this was the last of the killer bears, and maybe now, the valley would be a safe place to live. Not having to watch over his shoulder every time he left the cabin would feel good. As his tired body relaxed, complete exhaustion settled across his bloody and haggard face.

The snow started falling heavier before Jed became aware of it and stood up. The bloody knife still protruded from the bear's throat where his last thrust finished her. Steam rose from his bloody shirt along with the sweat the battle with the bear had caused. Now, cooled down, he could feel the temperature was plunging. He had lost his blankets, everything but the bow, quiver of arrows, and his lance. Quickly skinning out enough of the bear to wrap himself in, Jed found the bow and turned back down the trail.

Jed wanted the claws of the old bear for a souvenir or trophy, same as a scalp meant to the Arapaho, but he was too exhausted to remove them. Jed knew that taking the claws would be impossible. He had lost blood, and with the weather turning bad, he knew he would be lucky to make the day long trek back to his cabin. Limping slowly down the beaten animal track, Jed knew it would be faster to go straight down the mountainside, but he didn't have the strength.

He still had his shot pouch which contained flint and steel, but he knew if he ever stopped and stiffened up, he may never get on his feet again. No one would come looking for him for weeks, and by then, he would be dead. He remembered Little Antelope's words to him on several occasions, "Walk proud, my warrior, walk proud." Smiling, he squared his shoulders and ducked his head into the falling snow. One step at a time, as he knew the journey would be slow and cold, but somehow he would find the strength to make it. Higher up on the mountain, the lonely call of a large grey wolf sounded across many miles, seeming to call out for him to have courage. Tired and exhausted, he still smiled, for the first time in months; he didn't have to search every blade of grass, expecting the old grizzly to come into view.

With his mind foggy from loss of blood and staggering from exhaustion, Jed didn't realize he had bottomed out onto the flatter grounds of the valley for several minutes. Somewhere, he didn't know where, he had picked up a stout stick to help him walk with. Blinking the snowflakes from his eyes, Jed studied the surrounding terrain, and he knew where he was. The cabin lay straight down the valley, but it was still many miles away. The snow wasn't helping, already covering the ground and beginning to fall heavier. Jed strained his eyes, hoping to see Roden out in the valley, running his trap lines.

Staggering forward, Jed tried to keep his footing, but twice already he had stumbled and fallen. Each time he fell, the harder it was to rise. He knew if he got down and couldn't get up, he would freeze to death. He could see the face of Walking Horse telling him, he was an Arapaho Lance Bearer and to be strong. His mind whirled as he fought for each step through the deepening snow. Going down on one knee, Jed wanted to rest, as he couldn't make another step. Suddenly, the moaning call of the great wolf called out again across the mountains. Jed nodded as the face of Little Antelope came before him, urging him to be proud and walk strong. Nodding, he staggered to his feet and continued down the valley.

How much further? His mind reeled, dragging his feet as he zigzagged down the valley. Only the walking stick kept him on his feet. How much further, his numb mind asked again and again. Ellie's smiling face flashed before him, causing him to reach out for her. Holding out her hands, she called to him through the swirling snow, "Come for me, Jed."

"Jed, what in the world?" Roden stood in the corral, feeding the horses, and spotted the weaving figure as it splashed across the small stream in front of the cabin. Racing to the stream, the scout caught Jed in his arms as he began to fall into the icy water. "Come on, hoss, you can make it the rest of the way to the cabin."

Struggling, the small trapper helped the wobbly Jed into the cabin and onto the bed. Quickly cutting away the frozen bear hide, and the blood soaked and shredded hunting shirt, Roden examined and washed out each wound. Only the shoulder wound where the old sow had bitten Jed and the long leg wound were serious.

Early morning found Jed limping around the cabin after checking over his prized piebald. Roden had already reported the horse was sound again and ready to ride. Returning to the cabin, Jed sat down at the table where Roden had placed his plate and coffee cup.

"Well, my boy, how are you feeling this morning?"

"Mighty sore but alive, and thankful for it." Jed thought about the old sow. "Very thankful."

Roden grinned. "Looks like she gave you quite a tussle for your money."

"You can say that again." Jed nodded. "Killed my horse, tracked me over two mountain ranges, treed me once, and put me in a cave. Yes, she was after me to the end."

"Looks of your body, she almost accomplished it too. You were very lucky."

Jed quickly gave Roden a running account of the fight with the bear. "I lost my rifle, Lem."

"I reckon you want me to go after it?"

"I'd appreciate it." Jed nodded. "Probably take you a day's ride there and a day's ride back."

"You got any idea where it might be?"

"Ride the south trail to the big river." Jed took a sip of coffee. "When you find where the old sow killed my horse on the high trail, the rifle, my coat, and robe should be about ten feet behind him."

"Well, at least I won't have to worry about them bears of yours on this trip."

"You be watchful anyway, never know what's back in them mountains."

"I didn't get to be this old without being watchful." Roden grinned. "I'll leave come first light."

"You get any traps set out?"

"What I was doing when it started snowing yesterday."

"Good."

"The beaver have really made a comeback from the shining times." Roden thought back many years. "We'll take plenty of plews out of them ponds this season."

"Bate Baker says he ain't buying beaver this year."

Roden snickered. "That old crook says that every year, he'll buy."

"He will if he wants our other pelts." Jed shrugged. "If not, we'll sell them at Fort Bridger."

"Fine with me." Roden finished his plate. "I'll go set yours on the north end, then come morning, I'll ride out."

"I'll help you."

"No, you rest until I get back, then you'll be in shape to trap."

Nodding, Jed moved his sore, tired body back to the bed. He didn't like laying up when there was work to be done, but he had to rest. The hard race over the mountains, then the fight with the old grizzly had taxed his strength to the limit. Several times during the night, he sat up on the bed as the savage roar and blood shot eyes of the sow awoke him from a bad dream.

After fixing breakfast the next morning, Roden saddled up and headed to the south pass. Jed hated to ask him, but the Hawken was too fine a rifle to leave under the snow to rust. He knew it would be several days before he would feel up to making the long ride.

Moving outside, Jed watched Roden disappear over the far valley swell. Turning his attention, he led the horses, including the piebald and the black mule, out to pasture. He left one of the Blackfoot horses in the corral, in case he was needed. Pegging the half skin of the old sow next to her cubs on the barn, Jed stepped back and nodded. They had been a dangerous trio to deal with. He and Roden had been extremely lucky in their encounters with them. He was thankful and glad they were hanging right where they were.

Moving back inside, Jed sat down at the table and started on another bear claw necklace. Looking over at the one from the first cub, he shrugged, as he didn't know what they'd be worth in town. Now, he wished he had taken the larger claws from the older grizzly sow. Even if they weren't worth a plug nickel, he'd still have the necklaces from the killer bears, proving that they had actually existed. The hides would slowly deteriorate, but the claw necklaces would survive forever if taken care of.

Roden pulled his parka up tight around his face, keeping out the blowing snow that started falling again. The sorrel horse ducked his head against the cold winds as he plodded south to the pass. The weather was turning colder, but the old scout had ridden this kind of wintry days many times in the high mountains. With the early start, he figured on being at the pass, above the big river, by dark. He shook his head, wondering how Jed had made the long trek, wounded and exhausted, in this weather. However, the old scout knew if a man had courage and strong will, he could work feats of endurance far beyond belief. He knew Jed was one man with that kind of mental and physical courage.

The place Jed spoke of wouldn't be hard to find. If he remembered correctly, there was a heavy stand of trees where he could make camp for the night. Thinking about how bad Jed had been cut and chewed on by the old sow, he shook his head. Yesterday, the youngster had been lucky and he hadn't been killed. Since Roden met the young Arapaho, known as Crow Killer, good fortune seemed to smile on Jedidiah Bracket.

Late in the afternoon, the wind stopped blowing and the snow almost quit falling. Kicking the sorrel into a trot, Roden pushed the horse down the last grade, leading to the big river. As full dark covered the mountains, Roden rode into the grove of trees he remembered and dismounted. The snow had already blanketed the dark pass, and it was too late to look for the rifle, so he unsaddled the horse and made camp. As he pulled dead wood from under the heavy limbed spruce and cedar trees, Roden straightened and sniffed the air. Searching the surrounding darkness, he noticed the sorrel was looking down the trail leading to the river.

Forgetting the fire, the old scout quickly took his rifle and worked his way down the snowy path, leading to the river's edge. After an hour of moving silently through the darkened night and down the rough trail, Roden saw a small campfire flickering. Several robed warriors moved about in the firelight, talking and laughing. Moving nearer, trying to get close enough to hear what they were saying or who they were, the old scout squatted behind snow covered bushes and listened.

Six Pawnee warriors, one the others called Wet Otter apparently a chief by his arrogance and actions, silhouetted themselves against the backdrop of the fire. Roden could not understand why Pawnee warriors were so far north, this time of year. They had to cross Crow and maybe even Arapaho lands to reach this trail to the north. Jed had been too weary after the fight with the grizzly to tell him about the fight with the Pawnee. Roden recalled Jed speaking earlier of having met a warrior named Wet Otter at the Blue water, where Bow Legs was killed. Slipping closer, he could make out only a spattering of their words, but he heard the name Crow Killer spoken several times. The scout shook his head, as he remembered Jed and Hatcher talking once of him having trouble with the Pawnee tribe, but he understood a truce had been struck and all was well. Nevertheless, before him sat six fierce Pawnee warriors bragging about how they would kill the Arapaho Crow Killer. The warrior called Wet Otter was doing most of the boasting, as he bragged about how he would take Crow Killer's scalp.

Moving silently away from the fire, Roden quickly retreated the way he had come down the pass. He knew he had, no time to waste, to find the rifle in the dark, providing he could, then return quickly, back up the treacherous trail. Come morning, the Pawnee would find his tracks and know they had been seen. He knew once he was discovered, the journey would be a footrace back to the north. Roden had seen the rifles standing around the Pawnee fire, so they were every bit as well-armed as he was. Indian tribes that didn't have the white man's rifle were scared of their power, but the tribes that did have them weren't afraid of the thunder guns, and these tribes were very dangerous.

He only had a few hours to search through the pass to find Jed's rifle, then head back to the north, and try to stay ahead of the Pawnee. Searching along the snow covered trail, Roden finally found the dead body of the horse under a large mound of snow. Tracks of many meat eaters, animals that had been feeding on the horse, showed all around the mound. Jed had said the rifle was on the ground, a few feet behind the horse. Feeling along the ground with his moccasined feet, Roden finally toed the rifle under the snow. Retrieving the rifle, he moved back to the dead horse to find the parka and robe.

Looking over at the darkened tree and rock ledge, Jed had told him of, Roden shook his head in disbelief. How the bear had killed the horse and missed killing Jed had been a miracle, and it could never happen twice. Wiping the snow covered rifle off, Roden quickly retreated to his horse and saddled the tired animal. Leading him, the scout started the long, dangerous trek back to the north. He hated traveling these trails at night, but he knew with the coming of day, the Pawnee could be on their way to the valley. Stopping along the pass, Roden pulled four branches out into the trail and propped them up for the Pawnee to find. He wanted them to see the branches as a sign they had been spotted and they had been warned.

Roden was baffled, wondering how the Pawnee knew where to find Crow Killer. The scout had no way of knowing the Pawnee followed Jed when he left the Arapaho Village and they had scouts hiding along the crossings of the Yellowstone. Why was Wet Otter and his warriors this far north and what did they hold against Jed to seek revenge so badly?

Wet Otter reined in as he spotted Roden's tracks, left near his camp during the night. Dismounting, he backtracked, finding where the tracks stopped in the nearby bushes, within hearing distance of their campfire. It was a bad start and a bad omen for this trail. Shaking his head, he knew whoever had been there, must have heard their plans of killing the Arapaho, Crow Killer. Wet Otter had made a mistake when he first challenged the lance bearer. He would not make another mistake as he knew this Arapaho was protected by the spirit of the bear. The warriors followed Wet Otter, mainly because he was a wise, cautious leader, and one who would not lead his warriors into a fight they could not win.

"This a bad omen. If these tracks belong to the Arapaho, he will be ready for our attack." Wet Otter stood up. "For now, we will return to our village and come again when the cold times leave our lands."

As the sun came up in the east, Roden sat his horse at the top of the pass and watched his back trail. If the Pawnee were coming, they would cross the clearing far below on the winding trail soon. He knew they would have found his tracks in the snow, and they would know he had heard their plans. Roden knew the tribes were superstitious, and seeing his tracks so near their camp would be a bad omen to them. Roden figured they would return to their village and come again when they weren't expected. He knew the tribes well. Whenever they raided, they wanted surprise to be on their side, but now the Pawnee knew they had been discovered. If they did come as far as the warning branches across the trail, he hoped they would come no further.

Stopping to build a small fire, he warmed his hands and studied the trail far below. Finally, satisfied the Pawnee had given up and he wasn't being pursued, he mounted his horse and turned back up the trail. He knew it was not over, and in their own time when they figured their medicine was strong, the Pawnee would one day return. Like every tribe in these mountains, they also had heard about the killer bears and they feared them. Why would they dare ride into these lands to kill Crow Killer?

Taking one last look down the trail before topping the pass, Roden headed down the trail toward the valley. He knew the danger, from the Pawnee warriors, was over for the moment, and now they could resume running their trap lines. Roden was happy again in the tall mountains, his environment, but sadly he remembered his time in the cave in a drunken stupor over a woman. Seth Wilson and Adam Beale were bad men, but he knew he owed them a debt of gratitude. They had delivered him, in their own way, from the bottle.

The sun was bright overhead as Roden bottomed out into the valley. Reining in the sorrel, the scout studied the game trail leading back up the mountain to the east. This had to be the same trail, where Jed had killed the bear. Curiosity got the best of Roden as he turned the horse, wanting to see this killer bear close up. Climbing steadily, the scout was amazed Jed had been able to walk so far with his many wounds. He knew it took courage and a strong will to walk so far, enduring and surviving many miles of frigid cold weather as he crossed the valley.

Three hours later, after climbing steadily along a small game trail, the horse stopped suddenly, and before him lay the body of the killer. Slipping from the horse, Roden tied the skittish animal securely to a tree, as he sure didn't want to be left afoot to make the long walk back. The bear was covered in snow, but the stench from the dead carcass, polluting the air, spooked the horse. Pulling his skinning knife, Roden quickly ripped the remaining hide from the bear, and then took her claws. He had seen the claws of the other two bears in the cabin. Roden nodded, Jed deserved these as he definitely had earned them.

After sundown, the coal oil lamp burning in the window as a beacon sure looked good to Roden as he crossed the creek and dismounted. Unsaddling, he turned the sorrel into the corral as Jed opened the cabin door.

"Come on in, out of the cold." Jed greeted the old scout, relieved to see him back safe.

"I'm a coming, hoss." Roden carried his possibles and both rifles. "Hope you've got a gallon of coffee on the spit."

Jed nodded as he took his rifle and parka, then closed the door. "You made good time."

"Well, you might say I had a good reason." Roden gulped down a hot cup of coffee. "I brung you something to hang on the wall."

Jed grinned as Roden laid the old bear's claws out on the hearth. "You took the time to climb the mountain?"

"Yep, I brought you something else too." Roden walked outside and carried in the frozen hide of the bear.

"You skinned her?"

"Well, I sure wasn't about to bring the whole bear down here."

"Well, I don't know why not." Jed looked at the hide and smiled. "We'll hang that up with her other half, come daylight."

Roden picked up the hide. "You should check it out, three arrow wounds, one bullet hole, and I can't count how many times you stabbed the poor thing."

"Poor thing, my foot. She was wrestling me around like a rag doll." Jed shook his head. "Yes, I tickled her with my knife a few times. I wanted her dead."

"Shucks, I kinda feel sorry for the way you killed that poor bear." Roden teased Jed. "They called you wrong, instead of Crow Killer, it should be Bear Killer."

Jed shook his head. "If she'd been after you, I doubt you'd feel sorry for her."

"I imagine I wouldn't." Roden agreed. "Another thing, I met up with some of your friends, back on the big river."

"Who would be out there in this weather?"

Roden poured himself another cup and topped it off with sugar. "A band of Pawnee led by a subchief called Wet Otter."

"Wet Otter? He was the one I had trouble with over an elk." Hearing the name, Jed laid down the rifle. "Did you speak with him?"

"No, but I listened to him telling what he was gonna do to the great Crow Killer." Roden nodded. "Anyway, I figure they thought better of the idea after discovering my tracks close to their camp. They probably spooked and headed home for the time being."

Jed shook his head. "Wet Otter was coming here?"

"Was is right. I don't think the way he quit the trail so quick though, that he was real enthused with the idea of finding you." Roden laughed. "Injuns are a superstitious lot, as you already know. When they found my tracks, they skedaddled right quick."

"It's hard to believe." Jed shook his head. "Wet Otter here; are you plumb sure, Lem?"

"It was him, alright. His warriors called him by name several times." Roden picked up his cup. "I figure next spring, they'll pay us a visit."

"Why?"

"Can't rightly say, but he's dead set on killing an Arapaho named Crow Killer." Roden shrugged. "Leastways that's the way it sounded to me. Them Pawnee have a grudge built against one of us, and it sure ain't me."

The cold held, keeping the two trappers busy with their trap lines, and the small barn was loaded with stretched skins. Roden compared their catch every day to almost as good as the best trapping days of the shining times. During the long nights, two new buffalo robe coats had been finished and three bear claw necklaces now hung on the cabin wall.

"We've made a good catch already, Jed." Roden was working on new moccasins. "Old Bate's eyes will bug out when he sees this year's take."

"Hope so, but we may be headed for Bridger this spring." Jed remembered the last words from the trader about no beaver pelts.

"Not me, Jed, I ain't going with you."

"Why not?"

"I ain't lost a blasted thing in the settlements, that's why not." Roden looked at his handy work. "I'll give you a list of what I need from town."

Jed laughed. "You can't even write. You better go in with me."

"Come warm up, we'll see." Roden smiled. "I might change my mind by then, if not I'll tell you what to scratch down on paper for me."

Two weeks later, late in the afternoon, the cold times came with a sheer blast, as the norther hit with a vengeance. Blowing snow mingled with ice crystals pushed by heavy wind, steadily pounded the cabin, keeping Jed and Roden prisoner unless they were forced to go outside to feed and water the stock. This storm was far worse than the one Jed had waited out, last winter. The fire in the hearth kept popping and burning hot, keeping the cabin warm.

With the healing ability of youth, Jed's wounds healed and the soreness left his body. After four days, the cabin's confinement was working on his nerves, making him feel like the walls were closing in on him. Roden kept his hands busy, braiding ropes and working with the hides, anything to keep his mind from the howling winds. Several times, he warned Jed of men going stir crazy with cabin fever from being cooped up inside too long. Some had been locked up in their cabins so long, they went mad, and some had wandered aimlessly in a storm and froze to death.

Finally, as before, the wind suddenly stopped blowing, leaving the cabin in eerie silence. The storm abated, the snow finally stopped falling. Pushing open the cabin door, Jed stared in disbelief at the high snow-drifts as deep as the corral fences. Strapping his snowshoes on, Jed shuffled through the deep drifts to the corral where he tossed armfuls of dried grass to the horses. Fat and dry with heavy coats, the animals didn't feel the penetrating Arctic cold like the men did. Jed had built the lean-to and corral on the south side of the barn, toward the high ridge and trees. He knew the larger animals could keep warm from their body fat and thick hides as long as they could keep dry and out of the wind.

Roden carried two full buckets of thawed snow from the cabin into the corral for the thirsty animals. Giving each horse many swigs of water, it took several trips, before the horses turned from the water and started eating again. The two men trudged through the deep snow down to the creek, and looked out across the valley floor. Unlike last year, not a blade of grass showed out on the broad snow-covered plain.

"We'll have to dig out our traps in a couple days." Roden looked about the valley floor. "Looks of that deep snow, we'll have to use the snowshoes to reach them."

Looking up at the threatening sky, Jed shook his head. "I don't know, Lem, it could hit again."

"True, we don't want to get too far from the cabin and get turned around in another sudden storm." The scout agreed. "A man could freeze to death out here in minutes."

"I'm freezing now. Let's go get some coffee."

Another smaller storm followed on the heels of the first, but only lasting a day and night. Finally, later in the week, the sun broke out, letting the two trappers dig out their traps and reset them. Not used to the cumbersome snowshoes, both men were bone tired as they returned to the cabin. Even during the warmest part of the day, the temperature was well below freezing, keeping the snow from melting.

"Don't figure we're gonna do much for a few days." Roden stepped from his shoes. "I doubt the fur bearers will leave their dens in this cold."

"Yep, you're probably right, but we'll run the traps just the same."

"Suits me, I need the exercise." Roden looked down at his thin frame. "I'm starting to get fat."

Finally, the sun was shining through the clouds, allowing the snow to melt enough to allow Jed and Roden to begin taking pelts again, filling up the barn with more prime furs. The beaver ponds were completely frozen, but the land animals out hunting for food, fell everyday into their traps.

"How long you figure it'll be before breakup, Lem?" Jed stood outside the cabin watching a herd of elk crossing the valley.

"That's hard to say, maybe another six weeks." Roden shrugged. "Maybe less."

"We're gonna have a good haul this year." Jed looked over at the corral. "It'll take all our horses to tote all these pelts in."

"Yep, we may have to walk to the settlements ourselves. We may need our horses to tote all our plews." Roden pulled out his pipe. "This valley must have been overlooked during the shining times."

"Probably just restocked itself over the years."

"Maybe that too." Roden looked at the horses. "No matter, back in the time, we seldom rode horses and led them most of the time."

"Next season, maybe we'll trap over the mountain, and let this valley rest some."

"Sounds good, just a little more traveling is all."

The sun was shining brightly, melting the deep snow from the landscape and warming the valley. After oiling down the traps, Roden hung them from pegs inside the barn where the plews were stacked. Trapping season was over, and the two trappers had taken all the pelts they could transport to Baxter Springs. Snow showed in places across the valley, mostly under the broad cedar and spruce trees and along the mountain slopes. The old scout had brought in all the steel traps and sprung all the dead falls and box traps they had made. Jed was busy sorting, stacking, and pressing the different hides into bundles. Looking at the many well-tied bundles, he nodded, this year had been very productive and should be very profitable. The weather was warming up, and they had plenty of furs. Now, was the time to stop trapping and take their furs to the trading post.

Riding up to the cabin, Roden dismounted and nodded to where Jed was coming from the barn. "Well, I'm finished. I've checked everywhere, and all the trails and traps are cleared from the valley."

"You reckon the passes and the Snake will be crossable when we head out?"

Shrugging, Roden turned his horse out on the short grass in the valley. "This early, it's anyone's guess, but I say let's head out."

"What's your hurry, Lem?" Jed grinned. "I thought you weren't riding in with me."

"Jed, that's a dumb question. Remember, I've been cooped up here with you all winter." The scout turned to the cabin. "You're in a whirl yourself, wanting to go after Ellie and you know it, and I can change my mind if'n I want to."

"Ellie's in Slow Wolf's or Yellow Dog's village, not Baxter Springs." Jed reminded him.

"I know that, but you can't ride to Arapaho lands until we take our furs to Baxter Springs and unload them." Roden laughed. "So we better get a move on if'n you aim to see that girl before next fall."

"By golly, Lem, you've done persuaded me." Jed slapped his knee. "Come morning, we ride."

As they placed packsaddles on the loose horses, Roden remembered the old fur brigades and trapping with Bridger, Smith, and Sublette. This year was as good a catch as he had ever seen, even back then. He smiled, as old Bate Baker would water at the mouth when he sees this year's catch.

"Looks like we won't have to walk." Roden looked around at the loaded horses and black mule as Jed checked the latch on the cabin door.

"Good, that would have been a long walk." Jed picked up his possibles bag and rifle, then swung up on the piebald. "Let's get started then."

The Snake was bank to bank as Jed and Roden rode down to the water's edge and studied the broad stream. "It'll take two trips to get all the furs across, as many as we have."

Jed grinned. "That old river water is gonna be cold for sure."

"We crossing tonight or come morning?"

"Tonight, I sure don't want to be thinking about that long swim all night."

On the first crossing, Roden watched as Jed navigated the bobbing raft across the swift water. Then, he rode downstream on his horse to pull the raft back upstream as Jed recrossed. Piling the remaining bundles on the raft, Jed stripped his buckskins off and gathered the horses.

"I'll swim the horses across and meet you on the other side."

"Sounds good to me." Roden stepped onto the raft as Jed shoved him off from the gravel bank. "Water sure looks cold to me. I'm sure glad you had this here raft stashed, just for me to ride."

"Thanks." Jed knew Roden was just ribbing him.

Jed had guessed right, the water was cold as he swam alongside the horses, kicking hard to overcome the pull of the powerful current. Wading ashore, he looked to where Roden had beached the raft and tied it snugly to a tree. Riding downstream to where the older man waited, Jed quickly got dressed and hobbled the hungry horses on the new grass growing along the riverbank.

"You get a fire going, Lem, and I'll unload and hide the raft."

"We should be in Baxter Springs in a day or two if we get an early start." Roden started gathering wood for a fire.

"It'll be good to see Pa again." Thirty minutes later, Jed was leaning back against a bundle of furs, studying the hot coals in the fire. "Reckon how he is?"

"Ed Wilson will be doing fine. He's one strong man that Scotsman be."

CHAPTER 8

The sun was setting as the heavy-laden horses, led by Jed and Roden, plodded down the main street of Baxter Springs, stopping in front of the trading post. Several Nez Perce warriors sat their horses outside the post. Recognizing the Arapaho, their dark eyes stared nervously at Jed.

The warrior Squirrel Tooth exited the door, holding a bag of money. Seeing Jed, he stopped in his tracks, shocked, almost dropping his money. "Demon!" The word came out in a whisper.

Jed slid from the piebald and watched curiously as the warrior swung up on his horse, then raced down the street with the others following close behind him.

"Reckon them boys didn't want their supplies over at the mercantile." Bate Baker watched the retreating Indians curiously, then turned his greedy eyes on the packhorses. "I wrote them out a list for Elmer since he doesn't speak Nez Perce very good."

"Reckon they didn't, Bate." Roden looked down at the fat man. "You in the buying mood tonight?"

"Depends on what you have in them packs."

"Well, now, let's see here." Roden rubbed his chin whiskers. "There'll be coon, otter, silver fox, grey fox, lynx, two buffalo coats, robes, and about sixty beaver skins."

"I told you last year, I ain't buying beaver this time around." Baker pointed his pencil at Jed. "I'll take all but the beaver."

"Yes, I believe those were your exact words, Mister Baker." Jed admitted. "All or none."

Roden shook his head and dismounted. "Now, Bate, you sure could save us a long ride to Bridger if you thought on this a spell."

"I'll pay gold for everything, but not the beaver skins." Baker turned to his store. "Take it or leave it."

"Come on, Lem. Reckon, we'll be leaving this gentleman's offer." Jed reined the piebald and started down the street. "We'll pay our respects to Pa, then head east in the morning."

"You're a fool, Bate Baker, but then you always have been." Roden shook his head as he mounted. "There's a lot of prime plews in those bundles. Be seeing you."

Baker cussed as he watched the two trappers disappear in the long shadows of the street. He knew he had just cost himself a lot of money. "Dang hardhead, I told him I wasn't buying beaver skins this year."

"Bridger will durn sure buy them."

Thinking he was alone in the store, the words caused Baker to whirl in surprise. "Well, big Rufus Cross, I didn't know you were in town."

"Just got here. Me and the boys are camped west of town in the breaks." The big buckskin clad trapper walked to the counter. His huge frame made nary a sound as he crossed the wood floor. "We brought in some furs, nothing like that Indian was toting."

"This is the second year in a row he's come in heavy."

"Who he be?" Cross looked curiously through the door. "He's the same varmint that jerked knots in Luke and Willie's tail at the dance last year, ain't he?"

"Yep, same feller." Baker studied the uncouth hunter. "Name's Jedidiah Bracket. Indians call him Crow Killer."

"So that's the demon himself, is he?" The big eyes blinked. "Heard of him and I've seen him in action."

"So they say." Baker shook his head, remembering what Jed had done to Luke and Willie at the dance. "He's a bad one, dangerous."

"Do tell." Cross walked to the door and looked off into the darkness. "I'll bring my plews in, come daylight."

"I'll be here."

"You do that, Bate." Cross left by the side door, the same way he had come in, without being noticed. "You be here."

Scratching his head as he thought about Cross's words about Bridger buying, Baker hollered across the street at a man sitting before the saloon. "You, Billy Keene, come over here."

The unkempt man shuffled across the street as Baker beckoned to him. "Yes, sir. Mister Baker, you calling for me?"

"I'll give you a dollar to ride out to Ed Wilson's farm and deliver this note to Jedidiah Bracket."

"I don't know him."

"Just give it to Ed Wilson."

"Yes, sir, but I ain't got no horse." The string bean studied the paper.

"Take my mare, but you bring her straight back here." Baker didn't like letting this worthless bum use his horse, but he didn't have any choice. "Git and don't run her to death."

"Yes, sir, Mister Baker."

The Pennybrook was dark as Jed and Roden splashed across and rode up to the Wilson corral.

Hearing his blue tick hound barking at the strange riders, Wilson picked up his rifle and lantern, and walked out into the dark. "Who you be out there?"

"It's just us, Pa, don't shoot."

"Jed." Wilson trotted to the corral and grabbed Jed in a bear hug. Shaking hands with Roden, he helped them unload and tote the bundles into the dry barn, then turned them toward the house. "Man is this a surprise. I'm glad to see you boys."

"It's good to see you, Pa."

"Sit down, sit down, and I'll fix you up a bite to eat." Wilson grabbed some cups and the hot coffeepot.

"How you been, Pa?" Jed remembered Ellie's words of Wilson killing Willie Beck. "Everything okay here?"

"Everything is just fine now." Wilson smiled. "If you're speaking of Beck's killing? Everything's fine on that score too."

"Someone killed Willie Beck." Roden's hand stopped in midair as he raised his cup. "Who?"

"I killed him, Lem." Wilson rattled the stove lids as he pushed wood into the kitchen stove. "I did."

Roden looked over at Jed. "You didn't tell me."

"Nope, I didn't." Jed frowned over at Roden. "Weren't none of our business."

Shrugging, Roden turned to his coffee. "Nope, it weren't."

Halfway through supper, the men heard the hound barking again and the unmistakable sound of a horse coming into the yard.

"Busy night tonight." Wilson picked up his rifle and opened the door. "Now, who would that be this time of night?"

"Hello the house."

Wilson recognized the voice of Billy Keene the town drunk and loafer. "Is that you, Billy? What can I do for you?"

"Mister Baker sent you a letter." Keene kicked the mare closer and handed Wilson the note.

"I'm a thanking you, Mister Keene." Wilson watched as Keene turned the mare.

"Got to get Mister Baker's horse straight back."

"You do that, Billy." Wilson knew it was bad manners not to invite Keene inside the house to get warm. Keene was a drunk who failed to wash regularly so the man stunk. He was glad when he turned and rode off.

"See you, Mister Wilson."

Listening, as the hound bayed at the horse all the way to the Pennybrook, Wilson turned back into the house and studied the name on the paper. "Looks like it's for you, Jed."

Taking the letter from Wilson, Jed pushed it under the oil lamp to read. Shaking his head, Jed handed the letter to Roden.

Roden waved it away. "You know I can't read, Jed."

"It says, in short, Mister Baker has had a change of mind as is willing to give us top dollar for all our plews." Jed laughed. "All of them."

"That's mighty kind of him." Roden pushed back his cup. "What we gonna do?"

"We're gonna sell him some pelts, but it'll cost him extra for our work loading and unloading, plus transporting them all the way out here from town."

"That sounds good, Jed. I deserve something." Roden rubbed his back. "All that hard work, you know."

Early morning after breakfast while Wilson was milking, Jed and Roden cinched down the packsaddles and loaded the horses.

"Lem, I'm gonna stay here and talk with Pa for a bit." Jed rechecked the cinches on the saddles of the two packhorses and black mule Roden would lead. "I'll catch up with you before you reach Baxter Springs."

"I'm curious, Jed, how'd you find out about Beck?"

"Ellie."

Shaking his head, Roden mounted. "I'll see you at Baker's or before."

"I'll catch up."

Jed watched as the old hound made a run at one of the horses, who kicked and missed. He wasn't so lucky with the little black mule, who didn't miss, but landed a back hoof into his side.

"Silent One could have warned you not to try that, old man." Jed laughed as the blue hound returned to the house a whole lot slower, but a whole lot wiser.

Meeting Wilson coming from the barn, Jed stopped. "Is everything alright here, Pa?"

"The law's not after me, if that's what you're asking."

"And the neighbors?"

"Nah, after finding out what Beck was planning, they didn't blame me a bit."

"Good, now saddle up and we'll ride into town to pick you up some supplies." Jed had snuck a look in Wilson's cupboards. Coffee tins, sugar, salt, and his flour sack, every tin was empty.

"I could sure use a few supplies."

Rufus Cross and his men waited, two miles east of the Pennybrook, concealed in the heavy brush that lined the road. The previous day, Rufus had been listening in the fur trader's post, as Roden and Jed talked about the plews. After what he heard, he had all the information needed, from the conversation, to ambush Jed and Roden as they headed for Bridger.

"Place your shots where they count, boys." The big trapper grinned his toothless smile. "If they ain't breathing, they can't accuse us of stealing their pelts."

"They got a load of furs, Rufus?" A trapper named Bigfoot asked.

"They've got a pile alright. We'll make us a good bit of money."

"What about Baker, you think he'll put up a kick?"

"Nah, Bigfoot, you know he's greedy. I told him we had pelts to bring in this morning." Cross grinned again. "We take our pelts in, get our money, and no one knows the difference."

"What about the bodies, when they find them?"

"We'll be long gone and there'll be no witnesses." Cross held up his hand. "You two know Lem Roden, you take him."

"Alright, Rufus, but I ain't sure I like this set up." A smaller weasel of a man spoke up. "It sure beats trapping and freezing, I reckon."

"No, Fib, but you like to eat, drink, and laze around, don't you?" Cross frowned. "Now, get yourself ready and shoot straight."

The sun was up only a half hour when Roden came down the road, leading three pack animals. Enjoying the beautiful spring morning, he had no idea Cross and his men lay in wait yards up the road. Minutes later, two long rifles roared, knocking Roden backward into the road.

Racing out from his cover to catch Roden's horse and pack animals, Cross stared back down the road to the west. Shaking his head at the empty road behind Roden, he whirled and looked at his men. "Grab the horses and let's get."

"What about the other one?" Bigfoot looked up the road. "The Arapaho."

"We can't wait for him." Cross led out toward Baxter Springs. "Let's take these furs in and sell them, then get us a drink and ride."

The trapper, Bigfoot, shook his head. "Bate Baker is gonna know it was us that stole these pelts."

"Our word against whoever claims them." Cross swore. "These pelts are ours, we trapped them."

"I hope you know what you're doing, Rufus."

"Don't I always, Bigfoot?" Cross laughed. "Come on, perk up."

Bate Baker looked over his glasses as Cross and his men carried eight bundles of furs into his shop and laid them on the counter. Quickly, Cross cut the rawhide straps that held the furs tied tightly in their bundle. Even Cross had to nod his head at the high quality of the furs. Examining the pelts, Baker looked at Cross.

"Something wrong, Bate?"

"No, no, just admiring their quality is all." Baker coughed nervously. "Mighty fine furs, mighty fine."

Handing over his figures to the big trapper, Baker studied the big man as he went over the list. "Looks good, Bate."

Counting out the gold pieces on the counter, Baker smiled and waited for the men to leave. "See you boys, next spring."

"Yeah, you will." Cross grinned and picked up the money. "Come across the street and we'll set you up to a drink."

"I figured you boys would be riding out."

"We will, soon as we finish liquoring up and resupplying." Cross slapped Bigfoot on the back and laughed. "Ain't no reason to hurry, is there?"

Watching the trappers lead their horses across the street to the saloon, Baker picked up a fox pelt and examined the markings on it. Then, he picked up one of the inferior pelts from another bundle and examined it. For years, he had been buying furs from every trapper in the north. He knew every trapper had a distinct mark on their pelts and a different method of curing and skinning hides. Some took more care with them, making each pelt more valuable to the fur buyers. Six of these bundles were prime, well-cured skins, and the other two bundles were second rate, not taken or cured by the same man. Also, Baker knew who had trapped the beaver plews, and it sure wasn't Cross or his cronies.

Baker remembered the furs Jed had brought in last year, and these were the same quality with the same markings on them. Shaking his head, he looked out the window to where the trappers disappeared through the saloon doors. He knew these furs belonged to Jedidiah Bracket, but he didn't know how Cross and his men got them. Why did they leave the packhorses, black mule, and saddle horse tied to his hitch rail, in plain sight? Walking to the doorway, he squinted as he looked at the saddle, and blood showed plainly on the seat and cantle.

Quickly returning to his trading post, the trader busied himself nervously behind the counter. He didn't know the horse, but he was guessing it was the horse ridden by Roden. It had been almost dark when Jed and Roden rode away from the post, so he couldn't be positive. Did Cross and his men ambush and kill Jed Bracket and Lem Roden?

Looking down the street at the constable's office, Baker started to go around the counter. Changing his mind, he stopped and retreated to his desk and paperwork. He had no doubt, Cross would snap his neck like a chicken if he spotted him entering Constable Rourke's office. No, siree, he wasn't a brave man. Today, he would mind his own business and stay alive. He knew Constable Jim Rourke well, and the man was a coward at heart so he sure wasn't about to put his life in Rourke's hands.

As Jed waited for Wilson to saddle his horse, he faintly heard the sound of two rifle blasts off to the east. Figuring someone was out hunting, he disregarded the shots. Waiting until Wilson mounted and joined him by the corral, Jed turned toward Baxter Springs, kicking the piebald and the other two pack animals into an easy trot. He wanted to catch up to Roden before he reached Baxter Springs so they could ride in together. The morning was beautiful, and it felt good to be with his step-dad again, even if it was just for a brief ride into the settlement.

Trotting down the little used road, Jed's sharp eyes spotted the body of a man sprawled on the dusty road ahead. Reining in the piebald, he surveyed the surrounding grassland before cautiously moving forward. Riding closer, Jed could plainly see it was Roden. Handing Wilson the lead ropes to the pack animals, Jed kicked the piebald into a hard run to where the body lay. Sliding the piebald to a hard stop, he dropped from the horse and knelt beside the old scout. Turning the body over slowly, Jed examined the bleeding man. Two bullets had hit Roden high in the chest, covering his hunting shirt with blood.

"Lem, can you hear me?"

"I hear you, boy. What happened?"

Jed quickly cut Roden's leather shirt and stuffed the bleeding holes to stop the blood flow. "I was gonna ask you the same thing."

"I reckon someone wanted our plews, Jed." Roden swallowed, then coughed. "Felt like hot pokers biting into me."

Dismounting, Wilson knelt beside Jed and looked down at Roden. "Here, take my shirt, it'll stop the bleeding better than that leather."

"How bad is it, Ed?" Roden moaned. "Am I gone under?"

"You'll live, Lem." Wilson stood up. "Catch the horses, Jed, and hand him up to me. Let's get him to Doc Zeke."

"If I don't make it, Ed, it were Bigfoot Scott who done for me." Roden groaned as Jed rounded up the horses. "One other I seen was that snake called Rufus Cross."

"You sure, Lem?" No sound came from the bloody man as Wilson looked up at Jed. "He's passed out."

Bate Baker paled when Jed and Wilson rode past his trading post with the bloody Lem Roden held in Wilson's arms. Now, the fat was in the fire for sure, and he knew Jed would be back for answers. Jed noticed his two pack animals along with the black mule and Roden's horse tied outside the trading post as he passed. He didn't slow up, right now, they could wait. Lem Roden was his main concern. He had to get the wounded scout to the doctor before he bled out.

Taking Roden from Wilson, Jed carried him through the door and laid him on a long table as Doctor Zeke came from a backroom. "He's been shot, Doc, twice."

Adjusting his glasses, the old doctor removed the flannel cloth and examined the wounds. Ordering Jed and Wilson out of the way, the Doctor quickly went to work on the wounded scout.

"You see my horses, mule, and Lem's horse tied out front of Baker's?" Jed watched with Wilson from the doorway as the doctor worked feverishly over the wounded man.

"I spotted them." Wilson nodded. "Whoever done the shooting are a pretty crusty lot, aren't they?"

"They sure got their nerve. I'll say that for them." Jed shook his head. "Shooting a man, then selling his furs in the same town. Now, that takes some gall."

"Lem told me who they were." Wilson watched the doctor working over the table. "Whilst you were getting the horses."

Jed looked over at Wilson. "He seen them?"

"Yep, told me it were Bigfoot Scott that shot him." Wilson nodded. "He runs with a trapper called Rufus Cross, a real rough bunch."

"Surely they ain't that stupid?" Jed shook his head. "Shoot a man, steal his furs in daylight, and sell them in the nearest settlement."

"They figured there were no witnesses." Wilson shrugged. "Bigfoot probably figured Roden was dead."

Jed looked to where the old doctor was furiously working over the wounded man. "If Bate Baker bought our plews, he'll know for sure who sold them."

"Yeah, but if Lem goes under, it'll just be your word against theirs."

"No, it won't Pa, you heard Lem."

Wilson nodded. "I heard him."

Doc Zeke turned to where Jed and Wilson waited in the doorway. Wiping his bloody hands, he nodded tiredly. "I've done what I could for him, for now."

"Will he make it, Doc?"

"Too soon to know. I'll know by morning." The doctor pushed the two outside. "I'll let you know whenever he takes a turn, good or bad."

Turning, Jed started out the door. "Where you headed, Jed?"

"Gonna have a little talk with Mister Bate Baker."

Entering the trading post, Jed found Baker and another man standing beside the counter. Letting his eyes rove around the post, Jed noticed his pelts stacked along the wall. Walking over to the bundles, Jed picked up one and carried it back to the counter where the fat man stood sweating.

"I've got four more bundles with these same markings outside, Mister Baker." Jed held the pelt up in front of the fur buyer. "These pelts belong to me."

Wiping his wet face, Baker nodded over at the other man. "He's Jim Rourke, constable here in Baxter Springs."

"I've got a wounded, maybe dying partner down at Doc Zeke's." Jed's dark eyes penetrated the constable. "Why aren't you down there?"

"Bate asked me here. I didn't know anything about a wounded man." Rourke lied. "Who is it, and who shot him?"

"Lem Roden is the one shot, and he said Bigfoot Scott was the one who done the shooting." Jed looked over at Baker.

"Lem Roden, well, I'll be." Rourke shook his head. "Will he make it?"

"Who sold you my pelts, Baker?" Jed touched his skinning knife, ignoring the question. "Don't forget, I've got four more bundles just like them outside those doors."

"I bought these pelts from Rufus Cross." Baker mumbled. "I don't know that they're yours."

"You know my mark don't you, fur buyer?"

"Yes."

"Is this it?" Jed held the pelt up to Baker's face. "Don't lie."

Nodding his head slowly, Baker paled as he looked at the mark. "Yes."

"You knew they were mine and Roden's when you bought them, didn't you?"

"I was scared to not buy them, plumb scared." Baker dropped his eyes. "Cross would have killed me for sure."

"I'll be taking my plews back, now." Jed looked across at Baker. "You got any objections?"

"I do, Bracket. Bate paid cash money for them furs." Rourke straightened. "They're his and they're evidence."

"You aiming on stopping me from taking what's mine, Constable?" Jed turned to face Rourke.

"Let him have them, Jim. They belong to him." Baker held up his hand. "It's my fault for being a coward, and my loss."

Rourke relaxed, as Baker got him out of this mess without having to face down the man called Crow Killer. "You heard Mister Baker. Take your property and get out of Baxter Springs."

Jed smiled and looked dead into the constable's wavering eyes. "I'll take my furs, Constable, but I'll leave town when my partner is well enough to ride. Don't push me, Rourke, not one inch."

"Well..." Rourke hesitated, looking over at Baker. "I reckon that'll do."

"What are you gonna do about Bigfoot Scott and the men with him?"

"What about them?"

"I told you, they're the ones that shot Lem Roden." Jed's face hardened.

"Just your word against theirs, ain't it?"

"Tell him, Baker." Wilson spoke up from the doorway. "They shot Lem Roden and stole his plews, and you know it."

Rourke shook his head as Baker nodded. "Can you prove that?"

"Came right out of Lem's mouth." Wilson moved inside the room. "Now, Mister Constable, what are you fixing to do?"

"I'll have to speak with Roden." The constable was scared.

"You can't right now, he's in bad shape." Wilson spoke up. "Doc Zeke won't stand for it."

"You can go across the road and speak with Bigfoot Scott and Rufus Cross." Jed added.

"I can do that." Rourke swallowed nervously. "Providing they're still in town."

"They're over there alright, Jim." Baker nodded at the window. "I seen 'em go in and they haven't come out. Those are their horses tied out front of the saloon."

"How many are over there, Bate?"

"Rufus Cross, Bigfoot, Fib, and another trapper." Baker shook his head. "Probably got themselves liquored up and forgot to leave town as they were planning."

"You plumb sure these pelts belong to this man?" Rourke looked across the counter at Baker. "Plumb certain, no maybe?"

"Yes, I'm certain."

"Then I reckon we better go have a talk with Mister Scott."

"Then do it, Rourke." Jed spat out. "Quit your stalling, I'll back you."

Wanting to get Wilson out of harm's way, Jed sent him to check on Roden. Tying his horses to the corral fence beside the trading post, Jed joined Rourke when he appeared outside the door.

"Alright, Constable Rourke, I'm right beside you."

Visibly scared, Rourke looked over at Jed. "I know these men, Bracket. They're ornery and mean."

"And killers now, and Mister Constable they're in your town."

Visibly shaking, Rourke shook his head. "I'll go speak with them."

"Now, that's just fine, like I said I'll be right alongside you."

Jed could sense the man's fear. If he could dig a hole and crawl into it, he'd be there already. The man was afraid. Jed was surprised he was even heading to the saloon. Pushing open the door, it was as Baker had said, four men sat at the rear of the room, sitting around a table drinking spirits. All four looked up as Rourke and Jed entered the saloon and walked toward them.

"Well, Jim Rourke..." The big trapper Cross greeted the constable. "I hear you're the Constable of Baxter Springs now."

"Howdy, Rufus." Rourke looked at the man. "We got a problem."

"And what would that be, Jim?" Cross smiled broadly and laughed drunkenly. "You sick or something?"

"He sure looks sick, don't he, Rufus?" Bigfoot cockily reared back in his chair. "Why, he's done turned pure white."

"We got a wounded man down the street and some stolen pelts you sold to Bate Baker." Rourke nervously fingered his rifle.

"Now, Jim, we wouldn't know anything about stolen pelts or that shot man. Would we boys?"

"The wounded man named Bigfoot as the shooter, Rufus." Rourke motioned to the door. "I'll have to take you and Bigfoot over to the office for a talk."

"Sure, sure, Jim. We always cooperate with the law, don't we, Bigfoot?" Cross winked at the man across from him. "We're downright peaceable citizens."

Suddenly, the big man pulled a knife and stabbed Rourke, causing the constable to fire his rifle with a dying reflex. The wild shot hit Bigfoot in the stomach, killing the trapper where he sat. Lunging at Jed, one of the other trappers took the force of Jed's Hawken straight through his face. Swinging sideways, as Cross lunged at him with the razor sharp skinning knife, Jed clubbed the big trapper hard with the Hawken.

Turning his attention momentarily to the fourth trapper running from the saloon, Jed caught the huge figure of Cross lunging at him again from the corner of his eye. Powerful muscles bulged as they strained, gripped in each other's clutches. Tables crashed and chairs were turned over as the two men fought around the room. Finally, Jed jerked free of the big trapper and pulled his own knife. Blades clashed, ringing out across the room as both fighters parried and thrusted at each other. For a big man, Cross was fast and nimble on his feet, attacking then retreating out of harm's way as Jed sliced the air where he once stood.

Retreating from the dangerous blade of Cross, Jed tripped over an upturned chair and fell backward, sprawling on the floor. A shot rang out, filling the saloon with a roar, putting a surprised look on Cross's face as he started to stab at Jed. Staggering backward, Cross looked at Wilson, then slowly fell face forward across the jumbled floor. Looking over at the door, as the smoke from the rifle cleared, Jed raised to his feet.

"Lem's dead, son, murdered by this scum."

The trapper called Fib tried to run from the saloon and was clubbed senseless by Wilson and lay outside on the boardwalk.

Picking up his rifle, Jed looked down at the unseeing vacant eyes of Jim Rourke, then took Wilson by the arm and led him from the saloon. Stopping at the door before exiting the saloon, Jed looked back at the shaken saloon owner. "You seen it all, mister saloonkeeper." Jed looked hard into the man's eyes. "When you tell it, tell it straight."

"I will."

"You better or I'll be back to deal with you." Jed warned.

Wilson looked at several men standing around the unconscious trapper. "Lock this one up. The charge is the murder of Lem Roden and Jim Rourke."

Repacking his pelts, Jed led Wilson and his horses back to Wilson's farm after paying for Roden's burial. Already, in less than an hour, the swinging body of the last trapper called Fib decorated one of the larger limbs of a lone oak tree outside Baxter Springs.

"That was quick and sure justice." Wilson looked over at the body as they passed. "Couldn't have happened to a finer feller."

Unloading and turning the tired horses into the corral, Jed put out corn and hay, then followed Wilson into the house. It had been a long, sad day. He had lost another close friend. It seemed every time he came to Baxter Springs, something bad happened.

"That was too bad about Lem." Wilson placed the coffeepot on the wood stove. He was still upset and needed the hot coffee bad. Cross was the second man he had killed in the last month. Third, if he counted Fib, the trapper he had knocked cold and was hanging from the oak.

"Yeah." Jed shook his head. "All he wanted was to get back to the valley."

"What will you do now?"

Jed shrugged. "I'll take my furs to Fort Bridger, then I'll pick up Ellie and go home."

"Sounds good."

"Why don't you come with me, Pa?"

Wilson poured the cups full. "It's sad, Jed, just this morning Lem was having coffee with us, right here at this table."

"Yes, he was."

"I can't leave my farm just now, son." Wilson shook his head. "Maybe later."

"Get your neighbor to tend it for you and come with me." After all the problems of the last months, Jed wanted to get Wilson away from Baxter Springs. "Just for the summer, and you can come back anytime you get ready."

Drumming his fingers atop the table, Wilson looked around the room. "The farm doesn't hold the joy I once had for it."

"Then come with me."

"Do you have room for me?"

"We'll let the horses rest another day while you get your neighbor rounded up, then we'll pull out." Jed looked at the confused man. "But, only if you want to go."

"Let me think on it tonight, son." Wilson walked to the door and looked across the yard at Seth's grave. "I still have so many feelings attached to this farm."

"I know you have, Pa. You sleep on it."

Jed sat under the Jersey cow, deep in thought, as he milked the cow. He would say no more about his step-pa going to the mountains with him. He had asked, and now the decision was up to Wilson. He worried about his safety, in Baxter Springs, not only from the locals, but from himself. Jed wanted him to go back to the valley so he could watch over him, but now, it was up to the farmer. Jed knew men of the land, and a farmer's love for the ground they worked was almost like family.

Coming from the barn with a bucket of warm milk, Jed looked over to where Wilson stood over the grave of Seth Wilson. Taking the milk into the kitchen, Jed strained the warm milk through a clean flour sack into a large jar, then poured himself some coffee and sat down at the table.

"I reckon you're pulling out this morning?" Wilson entered the house and walked to where Jed sat.

"Yes, sir, I've got to get my furs to Bridger before it gets hot." Jed studied the sad face. "I hate to go, but I've got to sell my plews. I can't let them go to ruin."

"I guess I won't be going with you this time, Jed." Wilson's face dropped. "I can't leave this place, not right now."

"Okay, Pa. I understand."

"Will you be headed back to the valley after you leave Bridger?"

"Yes, sir, after I make a couple stops."

"Can you handle the pack string alone?"

"I can handle them just fine." Jed nodded. "I'll leave Lem's saddle horse with you. Lem said he owed you for him."

"Thank you, son." Wilson nodded. "He'll be easier to ride into town than my work horse."

Jed didn't tell Wilson, he left a bag of gold coins on the kitchen table. "He's got a running walk that sure is comfortable going down the road."

"Will you do me one favor, son?"

"Whatever you need." Jed knew what Wilson was fixing to ask.

"Take me to Billy's resting place so I can bring him home." Wilson shook his head. "I know what kind of man he was, but he was still my son."

"I'll come for you in the summer." Jed nodded. "I'll be here, soon as I get my place ready for the cold times next year."

"Thank you, Jed. You are all I have left, you and the grave out there." Wilson smiled. "And thank you for all these supplies."

"Pa, will you be alright here by yourself?"

"I'll be fine. You've helped me over the rough part with my crops and supplies." Wilson smiled. "I'll be fine."

CHAPTER 9

Bate Baker watched from his trading post as Jed rode the big piebald horse, with his pack train, down the middle of town. Shoulders squared and head held high, Jed sat the beautiful paint horse proudly as the piebald pranced through Baxter Springs. Afraid to show his face on the street as others were doing, Baker watched from his store's open doorway. He had seen the carnage Jed could do when riled. The dead bodies of three trappers and a constable were carried from the smashed saloon. The fourth trapper still hung from the large oak outside town where all could see. He had been stupid in his dealings with Jedidiah Bracket, and would not add to that stupidity by showing himself.

The eastbound immigrant road Jed traveled was far easier to navigate than the steep mountain passes, but he kept a leisurely pace to save the heavily laden horses. Even though he made camp early and let the horses rest, graze, and fill up with water, Jed was still making good time. Fort Bridger was only hours away, but he wanted an early start in the morning.

Jed thought of Ellie and wanted to sell his furs quickly so he could push on to Arapaho lands. Staring into the small fire, Jed listened as several coyotes chorused their voices, probably in pursuit of a rabbit or some prey. The bright stars overhead shined brilliantly as they covered the skies by the millions. Relaxing against a bale of furs, he bit into a stale cracker, thinking he would be back home in his cabin soon. Although, saddened by Lem Roden's death, he hoped the valley would now bring him the peace he sought.

After an early start, the trading post most called a fort, built by Jim Bridger years before, came into sight by noon. Jed was slightly shocked at the buildings and surrounding stockade, as it wasn't quite the sight he expected. It wasn't the haven of rest people spoke of when they described Bridger. Jed understood their feelings, after weeks of difficult travel, any place offering respite from the wind and heat, would seem like an oasis.

Passing through the heavy gates of the post, Jed noticed many Indians and fur trappers loafing around the compound. Reining in at the trader's store, he slid from the piebald. Jed couldn't help noticing there were several warriors with blank stares as they stood up, noting his presence. Sioux, Cheyenne, Assiniboine, Arickaree, even a smattering of Pawnee, and others Jed didn't know, passed in and out of the trading post. How Bridger kept the peace was a miracle in itself, considering all the enemy tribes present, occupying the post grounds.

Jim Bridger welcomed all tribes at the post to trade their furs as long as they didn't carry out their blood feuds within the post or surrounding lands. All knew Bridger wasn't a man to be trifled with, as his word was law. Nobody crossed the cantankerous old mountain man, unless they wanted to reap his outrage and that could be disastrous. If banned from the post, they would have no other place within several days ride to trade their furs. At the other posts, they might not be as welcome as they were here, nor would their profits be as great. Bridger was a trader, so he needed the furs brought in by the tribes as much as the tribes needed Bridger to buy them.

After selling his furs, Jed stepped out into the late afternoon sun, hefting the heavy bag of gold eagles. Looking about the busy post, he pushed the heavy bag down inside his hunting shirt, securing it to his leather belt. The long ride to Bridger had been tiresome, but his pelts were sold and he made a good amount of money, well worth the ride. Half of his profit belonged to Lem Roden, so Jed would try to find out if the old scout had any kinfolk to give it to. Never again would he trade his winter catch with Bate Baker, back in Baxter Springs. Jed had no proof, but he suspected Baker had somehow been responsible for Cross and the other trappers killing and robbing Lem Roden. He didn't believe the fur buyer was directly involved in the shooting, but he didn't try to warn Jed or tell the dead constable about Cross and Bigfoot.

Walking about the stockade with the Hawken across his arm, Jed noticed what looked like a band of Assiniboine camped outside the fort's gates. Checking on his horses, standing in the post's corral, Jed ordered them another good feed of corn and hay, then walked out the gate. Several women stood around the lodges, working as Jed approached. Seeing him, most stepped back, eyeing him with distrust and fear. Before them, walked the demon, the Arapaho, Crow Killer himself.

Quickly signaling with his hands, Jed asked the squaws if any knew of the youngster, Silent One, or anything of his mother. Shrugging and dropping their heads, most of the women moved away at the mention of the name. Jed could tell by their actions, they knew Silent One, but were reluctant to speak. Stopping one of the shy women, Jed quickly signaled to her about the youngster's death, and that he wanted his mother to know. Getting only a blank stare at his words and no response, he turned back to the stockade.

"You are the Arapaho called Crow Killer, the demon." Jed turned to where an Assiniboine warrior was standing beside the gate. "We know of your friendship with the Silent One."

Jed turned and faced the warrior. He couldn't figure how the warrior could possibly know of his friendship with the youngster. "He was a good friend."

"It is told the white eyes killed him." The warrior nodded. "Word came here."

"No more than his own people." Jed looked about the stockade walls. "They pushed him out."

The warrior nodded. "Silent One ran away from his people in shame."

"Because of something he couldn't help." Jed looked at the warrior. "He saved my life two times. As young as he was, Silent One was a great warrior and my friend."

"He was Assiniboine, but the evil spirits entered his body and left him with no speech and no ears." The warrior shrugged. "He was cursed."

"So you cast him out to work for the squaws." Jed shook his head. "The Assiniboine lost a great warrior with their foolish beliefs."

"His mother's new husband sent him away." The warrior spoke again. "He was ashamed of his touched son."

"Tell this one, he should be ashamed of himself, but tell all, Silent One died a brave and courageous warrior."

"I, Black Elk, thank you for your friendship to the young one."

"Now, why would you do that, Black Elk?"

"The Silent One was my nephew, son of my dead brother."

Nodding, Jed continued to the post. The tribes of the north had superstitious beliefs. Jed knew they would never change, no matter what he said, and it didn't matter now. Silent One was dead and Jed had lost a good friend.

With his pack string strung out behind him, Jed turned the piebald back southwest as he left the stockade. While at the post, Jed had learned Yellow Dog's village of Cheyenne were camped in a valley only two days distant from the post. At least they were close when they had come in to trade their winter's catch and buy supplies three days prior. Riding unknown trails, he would pass through new and sometimes hostile territory. Yesterday, back at the post, an old mountain man working the stable and corrals as a hostler had drawn out the trail to the Cheyenne Village. Watching, as the old man drew out a map in the dirt, Jed didn't figure it would be too difficult to locate. With a dire warning to be watchful and vigilant, the mountain man said the village was on the south trail, several miles from Fort Bridger.

Jed knew out there alone with the string of good horses, he could fall victim to any passing band of raiding warriors. He needed a guide across the mountains to Arapaho Country and Yellow Dog's Village was his best chance to find one. The old man had said the tribes along the grasslands were mostly friendly to white trappers, but not to trust them, never let down his guard, and always ride with caution. Jed smiled, as the old man sounded almost like Walking Horse.

Several miles from the post, Jed spotted several mounted warriors riding toward him at a slow lope. Cocking the Hawken, Jed reined the piebald in and waited. Recognizing them as Cheyenne, Jed relaxed as some had been with Yellow Dog when they were in the Arapaho Country months before. Reining in their war horses, five Cheyenne Dog Soldiers sat their horses motionless, staring across the short space separating them. Flattening his hand, Jed made the piece sign and waited.

"You are Crow Killer the Arapaho, brother of the Cheyenne." A warrior nodded over at Jed.

"I am Crow Killer, friend of Yellow Dog and Crazy Cat."

"Crow Killer, the demon?" A young warrior, not recognizing Jed, seemed stunned as he heard the name spoken. "You are the blood brother of Walking Horse the Arapaho?"

"I am Crow Killer. Take me to Yellow Dog."

The Cheyenne Village was spread up and down the banks of a small stream, surrounded by tall trees and high grass. The white hide lodges stood tall and stately along the banks. Their darkened smoke holes emitted wood smoke up into the clear sky.

Walking through the village, He Dog let out a whoop when he recognized Jed riding into the village with the Dog Soldiers. Smiling, Jed slid from the piebald and grasped the youngster's shoulders.

"It is good to see He Dog again."

Raising his hand, He Dog yelled out to the watching villagers. "This is my friend, the great Crow Killer, Arapaho Lance Bearer, killer of enemies, great warrior, and good friend of Yellow Dog. Everyone will treat him as a friend and with respect."

Jed laughed as the youngster took charge and ordered the older people on how to conduct themselves. "Thank you, He Dog."

Villagers pushed closer to Jed, trying to touch his arms, fascinated with the warrior they have heard so much about. Everyone knew of the Arapaho, Crow Killer, who some thought was a demon, but they knew he was a friend and ally of the Cheyenne. Here, he was an Arapaho, not a demon like some feared.

He Dog grinned broadly as the warriors and villagers surrounded Jed. "What does the warrior, who saved me from the Crow women, do here in this far land?"

"I traded my furs at Fort Bridger. Now, I come here to visit with my friends, the Cheyenne."

"Where is the medicine woman and her father, Rolling Thunder?"

"They are still in the Arapaho Village where you saw them last." Jed looked about the village. "Soon, Rolling Thunder will come here to Fort Bridger."

"He leads more white eyes to the west from Bridger?" A listening warrior spoke up disgusted. "We do not need more whites in our country."

Jed shrugged. "I understand your feelings."

"Come, we will turn your horses loose, then we will fill our bellies." He Dog pulled Jed away from the warriors. "Does the medicine woman come with her father?"

"I'm not sure, but I think she waits in Slow Wolf's village until I return for her."

"She is a beautiful woman. Will Crow Killer make her his woman?"

Jed grinned, for one so young, He Dog was very vigilant. "I will."

"Rolling Thunder will ask more for her than these few horses you have here with you, I think."

"Probably. Tell me, He Dog, where is your brother, Yellow Dog?"

"Yellow Dog, Crazy Cat, and several others hunt for the shaggies to feed the village until we ride east." He Dog turned Jed's horses in with the herd. "They will return soon. Yellow dog will be surprised you are here."

"I imagine. I'm surprised I am here."

"Come, we will eat." He Dog noticed Jed studying the piebald. "Do not worry for your horse. We have many horse guards posted around the valley, and they will stay awake."

Laughing at the youngster's joke, Jed followed He Dog to a large lodge and ducked inside. At He Dog's command a comely young woman quickly spooned up heaping bowls of buffalo meat and wild turnips. Thanking the woman, Jed dipped into the meat hungrily.

"She is our sister, Bright Moon." He Dog noticed Jed looking at the woman. "She would cost fewer horses than the medicine woman."

"Thank you, He Dog, but I have already asked for the medicine woman, and a gentleman cannot back out on a marriage proposal." Jed grinned over at the youngster.

"What is a gentleman?" He Dog tried to pronounce the word.

Jed laughed as he ate, then looked over at the woman. "A gentleman is a good warrior."

He Dog shrugged. "She is very pretty, is she not?"

Bashfully, Jed looked over at the young woman. "Yes, she is very beautiful."

"And she is strong, hardworking, and a good cook."

"That is true." Jed agreed, curious at what the youngster was getting at.

"If she was your squaw, you would be my brother-in-law."

Jed laughed. "This is also true, He Dog, but I feel you are already my brother."

Seeing a frown come from the young woman, He Dog quieted and concentrated on his food. The youngster was right, Bright Moon was very pleasing to the eye and would make a warrior a good wife. However, his heart was set on Ellie Zeke, even though his feelings at times made him feel guilty about the memory of Sally Ann. Maybe it was too soon for him to have such feelings for another woman, since Sally Ann had died such a short time ago. As He Dog motioned for him to leave the lodge, Jed found the eyes of Bright Moon studying him.

Walking through the village, Jed grinned as He Dog seemed to strut with his chest pushed out, proud to show off his friend, Crow Killer. The Cheyenne people were taller in stature than the Arapaho. Other than their height, the Cheyenne and Arapaho were almost identical in appearance. Painted lodges showed off their owner's great deeds of valor and courage. Each lodge, by the paintings on them, identified the high warrior that occupied it.

From the end of the village came loud shouting, women calling out their shrill cries, dogs barking, and the general hubbub of new arrivals took their attention.

"Yellow Dog is here." He Dog turned and yelled his war cry. The youngster jumped into the air, trying to see the horsemen riding into the village. "Our chief, he comes with his warriors."

"I thought your father, Flying Eagle, was the chief of the Cheyenne people?"

"My father went to live with his ancestors two moons ago." He Dog shrugged. "Now, Yellow Dog is our chief."

"I am sorry." Now, Jed knew why He Dog walked so proud and could talk to the older Cheyenne women the way he did. He was next in line to be the hereditary Chief of the Cheyenne.

"Yes, he will be missed."

In a grand entrance with racing horses, women screaming in anticipation, dogs running and barking, and children hollering, the entire
village was in complete hysteria. Jed smiled, as he had seen the same
turmoil in the Arapaho Village when their Lance Bearers returned
victorious from a raid on an enemy tribe.

Sliding his grey horse to a stop, Yellow dog stared down at Jed in
complete surprise. Sliding from the horse, the warrior grabbed Jed's arm.
"My brother, Crow Killer, I am glad you visit our lodges."

"My brother, Yellow Dog, I am glad to be here in your village."

Handing his horse to He Dog, Yellow Dog spoke to his warriors
then propelled Jed toward his lodge. "Have you eaten, my friend?"

Jed nodded. "Bright Moon fed me and He Dog just before you
arrived."

"You came here from Bridger?"

"They say I missed you at the post by only a couple days."

Ducking inside the lodge, Yellow Dog motioned to a pile of blankets
with a backrest, then sat down. Bright Moon dished him out some food
and retreated to let the warriors talk alone.

"Thank you, Sister." Yellow Dog looked across at Jed. "Bright
Moon tends to my lodge while my woman is in the squaw's lodge."

"She sick?"

"She will have a little warrior very soon, maybe tonight." Yellow
Dog grinned.

"Well, congratulations." Jed looked over at Bright Moon. "It is a
great thing to have a son."

"Thank you, my friend." The warrior nodded. "How is my brother,
Walking Horse, and my sister, Little Antelope?"

"Walking Horse grows strong again and Little Antelope is as beautiful as ever."

"Bright Moon is Little Antelope's sister." Yellow Dog nodded at the
young woman. "They are both beautiful."

"Yes." Jed cleared his throat. "He Dog has already suggested what
you are thinking."

Yellow Dog laughed. "I knew he probably already did. He thinks
much of you, Crow Killer."

"How many suns is it to the Arapaho lands?"

"Six or seven sleeps, maybe more, if you don't know the shorter trails and just follow your nose." Yellow Dog set his empty bowl aside.

"I will listen to your directions closely."

"No, I wish to see my brother, Walking Horse, and my sister, Little Antelope." Yellow Dog looked across at Bright Moon. "We will ride with you to Slow Wolf's village."

Jed knew Yellow Dog was lying about wanting to see Walking Horse. The warrior would ride with him west to make sure he got to the village safely. There were many dangerous tribes on the trail to Yellowstone Country. Many had heard of Crow Killer the demon, but very few knew what he looked like, and many would attack a lone warrior leading a string of good horses. Stealing horses was a way of life to an Indian and a way of gaining respect, fame, and wealth.

"We will leave for Arapaho lands after the little one arrives and my woman is strong again." Yellow Dog looked over at Bright Moon. "My sister also wishes to see her sister, Little Antelope."

"Bright Moon is coming with us?"

"She is a good cook, my friend, and she is not hard to look upon." Yellow Dog smiled.

"No, she is not." Jed was embarrassed.

The weather was warm and clear. After checking on his piebald horse, Jed pitched his robes under an oak tree, and crawled tiredly into them. Sleep came easily, as the last thing he remembered was staring up at the clear sky before falling into a sound sleep. Awakened late in the night, as stampeding horses thundered from the darkened encampment, Jed sat up groggily. Following the drumming of the running horses, came yelling war whoops and screaming women, yelling of raiders. Throwing off his blankets, Jed sprang to his feet, holding his strong bow and quiver of arrows. The yell of raiders came again from the yelling villagers as loose horses raced by him, followed by mounted warriors.

Lunging out of the dark as a screaming mounted rider passed, Jed pulled the rider from the racing horse. Slashing with his knife, he quickly killed the warrior as Yellow Dog raced from his lodge. Taking a torch from Bright Moon's outstretched hand, Yellow Dog looked at the dead warrior Jed had killed.

"Arickara."

"They got away with many horses." Jed watched as the women lit the cook fires, throwing light across the village.

Bright Moon looked down at the dead warrior, then over at Jed. Smiling, she took in his calm demeanor as he replaced his hunting knife.

Several of the younger night herders led what horses they could catch into the village. "We are sorry, Yellow Dog. They took most of the horses and killed Small Calf."

"Small Calf?"

"He is dead." The youngster nodded. "They took his hair."

Looking around at the gathering warriors, Yellow Dog took the weapons Bright Mood handed him. "All who have horses and wish to kill enemies, ride with me."

Leaving his rifle with Bright Moon, Jed only carried his strong bow and quiver of arrows, then took a lead rope from one of the horse herders. Quickly fashioning a rope Hackamore, Jed swung up on the horse.

"Follow me, brave warriors!" Yellow Dog screamed.

Through the moonlit dark, Yellow Dog and his warriors raced into the night, following the dust trail and noise of the fleeing herd of horses. Trying to push the stolen herd through the narrow passes was much slower going than the warriors racing to catch up with them. Jed could hardly see the warriors riding beside him, as his eyes were fixed on the trail, making sure a limb didn't come out of the dark and unseat him. As the racing warriors gained on the fleeing raiders, several head of tired horses swung away from the herd and were overtaken as they slowed to a stop on the trail.

The horse Jed rode was a powerful buffalo runner with speed, stamina, and a good handle. Jed knew the Arickara would have no choice on hearing the oncoming maddened Cheyenne yelling behind them. To save themselves, they would have to abandon the stolen horses and try to outrun their pursuers. Their plan to steal the Cheyenne horses had worked well except for their escape. The Arickara failed to keep horses out of the hands of the young horse herders who caught the few missing horses. The Cheyenne were expert horse thieves themselves and they knew exactly how to catch up with the raiders.

Yellow Dog called out to his warriors, gathering them around him. "Our horses are tired, catch a fresh one when you can, and then we will catch these thieves."

"How far will we chase these warriors?"

"All the way to the north, to the Grandmother's land, if we have to."

"We have most of our horses." Another warrior spoke out.

Yellow Dog turned on the warrior with a vengeance. "They killed one of our horse herders, only a boy. Now, they will all die if we can catch them."

Jed swung up on a fresh horse, he managed to catch as he passed it on the trail. Riding up beside Yellow Dog in the shadow of the moon, Jed called out. "We must wait until the new sun or we may kill our own warriors in the dark."

"I agree, but we will ride on and stay close to the Arickara." Yellow Dog kicked his horse. "I will not lose the ones responsible for the death of Small Calf."

"We'll catch up, my brother." Jed whipped his powerful horse.

With the coming of a dusky dawn, Jed looked around to find only six warriors, besides himself, still riding alongside Yellow Dog. Jed shook his head sadly as he passed a few horses, mostly older broodmares and colts, too old and tired to run further, and played out with exhaustion alongside the trail. Seeing their ruined condition, many were wind broke, some stone bruised from the rough ground, caused Yellow Dog to let out a yell of rage. These horses were his tribe's riches, their means of transport for hunting, and for keeping the Cheyenne people safe. To see them in this shape, enraged the warrior. By the tracks along the sandy trail, very few horses still ran before them. Jed watching the trail, counted at least a dozen raiders racing ahead. He couldn't be sure, but it looked like the tracks of the piebald running with the raiders.

Spotting a loose gelding grazing alongside the trail, Jed caught the animal and quickly changed horses for the third time of the night. Whipping the horse with his bow, Jed charged down the trail ahead of the other Cheyenne. Rounding a sharp bend, Jed found himself close behind two Arickara warriors whipping their fatigued horses frantically, trying to escape. Notching an arrow, Jed sent the missile deep into the back of the last rider. Whipping his horse, Jed closed in on the other racing warrior and knocked him from his horse with his war axe.

Less than a mile down the trail, Jed blinked, before him stood the piebald grazing beside the trail. Reining in his heaving bay horse, Jed dismounted and patted the piebald's neck, quickly haltering him. The paint was hardly sweating from the long run. In the dark of night, the raiders had overlooked the powerful animal. Swinging up on the horse, Jed kicked him into a hard run down the trail.

The piebald felt strong, and the long run through the night hadn't tired the powerful horse in the least. Astride the piebald, he would be able to run down the remaining Arickara. He lost sight of the raiders, and now only the deeper cut tracks of horses carrying riders were ahead of him. Apparently, all the stolen horses had stopped alongside the trail exhausted from the long run, some with broken legs and split hooves from the harsh trails. The raiders, knowing they were being overtaken, had given up on keeping any of the stolen horses. Now, they were intent on only saving themselves.

Riding the powerful piebald, Jed pulled far ahead of Yellow Dog and the other warriors, and was alone against possibly ten or more Arickara. He knew his pack animals were behind him, somewhere on his back trail, as he had seen one or two of them as he passed. Now, he raced on after the raiders, to punish the warriors ahead for killing the young Cheyenne boy and the theft of the horses. Jed knew the Arickara had to be punished for their actions, or other tribes would be emboldened to raid the Cheyenne as well.

The trail leveled out on a long straightaway, revealing the Arickara warriors fleeing to the north, trying to reach Fort Bridger and safety. Jed counted nine Rees on the trail ahead, whipping their laboring horses and looking behind them to see who was in pursuit. Seeing only one lone rider following them, the warriors slowed and turned their blowing horses. Without slowing the powerful piebald, Jed hit the waiting warriors head on, throwing riders from their horses and knocking two horses sideways to the hard-packed trail. Quickly, reining the well-trained warhorse around, Jed charged in among the raiders with his war axe, cracking bones and bringing death wherever it landed. His attack was so sudden and vicious, the Arickara didn't know how to defend themselves from this demon. Their horses were too exhausted to respond to their frantic riders whipping them, trying to get away from this menace, and the powerful piebald horse.

Yellow Dog and his warriors reined in and looked ahead, amazed at the carnage the Arapaho Crow Killer had left laying on the trail around him. Both warriors and horses lay dead or dying in the dust. Watching the remaining five Arickara race away frantically in fear for their lives, Jed reined in and sat the piebald. His fury abated and blood lust cooled, he would not pursue the beaten Rees further. Turning the piebald, Jed rode by the stunned Cheyenne without a word or even a nod, as he knew they were there.

Crazy Cat turned his head, looking at Jed's back as he passed like he had never seen him before. "This one is truly a demon. The Rees are powerful warriors and today he killed six of them like he would destroy a fly."

Yellow Dog could only shake his head as he kicked his tired horse back to the south. "We will pick up our horses as we go back."

"We do not pursue the Rees?" Crazy Cat looked over at Yellow Dog.

"No, they have been punished enough."

"Many of our horses are crippled." Another warrior shook his head sadly.

"We will save what we can and destroy the ones that cannot return to our village."

Luckily, Jed found the little black mule and one other of his horses as he followed the trail of horses back to the village. Villagers stared in curiosity as the Arapaho, covered in blood, with his hunting shirt slashed in many places, passed by them without speaking, then dismounted in front of Yellow Dog's lodge.

Quickly gathering his rifle, bags of supplies, money, and packsaddles, Jed saddled his pack animals. He then tied the extra saddles on top of the already saddled horses and mule. Turning to find Bright Moon staring at him, Jed nodded and turned to the piebald.

"Is Crow Killer hurt?"

"No, it is not my blood, Bright Moon."

"Were any Cheyenne warriors killed?"

"No, Yellow Dog and his warriors will return as soon as they gather the horses." Jed stared down at the pretty woman.

"Are you leaving our village now?"

"Yes, I will ride to Arapaho lands."

Turning, she passed the words the waiting villagers wanted to hear, then turned back to Jed. Relieved that none were killed, the villagers started chanting and some touched him as they passed.

"Do you leave before Yellow Dog returns?"

"I must." Jed felt embarrassed, guilt or something, he didn't know which. The way Yellow Dog and his warriors had stared at him, in passing on the trail, Jed just wanted to get away and be alone.

"You should wait for Yellow Dog to return."

"I go." Jed nodded as she placed her hand on his bloody sleeve. "Tell my friend, Yellow Dog, I will see him again."

"You do not have all of your horses." Bright Moon shook her head. "Wait, my brother may bring in the others."

"Good-bye, Bright Moon." Jed swung on the piebald and reined him to the west. "Tell no one to follow me."

The tall woman shook her head as Jed passed from her sight through the lodges. She knew there had been a terrible fight, as he turned the piebald, the war axe of Crow Killer took her attention. The heavy weapon was covered in blood as well as his clothing, arms, and face. She shivered, his face looked like the face of death, and she could smell death on him.

Jed slowly calmed and relaxed as he trotted his animals to the west. He didn't know this country, but by his natural instinct of direction, he knew this trail would take him back to the Arapaho. He had to leave the Cheyenne encampment and be alone today. He was in no mood to listen to the warriors brag on his courage or tell of the deaths of the Arickara. Jed shook his head, as he didn't know what possessed him at times in battle. Perhaps, his killing lust did turn him into a demon as most tribes believed.

"He would not stay until you returned." Bright Moon looked up at her brother as he slid tiredly from his horse. "He acted strange, different from last night."

Yellow Dog shook his head as he handed He Dog his horse. "He killed many enemies today, all alone. He is a mighty warrior in battle, mighty."

"He is a demon." Crazy Cat shook his head. "I have seen this myself today."

"Maybe this is true, but he is our friend." Yellow Dog turned away. "With the new sun, we must follow him."

Bright Moon put her arm on Yellow Dog's arm. "No, my brother, he said for you not to follow him."

"You seem to fear Crow Killer, my sister."

"I do not fear Crow Killer, our friend, but the demon, I do fear." The woman held up her hand. "Do not follow him, my brother. Let him ride alone and sort out his mind."

Nodding, Yellow Dog walked away. "We will gather our horses, then we will return to our lands."

Bright Moon looked off to the south where Jed had ridden out of sight only minutes before. Never had she seen a warrior like him. He Dog had told of his prowess in battle, but she thought her little brother was just making up another story. Now, she knew better. Crow Killer was a mighty warrior, but she wondered if he was dangerous and indeed a demon.

Ellie walked beside Little Antelope as they toured the village looking through the lodges, making sure all the people were okay. Some of the villagers did not trust a woman to treat their ailments, even with Slow Wolf telling them she was their medicine woman now. Little Antelope smiled and told Ellie, soon they would all come to respect her when they saw the others healthy and happy.

Her medicine supply was running low. Ellie hoped Jed would return soon and bring her a new supply from a list she had given him.

Little Antelope sensed what she was thinking. "He will return soon. The warm times come, and his furs have been sold."

"I hope so."

"I miss him too, Sister." Little Antelope smiled.

"I know you two are close."

Nodding, Little Antelope smiled. "From the first day he came here."

"Does Jed feel the same?"

"Crow Killer is a proud man, and Walking Horse is his brother. Yes, he feels the same, but that is all, nothing more."

"I didn't mean."

Little Antelope smiled. "It is okay, my husband knows my feelings and he understands."

Ellie looked curiously at the little woman. "I understand too."

From the end of the village, a shout went up causing several warriors to spring on their horses and encircle two warriors riding between the lodges. Ellie shadowed her eyes as she recognized one of the riders.

Little Antelope frowned. "Big Owl brings the pretty one, Red Hawk, the Crow here."

"Why?" Ellie watched as Big Owl pointed at them, then toward Slow Wolf's lodge. "Something must be wrong."

"Let's go see." Little Antelope turned. "Big Owl motions for us to come to Slow Wolf's lodge."

Ellie grinned. "I think you kinda like the Crow."

"Bah, he knows he is pretty." Little Antelope shook her head. "All the unmarried ones parade themselves in front of our enemy, like girls will."

"Well, Sister, he is very handsome."

"Yes, but he doesn't have to know it."

"He's a man." Ellie laughed. "Men will be men."

"Red Hawk is impossible." Little Antelope looked over at the Crow. "He is pretty, but he doesn't have to act so conceited."

Little Antelope sensed Red Hawk wasn't in one of his normally happy moods. The face was worried, and for once, his voice serious. Talking to Slow Wolf, he motioned at Ellie several times. In her days with the Arapaho, Ellie had picked up quite a bit of sign language and the Arapaho tongue. She could understand a few of his words. Someone was sick in the Crow Village.

"Red Hawk has come for you, Ellie." Little Antelope translated the words she was hearing.

"Why?"

"He tells Slow Wolf his father, Plenty Coups, is very sick. He asks permission for you to ride to the Crow Village with him."

"What does Slow Wolf say?"

"He has sent for Walking Horse to decide." Little Antelope looked into the proud face of the warrior. "His father must be very sick for him to ask such a thing of an enemy."

"Who is the young girl?" Ellie looked at the little girl standing beside Red Hawk.

"She is his daughter." Little Antelope answered. "He will leave her here, for your safe return."

Stepping forward, Ellie knelt down in front of the scared little girl. Holding out her hand, she took the small hand in her own. "I am, Ellie."

"Her name is Butterfly. She is my daughter." Red Hawk nodded. "She will be a hostage until your safe return."

"It is good to see Red Hawk again." Ellie stood up and looked down at the small girl. "I didn't know you had such a beautiful daughter."

"I didn't know you had a squaw, poor thing." Little Antelope spoke up.

"And it is good to see you again, little one." Red Hawk wouldn't be drawn into an argument today.

"Tell me, Red Hawk, what is wrong with Plenty Coups?" Ellie questioned.

"His stomach hurts on this side." Red Hawk pointed to his left side. "He will not eat. He is in much pain."

Big Owl pointed across the village. "Walking Horse comes."

"I cannot let her go." Slow Wolf shook his head. "How long has Rolling Thunder been gone from the village?"

Big Owl looked at Red Hawk. "We do not have time to go after Rolling Thunder, my chief."

"What will we do?"

Walking Horse dismounted and nodded at Red Hawk. "What is wrong?"

"Plenty Coups is sick. Red Hawk asks for the medicine woman's help." Slow Wolf spoke up.

"What does our chief say?"

"The decision is yours, Walking Horse."

"When I was sick, Plenty Coups offered his medicine man to help me." Walking Horse argued. "Can we do less?"

"He helped protect our village while Walking Horse and Crow Killer were away to the north." Big Owl spoke up.

"Ask my sister." Walking Horse shrugged. "It is her decision."

"No, it is your decision." Slow Wolf frowned.

Walking Horse smiled. "You worry about Crow Killer. She is his woman."

Little Antelope had been helping Ellie understand what they were saying. "While we stand here arguing, Plenty Coups is dying. I'm going with Red Hawk."

Walking Horse spoke to some boys who quickly brought fresh horses for the ride to Crow country.

Slow Wolf after hearing Ellie's words, shook his head slowly, then looked over at Walking Horse. "You will go with her, my nephew."

CHAPTER 10

After retrieving her medical bag and supplies, Big Owl helped Ellie onto the back of a horse. Pointing down at Red Hawk's daughter, Ellie had Big Owl put the little girl in front of her. "A hostage is not needed between friends."

Nodding, Red Hawk thanked Ellie and led them to the Yellowstone in a short lope.

Several Crow warriors came down from the high ridge, leading spare horses, and joined them as they rode from the river. Keeping the horses in a slow lope and breaking down to a steady trot, Red Hawk kept the small party moving fast, as concern showed on his face. Midday on the second day, the village came in sight in the lower valley.

Quickly dismounting, Ellie was about to enter the large lodge of Plenty Coups when an elderly man, shaking rattles and screaming, stepped between Red Hawk and the door. Screaming and pointing at Ellie, all she could understand of the Crow language was the word squaw.

Pushing the old one out of the way, Red Hawk motioned Ellie and Walking Horse into the lodge. The huge body of Plenty Coups lay on a bed of buffalo hides.

"My father, this is the medicine woman who cured this warrior, Walking Horse." Red Hawk knelt beside the bed. "If you would permit an Arapaho Medicine Woman to give you medicine, maybe her medicine can heal you."

The huge head rolled sideways to look into Ellie's face. "Can you make a dead man well, woman?"

"Crow Killer has told me you are the bravest of the brave." Ellie took the huge hand in hers. "Be brave and let me help you, Chief Plenty Coups."

Plenty Coups looked up at her from his pain-racked eyes and nodded. "Do what you can. I hope your medicine is strong and takes away the pain."

Ordering Walking Horse and Red Hawk from the lodge, Ellie motioned for the old woman to help her remove the blankets from Plenty Coups. Pushing and feeling the chief's sore and swollen side, Ellie sat back and nodded. Calling for Red Hawk to come back in the lodge, Ellie pulled out a bottle of medicine from her bag.

Looking up at Red Hawk, Ellie showed him the bottle. "This is laudanum. Tell Plenty Coups it tastes terrible, but it will make him feel better."

"What is wrong with my father?"

"His stomach had something in it he cannot pass." Ellie held up another bottle. "I will give this to him, to help him get well."

Quickly explaining her words to Plenty Coups, Red Hawk laughed as the chief made a terrible face when he swallowed the bitter tasting medicine. Within a couple hours, the chief's pain subsided as the laudanum started working. Next, she dosed him with the foul smelling castor oil.

"Daughter, your medicine is worse than the pain." Plenty Coups shook his head, trying to dislodge the awful taste. "Ugh, it is terrible!"

"Soon, you will be well, my chief."

"What is in my stomach that causes so much pain?"

Ellie had heard her grandfather talk of kidney stones, and she was hoping that was what ailed Plenty Coups. She was only guessing, as medicines dealing with internal ailments were new to medical books. She had heard Doctor Zeke tell patients with kidney stones that they would pass in a few days. All she could do for now was keep him pain free, while dosing him with castor oil.

At the end of the first day, after taking the medicine, Plenty Coups was out of pain and feeling much better. On the morning of the second day, the medicine was working and he was on his feet. Seeing the chief improving gave the villagers a sense of hope as Plenty Coups walked slowly about the village, greeting his people. For three days, Ellie watched over him as he moved about, holding his side.

"Soon, you will feel better, my chief." Many times she promised the same words. "Soon…"

Late in the night, Ellie watched as Plenty Coups made his way slowly from the lodge, then suddenly let out a loud moan outside the lodge. Seconds later, the chief made his way back to his bed.

"Your medicine will either kill me or cure me, but I do feel much better." Plenty Coups called from the dark.

"Soon, you will feel better."

Waking early the next morning, Ellie was surprised to find Plenty Coups sitting outside the lodge, smoking his pipe. Several warriors sat talking in a circle, around him. Red Hawk pointed to a folded blanket and asked her to sit. Looking over at Walking Horse, she was hesitant as she knew a woman was never allowed to sit in council with warriors.

"Sit, Medicine Woman, you have saved our chief's life, and have earned the right." Red Hawk smiled up at her. "You are a great healer."

Ellie studied the smiling face of Plenty Coups. "How is your side, my chief?"

"I have no pain. Sore, but no pain." Plenty Coups stuck out his tongue. "The taste, I will never forget it."

"You should eat my woman's cooking." An older warrior laughed.

Ellie was relieved, as she wasn't sure Plenty Coups would recover. She wished her grandfather, Doctor Zeke, was there to advise her. This time, she was lucky, as she had only guessed. For now, Plenty Coups was over his problem, whatever it was.

"I am well. Tomorrow, Red Hawk will see you safely back to your village."

Shaking her head, Ellie held up her hand. "I will wait a few days, my chief. I want to make sure you are well."

"Thank you, Daughter." Plenty Coups smiled. "I am glad you will stay with this old man a few more days."

Plenty Coups had grown fond of Ellie in the few days she had been in the village. His pain was gone, so now he proposed an assembly of the village and a large feast to celebrate his health and the young medicine woman.

For three days, the dancing, celebrating, and feasting kept the village in a frenzy as the Crow celebrated their chief's return to good health. Plenty Coups refrained from dancing and, with Ellie's warning, from eating like he used to.

"You will starve me to death." Plenty Coups pretended sadness. "I am a big man. I need plenty of buffalo, elk, and deer to keep my strength."

"Yes, Chief, but if you eat these things, I will have to give you more foul tasting medicine." Ellie smiled.

Halfway to his mouth with a piece of buffalo meat, Plenty Coups stopped and dropped the meat back onto the plate. "You would do that to me, Daughter?"

"Yes, I would, to save you from yourself."

Red Hawk, listening to the exchange, could only smile to himself. He knew his father's large appetite, which consisted mostly of meat with few greens. Tonight, Ellie won the argument, but when she left the village, he knew his father's voracious appetite would get the best of him.

Hatcher blinked his eyes as he looked down the steep mountain trail. He would know the piebald paint with his white bald face at any range, day or night. Coming up the narrow pass toward him was Jed Bracket himself, astride the horse. Raising his rifle, Hatcher let out with a yell and waited at the top of the trail. He couldn't believe Jed was there, crossing the mountain range to the west.

Stepping down from his horse, Hatcher waited as the piebald picked his way slowly up the rough trail. "Jedidiah Bracket, you young whippersnapper, what are you doing way up here in the clouds?"

"Looking for an angel." Jed slid from the paint and took Hatcher's hand. "I believe I'm high enough to find one, Lige."

"I left her back at Slow Wolf's village."

"She is an angel alright." Jed smiled. "The prettiest angel in these mountains."

"Yes, she is." Hatcher nodded as he studied the bloody figure standing before him. "You're so bloody, what happened? Why are you on this trail?"

"Let's get a fire going, Lige." Jed hobbled his horses on grass and started kicking a fire together. "I could eat."

Sipping coffee, Hatcher reclined against his saddle and studied Jed as he ate. "Now, tell me, what happened?"

Slowly, Jed told of selling his furs at Bridger and the fight with the Arickara. "Now, I'm headed to Slow Wolf's village."

"For Ellie?"

"Would it bother you, Lige?" Jed looked at the old scout. "Do you approve?"

Looking into the small fire, Hatcher shrugged. "I am concerned, Jed. In these mountains you have a killer reputation. Now, from what you say about your fight with the Arickara, your reputation could be even worse."

Nodding, Jed tossed another stick on the fire. "You're probably right about that, Lige."

"I just want her happy and safe." Hatcher didn't want to bring up Sally Ann Duncan, but her death was on his mind. "Can you keep her safe, boy?"

Jed couldn't answer, but he understood Hatcher's feelings. "I will think on your words, my friend."

"It's not you, Jed, you know that." Hatcher looked across the fire. "I have always been fond of you, but she is my daughter and I just want her safe."

"I understand, Lige."

"Speak with Ellie, then decide." Hatcher shrugged. "That is all I ask."

"I will speak with her." Jed nodded. "I will tell her your fears."

"Thank you, Jed." Hatcher was embarrassed. "You know, I'd be proud to have you for a son-in-law."

"Thank you, Lige. We will talk it over."

After coffee and biscuits, over an early morning fire, Jed quizzed Hatcher about the trails leading to Arapaho lands. "You'll find it, Jed, just follow your nose, then turn due west at the granite crossing, two days south of here."

"I'll make it fine, Lige."

"I know you will. I'll see you next summer." Hatcher cinched his horse.

"You fixing to move into Fort Bridger for the winter?" Jed questioned.

"Nah, I'll winter with Yellow Dog and hook up with Chalk for the westward trek, come early spring."

"Who guides Chalk to Bridger?"

"Charles B. Sawyer, that's who."

"I've heard that name." Jed nodded. "Why doesn't he lead the train all the way west, then we could do some hunting?"

"He up and got himself hitched to a widow back in Nebraska, and she won't let him stay out no longer than Fort Bridger."

"You're kidding." Jed laughed. "A halfway guide, never heard of such."

"Wish I was, but I ain't." Hatcher laughed. "Yep, you might call him a halfway wagon scout."

"Told what to do by a woman?"

Lige laughed. "Let me tell you, that woman is about six inches over six feet and as broad as a wagon beam. I seen her throw a man clean over a hitch rack one time. She scares the daylights out of me for sure."

"Well, for Pete's sake, why did he marry her?"

"Drunk."

"Drunk? Well, divorce her then."

"Ha, last fella done that wound up six feet under."

"Whew, reckon he better toe the mark then."

"For a fact." Hatcher laughed. "He's in big trouble if'n he don't."

Jed heard Lige whistling halfway down the mountain, and wondered if the old scout wasn't pulling his leg about Sawyer and his big wife. Still, about Ellie, the old scout was right, as trouble followed him around like a sour smell throughout the mountains. Even back in his valley, how could he be sure she would be safe? If it weren't for him, Sally Ann would still be alive.

Three days after leaving Hatcher on the mountain, Jed reined in and looked across the flat valley where several Arapaho boys watched over their large horse herd. Nudging the piebald forward, Jed split the horses as he crossed the small stream that bordered the village. The herders, alerted to his presence by the moving horses, started to give the alarm, then recognized Crow Killer, the famous Lance Bearer. They gawked with their mouth's open as he passed through the horses.

A yell of recognition rang out as the villagers glimpsed the rider coming to the village was Jed. Exiting her lodge, Little Antelope heard the yelling of his name and watched as the people hurried to the end of the village. Running to Jed's lodge, Little Antelope woke up Ellie, who had been resting from her long hard ride from the Crow Village.

"He comes, Ellie."

"Jed?"

"Yes, hurry. We will go meet him at Slow Wolf's lodge." Little Antelope looked about the village for Walking Horse. "Hurry, Ellie, hurry."

Both women looked in shock at the bloody hunting shirt Jed wore as he slid tiredly from the piebald in front of Slow Wolf's lodge. Looking around, he smiled as his eyes located the two women.

Turning, he greeted the old chief coming from his lodge. "I have returned to my people, my father."

Slow Wolf looked at Jed's shirt as he greeted the tall warrior. "It is good you have returned, my son."

"Yes." Jed nodded. "Thank you, my chief."

Looking about at the watching villagers, Slow Wolf motioned Jed inside his lodge. Seating themselves, the two warriors sat across from each other solemnly.

"I do not have to ask, my son. These old eyes can see for themselves. You have been in a fight in the last few days." Slow Wolf nodded slowly. "Tell me of this battle."

"Arickara warriors raided Yellow Dog's village, killed and scalped one young horse herder, and stole many horses." Jed looked into the small fire burning in the middle of the lodge. "We killed many and recovered the horses that weren't crippled."

"The Arickara are great warriors and very dangerous enemies."

"The ones I fought were not warriors, nor were they great."

"I see." Slow Wolf smiled. "Tell me, my son, how is Yellow Dog and the Cheyenne people?"

"They will be fine." Jed picked up a small stick, tossing it into the fire. "No Cheyenne were killed except the young horse herder."

The doorway of the lodge darkened as Walking Horse's large frame ducked through the lodge hole. Taking a seat beside Jed, the warrior took in his bloody shirt and leggings then smiled. "You have been fighting again."

"Seems like that is all I do anymore." Jed shrugged. "I fought for the Cheyenne people this time."

"Who was the enemy?"

Again, Jed quickly related the story of the Arickara, his journey to Forth Bridger to sell his furs, his visit with Yellow Dog and the Cheyenne, and his journey back to the Arapaho. "Now, I will return to my valley and hopefully peace."

"Did not White Swan say you would never have peace?" Slow Wolf asked. "You are a Lance Bearer. The people's enemies are your enemies."

"I will always defend the Arapaho people if I am needed." Jed looked at Slow Wolf. "But, I would like to have peace for a change."

"This is good to hear." Walking Horse smiled. "Crow Killer is needed by his people."

"You look strong again, my brother." Jed looked over at Walking Horse.

"I feel strong."

"Go, both of you and leave an old man in peace." Slow Wolf knew the two warriors needed to talk alone. "I will speak with you with the new sun."

Exiting the lodge, the two shook hands and smiled. "I think you need a new shirt. You are an embarrassment in your condition."

Turning toward their lodges, they almost collided with Ellie and Little Antelope. Ellie seemed to shrink back as she took in his bloody clothing and wild appearance.

"Are you hurt, Crow Killer?" Little Antelope looked him up and down. "Is it your blood?"

"No, little one, it is not my blood." Jed looked at Ellie, who didn't say a word.

"Come, Little Antelope." Walking Horse could see Ellie's reaction to the blood. "Let's go find Crow Killer another shirt."

Looking into Jed's eyes, then over at Ellie, Little Antelope followed Walking Horse to their lodge. Cringing back as Jed reached for her, Ellie turned and walked toward the small creek, away from the lodges.

"How many have you killed this time?"

"Only those who attacked Yellow Dog's Cheyenne, and who deserved killing." Jed couldn't understand her question. There, among the Arapaho, killing one's enemies was honorable. "What is wrong, Ellie?"

"Wrong? Look at yourself, Jed. How many have you killed in the little time I have known you?"

"I am an Arapaho Lance Bearer. My job is to protect the people and to do less would bring dishonor on me and the Lance Bearers."

"You are a killer, Jed. You like to kill." Ellie cringed from his touch. "I called you a heathen once. I thought I was wrong, but now I know I wasn't."

"I met your father on the trail here. He said for me to tell you he would come in the summer to get you."

"That is good. I will be here."

"You will not come back with me to the valley?"

The tall woman shook her head. "My place is to save lives, and yours seems as if it is to take lives."

"I thought we were to be married."

"I love you, Jed, but I do not love Crow Killer." Ellie shrugged. "I will not marry a heathen killer, never."

Turning, Jed walked back to where his horses stood beside Slow Wolf's lodge and swung up on the piebald. Kicking the horse, he turned south toward the Yellowstone, leading his pack animals.

"He leaves." Little Antelope spoke to Walking Horse, then her eyes followed Jed from the village. Walking to where Ellie stood, Little Antelope looked curiously at her. "What did you say to him?"

Shrugging, Ellie kept her attention focused on the creek. "I will not marry a killer."

"You fool. He is the greatest and kindest warrior in all the Arapaho Nation." Little Antelope shook her head. "Any woman in this nation would be proud to have him for a husband."

"You too, Little Antelope?"

"Yes, me too." The little woman straightened her shoulders. "If I wasn't married to Walking Horse, I would marry Crow Killer if he asked me."

"He is a killer. He has killed many."

"Yes, and he will kill more." Little Antelope looked to where

Walking Horse mounted his horse and raced from the village. "He killed to save me, Walking Horse, Red Hawk, and even you, Sister."

"He likes killing." Ellie shook her head. "I hate what he stands for."

"Your Arapaho blood is weak. Go back to your white blood."

"My father will come for me in the summer."

Little Antelope couldn't understand Ellie. Crow Killer was a warrior. In Arapaho society, warriors were taught to kill their enemy. "Go back to your white people. You are no longer my sister."

Ellie looked over as the small woman walked away. She would have to wait until Hatcher returned in the fall to take her from these people. She couldn't understand the Arapaho people, and their lust for blood.

After hearing the hard running horse come up behind him, Jed reined in the piebald as Walking Horse reined his horse to a sliding stop beside him.

Looking over at Jed, the warrior shook his head. "You leave without saying you are going, my brother."

"Yes, I'm leaving."

"She is half white, raised by the whites." Walking Horse looked over at Jed. "She does not understand our ways, this country, or our warring tribes."

"She despises me." Jed nodded. "I return back to my valley where I belong."

"I am sorry." Walking Horse shook his head sadly. "I will come to see you and we will hunt in a few suns."

"You will always be welcome." Jed reached out and shook hands with the warrior. "Take care of her until Rolling Thunder returns."

"I will do that." Walking Horse watched sadly as Jed turned the piebald. "I am sorry, my brother. I am sorry she thinks as a white, not like an Arapaho woman."

Nodding, Jed raised his hand, then kicked the horses into a lope.

Reaching the Yellowstone, Jed didn't hesitate or let the horses rest before kicking them into the deep river. He already spotted the Crow warriors watching him from the high ridge. He hoped the warriors that had followed Two Tails weren't among the mounted Crow. He didn't want to fight the Crow, but in the mood he was in today, he would kill them all. Jed shook his head, wondering if she was right. Has he turned into a killer?

Passing close by the waiting Crow warriors, Jed noticed they were younger men than the ones Two Tails had ridden with. Perhaps, Red Hawk had refused to let the warriors of Two Tails guard the Yellowstone crossing. Nodding, he reined in beside the warriors.

"You are leaving our lands, Crow Killer?" The Crows stared at the bloody shirt.

Nodding, Jed looked at the warriors. "Tell my brother, Red Hawk, and Chief Plenty Coups that I am returning to my lodge."

"Come with us and tell Red Hawk this. He would like to see you." A young warrior named Tame Goose spoke up. "Our chief regains his strength."

"Plenty Coups was sick?"

"Yes, the medicine woman from your tribe came to our village and healed him." Tame Goose looked surprised that Jed knew nothing of this. "You did not know?"

"No."

"But, we thought she was your woman?"

"No." Jed shook his head. He hadn't lingered in the Arapaho Village long after Ellie once again called him a heathen and killer. He heard nothing of Plenty Coups sickness. "I am glad Plenty Coups is well."

"Your shirt is bloody. Are you injured?"

"No, it is not my blood."

"We will tell Red Hawk your words."

"Good-bye, my friends." Jed nodded. "Tell Red Hawk to come and hunt with Crow Killer."

Jed reined his horses in at the same place the old sow had attacked and killed Billy Wilson. Looking around, expecting to see the grizzly emerge from the thick brush, Jed's skin unexpectedly tingled. Tying his horses, Jed took down a leather bag from one of the packsaddles and walked through the tall grass and brush to the last place he had seen Billy Wilson's body. Jed knew he had lied to his stepfather about burying Billy's remains. He just thought too much of the man, and couldn't bring himself to tell him his son's bones lay scattered and uncovered on a lone mountain.

Pushing through the rough brush and bushes, Jed searched the ground closely as he moved forward. Finally, he found what he was looking for. Scarred bones, showing teeth marks from the grizzly, were scattered about the flat ground. Moving the grass aside slowly, Jed picked up all the bones he could find of the dead Billy Wilson. It was terrible work to pick up the bones of a man you knew. Jed had promised to bring Ed Wilson's son back to the Wilson farm for burial this summer, and he wouldn't break his promise.

This way was easier, as Jed didn't want Wilson to see his son's bones unburied. Hefting the leather pouch, Jed searched the grass for more bones but found none. Turning to the horses, Jed tied the bag to the packsaddle of the black mule. Later in the spring, after selling his furs at Bridger, he would take Billy Wilson home for burial.

Jed sat studying the cabin from across the valley, and everything seemed peaceful. The piebald pawed the ground, as he knew he was home, eager to reach the corral. It was barely past noon, so Jed decided as soon as he unloaded his supplies, he would turn the horses loose on the lush valley grass. They had been ridden hard and far over rough and treacherous terrain. They deserved a good rest and plenty of lush grass.

Opening the door, Jed stepped inside the dark room and looked around the familiar cabin. With Silent One gone, then Lem Roden, and now Ellie Zeke, the cabin was empty, but still it was home. After placing the sacks of supplies on the cabin floor, Jed walked the piebald to the creek for a drink. He hobbled and turned him out on the grass with the other horses and the little mule.

Taking a new bar of lye soap, he had bought from a trader at Bridger, Jed took a new pair of leggings and hunting shirt, then walked to the deep pool above the cabin. Quickly stripping, he waded into the water and submerged himself. He had seen soap, but he never smelled anything as strong as lye soap. Sitting on a flat rock to dry off, he could still feel the sting of the lye in his eyes. Nevertheless, he had to admit, the strong soap did get him clean and smelling better.

Pulling on his new doeskin clothing, Jed tossed the bloody ones on the outside campfire and returned to the cabin. Sorting and putting his new supplies on the oak shelves, Jed knew he had more than enough to see him through the cold times. After next trapping season, in spring, he would take his furs to Bridger using the Blackhorse Crossing on the Snake. Later, he would ride west to see his stepfather and take home the remains of Billy Wilson.

All summer, Jed cut grass and filled the barn, then turned his attention to his traps and trap lines. Soon, the days would turn shorter and colder, and it would be time to turn his full attention on his trapping. He studied the three horses and mule grazing out on the valley floor. If his trap lines produced pelts as they did last year, he would need more pack animals.

The blissful days of summer passed peacefully, as the bears were gone, and the ponds and streams abounded with beaver and fish. The woodland trails, running through the tall, stately trees along the mountain ridges, were alive with the tracks of many fur bearers. Jed knew this trapping season would perhaps be even better than he and Roden had enjoyed last season. Even with the loss of his friends and Ellie, Jed still loved his valley but not the solitude. With Ellie gone, some of the joy left and in its place loneliness came. With the passing of time, perhaps the happiness he once felt would return and he would forget the sadness.

Near sundown, hearing the braying of the black mule, Jed took up his rifle and opened the door. Across the valley, several warriors rode in a line loping their horses toward the cabin. Watching the approaching riders, Jed smiled when he recognized Walking Horse and Big Owl riding at the front. Stepping into the yard, Jed raised his hand in greeting as the riders reined in, smiling at him.

"My brother, we have come as we promised." Walking Horse dismounted and walked to where Jed stood. "It is good to see you."

"It is good to see my friends." Jed nodded at the assembled warriors. "Turn your ponies into the corral and I will fix you some deer steaks to eat."

"Yellow Dog brought your ponies to our village." The warrior nodded at the two riderless horses. "He found them after you left the village."

"He did not come here with you?"

Walking Horse shrugged. "He would not come. His warriors fear you, my friend. The stories of how you killed the Arickara."

"They fear me for killing their enemies, fighting for them?" Jed was in shock as he heard the words. "I am not the Cheyenne's enemy."

"They do not know you as the Arapaho do." The warrior nodded. "What they saw was one lone warrior defeating many Arickara, so easily."

"They think I am a demon."

"They are superstitious. They fear the demon." Big Owl frowned. "They told of watching you kill many Arickara, while the mighty Rees sat helpless under your trance."

"Seems everyone hates killings." Jed thought of Ellie. "What of Yellow Dog, does he fear me too?"

"No, Yellow Dog and his sister, Bright Moon, defends you." Walking Horse smiled.

"Bright Moon defends me?" Jed looked at Walking Horse. "Does anybody else?"

Walking Horse knew he spoke of Ellie. "My sister is well and she treats the sick ones in the village while she waits on Rolling Thunder to come for her."

"And Little Antelope. How is she?"

"She is well, but my wife and my sister no longer speak." Walking Horse shrugged. "Women can be worrisome at times."

Jed looked over at the warrior. "Why, what has happened?"

"I do not know, neither would tell me, but I feel they had words about you." The warrior shook his head.

"Me?"

"Little Antelope is an Arapaho woman. She defended the battles you have had for your people and me." Walking Horse shrugged. "My sister was raised white. She does not understand our way of life, and in ways, she is soft."

"Yes, she told me that plain enough." Jed remembered her words. "She thinks me a killer and a heathen."

"Maybe she will change her mind."

"I don't think so, my brother." Shaking his head, Jed walked into the cabin. "Maybe it is too late."

"It is never too late." Walking Horse followed Jed. "If it is in the smoke, there is another who looks upon you with great pride."

Jed knew Walking Horse spoke of the young Cheyenne maiden, Bright Moon, sister of Yellow Dog and Little Antelope. Walking Horse said she had ridden with Yellow Dog when they brought his horses back to the Arapaho. Probably, she had spoken about him to Little Antelope, and that's how Walking Horse knew of her feelings. In his short time around her, Jed could sense her feelings for him. She is Cheyenne and they don't try to hide their feelings as white women would. But, she was young yet, so perhaps it was just infatuation that she felt.

Entering the cabin, Jed quickly placed deer steaks in the iron skillets and rolled pan biscuits in the Dutch oven. The words of Walking Horse went through his mind about Bright Moon as he prepared supper for the warriors. He had no doubt Ellie was lost to him, and he tried to understand her way of thinking. Still, she was on his mind, and it would take a long time to forget his feelings for her, providing he ever would be able to.

Watching the warriors sitting around, enjoying the meat and biscuits, Jed felt relaxed for the first time since coming home, as he enjoyed their company. Big Owl and the others swallowed chunks of deer meat hungrily as they told stories of their escapades against the Crow, Pawnee, and other tribes. Before coming into the cabin, they examined the skins of the grizzlies nailed to the barn wall. Shaking their heads, almost in awe and disbelief, they studied the huge skins nervously, then retreated to the cabin. Eyeing the three bear claw necklaces, hanging next to the chimney, they shook their heads again in wonder at their size, but none offered to go near or touch the claws.

All were curious, as they had seen the arrow, knife, and bullet holes in the hides, telling of the terrible fight the bears had put up before dying. Many tales of savagery of the man killers had been told and retold around the fires of the Arapaho. The warriors were not only proud of Crow Killer, but they were honored he was one of them. Most warriors looked upon the warrior with deep respect, others with awe, and a little nervousness.

Big Owl burped loudly, then smiled at Jed. "Tell us, Crow Killer, now that my hunger is satisfied, speak of your battles with the grizzlies."

"No, my friends." Jed shook his head. "It would be boring for me to talk of it."

"Tell us. We wish to hear of your victories over the enemy." Walking Horse laughed. "We are your guests, my brother. You must honor us by telling us this tale."

"Tell us, tell us." The voices resounded throughout the cabin.

Raising his hands as the chorus of voices rang out, demanding he tell the story, Jed poured each warrior a cup full of coffee, then sat down next to the hearth, the center of attention. The warriors squirmed where they sat, waiting eagerly to hear the story of the killer bears and how they had finally been killed.

The Arapaho Lance Bearer, Bow Legs, had been there with Jed when the old sow had chased them from the body of Billy Wilson. Bow Legs was small in stature, but he used to spin tales of intrigue larger than life for the Arapaho back in the village. Every Arapaho warrior enjoyed a good story, almost as much as a battle or stealing horses. For hours, during the cold times, the storytellers of the village entertained children, squaws, and warriors with their tales of the unknown. Sometimes, their stories were so believable that many were afraid to return to their lodges alone in the dark.

Now, the gathered warriors were engrossed as they listened to the story told by the demon, the man, who had defeated the killer grizzlies. Starting from the beginning when the grizzly had killed Billy Wilson, for two solid hours, Jed retold the story of the she bear and her two cubs, keeping the assembled warriors mesmerized by the tale. Jed kept his listeners spellbound, completely engrossed, as they could actually smell the stinking breath of the bear, and in their mind, they could see blood dripping from his jaws. Big Owl was booed down by the others as he asked Jed for more coffee, breaking their train of thought as they sat listening. Passing the bear claws around the room, Jed then showed his listeners the ripped, bloody hunting shirt, which added to the unfolding tale of drama and death. Finally, as Jed finished, the warriors sat around half fascinated and half unbelieving the tale.

Walking Horse smiled to himself, then poured Big Owl his coffee. He could tell by the way the others looked around the cabin, at the necklaces, and the bloody, ripped hunting shirt, they expected to see the bears break through the cabin door at any minute. Walking Horse picked up the hunting shirt. "That was a good story, my brother. I wish I could have been with you to watch."

"No, you don't." Jed shook his head. "If I had been able, I would have run from that place as fast as I could."

Walking Horse smiled. "I know Crow Killer better than that. An Arapaho Lance Bearer runs from nothing."

"I thought of it, sure enough." Jed laughed. "Just didn't have any place to run to at that moment."

"Uh huh." The warrior laughed.

Listening, as the warriors walked outside to talk and discuss the bears, Jed smiled. Far out on the mountain, the grey wolf called out his lonely cry, which rang sad and forlorn across the valley. All the warriors became deathly quiet as they heard the lonely hair-raising cry. Looking around, the warriors shivered, as they thought the wolf was calling out to them, warning them she was coming back from the afterlife. Several times in his story, Jed spoke of how the wolf would call out a warning when the bear was near. Walking Horse knew his warriors and how superstitious they could be at night in the dark. Fearless when facing any number of enemies in the daylight hours, but the unknown evil ones from the night frightened some of the most brave and stouthearted. To lose one's life in the dark hours of the night was taboo because a warrior's spirit would wander forever in the afterlife.

Big Owl looked around the dark. "Are you sure, Crow Killer, that all the bears are dead?"

"Not all, my friend." Jed smiled. "There are plenty, still out there."

"He means the demon grizzlies." Plenty Feathers added shaking his head. "The man killers."

"They are all dead, my friends, but I would sleep lightly tonight." Jed laughed, but was relieved the warriors didn't discover the bag filled with Billy Wilson's bones, hanging in the barn. They probably would have stampeded back to the south before he had time to explain why he had them.

"The bears would like your fat body, Big Owl." Plenty Feathers pushed the fat warrior in play. "They might find you tasty."

"This is not funny." Big Owl frowned, looking around nervously, then down at his big paunch. "Are you sure they are dead?"

"Three are, for sure." Jed grinned.

"No, it wasn't funny." Plenty Feathers laughed at Big Owl's nervousness. "I am tired and would like very much to sleep."

Walking Horse shook his head as he walked with Jed to help him bring in the horses to the corral for the night. "My warriors will leave me and ride back to the village if you tell them anymore tales."

"You asked for me to tell the story. Remember your words?" Jed rolled his eyes. "You are my guests, and as a good host, I should tell the story."

Walking Horse grinned. "I did want the story told, but not so much of it."

"You have ridden a long way, and I do not think it was to hear me tell of killing some bears."

"It was indeed a very good story." Walking Horse continued. "It made the hair stand on my neck."

"Tell me, why are you here, my brother?" Jed turned the piebald into the corral. "To hunt, raid, or just to get a free meal?"

"We came to see Crow Killer, and to hunt." Walking Horse patted the piebald with admiration. "Only the spotted horse of Red Hawk is as great as this one."

Jed nodded. "Yes, he is a great one. I feared I had lost him when the Arikara raided the Cheyenne pony herd."

"That is why you killed the Arikara, because they took the horse?"

"Partly, I reckon, but they killed a young boy." Jed shook his head. "They didn't have to kill him to steal the horses."

"I do not blame you for killing the Arickara, my brother." Again, Walking Horse looked over at the piebald. "Yes, he is a magnificent animal."

"Tell me." Jed knew the warrior was stalling. "What other reason does Walking Horse and his warriors come here for?"

"When you come again to our lands in the spring, we wish you to bring many rifles to us, as much as you can carry." Walking Horse became serious. "Many."

"Rifles?" Jed was curious.

"Many rifles, as many as we can trade for."

"Rifles like mine cost a lot of white man's gold."

"We will meet you at Yellow Dog's village in the spring and ride with you to the traders post at Bridger." Walking Horse nodded. "We will trap during the cold times. We will bring many furs, robes, and buffalo coats to trade for the fire guns."

"Why do the Arapaho need so many rifles?"

"We have watched our enemy, the Pawnee, cross our hunting grounds and show no fear. Now, many carry the deadly fire weapon." Walking Horse nodded. "Rolling Thunder told us how easily you defeated the Blackfoot when you battled them with the help of the rifle."

"The rifles helped alright, but the bears did their work too." Jed remembered the fight with the Blackfoot Deep Water and Lone Bull."

"I know, I have heard the story of the battle." Walking Horse shrugged. "We need the fire rifles to protect our people. We don't have any demon bears, my brother."

"Alright, I will get the weapons for you in the spring, but it will take many furs." Jed agreed, warning Walking Horse they were very expensive.

"Our women work on buffalo coats now." Walking Horse nodded. "Rolling Thunder told of the value the white traders put on the heavy coats."

"They do that alright." Jed shook his head. "Why do you not trade for the rifles yourselves?"

"We know nothing of these weapons. We would be cheated by the traders at Bridger." The warrior looked at Jed's Hawken in disgust. "We do not even know how to make them kill."

"I will let you fire this rifle, tomorrow."

Walking Horse looked over at the Hawken and shook his head. "I do not want this for myself, but I know it is the only way our people will survive."

Jed knew the powerful rifles were the weapon of the future. Among the tribes, the warriors knew their bows and arrows were now obsolete. The bow was an ancient and well-used weapon for war or hunting. However, the bow didn't have the long range or the accuracy of the rifle. To own a rifle, would give a warrior much prestige among his people. Every warrior would trade many horses or furs to own one.

Jed knew he spoke the truth. "I will meet you at the village of Yellow Dog when the passes clear and the rivers run free again."

"That will be good." Walking Horse smiled. "Tomorrow, we will hunt. We have to feed Big Owl."

"It is good you have come here with your warriors." Jed nodded. "This has been a lonely time."

"There will be other women, my brother." Walking Horse smiled. "Like I said, in the Cheyenne lodges there is one maiden who has set her eyes for you. This one honors you above every other warrior."

Jed didn't answer, as he knew the warrior spoke of Bright Moon. Still, his mind thought of Ellie and her last words to him. She had taken his heart as Sally Ann had, and it would take many days, if there was enough in a lifetime, for him to forget either of them.

CHAPTER 11

Walking Horse's strength seemed as great as ever, even though his full weight and muscle mass hadn't fully returned. Running across the high ridges at a rapid pace, the warrior didn't tire as they crossed the valley in search of the herds of elk that roamed the valley. Jed smiled, he was relieved Walking Horse had regained his strength. Watching the warrior crawl on his stomach, to look over the ridge, Jed eased up beside him quietly.

Lower, in the flats of the valley, several elk grazed contentedly on the tall grass. One huge bull grazed alone, alert to every movement and danger around him. Too far away and out of good bow range, Walking Horse studied the terrain, looking for a stealthy approach to the animal.

"This one is old and wise. He stays away from any enemy's hiding places." Walking Horse shook his head. "Our arrows cannot reach him where he stands."

Jed looked around the grassy knoll the bull stood on. "You go downhill along the ridge, and I'll try to spook him to you."

"It will be a difficult shot."

Jed grinned. "That is why I'm letting you do the shooting."

"If I miss, you will tell the others."

"But, if you kill him, I will tell of what a great shot you made."

Nodding, Walking Horse crawled downhill, hoping to get close enough for the kill shot. From where the bull stood, he realized, Jed's plan was the only way he could get close enough to the elk to get a shot. Moving into position, Walking Horse raised his hand, motioning he was ready. Slipping slowly through the grass, keeping low, he circled the huge bull, then suddenly stood up in full view. Watching the big bull race away with his harem of cows, Jed shook his head and walked to where Walking Horse sat on the ground.

"It was a good plan, Crow Killer, but it did not work out so well."

"He was a very foolish elk." Jed laughed. "He was supposed to run to you, my brother, not the other way."

"You should have told him your plan." Walking Horse shrugged. "We will try for another stalk."

"You know, if we go to the lodge without meat to fill Big Owl's stomach, we will be laughed at."

"We will kill something." The warrior looked about the valley.

"We promised an elk, not a deer or rabbit."

"Big Owl will eat anything."

"Have faith, my brother." Jed laughed. "Come, let's get the horses. We'll find another elk."

Late afternoon, found the two hunters riding back to the cabin with a yearling bull elk lying across the packhorse. Jed knew Big Owl would give them the old horse laugh when he spotted the small bull. For some reason, the elk, which were usually thick as fleas in the valley, kept out of sight all day. With seven hungry stomachs to feed, Jed knew the small bull would only feed them two meals. Tomorrow, they would ride out again to hunt for the wily animals.

Jed knew Big Owl, and the warrior liked to have fun. He knew they were in for a bad time when they rode to the cabin. "You know, Big Owl will laugh at our kill."

"It is not for Big Owl to say whether or not the elk is small." Walking Horse shook his head. "It is my kill."

"If he laughs, we will not feed him."

Walking Horse looked down at the bull. "At least the elk is young. He will be tender."

"I would rather have the old bull, then Big Owl would have to chew more and complain less." Jed grinned.

For three days, Walking Horse and his warriors remained at the cabin, telling stories, smoking their pipes, and eating. Jed and Walking

Horse, with the help of the Hawken rifle, had killed an elk and a deer on their second hunt, supplying plenty of meat for the warriors. Jed let Walking Horse fire the heavy rifle several times at the cabin before they rode out. The warrior was amazed as he fired the rifle, killing both animals at a far distance.

Looking down at the rifle and then over at Jed, he nodded and smiled. The warrior touched the smooth stock of the Hawken reverently. "Maybe I underestimated the fire weapon."

While Jed and Walking Horse hunted, Big Owl and the others, out of curiosity, rode to where Jed had killed the old sow. Only bones remained of the bear, and what they found had been scattered along the trail by scavengers, roaming over the mountains. In the evening, as the warriors skinned and cut up the meat, they told of finding the bear's remains. Jed shook his head, as he couldn't believe the warriors had ridden all the way up the mountain to look at some scattered bones. He wondered what happened to their superstitions.

Walking Horse sat and talked with Jed. "Will you come to see your people before the cold times?"

Jed thought of Ellie and shook his head. "No, I don't think that would be a good idea."

"You cannot come back together if you do not speak of this thing that she hates."

"She believes me to be a heathen, a killer." Jed shrugged. "I'm afraid there will be no coming together, and no talking."

"We must go back. The time to hunt the shaggies is near." Walking Horse looked over at the Hawken wishfully. "This weapon would kill many shaggies."

"You will have rifles for next year's hunt."

Big Owl rubbed his huge stomach. "Bring me a big one, Crow Killer."

"As big as your stomach?" Plenty Feathers laughed. "Impossible."

"Have you heard anything of Plenty Coups or Red Hawk?"

"Before riding here, Red Hawk sent word for me to meet him at the river for a council." Walking Horse nodded. "Plenty Coups has recovered. The Crow Chief sent word by Red Hawk, if Slow Wolf's people need to cross the Yellowstone to hunt the shaggies, it would be allowed."

"That is good news." Jed smiled. "Great news."

"Yes, thanks to my sister."

"She is a good healer." Jed nodded, remembering the young Crow warrior telling him of Ellie curing the sickness in Plenty Coups stomach.

"Red Hawk says to tell Crow Killer, maybe he will ride here before the meat taking time comes."

"It would be good to see him."

Early the next morning, after a heavy breakfast, the warriors gathered their sleeping robes and bridled their horses. Jed shook hands with each warrior, hating to see them go. Their tall tales of battle and arguing among themselves would be greatly missed.

"We must ride." Walking Horse swung up on his horse. "Good-bye, my brother."

"I am here if you need me. Send a runner."

"I know and Slow Wolf knows." Walking Horse reached out his hand as he looked at the cabin. "I wish things could be different for you, my brother. A lodge needs a woman to warm it."

"I will be fine."

"Leave this place, and come back to your people." Walking Horse nodded. "To stay alone by oneself can turn a warrior cold."

Jed thought of the words of Roden and of Little Antelope. "I wish I could, but for now, I must remain here."

"Good-bye, my brother." Walking Horse raised his hand. "Always watch the skyline and your back trail."

"I'll see you after the big thaw in the spring."

Grinning down at Jed, Big Owl rubbed his stomach. "You are a good host, my friend. Watch out the bears don't eat you."

Watching the warriors riding away, Jed waved, then turned to where his horses stood at the gate, waiting to be led out to pasture. He would wait until the horses of Walking Horse were out of sight so his horses wouldn't follow them. Thanks to Yellow Dog and Walking Horse, he had all his horses back again. They would be needed to take his furs to Bridger after the big break up and the snows melted. He looked up at the tall mountains, and for the first time, they seemed lonely and forlorn. He had a feeling this would be a long winter, made so by the loss of his friends. Hopefully, his catch would be heavy again this winter and keep his mind busy skinning, curing, and stretching hides.

Picking up the sickle blade, Jed quickly put an edge on the curved blade. Satisfied it was sharp, he picked up his rifle and walked to where the grass hadn't been grazed close. Once full to the rafters, the barn had been depleted while feeding the horses of Walking Horse and his Arapaho warriors. Jed laughed, the Arapaho or the Crow warriors would never lower themselves to cut and store hay, but they enjoyed seeing their horses filling their bellies with the grass from the barn.

The day passed fast as the hiss of the sickle cut through the tall grass, laying it out flat on the ground. Several times, as the horses looked up the valley, Jed would hesitate in his laborious work and study the entire valley floor. Mostly the horses were looking at elk and deer, but after the grizzlies, Jed was taking no chances. Lige Hatcher had told him many times that staying alert meant staying alive in this wild land.

With his winter wood cut and stacked, and traps oiled, ready for fall trapping, Jed had time on his hands as he waited for the grass to cure before hauling it to the barn. Early in the morning and with little to do, Jed rode south across the valley, planning out his trap lines for the coming winter. This year, he would be working alone, running the traps and doing the skinning by himself. Riding through the deep trees, Jed studied the smaller animal trails, making a mental note of where to string out the traps.

With all the traps hanging outside the cabin wall, Jed decided not to use box traps or deadfalls this year. Deadfalls were considerable work, and he would be busy enough, keeping the steel traps running daily and the catch of the day skinned out and stretched. When the heavy snow comes, it would be even harder to keep the traps checked every day.

Riding up on one of the heavy traveled beaver ponds, Jed sat the piebald and studied the pond. He thought about his beaver skins the last two years and wondered if they were worth all the work. The beaver plews hadn't brought enough last year at Bridger to bother with trapping the beaver this season. He remembered Baker, the fur trader back at Baxter Springs and his refusal to buy Jed's beaver pelts last season. When Baker realized he might lose all of Jed's furs to the buyers at Bridger, he changed his mind. Jed felt guilt, that the beaver pelts may have cost Lem

Roden his life. If he had sold his pelts to Baker minus the beaver, maybe Cross wouldn't have had a reason to rob them. Thinking of Lem Roden, he sure missed the old scout this year, as he had been a lot of help, same as Silent One. Both had been good company during the heavy blizzards that swept the valley.

For several moments, Jed sat the horse, pondering further on the beaver. The trapping needed to be done before the beaver ponds and streams froze over during the cold times. Beaver were plentiful in the ponds, but would be considerably more work skinning out the flat tails. Shrugging, he kicked the piebald and rode south. He had plenty of time to decide on the beaver plews, as the cold times were still many suns away.

The days were becoming shorter, as Jed sat outside at the split oak table, enjoying a cup of coffee and the quiet evening. Already, he could feel the nights were becoming cooler. Soon, it would be time to ride to the far valley and get his buffalo hides to make into warm coats. Jed knew it could be a dangerous hunt this year, after his two bad encounters with the Arikara warriors. The tribes were very vengeful, and they knew he hunted the small valley for the shaggies. In addition, they probably knew he was the one that had killed their warriors earlier in the year. Figuring he would return to Turner's Hole to kill the shaggies, Jed knew they might be there waiting to kill him. Everywhere a lone hunter rode in these mountains was dangerous, and only his sharp wits would keep him alive. A horse could fall with him on the treacherous mountain trails and break a leg, a bear could attack, raiding Indians could attack, or anything could happen to him so far from civilization.

The buffalo coats were valuable, much more than the beaver plews that lost most of their former value. Jed thought of Ellie, and her hate of fighting and killing. Would it be worth taking a chance of more fighting to go after the shaggies? Shrugging, he looked up at the mountains, as it didn't matter what he did or where he hunted. Ellie would never come here, and she told him that, so one more fight didn't matter. He had no doubt at all; if there was a fight she would hear about it. There were no secrets among the tribes, as tales of fighting and raiding spread like wildfire through the villages. Most times around the village fires, the stories were embellished by the storytellers to make them bloodier than they had actually been.

Tossing out the remainder of his coffee, Jed crossed the creek to bring in his horses. He made up his mind that soon he would travel east to the lower valleys to hunt. His profession and way of life was furs and trapping. He could not allow the threat of hostile tribes or Ellie's thoughts, to stop him from hunting these mountains, wherever and whenever he wanted. He wanted the buffalo, not only for their hides, but for their meat as well. Jed shook his head again, thinking of the woman. There was no doubt, if he was in a fight, word would get back to the Arapaho Village and to her. Jed knew it didn't matter as she was lost to him. Too many words had passed between them. Now, her life and his could not walk the same trail.

The summer months were past, and Jed had his preparations made for the cold times. Now, was the time for him to turn his thoughts to the shaggies. Frost appeared on the grasses and a few snowflakes came down softly across the valley. Preparations were made to go after the shaggies, and with the coming of day, he would ride east. The buffalo coats were very valuable and in great demand around the trading posts. He and Roden had brought back four buffalo hides last year, and this year he intended to bring back six.

As he started across the creek, leading the animals back to the corral, the black mule threw her long ears forward, raising her head. Quickly jerking the lead rope to keep her from braying, Jed hurried the horses inside the corral.

Something was on the valley floor, as the excited mule directed her attention to the south. It could be a band of wild horses, but Jed didn't think so, as something else held her attention. Whatever was out there, the mule was visibly nervous. With the evening sky turning dark, Jed didn't want to ride into the valley, not knowing what was waiting out there. If it was an animal, it would have the advantage of the night on its side. If it was human, they could have the advantage in numbers and secrecy.

Jed remembered Roden's warning of Wet Otter, the Pawnee, saying the Pawnee might come later in the fall and it could be him. He would wait until daylight, and if it were friends, they would ride on in tonight. However, if they didn't come in, they could be enemies. Quickly barricading the heavy gate of the corral, Jed took his rifles and bow up on the roof. He would spend the night up high to have the advantage on whatever or whoever was out there.

The morning mist shrouded the creek and valley in fog as it always did in the early dawn. Jed lay flat on the roof of the cabin and studied the valley floor. The heavy limbs of the large oak, covering the cabin, kept Jed hidden and gave him cover from whoever was below. Jed remembered Roden and Walking Horse speaking of the Pawnee having many rifles in their villages now. Rifles didn't scare him, since most warriors were better shots and far more dangerous with a bow than they were with a rifle. Jed listened for the slightest of noises. He could hear plainly the gurgling of the water flowing over the rocky bottom of the creek, but no other sound broke the silence of the morning. Normally, the small river was stirring with the calls of small night animals, birds, and crickets, but not this morning. Nothing moved out in the gloom of the fog and darkness.

Below, the agitated mule kept pacing back and forth along the corral fence, looking out across the valley. A natural watchdog, little escaped her long ears and sharp eyes. Jed's eyes strained as they roved the fog covered grassland, looking for any signs of intruders. Suddenly, before his eyes, several riders materialized out of the murkiness of early dawn. Still too gloomy to identify what tribe they were from; Jed hunkered down on the roof and stayed immobile.

Jed heard the horses as they splashed across the creek, then stopped when the mule brayed a greeting to the newcomers. Jed eased his rifle forward, preparing for whatever waited in the fog by the creek. Minutes passed and finally as the fog slowly cleared, revealing their faces, Jed recognized the Pawnee warrior from the Blue River, and it was Wet Otter. Five more Pawnee warriors sat alongside Wet Otter, staring at the cabin and corrals. Easing the hammer back on the Hawken, Jed waited. He could see the painted horses of the Pawnee, and he knew Wet Otter was here on a raid. Vengeance for their last meeting made the Pawnee ride the long distance and paint their horses. There was plenty of game in their hunting grounds so Jed knew they were after him.

Jed knew he had beaten Wet Otter and had taken the chief's pride, shaming him before his warriors earlier this summer. His shame must have been great enough to bring him all this way to retain his honor. Jed had lived long enough among the Arapaho to learn the Indian mind, and he knew without question that was exactly why Wet Otter came to his valley. No warrior or leader could hold his head up with pride after letting another warrior defeat him so easily. He hadn't seen many, but Jed had seen a few fights started between warriors when one challenged the other because of pride.

"What does the Pawnee want here in this place?" Jed spoke from the roof, hiding behind the oak limbs. "Tell me, Wet Otter, have you come here for another fight?"

Surprised to hear the voice coming across the open area in front of the cabin, Wet Otter tried to locate where it had come from. "I have come here for your scalp, Arapaho dog."

"Then come on up here and get it." Jed took dead aim on one of the warriors.

The warrior shrilled a loud war cry taken up by the others. Raising his rifle, he reined his horse in circles. "You will die for my brother, Touch the Sky."

Jed shrugged. "I do not know this warrior."

"He is the one that was killed at the Blue water." Wet Otter screamed. "The chiefs of our villages will not let us raid the Arapaho for revenge. So Crow Killer the demon, we come here for you."

"He was a brave and honorable man. Too bad his brother, Wet Otter, is not."

"Your taunts do no good, Crow Killer. I am not such a fool to fight alone against a demon like last time."

"Then go home coward. I do not want your weak blood staining my valley."

"You are wrong, Arapaho. This valley will be stained with your blood not mine. Then, I will burn your lodge and take your horses." Wet Otter screamed again.

The early morning peace was broken as several rifles discharged, breaking the silence. Jed could hear the heavy lead balls as they hit the oak limbs all around him. Taking careful aim, Jed knocked a warrior from his horse, killing him before his body hit the ground. Picking up the thirty-caliber rifle of Silent One, he killed another warrior's horse. Arrows began to thud into the log walls of the cabin and the limbs hiding Jed. He heard the little mule, spooked by the sudden heavy booms of the rifles as she tried to jump the corral fence, and he hoped she wasn't hurt.

Reloading both rifles, Jed stared down into the gloom. The Pawnee had dismounted and were silently stalking toward the cabin. A slight wave in the grass along the creek reminded Jed of the grizzly, hiding in the tall grass. Aiming slightly to the side, he gently squeezed the trigger. A scream came from the tall grass as a warrior toppled face forward onto the open ground.

Silence prevailed as Jed reloaded while watching the yard. Taking a quick look down at the mule, Jed grinned, as she didn't seem hurt, but she did pinpoint another warrior. The rifle sounded again, bringing a shriek from the bushes surrounding the cabin. Complete silence followed for awhile, as Jed watched the mule but she didn't alert on anything. Listening attentively, Jed finally discerned the sound of horse's hooves pounding the valley floor as they moved away from the cabin.

Lowering the ladder to the ground, Jed quickly climbed down and bridled the piebald. Leaving the smaller Hawken behind, and taking his bow and quiver of arrows, he swung upon the horse. Wet Otter and his Pawnee warriors had come to his valley to kill and rob, so Jed wasn't holding back this time. Now, it was his turn. Today, he would make an example for the rest of the tribes. After today, the tribes living nearby would avoid his valley. These warriors had come to kill without mercy, and now, he would show no mercy. Once at a tent service, he remembered hearing a circuit preacher saying to beware of reaping what you sow. These raiders were fixing to start reaping here and now.

The piebald raced across the valley, as Jed threw caution to the wind with his blood raging, he wanted to fight. The sun finally burned off the morning fog, and he could see the fleeing warriors crossing a swell ahead. Whipping the piebald hard, he felt the big paint stretch to his fastest stride as he closed in on the warriors ahead as if they were standing still. Two of the Pawnee were holding the third on his horse as Jed closed in on them.

Turning and finding there was no way they could outrun the powerful paint warhorse descending on them, the Pawnee warriors turned their horses. Jed reined in and walked the piebald slowly forward as the Pawnee death cry came from two of the warriors sitting their horses in front of him. Wet Otter sat as straight as he could on his horse, staring hard at Jed. Hate emanated from his eyes, and Jed could see blood covering Wet Otter's side, dripping onto the ground. No words were spoken as the Pawnees studied the Arapaho warrior before them.

"You come here to kill, Pawnee, now kill me." Jed motioned at the rifles resting across their horse's withers. "I'll give you the first shot."

"Wet Otter is wounded. He is weak." Another Pawnee spoke. "Let us go in peace. We will never come back to this place."

"Does Wet Otter beg for his life?" Jed spit out. The frustrations with the death of Roden, Silent One, Sally Ann, and the words of Ellie turned his face into a mask of rage. "Beg, Pawnee, and maybe you will live."

"I will not beg to an Arapaho dog eater." Wet Otter tried to throw his war axe.

Only the blast of the Hawken sounded as the Pawnee was flung backward from his horse. Jed pointed the empty rifle at the other two warriors and shrugged. "My fire gun is empty. Now, is your chance, Pawnee."

"We will leave this place. We will not fight a demon." One of the warriors dropped his rifle. "Kill us if your lust for blood is not satisfied."

Jed pointed down at Wet Otter. "Leave your rifles here and take your chief back to your village."

The warriors looked at their rifles then at each other. To fight one such as this warrior before them was foolhardy, as he could not be killed. Placing the last rifle with the other one, the two remaining Pawnee slipped from their horses and heaved the dead body of their chief across his horse.

"We go Crow Killer."

"I will bury your other warriors."

"We thank you."

"Tell your people, if they come back to this valley..." Jed looked across at the warriors. "Tell your chiefs, I will raid your villages with demons and kill all of you."

"Wet Otter was our leader, but he was foolish to come here." The warrior looked at Jed. "No Pawnee will come to this place again, ever."

"That would be wise."

Watching the two warriors ride slowly to the south, Jed gathered the Pawnee rifles and turned the piebald back toward the cabin. Again, he had killed. Again, his eyes had clouded in rage, driving him into battle without fear. He knew the Pawnee would have to pass back across Crow hunting grounds on their return to their village. The eagle-eyed young Crow scouts at the river would see the body of the dead Pawnee draped across his horse, then they would question the warriors and find out about the fight. The Pawnee would tell of the demon's bloodthirsty killing of Wet Otter, and soon the Arapaho would know. Jed shook his head, wondering what she would think of him when she heard and if it could be any worse than what she already thought.

CHAPTER 12

Jed sat before the hearth drinking coffee. Before him lay four Pawnee rifles and outside in the corral were three Pawnee horses. Shrugging, he downed his coffee. The Pawnee, Wet Otter, had come here to kill, and now he was dead along with three of his warriors. They had chosen to come to his valley, to challenge him to fight, and it was not his doing nor was it his fault. He didn't ride to their country to kill Pawnee, they had come here to kill and rob him. His conscience was clear, and Jed knew she would think differently, but he only defended what was his.

It didn't matter, as Jed knew she would not see the fighting his way. To Ellie, he was a heathen and a killer, as she had said with her last words to him. The red-hot pine knots in the fire popped, sending hot ashes out onto the rock floor. Tamping them out with his moccasins, Jed poured himself another cup of coffee. He wished White Swan still lived so he could look into the ashes and bones, then tell him what to do. Jed stared into the flames, as he thought he was destined to live out his life alone in the high lonesome.

Shrugging, he picked up his rifle and walked outside to check on the horses. He had built scaffolds for the three dead Pawnee beside Silent One. He hoped the Assiniboine wouldn't be offended by the Pawnee beside him. Tomorrow, he would ride east to bring in the buffalo hides and meat that he needed for the cold times, and try to forget what had happened. Looking over the horses, he decided to turn out the Pawnee horses. They might stay in the valley or run off with the wild ones, coming through the valley occasionally. His own four horses with the mule would be all he needed to carry the heavy green hides and meat, and enough to transport his furs to Bridger after warm up.

Jed thought about the four rifles in the cabin, and decided to hide them. If raiders came into the valley, he didn't want them stolen. He thought about hiding the traps, but Indians don't use steel traps and they were too heavy to carry without packsaddles. Jed doubted any of the wild tribes would dare raid in his valley again, especially if they heard about the last fight with the Pawnee. Even though his valley was remote, tribes would soon learn of the fight and how much of a demon he was. He had killed the greatest of the warriors from different tribes; Black Robe the Nez Perce, Standing Bull, Small Mountain, and Deep Water were Blackfoot, Two Tails the Crow, and now Wet Otter the Pawnee. Jed doubted any warrior or tribe would dare come into his valley. All knew him as a demon, and they were too superstitious to return.

Wrapping the rifles in trade blankets, Jed carried them to the dark barn and covered them deep in the hay. No one would look in the hay so they wouldn't be easily found. If anyone came here to set fire to the hay, the rifles would be lost, but Jed couldn't do anything else with them.

The trip east to Turner's Hole had been uneventful and Jed enjoyed the hunt and the ride to the east. Behind him on the steep rocky trails were four horses and the little black mule, heavily loaded with green hides and buffalo meat. The temperature fell several degrees and snow was falling lightly as he rode the piebald back west to his valley. His hunt had been peaceful, and no enemy warriors had been seen while he camped in the valley where the shaggies grazed.

The horses were eager as they crossed the valley floor in a hard trot, wanting to get back to the barn. Reining in front of the cabin, Jed smiled, as it was good to be home. Unloading the frozen meat and hides, Jed unsaddled the horses and led them out on the dead valley grass. The weather was well below freezing, and already solidly freezing the fresh killed buffalo meat. Jed looked up at the sky, then hoisted the frozen meat high into the trees, out of reach of the varmints. Dragging the green hides into the barn where they would be safe from night animals, Jed secured the door. Later, he would bring them into the cabin, when he had the time, to start curing them for coats. Now, time was short, and tomorrow he would begin setting his trap lines and beaver sets.

Later in the evening, as Jed brought in the horses, he found the three Pawnee horses had returned when they saw Jed's horses grazing out on the valley floor. He didn't want to feed the extra horses over the winter, but he had no choice. Come spring, he would sell them at Bridger's Post. In white society, the horses would be considered stolen property, but in Indian culture, they were considered what the whites called the spoils of war. He doubted Ellie would see the Indian side of it.

Jed had sixty traps set, some in the beaver waterways and ponds, and other traps set both south and north on the small animal trails he had scouted out during the summer months. Already, he was harvesting beaver plews and many fur bearing animals that hunted the land. He was tired, and his hands were sore and feet were cold, but he was taking many furs that would bring cash money at Bridger in the spring.

Sitting back in his comfortable hide chair, Jed stared into the fire. He wondered how Walking Horse and Little Antelope were and how Ellie was taking the cold, living in a hide lodge. Returning to the long table, he had put together to work on the buffalo hides, Jed marked out the cuts he would make on the soft robes. Making coats was time consuming but well worth the work. Fur buyers and traders would pay lots of money for the heavy warm buffalo coats and they were in great demand by the white immigrants coming west on the trains.

This year the snowstorms held off, and none were forthcoming as they had been for the last two years. The temperature remained below freezing as the small creek was almost frozen solid, but no snow yet. Jed kept a hole chopped through the ice so he could water his horses and dip out his drinking water for the cabin. The ponds were freezing in the valley, and he had to pull his traps from the beaver ponds soon. He already had over fifty beaver pelts stretched and ready to take to Bridger. Tomorrow, he would retrieve his traps from the frozen ponds and waterways.

His catch of land animals was better since the heavy snows held off, as the meat eaters didn't go into their dens yet. Standing in the icy cold pond water, Jed pulled up an empty trap, then tossed it out on the bank.

The ponds would be frozen solid in a few days, ending this year's beaver season. The mule was loaded with the steel traps and Jed would take them to the cabin, clean them, and reset them on land to trap other animals.

Earlier in the morning, he ran his land trap lines. Later that day, Jed looked up and could see dark clouds approaching from the north. Turning the piebald toward the next pond, he knew the storm would reach the cabin before nightfall. By the snow clouds building, Jed was aware the weather could be as bad as the storm that had blown across the valley for four days the previous winter. Still, there was no hurry, as everything at the cabin was prepared. Now, all he had to do was finish picking up his traps and ride back to the cabin. Later, he would skin out his catch and get them on stretch boards.

Jed had his horses and the extra Pawnee horses lotted in the corral, and wood stacked inside the cabin as the wind started to blow in gusts across the valley. Taking one last look at the coming storm, he fed the horses, then carried in two full buckets of creek water for the morning. During the long summer, he had hewed out a large oak log for a watering trough. He had seen water troughs in town made from oak lumber so he didn't see any reason a log wouldn't do as well. He filled it half full, so come morning, he only had to pour hot water into the trough to water the horses. Eight horses and one mule stood in the corral now, and the trough would be much easier than toting buckets of thawed water to each horse.

Moving back inside the warm cabin, Jed ate his supper, and went back to work on his plews and buffalo coats. By the look of the deep boiling clouds and the raging storm heading his way, he figured he may not be venturing outside for many days, except to feed and water his horses.

Jed didn't miss his guess, as a strong storm hit right after full dark. Winds blew hard against the heavy door and the snow blew sideways as Jed looked from the cabin. He loved the high mountains and his valley, but the storms were something else, and he sure didn't love them. Winds raging just beyond the door and screaming eerie sounds as it moaned through the oaks outside, could drive a man mad if he allowed it. Only the sound of the popping fire in the hearth and the wind driving particles of ice and snow against the cabin could be heard as Jed worked.

The storm was bad, and twice a day, Jed fought this way to the corral, feeding and watering the horses, then returning to the cabin to work on his furs. One coat was finished and it was a thing of beauty. The coat would keep a man warm in the coldest and wettest weather. Jed counted the furs, and figured he had already cured enough for at least three bundles weighing a hundred pounds each. If his luck with the traps held after the storm, he would have a good catch for the season.

Finally the storm was over, and only a light snowfall continued after the heavy winds and snow subsided. Jed walked outside and looked about the cabin. The horses were all huddled under the lean-to beside the barn. Tossing them more hay, he returned to the cabin after examining the ground around the corral and cabin. Since the bear threat, checking the ground for tracks became a habit for him.

The snow on the valley floor was deep with snowdrifts covering the valley and mountain slopes. The snow was too deep to put the horses out on pasture. The corral was big enough to accommodate the nine animals and a barn full of hay so he could keep the horses up until the snow melted.

Two days later, Jed put on snowshoes, then started running his trap lines and carrying his catch back to the cabin after cleaning them. The work was cold and tiring. His muscles ached from the penetrating cold as he sat before the hearth at night. Still, he was satisfied, as his traps had produced many fine furs and in the spring they would bring many dollars in gold. Next year, he would try to find another skinner to replace Lem Roden. Jed did all the work himself. Trapping, skinning, and stretching all the hides, from his traps had become too much for one man.

The long winter nights seemed to grow even longer as Jed passed the winter, busily working with his furs and taking care of the horses. Cooped up inside the cabin, during the worst of the storms, Jed worked steadily on the coats and plews to placate his mind. With the passing of each storm, he went back to running his trap lines. The long months inside the cabin or wading through the deep snow and freezing temperatures had been a real test of Jed's love for his valley. Through the quiet and solitude of the cabin, Jed kept himself busy, as the many bundles of furs stacked in the barn showed he had been working.

The weather turned and spring was coming. The long icicles hanging from the cabin began to drip and the snow covering the valley started to recede. Today, he would use the black mule to run his trap lines. Soon, the trapping season would be finished, then he would have all his furs pressed into bales of prime pelts ready to haul over the mountains to Bridger. As soon as his pelts were sold, he would help Walking Horse buy his rifles, then head back to Baxter Springs to check on Ed Wilson and bring Billy Wilson's bones home.

Another month had come and gone, and the snow was almost completely melted. Jed had everything ready to head east to Bridger. He sat hour after hour at his table, working on his fourth buffalo coat late into the night, wanting to finish it quickly. When the last coat was completed, the hard work would be finished for the season, and then he would journey to Bridger to sell his pelts. He had told Walking Horse, he would meet him at Yellow Dog's village when the passes cleared.

Finally, the day to depart to the east and Fort Bridger had arrived. Counting the bundles stacked neatly in the barn, earlier in the day, Jed knew he would need all his horses and the black mule. At the break of day, Jed had the packsaddles on the animals and the heavy bundles of furs tied securely in place. Closing up the cabin and releasing the Pawnee horses back out on the valley floor, Jed turned to where his pack animals stood loaded, ready for the long haul to Bridger's Trading Post. Taking one last look at the cabin, Jed mounted the piebald and turned north to the steep passes leading out of his beloved valley.

The palisades of Fort Bridger came into view on Jed's sixth day from the cabin. Crossing the treacherous wet trails and dangerous raging river crossings had taken its toll, but Jed didn't get a single pelt wet. Sitting in front of the gates, Jed was content, as the passage over the mountains had been safe and uneventful. Entering the trading post, Jed noticed, same as last year, many tribes were represented as he crossed the flat grounds of the fort. Trappers, warriors, squaw's with papooses, and every individual from these mountains and grasslands were camped or standing around the post.

Many warriors stood up as Jed passed, whispering among themselves as he was recognized. The feathered Arapaho lance sticking out from his quiver and the huge piebald paint horse stood out as he rode by, telling all who he was. Many of the warriors feared and hated the Arapaho, but inside Bridger's Fort any act of violence would immediately get them banned from trading at the post. Most thought of Crow Killer as a demon, and the rumors of his powers of the bear were known by all. Few would dare challenge him in open combat.

Tying his horses to the hitch rail, Jed walked into the well-stocked trading post. Squaws with their small children lined the store walls waiting for any handouts the clerks thought ruined. Stale broken crackers, ruined cheese, and molded candy was plentiful, so it served to keep the women satisfied and the arrogant chiefs in a good mood. Sadly, mere morsels of useless leftover food kept the women happy and their warrior husbands trading their valuable furs for trinkets. The white traders were shrewd in their dealings with the tribes.

Getting one of the clerks to follow him outside, Jed showed him the bundles of furs and had him help carry them inside to be graded. For three hours, he argued and counted plews. After settling on the count and receiving his money, Jed produced the buffalo coats. The head clerk's eyes lit up as he handled the beautiful coats, but shook his head at Jed's price.

Jed purposely held back the coats until his other pelts were sold, as he didn't want his sale to depend on the coats. His price for the coats was high, but he had worked laboriously on them all winter. Finally settling on a price, Jed placed the gold pieces in his leather pouch and exited the store. Gathering his horses, he rode over to the post's black-smith and spoke to the old trapper that had helped him last year.

"Do you know if Yellow Dog is camped in the same place, old-timer?" Jed dismounted and nodded at the old mountain man.

"Yep, same place you killed all them Ree's last year." The old man grinned a toothless grin. "Boy, you sure done for them poor devils."

"Who told you that?" Jed wasn't surprised he knew of the fight with the Arikara, but he was surprised he knew it was him who did the killing.

"You and your lance sure ain't no secret around here, Crow Killer." The old scout pointed around the post grounds. "Look at them bucks just a glaring at you."

"Why are they staring?"

"That ain't staring, boy. I'd call it glaring."

"Alright, glaring."

"They've all heard the stories, boy. Some fear you, some admire you, but all want to kill you." The old man laughed. "Given the chance, someday they will."

"I reckon they'll try, but I doubt it'll happen." Jed shook his head.

"You're mighty cocky for one all alone."

"I'm never alone, mister."

"If'n I was you, I'd be mighty careful when you clear the fort." The old man spit a stream of tobacco. "Mighty careful. Bridger's law can't protect you outside these walls."

"Now, why is that?"

"Two things; they know your reputation as being the demon, and every buck inside this fort would like to have your hair and reputation. Second is all that gold you got for your plews." The old man laughed.

Jed looked at the trapper. "Indians ain't gonna try to kill me for gold coins, horses maybe, but not gold."

"Maybe not, but there's plenty of whites here that didn't do near as well as you done trapping this season." The man shook his head. "Most would cut your throat just for that horse you're riding."

"They might try." Jed nodded. "Tell me, why didn't these other trappers do well this season?"

"Lazy, that's why. They sure ain't making men like they did back in the shining times. Most are pure lazy now." The old one shook his head.

"Interesting, and now you're telling me I've got to guard against whites and Indians alike?" Jed shook his hand. "What's your name?"

"Name's Otis McGraw, and that's about the size of it, young feller."

"You seen Yellow Dog, or any Arapaho in here this week, Mister McGraw?"

"Nope, nary hide nor hair of them, but the day's still young yet." The trapper shook his head. "Them Cheyenne are downright unpredictable. You never know what they're gonna do. Shucks, most times they don't know what they're going to do themselves."

Jed nodded over to where he had unsaddled his pack animals to let their backs cool while they ate the corn and hay the old man fed them. "Give me a hand catching up my animals. I'll be riding out."

Helping Jed cinch the packsaddles down snug, the old man rubbed the ears of the black mule. "If'n you were a mind, I'd sure trade you outta this little jewel."

Jed laughed. Silent One would moan if he heard the man calling the mule a jewel. "No, she's kinda like family."

"Two horses, you pick'em."

"Reckon not this year, Mister McGraw."

"Three and that's my final offer."

"Nope, but I thank you for the offer." Jed knew it was a good deal, as the old trader had many good-looking stout geldings standing in the lot behind the barn.

"You must be pretty fond of her."

"Yes, sir, I am. Like I said, she's family." Jed thought of Silent One and how the mule had given him such a time, breaking her to ride. Yes, he was fond of her, but he didn't need the extra horses to feed and no horse could match her when it came to watching over the valley like a watchdog, day and night.

"Mighty fine then, but the offer stands anytime you want to get shed of her."

Swinging up on the piebald, Jed nodded down at the older man. "I'm a thanking you, Mister McGraw."

"They'll be waiting on you, somewhere out there, boy. You can count on it." McGraw scratched his beard. "Keep your powder dry and your eyes peeled on the skyline."

"I'll do my best." Jed thought of the Pawnee horses and the wild ones back in the canyon. "You buying any horses?"

"Always, if'n they're the right kind."

"Next time I head this way, I'll bring you some." Jed nodded. "Had too many to lead in by myself this trip."

"You do that, sonny." The old trapper smiled a toothless grin. "And don't be forgetting about that little mule."

"See you." Jed turned his pack string for the gate.

"Four horses."

"Nope." Jed couldn't figure why the old man wanted the mule so badly. The answer would be no, as she was too valuable back in the valley.

Passing through the post gates, Jed stared hard at the many warriors standing outside the palisades, and most glared back at him without blinking or turning their eyes. He wanted them to know he knew their thoughts, and he would be ready if they were foolish enough to attack him on the trail. His pack animals strung out behind him were loaded with the supplies he would need for the coming year. With one last look back at the trading post, Jed headed south toward Yellow Dog's village.

After leaving the fort, he had to be alert, watching for any enemy that might try to attack him along the narrow trails. Riding the trails alone, far back in the valleys and smaller hills, was always dangerous. The trail was fairly clear, but there was brush in many places where an enemy could hide. This year he carried both of the Hawken rifles, his and the one he had given to Silent One. A wide leather belt, hidden underneath his hunting shirt, snugly held the gold coins he had received for his pelts in small compartments, concealing them from prying eyes.

The little mule trotted alongside him, first in line of the pack train. Jed wanted her up front. If enemy horses were ahead, her sharp nose and long ears would detect them, even before the piebald would. He smiled, as he had complete trust in her ability to find an enemy lurking in ambush. The mule was uncanny, as Jed had never known anything, man or beast, able to evade her watchful eyes and ears. He had listened closely to the warnings of the old man at the stables, and knew many wanted to take his scalp and money. He shook his head sadly, wishing Ellie could be there to see for herself, who the real heathens were. He could say in all honesty, never once had he killed any warrior without provocation.

Late in the day, as the sun began to set, Jed rode into a small box canyon along the trail with only one exit. Quickly unloading the animals, he hobbled them on the lush grass that bordered a clear spring. Tonight, would be a cold camp. The hardtack and crackers he had bought back at Bridger and a handful of spring water would be his supper. Jed wasn't taking any chances, as tonight there would be a full moon, so he had to stay awake and keep guard throughout the night. Yellow Dog's village of Cheyenne wasn't far, but it was too far to make before dark, so he made camp and got ready for the long night. Tonight, he and the little mule would stay alert and awake. He could afford to lose a night's sleep, but his hair couldn't.

Picketing the black mule where he could watch her at the entrance to the canyon, Jed checked the priming of the thirty-caliber, then stood the rifle beside him against a rock. Wrapping his sleeping robe around his shoulders, he made himself comfortable and prepared for a long night of vigilance.

The night passed slowly as Jed listened to the sound of coyotes, sounding out across the trails as they pursued rabbits and other small game. He missed the long, full-voiced cry of the large grey wolf back in the valley, calling from the tall mountains. Jed looked forward to seeing Walking Horse, Little Antelope, and Yellow Dog, but thinking of the old wolf made him eager to get back to his home and valley. He wanted peace and to be left alone to live in his valley, where he could trap and enjoy his life. With the money he had earned from the last three seasons of trapping, Jed considered himself a fortunate man. He had made plenty of money from his plews to keep him in supplies for many seasons. Warding off sleep, his dark eyes strained as they looked out into the darkness, roving across the canyon entrance for any intruders.

Standing up cautiously, as the new sun rose over the eastern mountain, Jed surveyed everything in his sight, then brought up the horses and started saddling the animals. He was tired, as sleep had come only in small bits as he guarded over the small canyon. Swinging up on the piebald, Jed slipped the sling of the smaller rifle across his back with his arrow quiver. With the bigger Hawken laying across the piebald, he kicked the horse and led his pack string back out on the main trail.

The sun was almost overhead when the mule alerted her ears, sensing something ahead on the trail. Quickly reining to the side of the trail, Jed pulled the rifle from his back and waited for the oncoming riders. He could hear the sound of horse's hooves coming toward him on the sandy trail. Cocking both rifles, Jed watched as the mule switched her tail and threw up her ears, looking for the unseen riders. The small nostrils quivered as she was about to call out a greeting to the oncoming horses.

A smile crossed his face as Yellow Dog, Walking Horse, and Crazy Cat, with several other warriors, came into view around a bend in the trail. A yell went up as the warriors recognized him astride the great piebald warhorse and raced toward him. Dismounting, Jed grabbed the arms and hands of Walking Horse and Yellow Dog pumping them in happiness at seeing his friends and brothers. Turning to Crazy Cat and Big Owl, Jed shook their hands.

"It is good to see you, my brothers." Jed grinned happily, as he had missed them more than he knew.

Walking Horse smiled. "I am sorry we were late, my brother."

"You are early." Yellow Dog nodded. "We did not expect you for a few more suns."

"I was in a hurry to see all of you again." Jed turned his eyes and nodded at all the warriors. His eyes blinked as he noticed Ellie, Little Antelope, and Bright Moon were with the warriors.

"We needed women to cook for us." Walking Horse could see the curiosity in Jed's eyes. "Rolling Thunder will meet us at Bridger and take my sister to the white village to the west.

Jed knew the warrior spoke of Baxter Springs. Looking over at the women, Jed smiled. "It is good to see you again."

"And you, Crow Killer." Bright Moon smiled and stepped in front of Jed. "It is good to see the great warrior of the Arapaho Lance Bearers."

"Thank you, Bright Moon." Jed smiled at the lovely woman.

Little Antelope smiled as she walked her horse up beside Walking Horse. "It is good to see my brother again."

"And you."

Looking to where Ellie stood, Jed nodded solemnly as she returned his nod. "It is good to see you, Jed, and with a clean shirt on."

Jed recognized the coldness in her voice. "I changed it just in your honor, Doctor."

"That's nice. We heard about your killing of the Pawnee warriors." Ellie had to add. "Did you bloody up another shirt?"

Ignoring the question, Jed turned to where Walking Horse and Yellow Dog were listening, embarrassed by the exchange of words. "I will ride back to Bridger with you, my friends."

"This is good." Walking Horse nodded. "Maybe you should ride close to me for safety."

"I believe you. She ain't calmed down since I seen her last." Jed glanced over at Ellie. "She is pretty when she's mad, and she has learned the Arapaho tongue well."

"Pretty does not keep a warrior warm in the cold times or well fed any time." Yellow Dog whispered. "A squaw should please her husband, and they do not need to talk much."

"Maybe a husband, my friend, but I ain't her husband." Jed turned his head so the women couldn't hear what they were saying. "It sure don't look like I will be."

CHAPTER 13

Fort Bridger was less than a half day away at sundown. Reining in, Yellow Dog ordered a camp made and horse guards were put out. The women quickly built fires, cooking meat and wild vegetables over the open flames. Jed, Walking Horse, Yellow Dog, and Crazy Cat sat together, talking about the past year, as the women prepared their food.

"It was told; you killed Wet Otter and three of his warriors this summer." Walking Horse puffed on his pipe as he watched Jed's face. "The Pawnee say you shot Wet Otter dead even though he was wounded."

"Good news definitely travels fast out here." Jed nodded. "Yes, I killed Wet Otter when he was wounded, and I will kill any who raid my lodge again."

Yellow dog smiled. "They say you attacked them without warning."

"Six against one, and I attacked them." Jed laughed lightly. "That's a good one."

"They say, you are a demon and you are crazy."

"Maybe they are right." Jed looked over at Ellie. "I've heard that before, so don't forget the words heathen and killer."

"They claim you attacked them without warning. Now, their chiefs tell Red Hawk the truce is broken."

"They lie. They came to my lodge and attacked me there, far from their own hunting grounds."

"We have to watch closely for their raiders now."

"I am sorry for that." Jed shook his head. "You send word to the

Pawnee, if they attack the Arapaho, Crow Killer will personally ride against them and many will die."

"You're good at killing alright." Ellie mumbled hearing his words.

"They attacked my lodge in the early morning. Come and look for yourself." Jed shrugged. "My lodge is full of bullet holes and arrows. What was I supposed to do, let them kill me?"

"We believe you, my brother. We wish we could have been there to help you kill the Pawnee dogs." Walking Horse spoke loud enough to carry to where the women worked. "The truce means nothing. They would raid us sooner or later without provocation."

Ellie looked to where Walking Horse spoke as her glance took in all three men. Her face turned beet red, knowing she was being talked about. Neither Little Antelope nor Bright Moon looked up from where they were busy cooking deer steaks.

"He is the greatest of warriors and he is so handsome." Bright Moon whispered to Little Antelope.

Nodding, Little Antelope looked over at Jed and smiled. "He is a great warrior, but do not forget my husband, Walking Horse."

"Walking Horse is handsome for an old man, but Crow Killer is still young and pretty."

"Walking Horse is not old, Sister. He is mature." Little Antelope laughed.

Ellie looked at Bright Moon and shook her head. "He is a killer, and there's nothing pretty about him."

"Pretty is in the eyes of the beholder, the old ones say." Little Antelope spoke up. "And this beholder, says he is very handsome."

"You are married, my sister." Bright Moon stuck out her tongue. "Too bad, you can't have him."

"Who would want him?" Ellie shrugged.

"I want him." Bright Moon flashed her pretty smile. "Only a fool wouldn't."

Little Antelope looked over for Ellie's reaction. "Have you set your robes for Crow Killer, little sister?"

Bright Moon beamed again as she smiled and showed them a decorated piece of white doe skin. "We will see."

"What is that?" Ellie stared at the beautiful piece of beadwork.

Little Antelope shook her head and giggled. "When a maiden wants to get a warrior's attention, she makes a token of love for him; that is what this is."

"You mean she asks the man to marry her?" Ellie was shocked.

"No, I will not ask." Bright Moon looked over at Jed. "Crow Killer will know I wait for him to ask if I give him this."

"Well, Bright Moon, if you want a warrior that likes to kill." Ellie shook her head. "He's your man. Marry him."

"I would like that, Ellie, very much, but I hear he has eyes only for someone else." Bright Moon looked curiously at the woman.

"Well, he might as well set them somewhere else." Ellie frowned. "I'll never make one of those for him, never."

"Then, Sister, you won't mind if I take him for myself?"

"Do as you wish, Bright Moon. I'm sure I don't mind." Ellie turned to her cooking. "You'll be the one living with him."

"Yes, I will." The woman smiled dreamily. "I think that will be a fun thing."

Little Antelope stood up, announcing the meat was done. Picking up bowls, she started filling them with food. "I will feed the warriors."

"I will feed Crow Killer." Bright Moon took a bowl and filled it.

Walking Horse didn't miss the look that passed between Bright Moon and Jed as he thanked her for his food. Yellow Dog ducked his head as he smiled.

"I told you, my brother, there was another interested in you, and this one is very beautiful." Walking Horse whispered.

Jed remembered the warrior's words to him as he rode from the valley, but he thought Walking Horse had been speaking of Little Antelope. Looking over at Bright Moon, Jed shook his head. The woman reminded him of Little Antelope, a little taller, but their faces and way of moving were almost identical. The younger sister of Little Antelope was indeed a beautiful young woman.

After speaking about the rifles, Walking Horse wanted, Jed excused himself and walked to where the piebald stood hobbled, grazing on the spring grass. The horse nuzzled him softly as Jed scratched his ears. Jed was proud of the horse he had taken from the warrior, Black Robe, as he was a thing of beauty. Any warrior would be proud to ride the magnificent animal. In battle, the horse was powerful, and he had saved Jed's life many times in battle with his enemies.

"He likes you." Jed turned to find Bright Moon standing behind him. "The old ones say an animal knows the heart and courage of a warrior."

"He has saved my life many times."

"Are you afraid to speak with me?" Bright Moon looked up into his face. "Am I ugly to your eyes?"

Jed smiled. "No Bright Moon, you are not ugly, and I am not afraid to speak with you."

"This is good." The young woman turned and walked away, leaving Jed staring after her.

Patting the piebald on the neck, Jed turned back to the camp where the warriors still sat about the fires, telling their stories of fights and victories against their enemies. Almost into the firelight, Jed stopped as Little Antelope stepped in front of him.

"My sister is very beautiful is she not?"

Jed nodded. "Everyone seems to be telling me this, but yes, she is."

"Bright Moon has eyes for you, my warrior." Little Antelope looked to where Walking Horse was watching as she spoke to Jed. "She would accept you as a husband, and she will make you a good wife, Jed."

Jed looked to where Ellie sat by the fire. "You would like this?"

"I only want your happiness." Little Antelope followed Jed's eyes. "My husband's sister will not make you happy."

"I know, she does not want a heathen."

"She belongs in the white man's world." Little Antelope dropped her eyes. "Ellie is a good woman, but she doesn't understand our way of life."

Jed shook his head. "You mean kill or be killed."

"Sometimes this is true, not always." The little woman smiled sadly. "She is a healer, and she gives life. You are a warrior and you protect us, but sometimes that means taking life."

"I hear your words, little one."

"Think on this, my warrior, and think on Bright Moon." Little Antelope turned, then looked back. "I want you happy and at peace."

"Thank you, Little Antelope."

"I speak of this now because there may be no other chance in the days to come."

"I know, little one."

"I wish things could have been different." A small tear came to her eye as she walked away. "You know my feelings, and I will carry them to my grave, my warrior."

"And I." Jed watched the small woman walk away proudly, then rejoined the warriors.

Jed walked back to where Yellow Dog and Walking Horse sat talking. Both warriors looked over at him as he sat down. They could both see the sadness in his eyes. They knew the sadness in a warrior's heart over a woman could ruin him, as both had seen many times in the past.

"Tomorrow, we will ride to the post."

Jed felt the heavy leather belt around his waist. "We should be careful. Some may want to attack us."

"We are many." Crazy Cat looked across at Jed. "Who would dare attack us this close to Bridger?"

"I have been warned by the old scout at the fort." Jed nodded. "The white trappers may unite with warriors at the fort and attack us."

"Just to kill you, Crow Killer?"

"That and for the gold money I carry."

"What do you wish us to do?" Walking Horse asked.

"Tomorrow, we must be ready on the trail to Bridger."

"We will be ready."

Jed poured himself some coffee. "I don't know, but I have a feeling we are being watched, even now."

The early morning cooking fire was put out as breakfast was finished. The warriors were loading their pelts, preparing to leave for Bridger when a lone warrior rode in and dismounted beside Yellow Dog.

"Warriors and two whites wait ahead." Pony Wings pointed down the trail. "Their tracks show they came here last night, then retreated when they found our fires."

"How many?" Jed spoke up.

"Maybe this many." The young Cheyenne held up both hands.

"You see them?"

"Yes, two whites ride with the Arickara."

"Do they have the fire guns?"

"The whites have guns, and some of the Rees, but most have only bows as we do." Pony Wings looked over at Jed.

Looking at Yellow Dog and Walking Horse, Jed nodded as he looked back up the trail. "Will Yellow Dog be insulted if I tell you how we should prepare?"

Yellow Dog shrugged. "Tell us, my brother, and we will do as you say."

"Leave three warriors here to guard the women and horses. They will follow us but stay at a distance, back out of danger." Jed quickly laid out his battle plan. "The rest come with me."

Jed could see almost a mile along the flat trail. Nothing showed except the tracks of many horses along the trail, showing where riders had come close enough to see their campfires before turning back. Jed figured the enemy would be waiting, out of sight, around the far bend, hoping to surprise the Cheyenne with their rifles.

Holding up his hand, Jed looked around at the ten warriors close behind him. "If they choose to attack us, the enemy may be around the bend ahead." Jed motioned at the far bend. "They cannot afford to let us get closer to the trading post, where the noise from the rifles can be heard. They know Bridger will ban them from the fort if he finds out."

"What will we do, Crow killer?" Yellow Dog studied the far bend.

"Spread out behind me. If they charge us, free your horse and fight on foot." Jed noticed the shaking heads. "I know you always fight on horseback, but this enemy has rifles. Make yourself small, kneel down, and make every arrow count."

Yellow Dog shook his head. "This is not the Cheyenne way to fight, my brother."

"No, but it is the way to win and kill this enemy." Jed looked around at the warriors. "I do not wish my friends and brothers killed today."

"We will do as you say."

"Good, remember when they attack, dismount and fight on foot." Jed looked back down the trail. "Stay back many paces. Let me ride ahead and draw their fire."

The warriors behind Jed spread out as far as the trail would allow. Two of the younger warriors rode into the deep brush and timber that bordered the trail, making sure no enemy lurked there. Jed turned the piebald and moved down the trail with his back straight and shoulders squared proudly.

"There is the warrior you think a heathen." Bright Moon looked over at Ellie. "Again, he shows his bravery, putting his life in danger to protect his people."

Ellie watched as Bright Moon kicked her horse and rode forward, stopping beside Yellow Dog, who frowned at her. "Go back to the women, Sister."

"Do not ask me to do this thing, Brother." Bright Moon shook her head. "Since our father died you are my chief, but I must remain here."

"You think much of Crow Killer?" Yellow Dog asked.

Nodding, she smiled. "Yes, if I am lucky, he will be my husband."

Suddenly, with Jed less than a hundred paces from the bend, two whites raced their horses into view and reined to a stop, both firing their rifles. Thrown backward from the piebald, Jed hit the ground hard and rolled to his hands and knees, trying to regain the wind that had been knocked from him, from the force of the heavy bullet. Stunned and sucking wind hoarsely, Jed crawled forward in pain, gasping for air.

Whipping her horse hard, Bright Moon raced to Jed's side as the whites reloaded, screaming for the Rees to attack. Helping Jed to his knees and picking up both rifles, she placed the larger rifle in Jed's hand. "Kill them, my warrior. I will reload for you."

Jed took the rifle numbly as he finally regained his air. Jed's first shot knocked one of the whites from his charging horse. Handing the empty rifle to Bright Moon, Jed took the smaller Hawken from her. "Do you know how to load a rifle?"

"I watched Rolling Thunder teach Yellow Dog the use of the fire gun when he passed through our village on his way east." Bright Moon looked at the bullet hole in Jed's hunting shirt. "Are you hurt badly?"

"No, I don't think so." Jed fired again, then stood and plunged his war lance into the ground beside him.

Handing him the reloaded rifle, she smiled. She was proud to be there, fighting beside him. Today, she could be killed, but she had no fear. Arrows started flying into the oncoming warriors as Jed's rifle fired again, knocking another screaming Ree from his horse. Pushing Bright Moon to her stomach, Jed swung his heavy war axe, unseating another warrior as the rest turned back in a hasty retreat.

Walking Horse mounted his fast buffalo runner and caught the slower horse of the remaining white trapper quickly. Screaming his war cry, he lunged at the white, knocking both of them with their horses into a dusty tangle of hooves and bodies. Rolling atop the struggling trapper, Walking Horse held the man's long hair and plunged his skinning knife into his throat. Quickly removing the scalp, Walking Horse stood up and screamed, shaking the bloody long hair.

Eight dead Arickara lay about the trail while the remainder of the Rees retreated in fear from the battlefield. Jed helped Bright Moon to her feet, then looked questioningly at the disheveled woman.

"Thank you, Bright Moon, you saved my life." Jed touched her face, brushing dirt from her hair. "I will never forget this day."

Placing the white piece of tanned leather with the porcupine quill decorations across his arm, she smiled. "You are the bravest of the brave, Crow Killer."

Jed looked down at the beautiful piece of work. "Thank you, Bright Moon."

"May I look at your side?" She could see the holes, one small one and a larger exit wound coming from the shirt. "You do not bleed."

"No, but I will be sore." Jed knew the gold coins around his waist had deflected the heavy bullet, saving his life.

"Are you a demon as they say?" Her eyes questioned him. "You shed no blood."

"Do you fear me, Bright Moon?"

"No, Crow Killer, I love and admire you." The girl smiled. "There is no fear in my heart."

"Even if I am a demon?"

"Even if you are a demon." She repeated, then led her horse back to where Ellie and Little Antelope were approaching. "If you are, then you are my demon."

"Is Crow Killer hurt bad?" Little Antelope asked, as she saw Jed walking unsteadily toward the dead white.

"No, he is not hurt badly."

"Does he need me to help him?" Ellie watched Jed.

"Would you help him?" Bright Moon frowned at Ellie. "You haven't so far."

"If he needs my help…" Ellie replied.

Jed turned the white, he had shot, over onto his back and shook his head in surprise. It was Luke Grisham. He remembered the man clearly from Baxter Springs. What was he doing here so far from the settlement?

"Will you take his hair, my brother?" Walking Horse held the long scalp of the second trapper in his hand. "His scalp is not much."

Jed knew the warrior was referring to the hair being so short. "No, I do not need this one's scalp."

Walking Horse looked down at Jed's bullet torn hunting shirt. "The white man's bullet was weak, it did not kill you."

"No, I was lucky today."

"It was not luck, my brother. You have strong medicine that protects you." Walking Horse smiled. "The old one, White Swan, foretold this many moons ago, as he seen this in the bones and the smoke of his fire."

"White Swan." Jed smiled, remembering the old medicine man with fondness.

"He said Crow Killer would be wounded many times in battle." Walking Horse nodded his head. "But, he said you would never die by arrows or the white man's bullet."

Jed smiled, as the old one had been right. His body carried many wounds, covered in scars from his fights with his enemies, but he still lived. He looked forward to living in peace in his beloved valley, but would this wish ever come true? Would he ever be left to live in peace?

One dead horse and many small wounds from arrows and bullets were the only casualties the Cheyenne and Arapaho suffered. Eight dead Rees lay strung out on the trail, and Jed didn't know how many had been wounded. Gathering the Ree's horses and rifles, the warriors scalped the enemy warriors, screaming their war cries. Watching Ellie's reaction as the warriors danced around with their trophies, he wondered what she thought now of heathens.

"Will we be allowed in the post now?" Yellow Dog questioned Jed.

"I don't know. Bridger has strict rules against fighting anywhere near the fort."

"What will we do?" Walking Horse spoke up.

"I will ride ahead and speak with Bridger or his head clerk." Jed looked around at the warriors. "Bring the women and make camp within sight of the fort. I will return to you."

"Will the Arikara at the fort attack us if we are so close?" Yellow Dog looked over at Jed.

"No, Bridger forbids fighting between enemies." Jed shook his head. "I do not figure most of the Rees wanted these who rode against us to do this thing. They fear being banned from trading at the fort."

"Did they come after you for killing the Rees last year?" Yellow Dog asked.

"No, they came after my hair and the piebald." Jed shook his head. "The white men wanted my gold."

"We will do as you ask." Walking Horse looked around the trail.

"Stay alert, my brothers. I will be very close."

Ellie pushed her horse forward. "My father will be at the fort. I want to ride in with you."

"No, it is too dangerous." Walking Horse shook his head. "There are many enemies ahead. You will ride in under our protection."

Ellie looked down at the bullet holes in Jed's shirt. She was confused, and wondered how the bullet passed through his body, leaving two holes without blood.

"I'll see you as the sun passes from the sky."

"Still talking like an Indian, I see." Ellie shook her head.

"I am an Indian and remember, a heathen as well." Jed turned the piebald. "It is my way to talk now."

"He is a great Arapaho, Sister." Walking Horse watched as Jed rode away. "Did you not see the way he planted his lance in the ground, even as he was wounded."

"He's a killer, Brother." Ellie frowned. "He lives to kill, then says it is to help his people."

"Surely, you do not believe this?"

"He is cold, and a killer."

"Perhaps, but he just protected all of us while he was killing." Walking Horse looked down at her. "Out here, our people have to be hard, that is the only way for us to survive against our more powerful enemies."

"The white's say a man must not kill."

"If a man doesn't kill his enemies, then he will be killed." Walking Horse shook his head. "You should think on this, or lose him forever."

"In my heart, he is already lost to me." Ellie shrugged. "I cannot marry or live with a killer, no matter how you try to say it is a good thing."

"You are wrong, little sister, but you are still my sister."

"And you will always be my brother." Ellie smiled. "If the people ever need me, send for me and I will come."

"Thank you, Medicine Thunder."

Jed rode slowly through the gates of Fort Bridger, studying the faces of the sullen warriors as he passed them. He knew word of the fight had already been brought to the fort. Probably some of the wounded, that had participated, were now lying in the nearby Arickara lodges. Reining in at the post stable, Jed slid from the piebald and walked to where the old trapper was working over his forge.

"Well, I warned you, boy." The old man looked at the bullet holes in Jed's shirt. "Word's already been brought to Bridger."

"He put out?"

"You know the rules around here." McGraw pushed a horseshoe deep in the glowing coals of the forge. "No fighting."

"What about when a man is attacked without provocation?" Jed shrugged. "Don't that count?"

"I reckon Jim would figure a man has the right to defend himself."

"What about the Arickara, are they gonna be tossed out of here?"

"I doubt it. Pretty hard to tell which ones were involved."

"Well, looks to me like the ones lying in those lodges out there with holes in their bodies might be guilty." Jed leaned against the piebald.

"You hurt?"

"Nope, a little sore is all." Jed shook his head. He did have pain, maybe a bruised or broken rib. "You figure Bridger is gonna keep Yellow Dog and his Cheyenne from trading here?"

"Not today he ain't. He ain't here."

"When you expect him back?"

The old man scratched his beard. "That I can't rightly say. He's gone over the pass to see some of his Flathead friends."

Jed nodded. "Well then, I reckon I can bring the Cheyenne and Arapaho into the fort. We'll trade their furs, get supplies, and ride out."

"Reckon so. Nobody here to stop you, that's for sure." The trapper nodded. "What happened out there?"

"Nothing, I know of." Jed smiled. "What did you hear, old man?"

"Nothing, I reckon." McGraw looked back at the forge. "I just heard a couple whites and some Rees got themselves killed by some unknown warriors a few miles out."

"Do tell?" Jed pretended innocence.

McGraw looked behind Jed. "Where's the little mule?"

"Some unknown warriors are holding her for me a mile out."

"I was afraid you had lost her."

Talking with the old man, Jed didn't see the rider as he reined in at the stable. "You fellers ain't seen a lanky, string-bean Arapaho around here?"

Turning slowly, Jed let out with a shout and walked to where the man had dismounted. "Pa, what are you doing away out here?"

"Looking for you, son. Just looking for you."

"Well, you found me. Now, tell me what are you doing here?"

"A little chore for Lige Hatcher."

"What kind of chore, Pa?"

"Hatcher passed through here two weeks ago." The old man spoke up. "Said something about his daughter."

"Yep, the train was two weeks early and Chalk Briggs needed his help going on west." Wilson nodded. "Something about his help being sick and couldn't part with him."

"Yeah, his other scout came down with the pleurisy and was riding in one of the wagons." McGraw laughed. "Old Lige was mighty put out, I'll tell you. Something about missing a wedding."

"And?" Jed shrugged.

"Sent me here to bring Ellie back to Baxter Springs unless you two are already hitched." Wilson looked about. "Where 'bout is she?"

"About a mile outside the stockade by now, I reckon." Jed looked over at Wilson. "You hungry?"

"I could use a bite alright."

"Let's walk over to the post and fetch us something." Jed looked over at the old man. "You hungry too?"

"Nope, but thanks anyway." McGraw looked across the post grounds. "Watch yourself, boy. That topknot of yours is mighty inviting around these parts."

"Thanks, I'll try to keep it tied on."

Entering the trading post, Jed walked to the counter and helped himself to a hunk of cheese and a handful of stale crackers from the cracker barrel. A younger clerk watching him, motioned to an older man, then whispered something to him.

Walking to where Jed and Wilson stood eating, the older clerk studied them closely as he approached. "We traded a few days ago, Arapaho. Now, word has come that you broke Bridger's word when you fought with some Ree's near here yesterday."

"The fight was brought on us. We didn't start anything."

"I know, but I must follow Bridger's law." The clerk cleared his throat. "No exceptions."

"How long we got?"

"I figure Bridger will be back sometime next week, so you've got till then I expect." The clerk shrugged. "After that, I can't say."

"We'll be long gone by then." Jed paid for the crackers and turned to leave. "We'll be in come daybreak to trade, and then we'll ride out."

"We'll be here and you're welcome." The clerk smiled. "We heard what happened. That loudmouth, Grisham, has been spouting off around here for the last month or better."

Wilson looked over at Jed. "Luke Grisham?"

"The same."

"You boys kill old Kilmer too?"

"Long hair, no teeth, and a bad scar on his left cheek?"

"That be him, alright. No sorrier polecat ever lived in these parts than Kilmer." The clerk nodded. "You boys do for him?"

"Reckon so, he's minus his hair."

"Dang, he was a bad one for sure. Only ones worse were them Frenchies you killed over in Turner's Hole last year. Now, those boys were some real bad actors."

Jed looked over at the clerk in surprise. "Who told you that?"

"The Rees, boy. They described the demon down to your lance there." The clerk pointed at Jed's lance.

"You plumb sure it was me?"

"What's worse is Bridger is plumb sure."

"Put out is he?" Jed smiled.

"Can't blame him, can you?"

"Blame him?"

"Young feller, you keep killing off everybody and we could go broke." The clerk shook his head. "Old Gabe, he don't care about you killing Injuns and no account white trash, but he does care about you killing off his customers."

"Well, then I'll try to do better."

"When you come in tomorrow, I want no trouble from any of you. You understand?"

Jed looked over at the rifle rack standing behind the long counter. "You got any more rifles around here.

"Some in the back. Why?"

"We'll be in with the new sun."

"Who's we?"

"The Cheyenne with Yellow Dog, and the Arapaho with Walking Horse."

"Guns are expensive you know."

"I know."

CHAPTER 14

Several times, Jed backtracked and watched their back trail on the way from the post. He found no one following but was relieved to find Yellow Dog had posted guards, almost a half mile out from their camp.

Ellie was shocked when Jed rode into the campsite after dark with Wilson. "Mister Wilson, what are you doing here?"

"If that's coffee, Ellie, I sure could use some." Wilson pointed at the battered coffeepot and laughed. "At least we've taught your people one good habit, Walking Horse."

"Coffee is good when the cold times come." The warrior agreed, nodding his head as Ellie poured Wilson a cup.

"Anytime is good for me." Wilson thanked Ellie for the coffee. "To answer your question, Miss Ellie, your pappy asked me to come fetch you back to Baxter Springs. That is if you haven't gotten yourself married already."

"No, I am not married and don't intend to be." Ellie looked over at Jed. "Where's Papa?"

"He had to head the train clear to Oregon this year." Wilson reassured her. "He's fine, and he'll be back to fetch you late summer."

Jed looked over at Walking Horse and Yellow Dog. "We'll ride in and do our trading come sunup."

"The white trader, Bridger, is not mad?" Yellow Dog questioned.

"He's gone, so I doubt he has learned about the fight yet."

"He knows. The old man knows everything." Yellow Dog laughed. "We will trade our furs and leave this place before he returns."

Jed nodded. "That's the plan alright, come daylight."

Sipping on his coffee, Wilson noticed the cool reserve between Jed and Ellie. As Ellie moved away, Wilson looked over at Jed. "What has happened between you two?"

"She doesn't want to marry a heathen or a killer." Jed turned and walked away toward the piebald.

Arapaho and Cheyenne warriors rode proudly through the gates of the trading post as villagers watched while standing before the many lodges outside the fort. Longtime enemies of the Cheyenne and Arapaho, the warriors knew they had to leave their personal hatred behind, if they wanted to trade at Bridger. The one they hated most was the demon, Crow Killer, riding alone behind the column with another white. How many Arickara had this enemy killed? The older Arickara Chiefs, standing with their warriors, held up their hands as their hated enemy passed among them. They held the younger warriors in check as he passed. They too wanted the demon dead, but not at the expense of losing their only place to sell their furs and trade for the much-needed supplies. Before the white man's trade goods, the tribes were self-sufficient, but in the past few years, they had come to depend on the white man's trade goods more every year.

The older store clerk walked out on the porch with the other clerks, making sure no trouble started inside the post. He knew Bridger would have his hide if a fight erupted between the tribes. Bridger made his living trading with every tribe, and he could not afford to have them warring with one another in the post. Raising his hand as the magnificent Cheyenne and Arapaho warriors reined in at the store, the clerk welcomed Yellow dog. Turning his attention quickly, he watched the other warriors across the post grounds, relieved as they returned to their seats beside the palisades.

"Welcome, my friends. It is good to see you again."

"It is good to be here again at my friend, Bridger's Lodge."

"Come in, come in."

Jed chuckled to himself as the greedy clerk's eyes fell on the bundles of furs, the Cheyenne and Arapaho brought. Tying the piebald, Jed walked behind Ellie and Little Antelope into the trading post. He knew

Little Antelope, in her lifetime, had never seen anything like the store and its many supplies. He watched as her small hand touched the soft rolls of fabric. Bright Moon walking behind Jed wasn't impressed, as she had been to the post twice before with Yellow Dog to trade.

Jed stood beside the counter as a younger clerk quickly tallied the furs and then jotted down the price he would give. Jed could quickly tell the prices he just proposed were far less than he had paid for his pelts, only three days prior. Taking the paper, the clerk started to give to Yellow Dog, Jed made his own tally.

"You're a mite short on your figuring, clerk." Jed handed the paper back to the clerk. "I believe you meant it to read like this."

Clearing his throat, the man rechecked his figures. "Yes, I see my mistake."

Taking the paper back after the young clerk wrote on it again. "That's a little better."

After both Walking Horse and Yellow Dog received their money and Jed recounted it, the clerk had his helper clear the counter. "Now, that's settled. You look around and bring what you want to the counter and we'll settle up on that too."

"They'll be wanting several things, but first they want to buy rifles, shot and lead, and the necessaries that go with them." Jed looked over to where several rifles stood in a long rack behind the counter. "First, let's see the ones you have in the back."

"I done told you, they'll be expensive." The older clerk walked up.

"So you did, Mister Clerk."

"The name's Caldwell."

"Well, Mister Caldwell, my brothers will be spending a lot of gold here today." Jed smiled. "I hope they won't be too high and force us to ride to Baxter Springs."

"You're still welcome in Baxter Springs after killing Rufus Cross and Bigfoot?"

"They killed Lem Roden from ambush." Jed frowned. "You done heard about Lem being killed too, Mister Caldwell?"

"No, don't reckon I heard that." The face paled. "Grisham didn't tell that part of it."

Wilson shook his head. "Didn't expect he would at that."

"Well, how many will they be wanting?"

Jed spoke to Walking Horse and Yellow Dog in Arapaho for a few minutes, then turned back to the clerk. "They'll gather up what they need first, then take the rest of it in rifles."

"Help yourself, gentlemen." The clerk watched as different items were placed on the counter, keeping tally of the supplies. Blankets, pots, knives, coffee beans, and several cans of peaches Jed picked out and set on the counter. Looking over his glasses as Jed studied his figures, the clerk swallowed hard.

"How much is left for rifles?"

"They're figuring on spending everything they got?"

"Every ounce of gold you gave'em." Jed smiled.

Clearing his throat, the clerk did more figuring and looked up. "Yellow Dog's people can buy twelve rifles. The other gentleman has fifteen coming."

"You're throwing in enough powder, shot, bullet molds, and oil to keep them for a year?" Jed smiled. "That would be a good show of faith on your part."

"If they're trading with Bridger next year." Swallowing hard, the clerk nodded. "I reckon I can do that."

"Well, we're thanking you, and we'll all be back next season."

"You drive a hard bargain there, young man."

"Tell Bridger before he goes to throwing one of his tantrums to remember they'll be back next year, with plenty more pelts."

"I'll do that, yes sir, I'll tell him."

"You do that, Mister Caldwell." Jed smiled. "Meanwhile, I'll just pick out their rifles. That is, if you don't mind?"

Caldwell shook his head slowly. "No, you do that."

Bundles of supplies along with the rifles were piled high on the extra horses the warriors had brought with them. Jed stood alongside Ellie and Wilson, watching as the supplies were loaded.

"I reckon we'll pull out for Baxter Springs while the weather holds."

Jed looked over at Ellie and nodded. "It should take you about three days to reach the settlement, maybe less."

"I rode here in a little more than two." Wilson looked over at Ellie.

"Don't worry about Ellie, she'll be right behind you no matter how tough the going gets." Jed smiled.

"I know." Wilson could feel the tenseness between Ellie and Jed. He thought they were to wed, but something had come between them. "I'll let you two say your good-byes then."

Watching Wilson walk to where Walking Horse and Little Antelope waited, Ellie took Jed by the arm. "There have been many harsh words between us Jed."

"Yes, there have."

"I'm sorry." Tears came to her eyes as she looked at him. "I love you, Jed, but I can't live your life. I just can't."

"I know that now, Ellie." Jed nodded. "You're meant to heal people, be in civilization, and live among civilized folks."

"I'm sorry, Jed." Ellie held back the tears. "I didn't mean to hurt you."

"Nor I you, Ellie. You're right, my life in the mountains is no place for a cultured lady like you."

"Will I see you again, Jed?"

"You're still half Arapaho. Will you be coming to see your people?"

"You know I will."

"Tell Lige to bring you to the cabin. That is, providing you want to come." Jed smiled.

"I will do that. Be happy, Jed, and keep safe."

"I'll do my best, Doctor."

"Jed…" She hesitated. "In the last few days, I have learned a lot of things. You're not a heathen or a killer. I know that now."

Jed smiled. "Well, maybe a little of each."

"Good-bye, my love."

"Good-bye, Doctor Ellie."

Hugging Little Antelope and Walking Horse, Ellie pulled Bright Moon close and whispered to her quietly. "Take care of your warrior and make him happy."

"He has not asked for me yet."

Looking over at Jed, Ellie smiled. "He will, I know he will."

Shaking hands with Jed and the others, Wilson mounted his horse and looked at Jed. "You've come a long way, son. I'm a proud father."

"And I'm proud to call you father." Jed looked over at the bag hanging from the little mule. "I'll bring Billy home to you before I ride back to the valley."

"You'll bring his body home?"

"I promise, as soon as I see Walking Horse and Little Antelope safely back to Yellow Dog's Village, I will do just that."

"I would go with you and help." Wilson looked over at Ellie. "But, I promised her pa and grandpa to get her back safely to Baxter Springs."

"It's okay, Pa." Jed lied saving Wilson the sadness of knowing his son hung in a bag on the mule. "I'll tend to it and I'll see you in a few days."

"I'll be looking for you." Wilson nodded slowly as Jed lifted Ellie onto her horse. "Thank you, Jed."

Standing by Walking Horse and Yellow Dog, Jed watched as Wilson, with Ellie in tow, passed though the post gates, disappearing from his view. He would miss them but this time, he didn't feel the loneliness as they once again rode out of his life.

"You will come back to my village to show us the use of the new rifles?" Yellow Dog asked. "Rolling Thunder showed me a little of the use of such a weapon, but not enough."

Jed looked over at the smiling Bright Moon. "I will come long enough to teach you its use."

"We are slow learners." Walking Horse smiled.

"Two weeks, no more."

Walking Horse walked beside Jed, back into the trader's store. "You should take two more rifles back with you on this trail."

Jed looked questioningly at the warrior. "Why? I've already got two. Can a man shoot more than one rifle at a time?"

Walking Horse looked to where Bright Moon stood beside Little Antelope. "Maybe the bride price will be two rifles, who knows?"

"I swear, you and Little Antelope, always trying to get me married off."

"She stood beside you in battle and she would die for you." Walking Horse looked at Bright Moon. "She earned the right to be your woman."

"Yes, she did." Jed nodded. "Maybe I don't need a woman."

"Every man needs a woman to care for." Walking Horse argued

quietly, only heard by Jed. "Maybe you don't now, my brother, but in time you will learn to care for a woman. Think on this; a woman like Bright Moon that would die for you, cannot be found every day."

"I know you mean well, my brother."

"Heed my words, Crow Killer. A woman is very comforting in the cold times."

"I hear your words, my brother."

"You are hardheaded."

Jed fingered the beaded fur Bright Moon had given him, then turned to the counter as Walking Horse walked from the post. "Give me those two rifles, clerk, and wrap them up."

Exiting the store, he frowned when he found Walking Horse grinning broadly from the porch. Tying the rifles to the little mule, Jed swung up on the piebald and followed Yellow Dog and Walking Horse from the post.

"Watch out for your topknot." The old man waved as they passed the corrals. "I'll still trade you out of that mule, anytime you say."

"Maybe next year, old-timer." Jed knew he was lying as the words passed from his mouth. The little mule was family to him, same as the piebald. Looking at her brought back his fond memories of Silent One and their time together. Like him, the black mule would live out her days in the valley.

Passing through the gates, an older Assiniboine woman motioned him over to her. Reining the piebald to a stop, Jed looked down at the woman as she spoke and signaled with her hands.

"You were my son's friend?"

"Silent One was like my brother."

"He died well?"

Jed nodded, as he wouldn't tell of Silent One's murder, but he would tell of Silent One's bravery. "He saved my life. He was a great and brave warrior. A son for any mother to remember with pride."

"Thank you, Crow Killer, for being his friend."

"It was an honor to know one such as he, Mother." Jed felt her touch his leg. "If there's anything you need?"

"No, I am well taken care of." The woman dropped her head. "I just wish I could have done more for my son."

"He loved you, Mother, and that was enough." Jed smiled. "He spoke of you with affection."

"Good-bye, Crow Killer." The squaw nodded sadly. "Live a long life and be happy."

"Thank you."

"And I thank you for making Silent One respected among his people." She smiled. "Even if it is too late."

"It's never too late, Mother." Jed looked to the western trail, hoping to catch one last glimpse of Ellie. "Silent One will always be remembered in my lodge."

Jed kept his promise, and for two weeks he showed the Cheyenne how to fire and care for their new rifles. Walking Horse stayed for one week, but fearing his people may need him, he prepared Little Antelope and his warriors for their long journey to the west.

Little Antelope pulled Jed off to the side and yanked hard on his arm as she looked up at him. "Take my sister, Bright Moon, for your woman, my warrior."

"Everyone tells me this." Jed knew they all were trying to help, but he wished they would mind their own business. "Right now, I do not want a woman."

"You don't care for her?"

"I'm afraid to care for anyone, little one." Jed looked to where Bright Moon was working. "I've lost every woman I've ever cared for."

"You have not lost me, Jed." Little Antelope touched his face softly. "Never, will you lose me. It's just our lives together wasn't meant to be."

"I know."

"Do not spend your days alone and in sadness." Little Antelope looked up at him. "She will make you happy and she loves you, perhaps even more than I do. In time, I think you will learn to love her the same."

"It is too soon." Jed turned away.

"You need her, Jed." Little Antelope walked after him. "You have become hard, my warrior. Let Bright Moon bring softness back into your life and happiness once again."

"I am happy, little one."

Little Antelope looked at him. "Remember when you first came to the Arapaho, you were young and happy. I just wish to see my warrior happy again."

"I know, but…"

"Please, Jed, don't tell me it is none of my business." The little woman smiled. "You are my business. I cannot make you happy but my sister can."

Leading his horse to where Jed and Little Antelope talked, Walking Horse shook hands with Jed, then suddenly hugged him. "I hate to leave you, my brother."

"I will ride to see our people in the late summer." Jed watched as Little Antelope walked away.

"Little Antelope spoke with you?"

"She tried."

"I am proud you are my brother. I know if anything ever happened to me, Little Antelope would be well taken care of." The warrior smiled. "Think on her words. Bright Moon is Little Antelope's sister and a good woman."

"I will see you in the summer days." Jed shook his head as he listened to Walking Horse's words.

"If the bride price is to high, my brother, I will give you the horses Yellow Dog asks." Walking Horse grinned.

Bright Moon stood beside Jed as Walking Horse and his people waved from the high pass leading west. A lump came once more into Jed's throat as they disappeared from his sight.

"Will you miss her?" Bright Moon questioned.

Jed looked into her beautiful face and shrugged. "I will miss all of them."

"And my sister, Little Antelope?"

"We are close, that is all. She is the wife of Walking Horse." Jed could feel the soft fur of the porcupine token inside his shirt. "Let's go for a walk."

For another week, between teaching Yellow Dog's warriors to shoot and care for their weapons, and walking across the flat lands with Bright Moon, Jed kept busy. Slowly, his thoughts turned from Ellie and Little Antelope as he began to enjoy Bright Moon's company more every day.

Lying beside a fast, clear running stream, Jed looked down into her pretty face. "They say I am a demon."

"They fear you, so they say these things." She looked up at him. "I do not fear you, Crow Killer."

"Medicine Thunder, said I was a killer."

"You are a warrior. Warrior's kill to protect their people." Bright Moon smiled. "Medicine Thunder is only half Arapaho. Her white side doesn't understand our ways."

"My lodge is many suns from here." Jed touched her face softly. "Would you miss your people?"

"If I am with you, my warrior, how could I?" Bright Moon pulled him closer. "I will see them at times. Now, you will be my life and always will be, if you want me."

Laying the beaded token across her, Jed kissed Bright Moon softly.

The village drums were beating in rhythm as the wedding festivities rang out in the lodges for three days. A great feast was prepared and throughout the village, the people of the Cheyenne gorged themselves and danced until they passed out. One of their daughters was to marry the great Arapaho Lance Bearer, Crow Killer, binding the two great tribes, one Cheyenne and one Arapaho, even closer. Presents were piled high as Jed sat talking to Yellow Dog discussing the bride fee.

"Forty horses and ten rifles." The Cheyenne crossed his arms and stared into the fire.

"What? That's enough for ten wives." Jed pretended shock. "I will give one horse and one rifle."

"She is very pretty, is she not?"

"Maybe for some, to me she is ugly." Jed lied.

"I think my sister is the prettiest maiden in the Cheyenne Nation."

"I'm not marrying pretty. I'm marrying me a cook, skinner, and someone to keep me warm during the cold times."

Bright Moon walked by several times to see what they were arguing about. Frowning, she shook her head and walked back to her lodge. While they were fussing about what was already settled, the real wedding festivities were being held up.

"Twenty horses and five rifles." Yellow Dog flattened his hands.

"Yellow Dog knows I am poor. Two horses and one rifle."

"She is worth more."

"She has bowlegs and a bad temperament."

"But, she is a good cook."

"True."

Yellow Dog was about to speak when suddenly, Bright Moon stepped in front of them pretending rage. "Enough! If you do not want Crow Killer for a brother-in-law, I will live in your lodge until I am old and withered, and you will have to feed me."

"Okay, Sister, what do you consider a fair price for you?" Yellow Dog laughed.

Seeing Jed grinning, she glared at Jed. "Am I funny to you too, Crow Killer?"

"No, ma'am." Jed stammered. "Not one bit."

"Our people wait for you to announce my marriage. Don't make them wait longer."

Yellow Dog and Jed laughed as she walked away pretending to be upset.

Holding the porcupine beaded token up for all to see, Yellow Dog proclaimed his sister, Bright Moon, to be married this day.

"She was worth far more than two rifles, and you, my brother, know this." Yellow Dog smiled.

"I would have given much more." Jed announced.

Both men laughed and shook hands as the drums rang out through the village. Later, two of the older women of the village had Jed bathe, then they braided his long hair and dressed him in an all-white doeskin hunting shirt, quilled moccasins, and leggings.

Before Yellow Dog's lodge, the old Medicine Man of the Cheyenne called everyone together, then Bright Moon walked from the lodge. She was beautiful and radiantly dressed in an all-white doeskin dress with bells ringing from it. Jed swallowed hard as he took in the beautiful woman, more beautiful than he could remember.

Yellow Dog looked over at Jed and smiled. "I should have asked fifty horses, my brother."

"I would have given fifty, and more." Jed smiled.

Two days later, Jed and Bright Moon led their packhorses, traveling the immigrant road to Baxter Springs. Late, on the third day, Carter's farm came into sight. Bright Moon suddenly became nervous as they neared the white settlement. Except for Bridger's Fort, she had never been around many white people. At Bridger's there were a few clerks and a few white fur traders that came to the Cheyenne Village since she was a child.

Reining in at the farmer's house, Jed looked over at the beautiful woman and smiled. "Do not be afraid, Bright Moon. The whites are no different from the Cheyenne people."

"I am not afraid, my warrior. You are here to protect me." A big smile flashed across the dark face.

"Jedidiah Bracket." The name boomed out as the farmer exited his house. "It's good to see you again."

"Mister Carter, how are you?"

"Fine, fine." Carter looked up curiously at Bright Moon. "Get down and come in."

"Thanks, but no. We need to get on down the road and reach Pa's before it gets too late." Jed declined. "But, we thank you anyway."

"Ed said you'd be coming this way, but he didn't say when." Carter looked again at the woman.

"This is my wife, Mister Carter." Jed cleared his throat. "Her name is Bright Moon."

"She is very beautiful, Jed, and she is welcome. My wife would like to meet her." The farmer smiled.

"Thank you. Maybe when we pass back through this way."

"You staying long?"

"No." Jed shook his head. "I need to be getting back soon after I see Pa."

Waving, as Jed and Bright Moon kicked their horses and moved on down the road, Carter looked behind him to see his wife standing there.

"She is his wife?" The older woman questioned.

Nodding, the farmer turned his attention back on the road. "Yes."

"It's terrible, Mister Carter, a white man taking an Indian for a wife." The woman's tongue clucked. "Just horrible."

"Be quiet, Mrs. Carter. It is none of our business." Carter nodded. "Besides, Jedidiah Bracket is almost an Indian himself."

"Heathens." The woman stomped back in the house as Carter smiled and waved again.

"Maybe I should have been an Indian." The farmer mumbled.

Passing the first buildings in the town of Baxter Springs, Jed looked over at Bright Moon and smiled. "Sit tall and proud. Do not let the people see you are afraid."

Straightening her shoulders, Bright Moon smiled. "I will sit tall, and I am not afraid."

Jed had seen people look from the store windows before on his trips through Baxter Springs, but today the town was full of people craning their necks to see the Cheyenne woman with him. Quiet mumblings came to his ears, but nothing discernable. Passing by the doctor's office, he noticed movement inside, then Ellie and Doctor Zeke stepped out onto the walk. Never slowing the piebald, as he pranced through the settlement, Jed looked straight down the dusty street as he rode out of Baxter Springs. Jed didn't see Ellie's sad downcast eyes as he passed by without acknowledging her. He wanted to stop to say hello, but it could be embarrassing. No, it was better for them to ride straight through town.

Ed Wilson heard the blue hound barking and walked outside to find Jed and Bright Moon crossing the Pennybrook. Rushing to where they had reined in at the corrals, Wilson helped Bright Moon from the horse, then looked at her first, then over at Jed curiously.

"Pa, this is my wife, Bright Moon."

"Bright Moon, you are welcome and my new daughter." Wilson's voice choked as he took the surprised woman in his arms and hugged her. "Welcome, Daughter."

Jed quickly translated his words and shook hands with Wilson. "I have come as I promised."

Wilson looked over at the pack animals then let his eyes settle on the large leather bag, hanging on the black mule. Walking over to the mule, he laid his hands softly on the bag. "Is this my son, Billy?"

"It is." Jed watched as the shoulders shook softly. "We will put the horses in the corral and give you a minute, Pa."

"No, it is okay." Wilson looked over at Seth's grave. "We'll have supper, then I'll dig him a grave."

Wilson didn't have to ask about Bright Moon or Ellie. On their ride back from Fort Bridger, Ellie shared a few things that had happened between her and Jed, enough for him to understand they would not marry. She even mentioned Bright Moon, so Wilson wasn't shocked when Jed introduced her as his wife.

Bright Moon walked about the house, curiously looking at the way the white man lived. She was fascinated as Wilson cooked on the stove. She even had the men laughing as she jumped back when the large grandfather clock started chiming. Everything in the white world was a mystery to her, but in minutes, she came to like and trust the man Jed had introduced as his father and her new father. Sitting down on one of the beds, she shook her head as Jed explained it was what the whites slept on.

"It is too soft, my husband."

"You would get used to it."

"I don't think so." Bright Moon backed out of the room.

For three days, Jed stayed and helped Wilson catch up on some small chores, dig Billy's grave, and midday of the third day, Jed led his horses from the corral. Cinching down the packsaddles and loading the sacks of supplies, Jed turned to where Wilson stood.

"When Hatcher rides through, why don't you ride with him to the valley, Pa?" Jed looked to where Bright Moon was walking from the house.

Smiling, Wilson looked over at Jed. "If he rides your way, I will come with him."

"Is that a promise?"

"It is." Wilson laughed. "But, this old farmer sure couldn't find you back in all those mountains by myself."

Jed thought of Walking Horse, and knew Hatcher would probably ride back to the Arapaho sometime in the early summer to see about him.

"I want to stop at Baxter Springs and have the preacher marry us Christian-like, before we ride out." Jed smiled up at Bright Moon. "We would like for you to come to town with us."

Smiling, Wilson quickly saddled Roden's horse and joined them. The ride back to town seemed shorter to Jed than it ever did. Someone once told him that time passed by faster when you're enjoying yourself.

The preacher almost finished the wedding ceremony when Jed heard the big door squeak open. Turning, he saw Ellie standing inside the door.

"Amen, you may kiss the bride, young man." The old preacher smiled, then pronounced them man and wife.

Bright Moon had no idea what kind of ceremony the bald-headed man was saying, but as everyone started kissing her and shaking hands, she finally understood.

Walking up the aisle, Ellie smiled and kissed Bright Moon on the cheek. "My sister, I hope you will always be happy." Ellie spoke to her in Arapaho as she looked over at Jed. "Take good care of him."

Jed and Bright Moon, with the pack string strung out behind them, crossed the Snake River at the west crossing. Midafternoon, they topped out over the last mountain reining in at the outcropping, overlooking Jed's valley. Jed knew they would be home and sitting beside a warm fire by full dark. From high on the mountain, the Pawnee horses looked small, and Jed was thankful they hadn't left the valley. He planned on sending them to Yellow Dog for her bride fee. Looking over at Bright Moon, he smiled, as she was worth many horses.

"We are home." Jed pointed out across the far valley. "This is our valley."

"It is, as Little Antelope said, beautiful."

"Almost as beautiful as my wife."

Suddenly, as the horses started down the last steep part of the trail, the bright beckoning flash of light flashed its bright beam as it always did as Jed passed this part of the trail. One day, he would spend time here to find the light that was not to be found, but not today. Today, he wanted to get home to his valley, home with his beautiful wife. Somewhere to the south, high on a lonely ridge, the old grey wolf sent out his wailing howl, calling for a mate. Jed smiled over at Bright Moon, as he already had his, then kicked the piebald down the trail.

The End

CPSIA information can be obtained
at www.ICGtesting.com
Printed in the USA
LVHW10s1824260818
R13841600001B/R138416PG587340LVX1B/1/P